The Rt Hon Lord Hurd of Westwell, CH, CBE, PC was educated at Eton and Cambridge, where he obtained a first-class degree in history. He passed top into the Foreign Service in 1952, and served for fourteen years as a professional diplomat before joining Ted Heath's staff and working at 10 Downing Street as Political Secretary to the Prime Minister. He was elected to the House of Commons in 1974 and continued as MP for Mid-Oxfordshire (later Witney) until 1997. Following terms as Minister of State, he became Secretary of State for Northern Ireland (1984–85) and Home Secretary (1985–89) before his appointment as Foreign Secretary in 1989. Lord Hurd is the author of thirteen books, mostly political thrillers, and lives in Oxfordshire with his wife Judy and their son and daughter. He has three grown-up sons from his first marriage.

Sir Stephen Lamport joined the Foreign Office in 1974. After four years in Tehran, he was Private Secretary to Douglas Hurd from 1981–3. More recently he served as Private Secretary to the Prince of Wales.

'Here is a proficient and intelligent political romance'
The Times

'The authors are sure-footed guides to the palace labyrinths'

TLS

D0313909

The Palace of Enchantments

DOUGLAS HURD

and

STEPHEN LAMPORT

timewarner
paperbacks

A *Time Warner* Paperback

First published in Great Britain in 1985
By Hodder and Stoughton Ltd
Published in 1986 by Coronet
This edition published in 2003 by Time Warner Paperbacks

A CIP catalogue record of this book
is available from the British Library.

ISBN 0 7515 3459 5

Set in Berkeley by M Rules
Printed and bound in Great Britain by
Clays Ltd, St Ives plc

Time Warner Paperbacks
An imprint of
Time Warner Books UK
Brettenham House
Lancaster Place
London WC2E 7EN

www.TimeWarnerBooks.co.uk

Oh, the external world! Let us not be made dupes by the old slave . . . who promises us the keys to a palace of enchantments, when he only clutches a handful of ashes in his black fist.

Edmund Wilson, *Axel's Castle*

1

This is not a story about spies. There are too many spy stories. They attribute to that profession an absurdly dominant role in the world. Certainly Edward Dunsford, Minister of State at the Foreign Office, normally paid little attention to the intelligence reports which crossed his desk. A quick glance, a quick tick, and into the out-tray. He found them pretentious. A report was no more useful, and no more true, because it had been achieved surreptitiously and awarded a high classification and a codename. No spies had built Edward up as a competent middle-rank politician, no spies pulled him down. Nevertheless, a piece of intelligence work was the start of it all. A lazy, half-botched, pathetic little job, carried out by an American whom Edward never met.

It had started on a Saturday about a month before. Alfred Cross drove northwards parallel to the Hudson River through the unexpected rain of a mid-September morning. It had been clear enough in Manhattan, though even so Alfred had been surprised to hear his employer at breakfast time declare an upstate expedition. Joy-riding was one thing, making money out of oil prospecting another, and his employer up to now had shown every preference for the second. Anyway, despite the early onset of some fall weather, the leaves were nowhere near ready. He had told the boss they ought to wait another three or four weeks to see the brilliant reds, oranges and yellows. So why bother now? Why not wait a few weekends?

He had been ignored. That was the story of his life. So they cruised at speed along the Merrick Parkway. In Connecticut they flashed past the odd tree which had chosen its finery early. But once the Cadillac had cut west and then north again the clouds gathered, and any hint of the splendour to come was blotted out by the sudden rain. Here and there a wet leaf, early victim of the declining year, blew flat against the windscreen, and was shoved aside or mangled by the wipers. He expected his employer at any minute to tell him to turn back. It was an afternoon for watching football or a sexy movie on TV in a warm apartment But he was directed across the Hudson and into the grey, wet, indistinct Catskills.

'I'm having lunch with a friend.'

And so eventually to a tiny settlement deep in the hills, a garage with bunting to cheer up the used cars, a motel already closed for the winter, half a dozen wooden cottages in need of paint, and a single-storeyed dark brown restaurant behind a white carriage-wheel propped against an oak tree. The Stage Coach Inn, said the sign. Junk food, said Alfred Cross to himself. With surprise, because his employer cared for good food, and as Chairman of Arkansas Exploration he could command it.

A thin man in a dark suit got out of the Chevrolet as

2

Alfred parked in front of the diner. He had no raincoat, but opened an umbrella as he advanced towards Alfred's employer. He held it in such a way that both men would soon be half-soaked. The two men did not greet each other, but walked quickly towards the diner. Alfred's employer carried his black despatch case. About an hour, Alfred surmised. He had brought no sandwiches. After a moment's hesitation he marched into the diner behind the two men. The overheated room smelt vividly of all-American food. It was full of all-Americans, with a substantial proportion of noisy children. His employer and the thin man were already sitting at a table between shiny, high-backed wooden benches, which formed a cubicle protecting them from the world. Alfred advanced towards them, but was waved away as he expected. It was past one o'clock and there was no other table free. Alfred smiled lecherously at a fat young waitress in a tight black dress. Admiring his chauffeur's uniform and smart cap she let him hijack a Hamburger Special Plate and take it out to the car. He jerked a finger to show how it should be paid for.

Sitting in the Cadillac, damp and full of grievances, Alfred remembered that the Chairman of Arkansas Exploration was not his only employer. The truth was that his side employment had proved up to now wholly forgettable. Arkansas Exploration had, it was thought, been up to something. No one had ever explained clearly to Alfred the nature of the suspicion, except that it concerned Central America. AE had concessions in several Central American countries, and the Chairman visited them often. Alfred had been supplied with good money and some interesting equipment and told of his duty to

3

his country. He had travelled with his employer to Managua, Panama, San José and three times to Mexico. He had tasted the good life, and spent days in bed with dysentry. The money had been spent, but the equipment hardly used. The talk had all been of oil, and blameless. The assignment was now at an end, but Alfred was still owed a little extra money and had not yet returned the equipment.

He turned a switch below his driving seat. The receiver with the tool box there began to pick up and record on tape the conversation passed to it by the miniature transmitter concealed in the lining of Alfred's employer's despatch case. The reception was blurred and the words indistinct so even the equipment made no sense. The talk was clearly once again about oil, but this time in Africa, not in Central America. Meridia, Mangara, the Red Sea, names Alfred recognised only vaguely. He could not follow the technicalities. The two voices were low and even – no excitement. They might be interested when they got the tape in Washington, but more probably not. After about five minutes he switched it off again. Not worth being surprised by the two of them coming out of the diner. He would hand back the equipment tomorrow and go back to being a plain chauffeur/manservant again. The other job hadn't amounted to much. The cash had been handy; the excitement nil. Not at all like those long complicated thrillers by that English guy, what was his name, anyway he'd made a bomb pretending it was all sex and violence. Alfred Cross opened the car door and pushed the crumbs off his uniform out into the puddles.

2

Edward Peter Dunsford, Minister of State at the Foreign Office, licked the last envelope, sat back in his black official Ambassador car, and allowed himself an empty minute. He wrote a letter on House of Commons paper to every boy and girl in his constituency to reach them on their eighteenth birthday. The device had been his own idea, dreamt up shortly after he became an MP, and he was rather proud of it. The habit meant topping and tailing four or five letters each morning, licking the envelope, and sticking on a second-class stamp – second-class because Edward paid for the stamps himself. Though bad with money in a general way, he was careful in small things. It was convenient to do this chore while his official driver, Jack, drove him to the Foreign Office from his mews house in Eaton Close. He was friendly with Jack, but after one year of occasional chatter both now preferred silence.

A light rain was falling in the Mall, so the traffic was thicker than usual. The fallen plane leaves glistened in the gutter. The car slowed as the traffic light opposite St

James's Palace showed red. Edward recognised the cyclist alongside – a young man with red hair, white shorts and singlet, and a small tartan hold-all neatly strapped to the grid on the back of his bicycle. It was the second of his own Private Secretaries, new, raw, sometimes impertinent. Exhibitionism, grunted Edward to himself, to whom this was a crime. He turned away without a smile, as though he had not seen him. It was good that James Harrison was getting wet, and that his suit would emerge wrinkled and unsightly from that hold-all.

The car drew away from the lights in a slow-moving line of traffic. And there was the Foreign Secretary himself, coming down the steps from his house in Carlton Gardens. Despite the rain his umbrella was tightly furled. Patrick Reid wore no hat, and his thick white-yellow hair provided an effective setting for the hooked nose and fierce blue eyes under thick brows. Even from a distance he looked like prosecuting counsel in a TV serial. He recognised Edward's car as it moved slowly past him, and raised his umbrella in greeting.

'Here am I,' said the umbrella, 'nearly seventy, trim in figure and handsome in face, taking my constitutional in the rain as I have done man and boy in Edinburgh and London these fifty years – whereas you, Edward Dunsford, my inferior in years, breeding, station in life and ability, are putting on weight, and ride to the office in a second-rate car at the taxpayer's expense. And I hear you are on bad terms with your wife.'

'Pompous old windbag,' thought Edward. As the car turned right out of the Mall across the Horse Guards he took out of his breast pocket the blue slip of paper with the day's engagements. Good day or bad day?

11 a.m. Foreign Office Promotion Board.

12–1 p.m. United Arab Emirates National Day Reception.

He looked no further. It was enough. It was going to be a bad day. The Promotion Board, on which he was the only serving minister, comprised the senior officials of the Foreign Office and recommended senior appointments to the Foreign Secretary. To all those present except himself it was a sacred task. They spent hour after hour refining their judgement on their contemporaries before deciding who should be sent to where. A detail here, a reminiscence there, a very occasional hint of malice – there was no doubt that they greatly enjoyed themselves. Even light-hearted, quick-witted Under-Secretaries brought to these particular meetings a high sense of duty and great long-windedness. To Edward, the politician and outsider, they were a bore. He knew few of the people being discussed. Privately he thought that the differences between the candidates did not matter all that much.

Jack drove across the gravel of Horse Guards and dropped him at the park door of the Foreign Office. Edward paused for a second to examine the carved memorial to Sir Edward Grey. A good nose, much more convincing than Patrick Reid's. Grey had been Foreign Secretary for ten years, which was hopefully inconceivable for Reid. Edward knew that he himself would like to be Foreign Secretary one day soon. Such thoughts were silly because he could do nothing to forward them in present circumstances. He moved quickly up the little stairs which led past the portrait of Sir Henry Wootton to the main hall of the Foreign Office, then up the great central staircase. There was a lift, slow, creaking and unpredictable, but Edward never used it. He took no real physical exercise, but felt a mild access of virtue each time he tackled the stairs.

Sally Archer stood up when he entered the ante-room of his office.

'Good morning, Minister,' she said. He gave Sally a thin smile. Edward enjoyed the title in the abstract. But he was never sure whether he approved of the Office ritual of substituting the title for his name. He did not feel strongly enough to stop it. Young James Harrison's desk was empty. He would be climbing into his suit in the loo. Edward hung up his Burberry on an ancient peg, and moved quickly into his own room. It was not beautiful, but the sheer size of it gave him comfort. He had been in office six months, but already there was an accumulation of minor gifts from foreigners on every horizontal space – coffee pots, daggers, boxes for putting things in, ornate trays, and of course photographs. The portrait of George III by Ramsay, slightly larger than life, radiated a dignified lack of wisdom from the wall opposite his desk. The two big windows giving on to the park were obscured by white netting. Edward hated the genteel half-light this created, reminiscent of a midland suburb or a seaside bungalow. He had protested to the inarticulate far-off powers which govern the security of government. He had been told firmly that the netting, which disfigures the whole of Whitehall, could not be dispensed with in his case. It was needed to catch the glass which would otherwise hurtle into the room once a bomb or grenade had been thrown. He had complained and pleaded for common sense. But the netting had remained.

There was a heavy pile of papers on his desk, or to be

more precise in the second tray from the left, which was for current work. On the blotter in front of the trays was a small neat pile of blue folders, containing the morning's telegrams, sorted out into regions and subjects. Edward did not resent the telegrams, but he did resent the mountain of files in that second tray. This was Sally Archer's revenge because he had refused to take a red despatch box of work home with him last night.

There she was appearing round the door of his room, the senior of the two Private Secretaries, Sally Archer, Grade Five of the Diplomatic Service, aged thirty-one, slim, rather flat-chested, smiling, no lipstick; short, wavy, wiry dark hair, a good, clear, sympathetic voice. Edward had not got much further than outward appearances. It was partly deliberate. His own marriage was unhappy. His political career was important. Both might suffer if he began to find out whether Sally Archer was attractive or what she did in the evenings. She lived in Putney, and came in by underground very early each morning.

Indeed she was looking at her watch now. Edward was half an hour later than usual, it was well after ten. Damn the girl. To annoy her, he crossed the room to the big table and, neglecting the pile of work on his desk, picked up the *Daily Telegraph* from the neat array of that morning's newspapers. He began to read.

'I've tried to put the papers in some sort of order of importance,' said Sally. 'There are three immediates on top. Then the agenda for the Promotion Board.'

'So I see,' he said dismissively, still reading the *Daily Telegraph*.

As soon as she had left the room he put down the

9

newspaper, and sat at his desk. He pulled the second tray a few inches towards him. The three top folders with pink immediate labels on them began to slither forward until he checked them. He was suspicious of those who tried to add importance to their work by covering them with those labels. Deliberately he picked a folder without any label from the bottom of the tray. 'Meridia – Economic' – it sounded unappetising. But he began to read. He would not have civil servants trying to tell him how to organise his work.

In the ante-room Sally Archer blinked back her frustration. She shuffled papers on her desk without purpose.

'Cross?' asked James Harrison, who had slipped in while she was with the Minister.

'Maddening. He's in a foul mood. And you're late.'

'I know. Sorry. He splashed me in the Mall.' The pert young man paused. 'Don't worry, Sally. He'll relent once he's finished the Promotion Board. And you're going with him to the Arab party. Life's not all bad.'

Sally Archer blushed. It was infuriating that young James thought she was in love with the Minister. She had often told him not, but he had not believed her. She could prove it of course, but only by telling James something which he had no right to know and would not keep to himself. It was a trite, silly situation, a stock office joke. But she could not simply laugh it away. The truth was that she was troubled about her relationship with Edward Dunsford. After six months' sitting in the room next to his, she had not got it right.

Sally opened a telegram folder marked 'Arms Control Negotiations', and appeared to read the top telegram. In fact she was trying to think coolly about Edward Dunsford.

He was forty-three, had been a merchant banker, then a Member of Parliament for five years and a minister for the last six months. A reasonable rise, almost brilliant. He was not often written about by political correspondents. There had been great quarrels at the top of the Conservative Party, but he had taken no part in them. This made some rate him an opportunist, and Sally had crossed swords with this accusation at cocktail and dinner parties. This morning she did not know why she bothered.

Dark, hard-to-control hair, no grey yet, blue eyes, a strong chin, nondescript nose, lips somewhat thin, a tendency to wear flowery ties with striped shirts, a signet ring on the left little finger. She could continue the physical inventory of Edward Dunsford indefinitely, for she had a sharp eye; but it did not really help. She could perform the same inventory for Rosemary Dunsford, his wife, but would much rather not. Rosemary was resplendent, rich, well-educated, bloody. It was clear to Sally that Rosemary did not love the Minister. Whether the Minister loved his wife was obscure. He certainly treated her as a precious object which could easily come to harm; but that was not quite the same thing.

She always thought and spoke of him as 'Minister'. She knew this sounded pompous to Rosemary, indeed to everyone outside the Service and to many within it, such as the irreverent James. But it was easier than the alternatives. She did not feel like calling 'sir' a man only twelve years her senior. She could not imagine ever calling him by his Christian name.

And anyway it was as 'Minister' that he was important to her. She did not find him attractive, he had proved impossible to get to know well, and he took no trouble to get to know her. But he was definitely good at his job, and it was this which drew her. He handled the business of the Foreign Office with brisk skill. The meetings which he held never lasted more than half an hour. He was sure of his own judgement, sometimes too arrogantly. When he went against the views of officials it was almost always because he lighted on what they knew themselves to be a weak argument. He worked hard, but not too hard. He did not ask for more information than was readily available. His answers in the House of Commons were persuasive without being indiscreet. He understood that foreigners needed more politeness than the British. He had a useful range of outside contacts but was careful not to weigh too openly the gossip of the smoking-room or the lunch-table against the advice of seasoned officials. So he was competent in the way that officials liked, the way that Sally wanted to be competent herself. If she sometimes wished him to show some attachment to a cause, some sign of deep-rooted principle, some emotion over issues of peace and war, guns and butter, she let the wish fade away.

What worried her more was her failure to help him in anything except a routine manner. She ran the office well, and she knew that he knew it, though they rubbed up against each other on small matters of procedure. Occasionally he accepted her advice on policy, but not often. He liked to write alone and think alone. They talked when they had to, but never chatted. When they travelled side by side in a plane, he read and ate in almost total silence. For hours on end, day after day, she was close to him, at most a few yards away. She knew that people envied her this and said it must be a fascinating experience. She also knew that she was not close to him at all. She felt that she was failing in her job.

'You've been reading that telegram for four and a half minutes. I bet you can't tell me the first thing about it.'

Before she could rebuke James, the telephone on his desk buzzed.

'Minister of State's office, James Harrison speaking. Just a minute, please.'

He signalled to Sally.

'Who is it?'

'Didn't say.'

Sally picked up her telephone. 'Sally Archer.'

There was a pause.

'I thought we'd agreed you'd never ring me here.'

She looked slyly across the desk at James. He was searching earnestly for something in a drawer.

'Yes, of course I do. You know that already.'

James's eyes flickered momentarily in Sally's direction.

'All right. Sure. Yes, I'll be in. Okay, see you then.'

She listened intently to the person on the other end of the line.

'Me, too. I hope it doesn't go on too long for your sake. Good luck.'

She put the phone down, keeping a careful eye on James. She hoped she showed no flush of excitement. He was still rummaging aimlessly through his drawer.

The telephone buzzed again. James lifted it and grimaced.

'*La belle dame sans merci*,' he said, hand over the

13

receiver. Then he pressed the button which rang the phone on the Minister's desk next door. 'Your wife on the phone, sir. I'm putting her through.'

Then he put the receiver down. One or other of the two Private Secretaries monitored both incoming and outgoing calls, but the Minister's conversations with his wife were exempt.

'Good morning, darling. How are you feeling?'

'Lousy. I've got one of my heads.'

'You drank too much of that claret last night.'

'Don't be such a fool. I said I've got one of my heads. They've got nothing to do with drink. You ought to know that by now.' There was a short pause. 'Why didn't you come and see me before you left?'

'I waited half an hour, but you were still asleep. I couldn't wait any longer. I've a full morning here.'

'Work, work, that's all you ever think of. I suppose that silly Sally Archer is listening.'

'Of course she's not – you know they never do.'

'How can you be sure?'

Another pause. Rosemary was definitely not at her best. Then she resumed.

'Anyway, it's out of the question for me to go to dinner tonight with Garth Andrew. You know I don't like him. He is fat and corrupt and boring. You can go by yourself if you like him that much.'

'You agreed to go. I asked you specifically.'

'I hadn't got a head then. I have now. Do you want a doctor's certificate?'

'I want you to come. Please come.'

'Take Miss Archer with you if it's so important.'

14

A dam broke.

'For Christ's sake, Rosemary, listen. You will now bloody well take two Alka-Seltzers and go back to bed. You've got a hangover. You'll be fine by lunchtime. You've got to come to Garth's dinner. He will be upset if you don't. He's got the Elliotts. There's a division in the House at ten, three-line whip. Charles Elliott and I will have to leave then. That lets you out of another late night, you can go at the same time. Guy Carlton will be there too, so you'll be all right. Garth has laid the whole thing on for our benefit. I simply must keep in with that world if you want me to keep you in dresses. And I need you there too. So for God's sake stop whining and get yourself organised. I don't want to hear any more about it.'

Another pause.

'Well, Jack will have to pick me up at seven. You can't expect me to get a taxi.'

'Just make sure you're there.'

Some time ago Edward Dunsford had met someone at a party, he now forgot the name, who had talked to him at length about the debts of Meridia. It was a subject of which he knew nothing and it had riled him to be talked at. In a well-ordered society it was ministers who did the talking. Other people were there to listen. So next morning he had said he wanted regular reports on the Meridian economy. The fourth in a series now looked at him from the blotter, rescued from the bottom of his tray by his urge to thwart Sally Archer and her pink immediate labels. It aroused no interest or desire. He glanced at the covering minute, neatly typed on pale blue crested paper.

'*Recommendation*: That the situation be kept under

15

review.' Edward chuckled. Contrary to a common view, he had a sense of humour, and the inanities of official jargon brought it to the surface. Taking out his fountain pen for the first time that morning (he hated ball-point) he wrote steadily on the top, 'This series may now cease. EPD 5/x.' Then he flipped casually through the annexes to the minute. Annex F was an odd report of a rumour about a deal between the Meridian President, some American oil companies and the Russians. 'Not corroborated from other sources,' said the covering minute about Annex F. 'We include it for the sake of completeness but do not think it need be taken seriously at this stage.'

The Minister decided, in his present mood, to read it carefully. The secret report, from Washington, described an intercepted conversation. Its meaning was unclear and open to interpretation. The report hinted at a Soviet attempt to use American private funds to buy its way into Meridia. Such a conclusion was not there in so many words: the report was spattered as usual with conditional tenses and modifying adverbs. But the general message was clear. Other sources would have to be checked before a final view could be taken.

Edward crossed out his earlier instruction, and, wearing his thin smile, pressed the button for Sally. He was experienced enough to know that it was only journalists who had to pretend that something was important just because it had come to them in an irregular way. But today he was in a tiresome mood, and the report would serve as an instrument.

'I think Annex F is more important than some of your colleagues think. I think it needs to be taken seriously, don't you?'

16

She was an honest girl.

'I didn't get that far.'

'I see.' He did not push home the rebuke but his eyebrows were a little higher than normal. 'Please get that for now. Perhaps you can find time while I am at the Promotion Board.'

An hour and a half later, as the Horse Guards clock struck noon, Edward could bear it no longer. The Promotion Board had only agreed three appointments. Sir Reginald Anson, Permanent Under-Secretary, was summing up the discussion of the fourth. He sat back in his chair, and put his fingers judiciously together in front of his face. His voice was high, and he paused in the middle of each sentence as if to emphasise the fact that the second half usually contained matter which contradicted the first. The room was too hot. The three clocks on the mantelpiece showed London, Washington and Tokyo time respectively. Previous Permanent Under-Secretaries brooded from their canvases on the walls, and the portentous presence seemed to slow things down even further.

'Simmonds possesses a passable knowledge of Bulgarian,' pause, 'whereas Richards would have to convert from Russian. Some of the Board consider this gives Simmonds the edge,' pause, 'despite the fact that his wife, being Turkish, might prove not ideally suited for Sofia. Then the question arises what weight should be attached to that unfortunate security lapse in Prague fifteen years ago. The Chief Clerk quite rightly spared us the more intimate details, but, alas, they are in the file. It would not be right to disregard this entirely in considering Richards's claims;' pause, 'on the other hand fifteen years is perhaps a passable period for repentance. Whereas Richards has a blameless security record,' pause, 'though one may perhaps be allowed to question the depth of his commercial experience . . .'

Edward found that Alan Boyle, the youngest Under-Secretary present, had grimaced at him. He was not quite sure how to respond. Alan Boyle passed him a folded sheet of white paper. Unfolded, it showed a striking drawing of Justice and her scales. Sir Reginald in the foreground was busy loading the scales with files and books; already they were so heavy that the shoulders of Justice were buckling, and a rivulet of sweat ran from her forehead beneath its bandage.

Edward grinned, scribbled, 'I'm off' beneath the drawing, shoved it back across the table and stood up.

'I'm so sorry to interrupt, Sir Reginald,' he said, 'I've listened carefully and my vote is for Simmonds despite the Czech actress fifteen years ago. I have an Arab National Day I must go to.'

'We are all most grateful, Minister,' said Sir Reginald precisely, 'for the time and trouble which you devote to our affairs.'

One or two of them half-rose to their feet as Edward left the room, but it was a desultory gesture. They all knew that the Minister of State was bored with the personnel matters which they loved. They also knew that it did not matter a damn whether he reached the National Day party of the United Arab Emirates at twelve fifteen or twelve forty-five.

Hurriedly revisiting his outer office he noticed that Sally had put on a little lipstick during his absence.

'Arabs don't like lipstick,' he said at once.

In fact, he thought, she was altogether the very opposite of what Arabs liked. Too tall, too thin, too intelligent, too nice. They would greatly prefer Rosemary, as indeed did he, for purposes of bed and board. But life was not just bed and board. It entered his mind for a moment that Sally Archer, besides being a Private Secretary to be teased and contradicted, might also if tested prove a pleasant companion and friend. He dismissed the thought. The relationship between Minister and Private Secretary was defined down the ages. It suited his reserved, defensive temperament. He could not see Sally among his other friends. He could not imagine her using his Christian name. Sometimes he opened a door for her, but more often he found it more natural that he should go through the door first.

'Managed Annex F yet?' he asked as they sat side by side in the back of the car while Jack negotiated Hyde Park Corner. It was a continuation of the tease.

'Yes,' she said, simply. 'And I agree with you. It could be important.'

He looked at her sideways. There had been nothing deferential in her manner. She had not even called him 'Minister'. The satirist in him was disappointed.

'Oh, I don't know,' he said inconclusively. He was not really interested at that moment in Meridia and its intractable economy. 'The land where tomorrow never came,' someone had said. What kind of mood would Rosemary be in by the evening? It might have been better after all to go to Garth Andrew's dinner alone. Accompanying Rosemary when she was in a bad temper was like riding a whirlwind.

The Banqueting Room of the Inter-Continental Hotel was immensely crowded. At first sight you would not have realised that only soft drinks were being served by the Ambassador of the United Arab Emirates. The army of resplendent waiters, equipped with ice, buckets and immaculate napkins, bowed and scraped over each bottle of apple or grape juice as if it were champagne. It was not the drink which drew the crowds. Round the huge room, and in a circle at its centre, tables were set with an amazing array of meats, fishes and salads. Edward knew several of the Englishmen who had already piled their plates high with delicacies, and felt a mild disgust. There were few of them who lacked five pounds to buy their own lunch. He looked with distaste at the centrepiece of the whole room, a life-size swan made of ice. The swan presided over the dishes of smoked salmon, bowls of caviare, vaster bowls of huge, tasteless scarlet strawberries which probably came from Israel. The party had been going for some time, and the swan was beginning to drip discreetly from her beak and tail. One of the waiters tidied her up from time to time with a napkin. After many a summer dies the swan.

Among the guzzling Britons, he was glad to see a black familiar face, the Meridian Ambassador. A friendly grizzled man with a triple deck of scars on his left cheek. He had been in London for seven, perhaps eight, years. Because he wished to remain he did nothing controversial, and entertained in style the many Meridians who came to London for a wide range of duties and pleasures. But he was shrewd, and a patriot.

Annex F swam into Edward's mind. One of his techniques was to surprise diplomats with abrupt questions.

The soft juice in his hand made him less courteous than usual.

'Have you got anyone to invest in your oil yet, Ambassador?'

'Alas, Minister, the British companies are so slow . . .'

'Yes, yes, I know that. They were slow because they were fat. Now they're thin but still slow. I'm talking about the Russians.'

'The Russians?' The Ambassador lowered a slice of pizza which had been about to enter his mouth.

'There is a story. The Russians with American money . . . it sounds absurd. And dangerous.'

There was a flicker of alarm, surely, in the dark eyes.

The Ambassador had been a minister in his home capital Mangara once, and had kept up his contacts. He would know what was cooking. Or perhaps not.

'Absurd, yes, I think, Minister. An absurd combination.'

'And dangerous.'

The Ambassador ate the pizza. Then, through some crumbs, 'Yes, it would indeed be dangerous.'

Driving back with Sally, Edward made up his mind. The tease was over. Annex F should be taken seriously.

'Jack, drop me off at the bottom of the Duke of York Steps. I'll have soup and cheese at the Travellers.'

Jack nodded.

'Sally, I want a telegram to Mangara. Tell old stick-in-the-mud to check that story with the President. I think that Ambassador had a glimmer of it. He was alarmed, but not surprised.'

'You put it to him, Minister?'

Edward laughed.

'Don't worry. No sources, nothing definite. I'm house-trained, you know.' The car slowed. 'Let me see the draft telegram this afternoon. Draft it yourself. Don't let the department talk you out of it. If they try, you can tell them that it's ministers who make the policy round here.'

Sally watched him run up the steep slope. He had no raincoat, but there was only a light drizzle. For a minute or two she wondered if he might be enjoying himself.

3

Edward Dunsford walked from the Foreign Office and across a corner of St James's Park to the dinner party. Crossly at first, because he had sent his car to collect Rosemary, and his Private Office had failed to find him another. Pleasantly later, because the act of walking for more than a hundred yards was unfamiliar, and did him good. He crossed Birdcage Walk, disappeared up the Cockpit Steps, and made for Pimlico. Through the street openings he caught glimpses of green turf in Vincent Square. The sun was still bright on the grass, though it had begun to decline behind St Stephen's, Rochester Row. Was it a bomb or an impoverished congregation which had cut off the top half of that Victorian spire? Rochester Row itself was almost empty, despite the early hour. Outside the police station a drunk was shouting obscenities at two policemen trying to manhandle him inside. He appealed to the well-dressed stranger for help. Edward glanced at him. Conscience made him hesitate for a moment. Then he hurried past, carefully looking away.

He disciplined himself to use the last half-mile of his walk in useful thought.

First, about Garth Andrew, his host. A famous host indeed, at least among the few hundred citizens of Westminster who liked political meals and gossip. Garth was a thoroughly political person, but had never joined a political party, stood at an election, or even made a public speech. His politics were of the drawing-room, not the market place. They took the form not of a party, but of parties. He liked to influence and introduce. For him these were activities in their own right, regardless of any cause or philosophy. Causes were needed of course and he owned a PR firm which provided him with clients who in turn provided him with causes. They varied from year to year – Lebanese refugees, industry in Wales, Antarctic exploration. They were never pursued beyond a point that might have carried him into lasting personal commitment. They did not seem essential either to Garth's income or to his happiness. He spent money generously, but no one knew where it came from. The techniques of persuasion and of social life seemed more important to him than the results. He saw himself as patron rather than artist. Small, bespectacled, and unmarried, he looked like a monkey, yet had found a succession of splendid and obedient girls younger than himself to share his life and preside at his table.

Tonight's dinner would be good, yet it worried Edward. Garth's guest lists were drawn up with the greatest care, for his parties had to succeed. Sometimes success took the form of entertaining most of his guests by providing a gladiatorial contrast between two of them.

'Guy Carlton, I'm asking him,' Garth had said on the

phone, 'your old banking friend, and I know you still like him. Charles Elliott and Jane – not sure how you get on with them now . . . that might be interesting . . .' and the conversation had tailed away. By then Edward had accepted the invitation, and anyway he was determined not to be afraid of Charles Elliott. That was one reason why Rosemary had to be there. Present, she might drink too much and be disagreeable; absent, she would certainly provoke malicious questions from Charles and others. Turning into Warwick Square, Edward Dunsford thought, not for the first time, that life without women, though still difficult, would be a damned sight simpler.

Garth Andrew lived in one of the few houses in Warwick Square which had not been converted into flats. The door was opened by a self-conscious girl, evidently hired for the evening.

'Oh, hello. They're all upstairs,' she said, rather obviously. The staircase rose steeply in front of them to the noise above. Climbing the stairs, Edward could see guests out in the first-floor conservatory at the back, drinking among pink and scarlet geraniums. From somewhere he could hear Rosemary's clear laugh, and noted automatically that it did not yet have in it that note of shrillness which meant that she was upset or irretrievably drunk. Perhaps drink was proving a cure for her headache.

Garth appeared to greet him, looking more like a plump, educated monkey than ever: he held a glass of champagne in each hand.

'Late, but not the last, dear boy, not the last.' He affected the usual hearty tone quite out of harmony with either his appearance or his character. 'Hope you're keeping the world on its toes. I hear Patrick Reid gets lazier and lazier, and you carry more and more of the load.' He gave him a glass. 'I can't take you round the guests without barking my shins on the flowerpots. But you know them all. And those you don't will certainly know you . . .' – he reeled off the names. Indeed there were no surprises. A radical freelance journalist whom Edward disliked; Lord Templeton, an ass, but assiduous in the Lords and director of a company which used Garth's services; a wealthy manufacturer of biscuits who lived in East Sussex, in Edward's constituency; Charles Elliott – Garth paused over the name. 'And of course, where appropriate, their charming ladies. And my new number one girl-friend. Ruth, come and meet one of my oldest friends, Edward Dunsford.'

'Garth has so many oldest friends – but I am glad to meet you.'

She was like all Garth's girls – pleasant-looking without being glamorous, straight-eyed, straight-haired, long legged and nice. Their apprenticeship usually lasted two years. They then faded gradually into his background collection of past favourites. Edward remembered the mannerless excuse which he too often had to make.

'I'm so sorry but I have to go and vote in the House at ten. Don't ask me what about.'

Ruth smiled. 'I know. Rosemary told me. Don't worry. Come back if you can.' She was nice, definitely above average.

Edward moved from the landing, out into the warm glass-covered garden. The evening sky was pale lemon behind the big plane tree which dominated the tiny back gardens. Most of the guests were on their second drink. Edward found Rosemary entertaining a small circle of admirers which included Guy Carlton. He aimed a kiss at Rosemary's cheek, but she turned and took it on her lips. For show or for real, he could not tell, but at least it meant that there would be no immediate storm. She had decided to dress expensively that evening, a rather harsh, low-cut, blue and white dress lent by an American designer, diamonds at her neck and ears, a careful streak of fair hair across the front of her dark head. That too was a good sign.

'Hello, darling, here at last,' she said.

'You had the car.'

'God invented taxis, some time ago.'

'He created feet first.'

'You actually *walked*?'

On their honeymoon, Rosemary and Edward had tramped the hills of the Dordogne. That was a long time ago. For years now she had driven or been driven everywhere.

She turned to compliment the journalist on his last centre-page article. At this, too, she was skilful, when it amused her to take the trouble. Guy Carlton caught Edward's eye, and the two of them relaxed, like soldiers stood at ease. They were old friends whose paths had diverged. Guy Carlton wore a yellow rose in his buttonhole.

'Haven't seen you for a long time, Edward. We seem to bump into Rosemary more than you.'

'Bankers and politicians keep different hours.'

A pause.

'We miss you at Speyer's.'

'D'you still think of me as a renegade? Or like an investment that went wrong before you got your money out?'

'Nonsense.'

'There was a hint of that when I left. More than a hint in fact, from old man Speyer.'

'You were entitled to . . .'

'Of course I was entitled. But that's not what you all think. Half the money, half the prospects, always thought the fellow was unsound. I can imagine you all still intoning that round the lunch table.'

'Don't be so touchy.'

Another pause. Guy continued to grope for a friendship that was still within reach.

'It's true that we miss you. At least, I do. International banking isn't just a matter of figures as you well know. It needs political flair . . . I'm pretty sure, Edward, that if you ever want a job at Speyer's again, you could come back. That's all I wanted to say.'

Edward knew that it was generously meant, even if he did not understand the reason behind it. But he still felt a little nervous of Garth's intentions for the evening, and could not bring himself to react generously.

'To do what, pray? Fill old Speyer's glass and listen to his ancient stories. No thanks.'

Guy Carlton flushed. Speyer was his father-in-law.

'For Christ's sake, I'm trying to be helpful. You won't be a minister for ever, and as you well know we have our share of excitement, too. We're deep now into half a dozen countries where it's all politics. Take Meridia for example . . .'

'What about Meridia?' Edward's voice changed. He believed in coincidence. Guy Carlton relaxed.

'You remember how involved we were in the place before you left. Now even more so. We've worked closely

28

with the President for years. He's needed us, God knows, and our skill in putting money together. Sometimes he has paid on time, more often not. Not much profit for us, but we're used to him and it's become a habit. And one day, if it ever takes off . . .'

'You aren't the only ones.'

'No, but the closest. And all the time there was easy talk between us, comings and goings, Now suddenly there's silence.'

'What d'you mean?'

'No Meridians in London, no reply to our routine messages, no requests for new money. Yet they've begun to spend again. Not paying bills, you understand, but making new commitments. Big ones, needing big money.'

'Found a new banker?'

'No one would be so mad.'

'Oil companies, perhaps.'

'You've heard something?' Now it was Guy who turned sharp.

'The Foreign Office never hears anything.'

'There's talk about oil money. You've obviously heard it. But it doesn't make sense. Even if the oil companies wanted to invest, the President wouldn't allow it. Nor Washington, for that matter. Hamid hates the Americans, and the Americans won't touch him because of the wretched politics of the thing. You've been there?'

'Never. But I . . .'

Edward was not quite sure as he began the sentence how he meant to end it. He trusted Guy Carlton, but not the world in which Guy Carlton moved. In his loneliness he would probably have told Guy at least something about the story in Annex F – Soviet intrigue underpinned

29

by American oil money. But they were interrupted by Charles Elliott, and despite himself Edward froze.

'Ah, the Minister is here. We are indeed fortunate.'

'Don't be silly, Charles.' Guy almost interposed himself between the two politicians.

'Silly? The more experience I have, the more I realise that to be a minister, even a junior minister, is everything. To be a mere Member of Parliament is nothing.'

Charles Elliott was tall, saturnine, with an excellent profile, and good clothes. The story of his relationship with Edward had many ramifications, but was basically simple. It was also absurd. He and Edward had been close friends at Cambridge, and Charles had been the leader. He had had the larger following of friends. He had always enticed prettier girls to his parties. He had entered the House of Commons first. But now Edward had moved ahead, and into the job which the more experienced man had identified as his due. This was a blow to Charles which their friendship had not survived. Charles had to content himself with being Chairman of the back-bench Foreign Affairs Committee, a position of some power which Charles knew how to use, but which he always represented as powerless.

'Is Jane here?' Edward asked inanely for Charles's wife, wanting to say something but having nothing to say.

'Of course, of course, though I do not immediately see her. Some people say she is insignificant. Rosemary is of course by contrast unmistakable, unmissable . . .'

Rosemary chose that moment to laugh just a little too loudly in response to something said by the plump young journalist. Edward, who calculated her decibels with painful accuracy, noted that she had definitely drunk two gins more than was safe.

Fortunately Garth Andrew began to order the ladies out of the garden and downstairs to dinner. Charles Elliott followed close behind them, so that Guy Carlton and Edward by loitering had the chance of another word.

'Stupid to quarrel with him.'

'I don't.'

'It takes two.'

'Nonsense. He's absurd. You've just seen.'

'Listen to me. Charles Elliott is not a man to spend the rest of your life with on a desert island. But there ought to be a way of patching up a quarrel that does neither of you any good.'

'I don't see how.' They went downstairs side by side. 'Why was he so scathing about his wife?'

'Jane was always a mouse. A mouse with money. Now an unhappy mouse.'

'Why unhappy?'

'Because Charles has taken himself a girl on the side. All very private and discreet of course. Someone from the Foreign Office, the gossip says. You'd better watch your wastepaper basket.'

They parted with some sort of alliance reaffirmed, to the comfort of them both.

At the dinner table Edward was placed between Jane Elliott and the wife of Derek Headley, the biscuit-maker from his constituency. Headley was prominent in Edward's local party Association. Headley was proud, overbearing, intolerant, easily crossed. He liked his own way, both with his biscuits and his local politics. Edward had never crossed him, so far as he knew, but Headley clearly disliked him. Jane Elliott was silent, ate rather too much, and watched her husband. She smiled quietly

31

at Edward when they sat down, and out of curiosity he would have liked to talk to her. But at Edward's other side the unconscionable reminiscence from the biscuit-maker's wife was unstoppable. She had been to Kashmir in April and to a Royal Garden Party in July, and the material provided by these events was copious. Her narrative jumped between the two several times, so that Edward, listening with half a mind, was not clear whether it was at Srinagar or Buckingham Palace that the tea was so amazingly tasty. At the end of the table Rosemary twisted her glass of white wine, once or twice raising it, brushing the rim with her lips, putting it down untasted. She hardly touched her food. That was a bad sign. She must have had a secret supply of gin all to herself, up there on the terrace, concealed perhaps behind a scarlet geranium. The biscuit-maker's wife had veered on to motorways.

'My husband says it's really criminal that a road like that should be built. It's not as if the local people want it. Just think of the noise, and the damage it will do.'

Edward looked at his watch. Just on nine, and the meat still going round. He had to leave in fifty minutes. With luck they should be at coffee by then. He had lost all sense of enjoyment. It was a matter of getting through the next fifty minutes without disaster. He wished he had let Rosemary stay at home.

Tim Dowling, the plump, radical journalist, was illustrating a thesis with his hands. Edward could hear enough through the biscuit lady's chatter to gather that the thesis involved spending large sums of public money. As the sums became larger the hands moved more eloquently. The biscuit manufacturer was demurring. Since that holiday in Kashmir he was an expert on the Indian economy.

'Wouldn't give them another penny,' he said. 'The corruption's monstrous. Our aid just lines the pockets of the politicians.'

Garth Andrew glanced round his table. Now was the moment to take the argument, which had started in one corner, fan it into a general discussion, blow it up again if possible into a row, which would make his dinner memorable when dozens of others were forgotten. Edward had seen him do this before, and was fascinated by the technique. He started by disagreeing with what had up to then been said, slyly pushing the views of his unsuspecting guests towards extremes which, with greater foresight, they would probably have rather avoided. He addressed Mr Headley, the biscuit-maker.

'Surely that's not the point. But I don't agree with Tim Dowling either. India should get the money, but not because she's poor or third world or a victim of exploitation or any of that rubbish. She should get it because she's India. She's special. A country where eight generations of Englishmen fought and survived and ruled – and left behind something worth supporting. The only country east of Suez with decent institutions. That's the point.'

It was of course a point which offended the orthodox on both left and right. Tim Dowling for the left, the biscuit-maker and Lord Templeton for the right, began to mutter dissent. Edward noticed how the ladies kept silent. In the old days there would have been general chatter during the meal and politics for the men over the port once the ladies had retired. Not even Garth Andrew would organise an evening that way nowadays, but he

33

had his revenge on the feminists. Now there was politics during the main course – and the women were expected to shut up. His nice new hostess, Ruth, was evidently briefed to act as sheep dog. She briskly ended the separate chatter at her end of the table, and rounded up the whole flock into the same conversational pen.

'What do you think, Mr Elliott?' she asked. She had a calm friendly voice. The same sort of girl as Sally Archer, thought Edward, but more sexy. Everyone who wanted a second helping of the excellent beef had received it.

Charles quickly got into his stride.

'As politicians, Edward and I know this is a simple matter of politics. The Foreign Office has to wrap it up in a lot of humbug because that's their trade. But the truth is that there are a certain number of people in this country who have a conscience about poverty in places like India which persuades them that, because they're better off, they ought to do something to help. Not many, and few in the House of Commons. Normally it's a matter of bishops, charities, professional do-gooders, a few leader writers. They do not sway votes or win elections, but they are a nuisance if not humoured up to a certain point. They can organise a lobby of several thousand nice, well-meaning people for one afternoon. They can give a government embarrassing publicity. It is all nonsense of course, but a government has to do the minimum necessary to placate this group. It would not be honest to the taxpayer to do more than the minimum; but the minimum has to be provided. To calculate that minimum at any given time is a matter of nice political calculation. That's Edward's job.'

'It's not my job at all.'

'Then it ought to be.'

Edward was not a generous or an idealistic man, but he hated hearing his job and profession mocked. The different stresses of the day and evening were suddenly strong enough to snap his self-control.

'What nonsense you talk, Charles. You know that governments sometimes have to guide and educate. They make judgements on merit. It's not just a matter of political calculation. We have to think of what's right, sometimes at least. But you've reversed the usual rule. You were sensible at Cambridge, you talked well. Now you're in the House you talk like a silly undergraduate cynic.'

'That's rich,' said Charles. His voice had become harsh. 'Coming from a man helping to run a department which is notorious for its lack of principle – a man moreover who has never taken a decision of principle in his life.'

'Quite right,' said Rosemary, just audibly.

'Just like all those ghastly bureaucrats,' said Derek Headley, louder.

'What the hell do you mean by that?' Edward aimed at Charles before he heard Rosemary and the biscuit-maker.

But Garth had achieved his purpose. There was no need for more. The dinner was memorable.

'We must change the subject,' he said authoritatively. Empty plates were being removed. At her end, Ruth plied her neighbours with chocolates from a complicated silver dish. Jane Elliott turned a flushed face towards Edward.

'I'm sorry. It was silly of you to have tangled with him. But he shouldn't have behaved like that.'

Edward was seething. 'That's all right,' he said, meaning the opposite. He looked at his watch. 'I must go,' he said loudly. It was not true, for it was not yet a quarter to ten, and the car would take five or six minutes to reach the Commons for the vote. But he could not stand Garth Andrew's party any longer. He got to his feet.

'You're not going now?' Rosemary too was on her feet, though a little unsteady.

'You knew there was a vote at ten.'

'What a bloody uncivilised way to behave. You're beaten in a fair argument, and then you slink off into the night leaving your wife to face the humiliation. My God, you can be insufferable.'

This was hurled across the coffee cups. The rest of the company sat in embarrassed silence – Garth had achieved two rows for the price of one. Edward made no attempt to argue. After twelve years he knew the futility of it.

'I'll send the car back.'

He muttered some words of thanks to Ruth, and found the door. Garth came with him, and so to his surprise did Charles.

'Can I cadge a lift?' Charles spoke as if they had not just quarrelled.

'Don't you have your own car?'

'I'll leave it for Jane.' He turned to Garth. 'I'm so sorry I can't come back.'

'I'm afraid I can't either,' said Edward. 'I have a boxful of work to cope with before morning.'

'Good night, my children, and thank you for coming.' Garth spoke enthusiastically as if the evening had been a great success.

Edward's practised eye could see Jack and the car parked at the edge of the square.

'Why did you say I was unprincipled?' They walked briskly side by side towards the car. Edward had regained control of his temper.

36

'I did not say that. I said you had never had to take a decision of principle.' Charles paused. 'You have risen on an escalator, not a staircase. You have never had to fight for a cause or face a difficult choice. No one can know what will happen when you do. One can only guess.'

They reached the car without further talk. The drive to Westminster was also silent. Edward thought of a further remonstrance, but Jack would hear, and anyway his anger had ebbed. He thought of what Charles had said.

It was true, of course, put like that. He had never had to take a decision of principle. But then it was true of most politicians. It was certainly true of Charles himself. The ordinary warfare between the parties worked as a haphazard system of selection. Men lost their seats or floundered in debate. They were discovered in brothels or with guardsmen. Or they failed even with the civil service prop to achieve the low minimum of competence required in office. Others conversely did well. Often it was a matter of luck, sometimes of skill. But none of this had anything to do with beliefs or principles. Only occasionally, perhaps once in twenty years, a great cause swept across the political landscape like a flood, changing its features – Home Rule for Ireland, free trade or protection, Europe. Rather more often, an individual politician found himself having to make an isolated decision of principle. It would, Edward supposed, be like coming under fire for the first time in war, or going to bed with the first girl. One could not tell in advance how one would perform.

'Thanks for the lift,' said Charles, and moved swiftly past the policeman into the Members' Entrance of the House of Commons. Edward was conferring with Jack.

37

'Just one vote, I'm paired after that. But I expect I'll be half an hour or so. Can you go back to Warwick Square and take Mrs Dunsford home?'

'Maybe she won't be ready.' Jack never complained about the late hours, which brought him substantial overtime and Mediterranean or even (once) Caribbean holidays. But he compensated with a mild pessimism about the feasibility of his instructions – in this case, almost certainly justified.

'Let her know you're there, then wait. That's the best. I've got plenty to do here. Come to my room when you're back.'

'Okay then.' Jack never called him 'Minister', or indeed anything. This was refreshing.

Glancing at the indicator above the entrance, Edward saw that John Fletcher was still winding up the debate on hospital expenditure. The time figure flicked to twenty-one fifty-six as he watched. Four minutes to go. The Opposition would by now be drumming up some artificial noise designed to destroy Fletcher's peroration and get a mention in the late editions of the papers and in the early morning radio programmes.

'Scrooge' they would be shouting, and 'Resign'. The Speaker would ask them to give the Minister a fair hearing. Fletcher would have his head down ploughing through the departmental text in front of him, producing figures of higher and yet higher expenditure on the nation's hospitals, until he felt the Chief Whip tug at the hem of his jacket, meaning that it was ten o'clock as near as dammit and he must finish a sentence, any sentence, and sit down. Edward had no wish to join in all this. He paused at the tickertape at the foot of the stairs.

Cairo. Speaking today to the International Conference on Resources and Development in Cairo, President Hamid of Meridia hit out hard at Western banks and governments which had failed to understand the developmental needs of poor countries. In a colourful address the fifty-eight-year-old President told the eighty-three-member UN agency that his own economic strategy had been constantly thwarted by the West's inability to devote sufficient funds to meet Meridia's needs. 'They squeezed the lemon till the pips squeaked,' declared Hamid amid laughter, 'and now they complain there's no lemonade.' He warned that Meridia would look elsewhere for assistance. 'Money doesn't stink,' he said, 'we'll cash the cheque first, and worry later about the politics of the man who signed it.'

Gratefully Edward switched his mind away from Rosemary and Charles Elliott and the awful dinner party he had just left. It was much easier to cope with the problems of work than those of personal life. The facts clicked together, though there were still missing pieces. That American report in Annex F, Guy Carlton's information, Hamid's knockabout turn in Cairo – looked at one way they all pointed to new money for Meridia, enough to make its ruler cocky, enough to turn him into dangerous ways. How much aid were we giving to Meridia this year? He jotted the question on a card in a slot in his wallet.

Edward turned right through a side door into Westminster Hall. He sometimes did this at night when he wanted to clear his mind. To him it was the most impressive place in London. Impressive even in the day, when it was a thoroughfare for Members of Parliament and their secretaries, and a refuge of tourists from the rain. Impressive because it had no everyday function, reserving itself for jubilees and trumpeted occasions, the trial or lying in state of kings, duly recorded on the brass tablets set in the brass floor. Impressive above all at night, when one had to imagine looming through the dark the great rafters and bosses of Richard II's roof, and where every step set up an echo from the grand and dangerous past. For Edward the nineteenth-century Palace of Westminster next door was a place of work. He found its architecture eccentric, its furnishings seedy and its rules often as absurd as its ornaments. It had gradually won his affection as a fundamentally good-hearted place, but he was always surprised when constituents found it awe-inspiring. The real thing was there in Westminster Hall. Edward's shiver did not come only from the cold.

He did not linger, but walked towards and then up the dimly lit steps which led to St Stephen's Chapel and in turn to the Central Lobby. He did not need to cudgel his brains into any great decision that night. He wanted to save his marriage, but he knew that unlike one or two of his friends he could not do that by giving up politics. Rosemary had married plain Edward Dunsford, but long ago she had shifted her loyalty, such as it was and despite many complaints, to the Member of Parliament and now Minister. He now had few friends outside politics, but that was something he could attend to later. He drove a troika: the Foreign Office, his parliamentary life, Rosemary. All three horses were high spirited and neces-sary and he would have to improve his horsemanship if the sledge was not to overturn. He pursued the metaphor too far. There were plenty of wolves in pursuit, mostly

40

looking like Charles Elliott, but Edward Dunsford had the wit and courage to outpace them.

At moments of private despondency Edward sometimes let his shoulders slump so that all the muscles of his upper body went slack. At moments of private determination he threw his shoulders hard back. Both movements were a parody, designed to bring to an end a particular phase of thought or feeling. As he threw his shoulders back in the central lobby, the division bell rang, high and strident, and a policeman took up the message with a bellow, 'Dee-vision'. Edward moved quietly to vote.

He could tell whether to go left into the Aye lobby or right into the No lobby simply by noticing on which side the Government Whips were standing. The members waited to pass through two narrow channels where the tellers marked their names, like sheep passing through a dip. Some jostled to get through in a hurry, others gossiped on the long upholstered bench which ran most of the length of the lobby on the window side. The Foreign Secretary stood in a group of Cabinet Ministers talking about the debate which had just finished. It had clearly not gone well; the Cabinet Ministers looked sombre, and Fletcher, the junior Minister who had wound it up, stood by himself, fidgeting with his notes, receiving no congratulations. Edward wondered whether he should say something to Patrick Reid about Meridia but decided not. The story was by no means clear cut, and if the Foreign Secretary gave a quick off-the-cuff reaction it would be difficult to change his mind later. A member whom Edward did not like came up and congratulated him on a recent radio interview. For a minute or two he chatted about the impending motorway with a neighbouring

Sussex MP. Then as the crowd waiting at the sheep dip began to thin out, he moved forward to do his duty.

After he had voted, Edward went down the stairs behind the Speaker's chair to his own small room on the ground floor.

'Edward Dunsford, Minister of State, Foreign & Commonwealth Office' said the label on the outside of the oak door. There on the desk was his red box, locked, and full of work to be done before he went to bed. There beside it was a fat buff envelope full of constituency letters to be signed. On the wall hung three prints of Queen Victoria's golden jubilee procession through the streets of London. It was a bare room, a brown room, a bachelor's room, and for Edward a refuge. Rosemary never came there, or indeed anywhere in the Palace of Westminster except the dining-rooms, and in summer the Terrace. Sally Archer and other Foreign Office officials rarely came there, fearing the contagion of party politics. James Harrison, the most junior member of his Private Office, occasionally came to look after the contents of the drinks cupboard. It was the room in which Edward was most often alone. He needed a good ration of privacy in his life, and Room Thirty-One in the Lower Ministerial Corridor often provided it.

He found the key to the drinks cupboard and poured himself a strong whisky. There was no point in going home yet, indeed Rosemary would be at Garth's party for at least half an hour, perhaps more. He ought to work at his box and sign his letters, and normally enjoyed doing both. He found the box key in the pocket of his trousers. But instead of unlocking the box he moved to the other side of the room and stretched himself out on the sofa, irritated by its angular, uncomfortable corners which had so often prevented him from stealing sleep during all-night sittings. He tried again to think straight about Meridia, but the facts had now lost the earlier pattern which had formed in his mind. A wave of tiredness swept over him, and he dozed. He thought of Charles Elliott, the undergraduate, standing one summer night on the edge of the cut in a Cambridgeshire fen. Charles's body, tense before he dived into the black cold water, was in silhouette against the sharp orange edge of what had been a brilliant sunset. They had been close then, before the poison came, and the friendship had meant much to him – and, he thought, to Charles too. He thought of Rosemary. She would be flushed and beautiful, reluctant to leave Garth's party, excited by the quarrel and no doubt by much later flattery. She would be devastating to any man who caught her in that mood. She would attract and fascinate her prey as surely as any cobra. Jane Elliott would be brushing her teeth, folding her clothes, perhaps saying her prayers, anxious, miserable, waiting for Charles. And would Charles go home tonight? Or would he have other plans which ignored any place that Jane had once held in his life? Sally Archer – why the hell did he need to think of Sally Archer? He jerked himself awake. He had been for drinks once in her flat in Putney, and it was exactly as he had expected. A million paperbacks up the walls, an antiseptic kitchen, a few pieces of country furniture too big for their surroundings, a bright carpet from Morocco, and across the hall (he had looked) a narrow, white bed in a narrow, white, single-girl's bedroom. Nothing of interest could ever happen there.

But in this Edward Dunsford was wrong. For at that

moment, in her little flat in Putney, Sally Archer was listening to a tall, serious-faced man telling her the story of his evening. His jacket hung over the back of an armchair. She had loosened his tie for him and unbuttoned his collar. They each had a large tumbler of duty-free whisky in their hands. Sally looked worried at first.

'But why were you so beastly to him? And so deliberately?'

'Why should you worry? You said yourself how impossible you find it to get on with him. Perhaps you're not the only one.'

He smiled and sipped at his drink, keeping his eyes on her.

'All you politicians are as bad as one another. It's just envy. Of the successful for the –' she hesitated, '– well, the bit more successful.'

'Come on, Sally dear, grow up. We're all just playing a game. It's what's expected of us. If we don't give the audience a good laugh we don't earn our supper and we don't get asked again.'

She laughed. 'Don't tease. There's more to it than that.'

'You're right.' He leant forward, fumbled with the buttons of her nightshirt and tried to kiss her, but she backed away.

'Oh no. You'll have to admit the truth first. Why don't you two hit it off?'

'But we do. We used to be the best of friends, once upon a time.' He gave her a rather lecherous look. 'When we were both about as young and as innocent as you.'

This time she stayed where she was on the old horsehair sofa. He kissed her with the passion of a man whose enjoyment was increased by the possession of their mutual secret. The remnants of her whisky spilled on to a cushion as she let her tumbler slip from her hand. She murmured something into his ear. The nightshirt slipped from her shoulders. Not for the first time it was left behind on the bright red Moroccan carpet as Sally led Charles Elliott to her narrow, white bed.

4

Julian Sandford-Smith had been British Ambassador in Meridia for five weeks when a long telegram of instructions, marked 'Immediate and Confidential' and heavy with phrases like 'Ministers attach great importance to . . .' arrived from London. It was Sandford-Smith's first ambassadorial post. He had never before served in Africa, and felt desperately unprepared for the task. To him Africa was a perplexing tapestry of tribal customs and darkly-held secrets. As a young man he might have mastered them more easily. But he was fifty-six and it was difficult now. Of course he knew the outlines. He had read the chapters of those fat colonial histories which dealt fleetingly with the dull and uninspiring story of British Mid-Africa. Not a particularly glorious episode. No memorable battles. No deeds of legendary daring or courage. No great soldiers or administrators. No Gordon, no Kitchener, though the latter had once diverted an army to deal with a tribal uprising in the north-east. Somewhere, too, he had read that Livingstone had once explored part of the forests which jutted into its south-western corner. But the explorer had soon realised there were more important parts of the continent. Sandford-Smith could understand why. Imperialists, on the other hand, had thought Meridia worth a small investment at the time, for the country had minerals, good cotton-growing along the river, and one port sitting remotely on its eastern flank. But on the whole it was a routine story of colonial exploitation and administrative competence.

Britain left Meridia long ago when it no longer had any further use for it. Evidence of the country's brief moment of Victorian prosperity had all but disappeared. Now Meridia chose to ignore its past and its imperial connections. Its government, authoritarian, independent, self-consciously non-aligned, shunned membership of the Commonwealth while relying heavily on the goodwill and expertise of the London banks and, to a lesser extent, on British aid. Its people, if not always its governments, kept some small affection for Britain. Yet by and large it was arid, poor and forgettable. There might be new potential one day in its minerals. But not this century. Not until the world grew even smaller and began to look around for new mineral supplies as had Meridia's first conquerors a century before. It was a country, in short, requiring a competent and elderly ambassador, someone to mind the shop and generally keep things going. Flair and determination could be saved for more deserving and demanding posts. So Sandford-Smith had been appointed to Mangara.

And this morning there had arrived this long and difficult telegram instructing him to call immediately on President Hamid. The Ambassador disliked its peremptory tone. Nor was he certain he understood exactly what he had to do. He knew only that he had to raise some delicate and difficult points, and he did not look forward to it. Though he had only exchanged with Hamid the blandest civilities when presenting his credentials a few weeks before, he was already well aware of the President's reputation for total self-confidence and a remarkably unpleasant temper.

As the British Ambassador's ageing black Daimler bounced sedately through the decaying streets of the city and headed towards the river, Sandford-Smith sprawled on the back seat trying to master his instructions. Beside him sat a Second Secretary who had been nearly three years in Mangara and was inclined to take seriously the story in the telegram. But the Ambassador did not intend to listen to Second Secretaries for 'political' advice. Although it was autumn in this part of Africa, the heat was still great. Sandford-Smith was perspiring profusely in his heavy black three-piece suit. He took a large red silk handkerchief from his breast pocket and mopped his brow vigorously. It was a rounded brow on a round red fleshy face squatting on a round heavy body. The predominant appearance of the Ambassador's frame was taken up in miniature by the round owlish glasses which clung precariously to two small pink ears. During bouts of nervousness – and there were many that morning – the Ambassador's fingers would search for the bridge of his spectacles, making sure they were still where they should be. He dreaded the intolerably hot summers of Africa, and cursed that his car did not even have an air-conditioner. The car, he thought, was rather more unpleasant than his faded, hot and dirty office. The outgoing Ambassador had joked to him in London about the smell of petrol fumes in the back of the car as reassurance in a country of shortages that the British Ambassador could still find his petrol. Now the fumes mixed sickeningly in Sandford-Smith's stomach with his own nervousness to increase his dread at the coming interview.

Had the Ambassador not been engrossed yet again in his impossible telegram, he might have noticed, as his car emerged from the canopy of plane trees which lined the banks of the river, that he passed a limousine driving away from the white stuccoed entrance to the President's palace. Had Sandford-Smith been in Mangara a little longer, he would also have recognised the stern, though on this occasion highly satisfied, features of the Soviet Ambassador. But that morning the eyes of the Daimler's distinguished occupant were searching a piece of flimsy, classified paper, and the Russian car glided past unremarked.

A few minutes later in the President's palace, Sandford-Smith sat uneasily on the edge of a large and once-lavish sofa. He was oppressed by the size and grandeur of the room in which he had to wait, and by the massive sprays of dusty plastic flowers with which it was adorned. Above his head a painting showed a group of British troops being speared and gored by a band of exulting black Meridians. A fan blustered on the Ambassador's face, but the sweat still trickled from his forehead. Eventually an attendant appeared noiselessly from nowhere and escorted the two Englishmen to the President's office.

The fact that Hamid always saw foreigners on his own reflected his one outstanding quality: he was his own master. Government policy, while it was appearing to work, was his policy. Discarded policies were the blunders of incompetent ministers, men who had failed to live up to the high responsibilities entrusted to them by the country's father figure. It was not that Hamid always knew his own mind. More important, and dangerous, was that he believed he did. This made him a dangerous man in the hands of others able to exploit a weakness.

Sandford-Smith did not quite see this at so early a stage of his posting. His senses on this morning were overwhelmed by the proportions of the President. He was immensely tall, and immensely black. Close-cropped hair, massive hands with the fingers of a large fat spider. His suit was as black as his skin. The effect was remarkable: all that Sandford-Smith saw as he entered was the white spread of the President's smile. He was appalled. Hamid was in an excellent mood – the change would be so much more dramatic and uncomfortable once his message began to sink in.

'Ambassador!' – the thought of the title had once excited him – 'I am happy to see you again so soon. The British never come to see me enough, yet I am a good friend of your country.'

The President beamed. Sandford-Smith wilted. The thing was impossible. All because of some over-eager counsellor in London anxious to please politicians who didn't understand the realities of the world, he was going to ruin his relationship with Hamid before it had begun. His fingers fumbled nervously with the telegram. Then there was a silence surrounding the President's smile, and he found himself stumbling into his speech.

'Mr President, you are a very busy man and I'm so sorry to have to bother you at this short notice. It's very good of you to see me, sir, on such an important matter, and my Government will be very grateful to you.'

This was awful. He was babbling. He mumbled an inappropriate introduction of the Second Secretary, but could not remember his name. If only the great man had not been smiling.

'The point is, sir, my Government has asked me to raise very privately with you a matter of some concern to us. But I must assure you that, in doing so, I am only reflecting the close friendship which exists between our two Governments. Indeed, our ties are such that British ministers themselves have been anxious that we might discuss this delicate matter.'

This mixture of the pompous and the craven did not make sense, even to Sandford-Smith, but he floundered on.

'You see, some information has come to my Government's notice – information which we are naturally inclined to discount – that the Soviet Government is trying to arrange with you some very privileged and far-reaching concessions to exploit your mineral resources. Of course this is entirely your own affair. But my Government would be very concerned if this information were true. The stability of your country has great importance for the whole of Africa, and Britain would not wish this to be threatened by a large Soviet presence here. This could have serious implications for both of us. We have close links with you. We provide substantial aid to you. We would not want all this jeopardised by Meridia turning itself against its friends in the West.' He paused. The President remained silent. 'And speaking personally, sir, it really would be misguided to put yourself in the

51

hands of a single foreign interest like that. Your people might well object. I remember the problems there were in Persia over the Reuters concession. I mean, of course, it's not for me to say. But . . .'

The smile remained. Perhaps its owner had not been listening.

'Well, Mr Ambassador, that is a very interesting report. But I'm disappointed that you think my country to be so unreliable that I might even consider such a thing. I am always very careful about my friends. I know the risks as well as anyone. I decide how closely I work with the Soviet Union – not them. So you needn't worry. I know what I'm doing.'

The Ambassador sat back a little in his chair. Everything seemed to be all right. Hamid had not lost his temper. Heaven knows why. And he had denied the whole thing. Well, it was true he had not actually spelled out the falsity of the supposed link. But he had as good as said so, and it would only be his sense of presidential pride that would have kept him from descending precisely to the wretched telegram's level of argument. Damn the Office. They ought in London to have realised what nonsense some senseless, garbled, third-hand rumour must have been. For Sandford-Smith had also seen the secret report which had lodged in Edward's mind as Annex F. And damn whatever minister it was who had asked the question in the first place. He supposed it must be Dunsford, whom he had seen before leaving for Mangara. Sandford-Smith remembered again the arrogant way in which the man had asked about Meridia, as though a new ambassador could have any considered opinions before spending at least six months in the post.

The man had hardly had the politeness even to listen to his attempts to speak sensibly about questions which had hitherto not occurred to him.

But the President was speaking again, and already in mid-paragraph.

'. . . you see, Mr Ambassador, it's the British – and the West – that could really help. You have helped us a little for many years, and I am grateful for that. But it has never been enough, and you have never understood that if my country is to develop properly it will need very great help. I cannot wait much longer before beginning this urgent task. My people will not be patient for ever. I have asked your American friends constantly for help. But they always talk about profit margins and political difficulties as though they can't trust me. Yet I must start somewhere. Anyway, –' a pause, '– it has been kind of you to come.'

Sandford-Smith shook hands with the smile, too wide a smile, he thought, to be always reliable, and retreated downstairs to his car. He was pleased with his performance. He began at once to draft in his mind a telegram which would put the Foreign Office in its place.

To FCO, repeated to Washington
Confidential
Your telegram number 214: Meridia
1. I had a constructive and friendly meeting with President Hamid at his palace in Mangara this morning. He was in good humour throughout our twenty-minute conversation.
2. I went carefully through the points raised in your telegram, emphasising that it was not our wish to intervene in Meridia's internal affairs. But our concern at this

report was natural, given our long friendship and close ties. In the absence of any supportive evidence we wished to consult the President discreetly on the matter.

3. Hamid replied briefly and to the point. He said he appreciated our concern. But he was well aware of the dangers of too close an association with the Soviet Union: his relations with them were fully under his control. We should have confidence in him. We need have no worries about the rumours I had raised with him.

4. It is clear to me from my conversation with the President that we can discount the idea of close links with the Soviet Union. Hamid is anxious to retain his close ties with us. He went out of his way at the end of our meeting to stress his appreciation for the help which we have given in the past (and mentioning in passing that more aid would be welcome if he was to meet the urgent need to develop Meridia's considerable natural resources). I do not think that damage has been done to our standing by raising with him this delicate matter. But I hope we can be much surer of our sources in future before again running such damaging risks unnecessarily.

SANDFORD-SMITH

5

That same morning after Garth's dinner party, a brilliant autumn sun hung over the gentle, rounded spine of the South Downs. A few miles from the county town of East Sussex a heavy, middle-aged man climbed a stile. He had the slow but assured movement of the countryman. He began the short climb up the steep slope towards Mount Harry. His face was red from the warmth of the sun and the thick brown tweed of his fading plus fours. A hat of equally fading tweed perched uneasily on his large head. A figure of fun to schoolboys, but for his confident, military bearing. He whistled for his dog, two notes in a descending scale that linked him to a young German pointer. The man smiled and snorted as the dog raced round a corner of the chalk path, stopping to bury its nose in a bank of grass, and then dashed on up the hill.

'Young fool,' the man growled good-naturedly.

As the figure climbed, the gorgeous plain of the Sussex Weald unfolded behind him. It stretched far into the shimmering distance. It was difficult to imagine the vast, ancient, Iron-Age forest which had once covered this rolling plain. But woods of more recent origin still meandered over parts of it. The man turned and ticked off in his mind the woods he had known for twenty years. Nothing intruded into the beauty of the picture but a handful of grey ugly buildings which, away in the distance to his left, marked the final destruction of the market town of Burgess Hill. The man stopped and picked up a fragment of chalk from the path. Then he frowned, and crushed the soft rock slowly in his hand.

A few minutes later he emerged on top of the Down. The dog raced to and fro as it snuffled out imaginary rabbits. To the left lay the little plateau on which the old Lewes race-course had been built. Though it was derelict and neglected, the remnants of a few inoffensive buildings blended easily into their surroundings. The man struck out now to the right, walking briskly. Another whistle and the dog raced past again. Larks soared above him. The usual breeze on the ridge was still. Slow time reigned. A peaceful, perfect autumn day, interrupted by the harsh shout of a modern technical voice:

'No, no, no. Back a few feet. Back, you idiot. I said back.'

The walker stopped. The man who was shouting stood pointing a tripod at a figure in the distance who stood to attention beside a giant ruler. The shouter was waving his arms now. The measurer was shifting uncomfortably from side to side. The dog, suspicious of this unorthodox behaviour, ran up to the giant tape measure and began to bark furiously. Her master paused a moment longer, called the dog off sternly, and hurried westwards, up a flank of Mount Harry towards Blackcap and the ridge which led to Ditchling.

He understood why the surveyors were there. As Edward Dunsford's constituency agent, Major Richard Peacock knew the passions and the politics which the surveyors aroused. There was opposition throughout Sussex to the construction of the massive eastward extension of the M27 from Portsmouth to Dover. It was an expensive elaboration of an earlier government's 1980 White Paper on road planning for England. It was the brainchild of a more recent Minister of Transport, his imagination fired by the glory of providing a South Coast temple, one hundred miles long, to the worship of the internal combustion engine. Every town which lay along the route of the existing main road had been suffocated since the 1950s by heavy traffic. Bypasses had been built, and extensions of bypasses. One village's relief was another's nightmare. But to the transport planners of Whitehall, none of this was enough, for they had had a dream. They saw a problem which needed a radical solution: an entirely new road, six lanes of tarmac cutting a path of progress for the benefit of a population desperate for relief, provided it was at somewhere else's expense.

Sections of the new motorway had already been built in West and East Sussex, near Dover and across the Romney Marsh. Funds were committed for other parts, some contracts for the less contentious sections let. But elsewhere people had not shown the gratitude which the planners had expected. The Department of Transport in Marsham Street had been in two minds about Edward's section of the road. Two preferred routes had been written into the draft Statutory Orders, a southern route, the creation of the pure visionary, and the northern route, the work of the pure bureaucrat. The southern route, so far as geography allowed, would run along the gentle southern slope of the Downs, but well below the summit of the hills. In this way it would remain hidden from the Weald, and stay just outside the boundaries of Edward's constituency. Firle Beacon, Ditchling Beacon and the Devil's Dyke would be skirted, and Chanctonbury Ring bypassed. But the cost would be enormous: the little valleys that cut north/south across the Downs would need to be bridged, and those parts of the bigger towns which had encroached short-sightedly on the hills would suffer mutilation.

Edward's interest lay in the northerly route. It ran inland from the scarp slope, cutting neatly through the flat Weald, forging across open fields, elbowing aside the odd village and the occasional farm, conspicuous, ugly and brutal. But the northerly route was cheap. To the planners of London it was sensible. By the people of the Weald it was hated, and those who opposed the Wealden route were the rich and the powerful of East Sussex, the barristers, the stockbrokers, the City men, the gentlemen farmers, well organised, well connected and vociferous. A public enquiry was granted and they made sure that they commanded the passions of every naturalist, every environmentalist and every conservationist in south-east England. Drainage, fog, a rare butterfly and an even rarer toad were pressed into the Wealden defence.

The final decision was still to be made.

The Major hated the issue. He was annoyed at the ugly reminder given by the two surveyors. But the Major was no sentimentalist. He had been the constituency agent for nineteen years. And he knew what its people wanted. Edward had to fight for those who opposed the northern route. The smart suits who thronged the up-line at Lewes Station at eight o'clock each morning expected it. Some of them were active and influential within the local party.

The Major was climbing now the soft turf which flanked Blackcap. His dog was rushing in and out of bushes of gorse, oblivious to their thorns, scenting rabbits. The Major turned once in the direction of the surveyors and the race-course and winced at the destruction which he knew the motorway would bring. He skirted the gorse and bramble which marked the summit of the hill and pressed on along the path. The fields and woods below and to his right lay helpless, fearing rape, hoping for a knight errant.

Across his line of sight the road to Ditchling meandered, keeping the respectful distance of a field or two from the hills beneath which it sheltered. The Major could see as he scrambled down the white path a black Austin Ambassador heading west along the road. In the back Edward Dunsford gloomily watched the last few miles to home and Rosemary slip past the window. He loved their house – or rather Rosemary's house – which nestled in a shallow valley a mile or two outside Ditchling. Rosemary had chosen it not long after they were married, and Rosemary's money had bought it and furnished it. She had good, comfortable taste, and the house had become a refuge from London which he prized more than he had ever told her.

It had been a bad day. Rosemary had been asleep

when he returned deliberately late from the House the night before. Nor had they spoken that morning. Edward had breakfasted alone. Last night's feud still festered. Rosemary would probably not let it go until she had provoked another argument with him. He had spent a tiresome morning in the Foreign Office, his frustration and gloom mounting with every piece of paper he had moved across his desk from the wooden tray at the left to the wooden tray at the right. Sally Archer had arrived late looking as if she had not slept for a week. She had made a mess of his programme for the morning by agreeing to three meetings within the same hour, each of which ran on into the one following. Finally she mislaid his briefing so that he met both the Roumanian Minister of Trade and the Egyptian Ambassador ignorantly unprepared. The Minister had bumbled incoherently through a piece of paper describing Roumania's wish to promote a new Joint Committee of Trade and Co-operation. Edward had been curt, dismissive and in command.

'Of course we shall look at the idea. But we need to know whether the Committee is to have a real function, or whether it will merely be another body making demands on ministers' time. I shall ask our Ambassador in Bucharest to go into the details with you.'

A fumbling of spectacles, a shuffle of papers, a hurried whisper with his accompanying delegation, some stilted courtesies, and the Minister had been led away.

The Roumanian Minister had merely annoyed Edward. But the Egyptian Ambassador had caught him unprepared and vulnerable on a difficult consular case. That had angered him. The Mediterranean Department's brief had explained the problem carefully. Sally, however, who had not had time to read the brief, and who could not find it in the scurry between one visitor and the next, had let him down. Edward was furious. He hated to look a fool. He had tackled Sally when she came in to clear his tray after the Ambassador had left.

'Why wasn't I briefed about that case? What the hell does that department think it's up to? I take it someone bothered to find out before the Ambassador came why he wanted to see me.'

She had backed away a little from his desk, her eyes staring at the papers in her hands. She found it difficult at the best of times to meet his eyes on the rare – and usually painful-moments when he bothered to look at her as he spoke.

'I'm sorry, Minister. It's my fault. There was a brief. But it was buried – among my papers, I mean. I'd hoped to have the chance before . . .'

The crucial moment had passed in the stumbled excuse. He relented slightly. He knew he had hurt her pride.

'It's just as well I'm leaving before lunch. You look as though you haven't slept all week.'

As Edward brooded in the back of the black government car he remembered how she had blushed as she had left his room. During the remaining half-hour before he had left, clutching a red box full of papers – 'weekend reading, Minister' – Sally had been bustling efficiently and confidently through the work. He had heard her giving instructions on the telephone. 'I'm sorry. The Minister simply won't accept that, and I'm not prepared to sound him out until you can show that you really have

61

tried all the alternatives.' He had smiled. He liked his women like that. As he was making his way down the red carpet of the Foreign Office's grand staircase on his way to the car, Sally had caught him up with an advance copy of a telegram from Mangara.

'Sandford-Smith's meeting with Hamid,' she had gasped. She was out of breath, and looking rather attractive.

Edward's head nodded against the window. Jack misjudged the sharp corner round the churchyard at Westmeston, braked hard and swerved, sending Edward's head crashing painfully into the little metal reading light which the Department of the Environment added to ministers' cars for the convenience of their occupants.

'For God's sake, Jack, be more careful. You do that every time you bring me down here.'

'Sorry, wasn't expecting it,' said Jack as usual. Edward rubbed his head.

The car turned carefully into the drive of Long Meadow and drove down the gravel with the respectful speed of a servant at the wheel. Edward removed the red box, arranged a time for Jack to collect him from the flat on Monday morning, and walked through the house into the kitchen.

'Hello, darling,'

Rosemary had come down mid-morning with the girls. She was busying herself among the thousand ingredients of a complicated recipe. Silence. Aggressive, deliberate, pointed silence. Eventually she looked up from the table, old scrubbed pine – 'very farmhouse' she had been told when she had bought it in a Lewes junk shop.

'Glad you could tear yourself away.'

'What does that mean?'

'Oh, I forgot. Let me count my blessings that Parliament doesn't sit on a Friday afternoon.'

'For Christ's sake, Rosemary. Can't we forget about last night?'

'That's fine for you, isn't it? You didn't have to stay on at Garth's party and apologise for your disgraceful, humiliating behaviour with Charles Elliott. Let me tell you, I don't actually enjoy clearing up after a spoilt little schoolboy.'

'I'm surprised you even noticed that absurd little tiff with all that you must have drunk by that time.'

'What?' A knife clattered on to the farmhouse pine. 'You idiot. Do you have any bloody idea how embarrassed I was after you left? If it hadn't been for Guy Carlton rescuing me from that crowd, I don't know what I'd have done.'

He was angry for the third time that day. But Rosemary had had her way. It was always her choice which decided when a silent argument lying between them should blow up.

'Shut up, Rosemary. You're making the whole thing into something it wasn't. And by some amazing process you seem to think it was you who suffered the embarrassment rather than me. No, not embarrassment – humiliation. How can you be so selfish? If you were ready to give a little of the energy you put into enjoying yourself, my life could be a great deal pleasanter.'

'And what am I to make of that?' She was looking at him carefully.

'Simply this, dear Rosemary. You may not have noticed through the haze of extravagance and luxury with which you surround yourself that all the various lives I have to lead could be greatly improved by a little help and sympathy from you.'

'That's good coming from you. Remember, it was my family which helped to get you into politics in the first place. You couldn't have done it at all without me.' She pushed past him, through the scullery and into the garden. Edward had no desire to follow her. No remorse. Not even a hollow feeling in his stomach this time. There was an orchard beyond the lawns, the trees heavy with the red fruit. Rosemary stopped when she reached it. There was a contradiction in what she felt as she ran her hand down the bark of an ancient apple tree. She looked back across to the house.

'Damn you, Edward Dunsford. Why the hell can't you see that I want you on top of this awful dung-heap, just as much as you do? I want the glory, too.'

While she stood picking angrily at the bark, a dog rushed along the gravel drive, followed by a man in a faded tweed suit. Rosemary waved and quickly turned away when she saw Edward appear to meet the Major. She went in search of her two daughters. She found them playing in the old stable and asked the elder to go and make tea for her father and Major Peacock.

The two men sat by the open window of Edward's study.

'Haven't seen your name so much in the local papers recently,' the Major said. 'There must be something happening in the outside world. That's the great blessing of having a government minister as our member. What he hasn't got time to see to locally, he makes up for by appearing on the television and radio, and being written about in the national press. But lately you haven't been in either.'

'Things are happening, building up.' Edward was vague, a little resentful, but he trusted Richard Peacock.

'Well, just try and make what you do a little more public occasionally.'

Edward had been gazing at the garden. He looked round sharply.

'Something's got at you. What's all this about keeping my end up? Is Lewes in uproar?'

Catherine appeared at the door with two mugs of very sweet tea. She was ten years old and embarrassed.

'Mummy asked me to.' She put the mugs down on a little table and went in search of some biscuits. Both men looked out towards the Downs. The Major thought of the two surveyors five miles away measuring the possibilities of destruction.

'It's the motorway that's on my mind.'

'It's on everyone's mind. My letters here are full of nothing else. There are seven among those I opened just before you came. They all want the same thing, Richard. But I can't help.'

'What? Of course you must help. That's your job.'

'We've covered this ground a thousand times. Of course I know I have to do what I can for my poor constituents who turn pale at the thought of this wretched road. I know what they expect. I know they think it's up to me to change ministerial decisions. But unless you and I play this very carefully, they're going to start wondering why they elected me.'

Major Peacock smoothed down the grey hair on each side of his head. Edward's gloom was new to him.

'I don't quite follow. Do you mean the stories are true about the final choice having been made?'

Edward paused. He felt the tension between his various lives. Catherine had not yet returned with the biscuits.

'Not on paper. The inspector has to report the results of the Enquiry first. But you understand the pressures, Richard. Money is tight. We both know there's no alternative, because of cost and because of plain good sense, in choosing the northern route.'

'And where does that leave you? Because . . .'

Catherine came sheepishly into the room again.

'Jane's hidden all the biscuits, and I couldn't find Mummy. But I've found some muffins. At least I think that's what they are. They're not very warm, I don't think.' They were presented with a plate of cold buttered muffins.

'Thanks, Katie. They'll be fine.' The girl smiled and skipped away. Edward handed the plate to the Major.

'It leaves me in difficulty, perhaps serious trouble. I can't quarrel with the choice. So when the time comes I shan't be able to question the decision. And that will land us – or me anyway – with a real problem of credibility. Friends like Derek Headley will have the Executive attack me. His feelings on this are abundantly clear, as his frightful wife told me at tedious length at dinner last night.'

'All right, so you can't fight the decision. But presumably it can't be announced until the inspector has done his Enquiry?'

'No, of course not. It probably won't be for six months or so. There will have to be a decent gap.'

'Edward, in my view, that gap is going to be crucial for

66

you. You didn't have an easy time settling in after you were adopted. It still rankles with Headley and his chums that they couldn't quite muster enough to vote down your nomination. But that's a long way back now. You've done damn well here since then. But you'll throw all that away if you get this issue wrong.'

'So my future depends on this bloody road. Its first accident victim, even before it's built. Seems a bit ironic to me.'

'You must be seen to be fighting until the decision is announced. There are meetings planned. Headley will bring it up in a big way at the meeting of the Executive Council on Thursday week. He wants to confront you and embarrass you. But there are others, who are equally important round here, who are passionate because it's their view it will spoil. You've got to convince them, too.'

Edward was out of his chair and at the window, staring into the garden. Two little girls were dashing round the only elm which disease had not claimed. Catherine started running towards the house. She was shouting at the top of her voice.

'Daddy, Daddy, come quickly. Major Peacock's dog has chased Mickey up a tree and now he can't get down.'

There was a silence in the study.

'I hear what you say, Richard. I've thought about all this a lot recently. But my heart's not in this fight. I don't believe in it. The Headleys of this country simply aren't facing up to reality.'

'That's not the point.'

'Of course it's not. But it's important to me. I can't do them any good. They'll be fools to think that I can.'

The Major was on his feet, too.

'Heavens, man, you must at least try.'

Edward smiled. Had he been blessed with warmer spirit he would have put his hand briefly on the Major's arm. But he did not.

'Of course I shall. Don't worry. I want to stay in this job, too. Come on. We've got a cat to rescue.'

6

The fall came earlier to New York that year. Early one Friday morning in October, a young, red-haired American lawyer sat in his office on the fifty-fifth floor of a black glass building on Wall Street. On his desk in front of him and surrounded by papers from the Meridia Energy Exploration Consortium MEECON, to those involved in the project – lay a letter from G. A. Carlton Esq of Speyer's, Bishopsgate, London EC2. The American looked puzzled and thoughtful. He read the letter for the third time. Around him lay the furnishings of young legal success and the symbols of a busy law firm which charged high fees. Deep carpets, polished wood doors, a glass-topped desk reflecting the colour of the ninety-storey building itself as it appeared to the passers-by in the street below. Round the walls of the office were hung a set of twelve abstract designs, an illusion of blue and red, printed from the original block. The young man was pale and drawn through overwork. He was thirty-two but his friends thought he sometimes looked older. He had come

into the firm from Harvard five years before. He had
worked hard and had been fortunate. His friends had
envied him. They knew that Moore, Harting &
Henderson had furnished more Attorney-Generals in its
eighty-four years of business than any other New York
firm. Neil knew this, too. He was ambitious. He had had
to push himself hard to get in. And since his first day he
had felt the pressure on him if he was to succeed. For
months on end he had worked sixteen or more hours a
day. So far he had survived and done well.

At least that was why, he thought, as he picked up Guy
Carlton's letter again, he had been given such a long rein
with the Meridia project. Bourton, the senior partner, had
warned him when he had first handed him the file, 'Don't
let this one go wrong. It's big and it's important. If it falls
apart, then so does your career.' That was the way
Bourton talked. So Neil had worked feverishly at the project, first in great secrecy and in the last few days more
openly. He had been amused by the early clandestine
meetings in ridiculous places, and rather discomforted
by the unpleasant Eastern Europeans who had been part
of the preliminary skirmishing. But that phase had
passed. It had been crowded out of his mind by the frenzy
of work which soon started. He had spent long nights
putting together the details of financing and loan agree-
ments, and long days at meetings with Texas oil men,
American bankers and Soviet officials. The boldness of
the undertaking excited him. Everyone agreed it was
daring. Most thought it was possible. And where there
were difficulties the oil men insisted that determination
would win out. Surprisingly, none of the difficulties had
come from the Russian side: at three meetings in New

York they had been candid, helpful – and in a hurry. The big problem was a capitalist one, not insurmountable but an annoyance. Raising money on satisfactory terms had driven the enterprise to the European banks. The Soviet side had not been overjoyed by this. Bourton thought they were partly afraid of the extra time required, and partly afraid of having to lift the wrap further from the unfinished sculpture. 'A necessary inconvenience,' was all that the Chairman of Arkansas Exploration had said.

That was a week ago. In four days of feverish activity the bait had been dangled privately among six selected European banks. There had been some bites. Not yet enough, but sufficient, it was thought, to be reassuring. The young lawyer thought that he too had been reassured, until the letter that morning from G. A. Carlton. Speyer's were experienced and well-known in Meridia. They had most to lose by staying out of the project, and most to offer and win if they came in. Why should they hesitate?

The American picked up the white telephone on his desk. A crisp, middle-aged female answered.

'Operator. Can I help you?'

'This is Neil Wainwright. I'd like a number in Moscow.' He knew it by heart after a month of telephoning.

'I want Viktor Radomsky.' He spelt out the name. 'If he's not there, leave a message in his office and have him call me back right away.'

He put down the telephone, picked up a bundle of papers and took them across to the window. They were his notes of Moore, Harting & Henderson's last meeting with Arkansas Exploration and the three other US oil companies who made up the American side of the

MEECON triangle. His notes, written in a large childish hand, were longer almost than the meeting had been, just as at college where they had always been longer than the books from which they were taken. He skimmed through them: oil reserve estimates, production targets, extraction costs, transportation proposals, markets, financing. Finance brought him back to the letter from Guy Carlton. It worried him as he stared out of the window waiting for his telephone call.

What he saw was adjusted by the height of the tower block to an almost human scale. Down in the street he felt he was sitting in the front seats of a theatre. There you could only peer at the world around you by throwing back your head until your neck ached. Up in his office he had the measure of his surroundings. His window looked north. Towering in the foreground he was confronted by the massive white wedding-cake of the Woolworth Building. He could look down and take in at one glance both the Hudson River and the East River. On the Hudson he saw the red and white model of the day's first Circle Line boat-trip creeping round the island. Between the two fingers of water he could see past the Empire State Building to the silver spire of the Chrysler Building. Away to the north pushed an endless succession of giant buildings, glinting in the sunlight. This was the junior lawyer's view. If he stayed with the firm and succeeded he would move across to the partners' view on the south side of the building. Life had treated you well if you could look from your office on to the twin towers of the World Trade Center.

'Neil? This is Viktor. How are you? No problems I hope.'

Radomsky had the ability always to imply that if there were problems they could only be someone else's fault.

'No problems as such. But we're getting a bit bogged down with some of the details. I'd like to come over this week to go through them with you. It's too difficult to talk about on the phone.'

'Come over? To Moscow you mean?'

Hell, why not, thought the American. This is business.

'Are you sure this is necessary at this stage? It's important that nothing should hold things up. Speed is vital.'

'It's nothing to worry about,' said the American. 'But I thought it would be useful for both of us. And I need some more help from you over the feasibility study. It's not proving easy to convince everyone in the West that it's a sound investment.'

'All right. We really must get on with the details. I am under pressure here. Come as soon as you can. I'll arrange a visa for you to collect tomorrow.'

Neil made some more telephone calls. A reservation for a flight the next day. An apology to his parents for a dinner to be missed. And a call to London. If G. A. Carlton was not going to be helpful he might at least explain himself. Bourton, the partner, had scoffed at the letter. 'Typical of Speyer's,' he had growled. 'They're so Calvinistic they wouldn't put money up for a summer camp in case the kids played ball on Sundays.'

Perhaps it's sour grapes, Neil thought. Or was it some sixth sense? Bankers might have it when even lawyers did not.

He took up the letter from Speyer's and dialled again. A moment later the middle-aged telephonist was back on the line.

'I have Mr Carlton for you.'

'Hello. Guy Carlton here.'

The confident, educated voice brought back to Neil how much he had always been unnerved by the Englishmen he had met at Harvard. He began to pour words unthinkingly down the telephone.

'It's Neil Wainwright of Moore, Harting & Henderson in New York. We got your letter about the Meridia project this morning.'

He paused for some kind of acknowledgment, not sure how he should best go on.

'Frankly, we're a bit puzzled. Felt this sort of thing would be a sure one for you. I appreciate you will have considered it carefully before deciding.'

There was no reply from London.

'Fact is, I'm going to Moscow tomorrow to sort out a few points. I thought I might stop off in London on the way back. Perhaps we could meet and have a talk?'

The cultivated voice came back at last, slower and more thoughtfully than the American.

'Yes. I'd like to do that, too. I hope you haven't misread my letter. There's a lot of interest here in the project. But it's some of the – well – arrangements which people aren't so sure about.'

'But, it's all perfectly straightforward financially,' Neil answered. 'Okay, it's imaginative, but that's no reason to be shy about it.'

'Frankly, Mr Wainwright, I'm not the only one with questions. I'd very much like to talk about it. Let me get together some of my friends and we'll have you here to lunch.'

'That sounds great to me. I'd appreciate that very much.'

They made arrangements. When Neil rang off he was pleased, but still uncomfortable. There was nothing new about deals with the Russians. Perhaps third-country arrangements like this were different. But if the Russians had the political influence, the banks the money and the American oil companies the skills, why not put them all together? Profit for everyone – lawyers included – and riches for a poorly-stricken part of Africa. Why not?

7

'Sandford-Smith is an ass,' said Edward. It was true of course, but this time Sandford-Smith was right. The conference in Mangara which President Hamid had suddenly announced over the weekend was not one which a minister should attend. A meeting of officials in Edward's room on the first floor of the Foreign Office was considering a departmental submission on the right level of attendance. The department had backed Sandford-Smith's recommendation.

Sir Reginald Anson, Permanent Under-Secretary, put the palms of his hands together on the highly polished table round which they sat.

'Let me attempt to recapitulate, Minister . . .'

He noticed Edward's gesture of impatience, suppressed a little too late. Sir Reginald himself was vexed at being made to sit on a hard chair round a table. There were plenty of deep comfortable armchairs at the end of the room under George III. It was not usual for the Permanent Under-Secretary to leave his fortress on the ground floor for anyone less than the Foreign Secretary. The compliment should have been acknowledged in some way.

He had come to a routine office meeting because he smelt something inappropriate in the air. 'Inappropriate' was his conclusive term of criticism. From long experience he diagnosed it accurately. It was a case, possibly even a serious case, of enthusiasm on the part of a junior minister. Edward Dunsford was becoming too interested in Meridia. Dunsford was having ideas of his own and that spelt trouble. Anson regretted the passing of the old days when junior ministers were allowed an office and a secretary, a little pomp and self-importance, in return for doing the chores of parliamentary work, but never a say in policy. Nor could he rely on Alan Boyle, the Assistant Under-Secretary sitting beside him, to keep control of his Minister. Boyle, too, showed occasional signs of enthusiasm. Not too serious in that case, natural indeed in a thrusting forty-five-year-old, and the fault would certainly correct itself as Boyle reached the last slow rungs of promotion. But it made him an unsuitable adviser to an ambitious young minister. So despite many other preoccupations Sir Reginald had assembled his papers and stiffly climbed the stairs.

'Let me recapitulate, Minister. President Hamid is bankrupt. He may or may not (we differ somewhat on the strength of the evidence) have put together some backstairs arrangement with the Soviet Union and some American oil companies. What is certain is that he is thrashing about, uncertain of the direction he will take. This conference which he has called at such short notice on Meridia's economic development prospects is an attempt to keep his options open, and above all to gain publicity. We must remember that publicity is an end in itself for most third-world leaders,' (and not only for them, he thought). 'The stage is more important than the play, indeed often there is no play worth noticing, let alone attending in person.'

He paused, pleased with the metaphor.

'Reginald, the invitation says it is a conference at ministerial level.'

Sir Reginald resented both the interruption and the unadorned use of his first name. He had been a knight for five years.

'None the less the French and Germans are sending senior officials. The Americans have not made up their mind, but will probably be represented by their Ambassador in Mangara. The Japanese . . .'

'The Italians are sending a minister, the Minister of Culture and Public Monuments.'

'Precisely. Precisely. I could not put it more plainly.'

Edward got up in irritation, crossed the width of the room and looked out on London through the half-drawn security net of grubby muslin. The weather had changed and mid-October was imitating February. A cold grey murk had settled on St James's Park. The window ledge was thick with pigeon droppings. Two men, working very slowly near the edge of the lake, were sweeping the fallen leaves into little heaps.

Edward imagined great heat and a wide, slow river, close to a city of courtyards and flat, white roofs. He imagined tree-lined avenues, and one house bigger than the rest, a palace with an outside staircase, at the top of which stood a curly-headed white man defying the upward surge of a black crowd carrying spears. Edward had not the faintest idea what Mangara was really like, and for a moment he muddled his hazy schoolboy recollections of African history, muddled romance with reality, the obscure with the famous. No doubt his picture was wrong. No doubt the flight would be an agony, the food bad, and the conference as confused and pointless as Sir Reginald Anson was predicting. The conference started on Sunday, only three days away. It would be a frightful scurry to get there so quickly. But he wanted to get away, be free and clear for a day or two of the encumbrances which he had loaded on to his life. Free from the constituency and the motorway, from the House of Commons and the malice of Charles Elliott, from the Foreign Secretary, his officials and the pigeon droppings, free above all from Rosemary.

Then there was the problem itself, which somehow out of perversity he had made his own. Edward did not care a jot for Meridia; but he was hooked on his Meridian problem. Most of the FO, and certainly Sir Reginald Anson, did not see it as a problem at all. They admitted that there were little scraps of evidence, diplomatic and secret. There was Hamid's unexpected international conference. There was bankers' gossip in the City. There was the sight of more Russian faces than usual on the streets of Mangara. It added up to nothing, Sandford-Smith claimed. Hadn't the President given him a clear assurance? It seemed most unlikely that anything of substance was taking place, said the Permanent Under-Secretary and most of his officials. So far, only Alan Boyle, the Under-Secretary who looked after Africa, was ready to agree with Edward that these scraps might assemble into an interesting and sinister picture.

There was another consideration, too. The problem was somehow more attractive to Edward because it was

79

his own property. So far as Whitehall was concerned it was his invention, his copyright. He would not make it over to others. He turned back into the room.

'I shall go,' he said. 'The Secretary of State will agree. He said he'd leave the decision to me.'

That surprised them, but it was more or less true. He had met Patrick Reid by accident at the park door that morning and had mentioned the conference in Mangara. He had seen the old man waver between his instinctive wish to thwart his junior, and his equally strong instinct that his own life was easier and more dignified when his junior was out of the country. The second instinct won narrowly.

'Do as you wish,' the Foreign Secretary had muttered, stepping with his detective into the creaky old lift.

'I'm right, aren't I, Alan?' Of course, that was unfair, pinning an official to choose between his Minister and his Permanent Under-Secretary, with a gaggle of juniors watching.

'Evenly balanced, I'd say, Minister.' Too glib, thought Edward. He liked Alan Boyle, his quick manner. His voice had stayed young even though his face was already folding into a cragginess which in ten years would be formidable. But he would have to learn which side his bread was really buttered.

The official machine moved into a different gear. There were practical problems of parliamentary business, of the motorway meeting in Lewes that following Saturday over which he was to preside. Sally scurried in with the big red master diary which contained the official version of Edward's future. Sir Reginald rose, adjusted the handkerchief in his breast pocket, and left

80

the room. It was not his habit to linger on the field of a battle which he had lost. Edward carried all before him. He spoke to the Chief Whip, and then to his Labour pair. His voting record was good, so he was allowed to pair the following Thursday. It was the second reading of the North Sea Oil Bill, but no serious trouble was expected. Sally left a message on Major Peacock's Ansaphone: 'Mr Dunsford is very sorry but he has to go abroad unexpectedly, and will have to miss the motorway meeting. Could you please get someone else to chair it, possibly Councillor Antrobus?' He would have to have malaria jabs, a book for the Ambassadress, possibly a formal letter of credentials, comprehensive briefing and diarrhoea pills. All within thirty-six hours. They would need to leave on Saturday morning. Next door in the private office the telephones buzzed happily on these various quests. Sally came back into the main room.

'Shall I get your wife on the phone, Minister?'

'No, I'll talk to her tonight.'

He sat for a minute at his desk. He was out of love with Rosemary, that was sure. He was still eager to go to bed with her at the right moment, but that was a different matter. Love was a stimulant, giving the lover a marvellous overflowing store of talent and energy which he could use not only to please his girl but to climb a mountain, make a million, become Prime Minister. By that test he had been out of love with Rosemary for several months. His marriage to her was now a depressant, which drained talent and energy out of the other parts of his life. He did not know if there would be a row when he told her he was going to Mangara the day after tomorrow, and he did not mind.

'Excuse me, Minister.' Sally was back in the room. It would be some trivial matter, interrupting his analysis. Would he ever feel that stimulus again? That was the important question.

Sally was slightly pink.

'Alan Boyle wondered if you would like him to come with you to Mangara?'

'No, certainly not.' Boyle should have supported him at the meeting. 'I suppose there'll be someone from the Development Ministry?'

'And from the Bank of England.'

'One or other, not both. Home Departments are always greedy when it comes to foreign travel.'

There was a pause, during which Sally grew pinker.

'As regards your own office, Minister, it's James's turn to go.'

In theory, the two Private Secretaries took foreign trips in turns. In practice, there had hardly been any, what with the tightness of the Government's majority in the Commons and the Foreign Secretary's usual cussedness. There had been the inside of days in Brussels, but these hardly counted. Edward thought of James Harrison as a companion. Lively, even cheeky, good-looking, more or less reliable, good-mannered when not excited, needed the experience.

'I think perhaps you'd better come yourself,' he said.

Sally turned away before he could see if she was pleased. Why on earth had he said that?

It was early on Saturday, very early, and they were passing Chiswick House on the way to London Airport. The motorway was up of course, but at this hour the excavations were still manned by winking blue and orange lights in place of men. There was a mist, but later it would be fine and warm.

Sally, sitting on the left of the Austin Ambassador, tried to still the turmoil inside herself. She was being very silly. It was partly that she had forgotten to leave a note for the milkman. She had remembered to stop the *Guardian*, but the milk bottles would accumulate. They would signal to the burglar that there were for the taking in middle-class Putney a rather expensive music centre, some good modern books, and two cases of a crisp Loire wine given by an indulgent uncle. Should she tell Jack to sort it out? But that would mean letting Edward know how silly she had been. And she was not at all sure how far Jack was to be trusted.

But the real trouble, of course, was not the milk lake. The real trouble was Edward Dunsford sitting beside her, separated from her by a red box. He had hardly spoken since Jack and Sally had picked him up in Eaton Close. He had consumed three newspapers quickly, gutting them neatly as politicians learn to do, and tossing the carcasses on to the rear ledge of the car without offering them to Sally.

It was the first time they had been away together for any length of time. She wondered if their relationship would change. At the moment it was professionally competent, and personally trivial. He was a good minister, she was a good Private Secretary. As human beings relating to each other, they were a failure. Anyway, what was it she was after? She had Charles – or so he told her when she asked. That was surely complication and excitement enough, given his position. And hers. But could she and Edward last four days in the tropics as they were, without going backward or forward? Yes, of course they could, because there would be plenty of people and noise, telegrams and anger to keep them from developing. Sally was a fan of E. M. Forster and rather fancied her grip of developing human relationships. In the abstract of course. But the abstract did not allow for the pressures of a man who, whatever the details of his relationship with his wife, had an uneasy and empty marriage. Edward, abandoning the last newspaper, began to search his trouser pocket for the key to the red box. He was clumsy, she thought, and though his suit was good he lacked the physical neatness of Charles Elliott. Thigh, knees, ankles were, on close inspection, all just a little too heavy. But then she had never seen Edward undressed, and of course never would. She wondered what he wore at night, and what was in the black leather suitcase with the elaborate lock which he had swung into the boot of the car. A present from Rosemary, no doubt. He was taking a stupidly long time to find his key. She opened her handbag, took out the duplicate and leant over to unlock the box for him.

He wondered from behind the *Daily Telegraph* what was in that cream Antler suitcase which he had seen in the boot of the car as he loaded his own. For the second time in their acquaintance Sally was wearing lipstick. And her hair was cut and new-washed. A new dress too, blue with some white unnecessary frills to distract attention from her flat chest. He thought of Rosemary as he had left her, sprawled asleep, hung over with Mogadon – ample breast half out of her nightdress, beautiful without effort. There was a draft letter in the box to a recalcitrant back-bencher which needed clearing before he left. He fumbled

84

in his pocket for the key, but took some time because his mind was still half on the cream suitcase. He found the key at last. As he brought it to the lock he met Sally's hand going in the same direction. They touched. Sally drew her hand away first.

'Sorry,' muttered Edward, fiddling with the box.

8

Edward and Sally missed the first day of Hamid's conference. It was no one's fault. Trouble with the engines of the Gulf Air Boeing and bad weather in Upper Egypt delayed them, and they were forced to spend the night in Cairo with the British Ambassador in his palace by the Nile. Next day they spent the five hours between Cairo and Mangara in almost total silence. Edward had read the department's briefs during his lunch over the Alps, and now seemed immersed in a novel. Sally tried to read through her folders a second time. She would rather have gazed out of the window but Edward had taken that seat. She was annoyed that he did not look out once before the runway was beneath them. They only spoke as the jet dipped towards the ground. And that was because Sally was trying to be private secretarial and efficient.

'You'll remember that Julian Sandford-Smith called on you a month ago, Minister, just before he came out.'

'I only remember him knowing nothing about the place.' Edward barely looked up from his book.

She was embarrassed. But her attention was taken by the sprawling brown city which was rising to meet them out of an equally brown land. Mangara, the capital of Meridia, population 471,000 (last census 1974). Topography: flat. Climatic group: semi-desert/savannah. The thin ribbon of the river glinted in the distance.

The aircraft stopped alongside two Aeroflot cargo jets. Edward was the first on the gangway steps. He felt more conscious of his dignity than he had ever done as a government minister, and asked Sally to carry his briefcase as well as her own brown official case. Of course he remembered Sandford-Smith. Why was Sally being so inane? There the man was at the foot of the steps, apprehensive, round, and three-piece suited. A bright red handkerchief was patting vigorously at his face. The Ambassador blinked up the steps at his Minister. He wore a forced, unconfident smile of ambassadorial authority, trying to say: 'It's all right, Minister, you're here. We'll look after you now. But please don't cause too many problems.'

Edward smiled too. He was glad to be there, partly excited by the travelling; partly hypnotised because he had come wishing to help the tall black figures who clustered round the Ambassador, some in shiny grey suits, others in white robes and head-dresses; partly because he thought he had the power to make that wish happen.

An immensely tall man in dazzling white shook his hand as he reached the foot of the steps.

'I am Mohammad Abdul Ahmad.'

'Deputy Minister of Commerce, Minister,' the Ambassador hissed.

'My Government welcomes you to Mangara. The President is delighted that the British Government attaches great importance to our conference and sends a so senior minister to be present.'

Beside the officials who had come to meet Edward, a camera team from Herald Television News pointed their equipment at the British Minister. They had their African correspondent with them. He was a middle-aged, fair-haired man with a well-known face. Edward smiled. Cameras clicked. There were many hands to shake, some black, some only bronzed, all warm and friendly. Only the Ambassador's was pink and damp. He was led across the tarmac to a low corrugated-iron building marked 'VIP'. Inside were fans, noisy air-conditioning, bright carpets and sofas of imitation velvet. An old, fading black and white photograph of the President hung on the far wall, over a table heavy with plastic flowers. The Minister who had greeted Edward at the aircraft steps sat on a sofa with his hands together, an enormous smile on his face. Edward noticed now that he was sporting a pair of leopard-skin carpet slippers. Sally sat on another velveteen sofa, trying to find a common topic of conversation with the Chief of Protocol. He sat silent and unsmiling, with the tired look of a man whose life is spent waiting and worrying at air-ports. Edward was offered a glass of thick, sweet peach juice. He sipped at the glutinous yellow liquid and smiled at another photographer. A microphone was pushed towards him, so he put together a few sentences to say how pleased the British Government had been to respond to the President's invitation; Meridia and Britain had long and close ties of friendship; we saw the conference as an occasion to show again the strength of our relations. Yes, he hoped to have talks with a number of ministers, and perhaps with the President himself. No, this was his first time in Meridia; unfortunately his visit would be too short to see all he wished. More smiling, and more flash-bulbs.

Five minutes later Edward was sitting in the back of the Ambassador's Daimler, inhaling the strong smell of petrol, and bumping at ten miles an hour along the road into the city. A drive of vivid impressions, he wrote that night in his diary. Sally sat in the front chatting about nothing to the friendly black chauffeur. Ahead a dirty and dented police car wailed and howled furiously through the empty streets. Occasionally a scruffy child stopped playing and turned to look. Nobody else took any notice. He saw filth and squalor, dust and decay. Rubbish piled at street corners. Long queues of people guarding their tin cans as they waited, patient, for their cooking paraffin. As many cars queued forlornly at petrol stations as crawled along the streets. Here and there, conspicuous and out-of-place, a white face and crumpled, ill-fitting suit strode along a dusty pavement.

The Daimler lurched towards the Ambassador's Residence. At a crossroads a huge triumphal arch of metal, plastic, cloth and tinsel spanned the road. It proclaimed on one side, 'Meridia welcomes the World Leaders'. In a lozenge at the top of the arch a smiling President Hamid in national dress beamed at the camera. His arm described an action between a wave and a clenched fist. A frozen dove fluttered on each side of his head. At the foot of the arch squatted an old man, urinating against the tinsel. Half a dozen thin, grey sheep scavenged among the neighbouring litter. Africa welcomes you, Edward thought. It was hot in the car. The petrol fumes were getting worse. The car jerked out of a pothole into which a swerving donkey cart had forced it. Edward's head bumped against the window.

'Sorry, Minister. Roads are dreadful. Nobody repairs them. Don't understand it. Wasting their money on the wrong things, as usual.'

Edward gave Sandford-Smith a weak smile. The red handkerchief reappeared and was flourished vigorously a number of times before the car turned off the road, swept down an unusually smooth tarmac drive, and stopped under the featureless, concrete and brick box for which a Ministry of Works architect, twenty-five years before, had won a prize as a reward for imaginative design.

'A zebra crossing of a day,' Edward wrote, pretentiously, in his diary. Black skins in white, flowing robes filled his memories of lunch and dinner. Sandford-Smith had done well to invite large members of friendly, joking Meridians to his house. The Ambassador's wife had bustled around in the background, straightening a flower here, chivvying a servant there, anxious that every detail should be according to plan. Edward had been flattered by the attention the Meridians had all paid him. Never in London would sixteen people have sat in silent respect round the dinner table whenever he spoke. He tried a number of times to sow the seed of his suspicions with a minister, a businessman, a university professor. He received only polite smiles, and silence. He tried the diplomat's game, conspiratorially steering the Minister of Industry, his dinner companion, into a quiet corner. What was the President really after? What were those vague threats about knowing who his real friends were? There were reports of Eastern Europeans being seen behind desks in government offices. What did Hamid have up his sleeve?

The Minister of Industry had nodded and smiled vigorously, said much and told him nothing.

They missed the conference that day because it only met in session in the morning. Meridia did not work in the afternoon. But to Sandford-Smith it was important that every minute of a minister's time should be properly occupied. He knew, he told his wife, an ambassador's duties, as he waved before her the four pages of closely-typed foolscap which purported to predict Edward's programme. He knew that no politician worth his salt liked a moment to be wasted. So Edward and Sally were bustled around the city. They went to the bazaar, closed during the afternoon. They inspected the rusting iron boat in which a British Governor had made a brief visit in much pomp nearly a century ago, and which now lay stranded pathetically on the river bank near the President's palace. They chugged in an aged motorboat down to the decaying bridge which an African Brunel had once exuberantly thrown across the river. Sally caught Edward's arm out of sheer excitement when their creaking boat was tossed about by the waters swirling around its massive piers. Edward was surprised at the gesture, and wondered whether Sally had noticed.

When they returned to the Residence, hot and dusty, Sally suggested a swim. Edward approved. The Ambassador consulted his programme and agreed there was a suitable gap, but asked to be excused. The Residence swimming pool lay to the side of the house, protected on two sides by walls, and on another by the house itself. They could only be disturbed by someone approaching through the garden. Sally had a black costume which plunged to a small chest and to the bottom of her back. Edward noted it suited her proportions. The water was covered in a film of fine Mangara dust. She slid gently into it. He dived in self-consciously. But they swam together, talking of Meridia, Africa, and the strangeness of it all. He wanted to touch her. But he put that down to the moral vacuum which travelling overseas, however briefly, seems to induce.

Edward woke early next morning. Below his window three figures were crouched on the lawn lazily sweeping the grass with bunches of twigs. At breakfast he told Sally what he had seen. She laughed. Sandford-Smith had eaten before them, and was now prowling around his house with the tense look of a man expecting an anxious day.

He worried with reason. The reports of the previous day's opening session of the conference betrayed utter confusion over its purpose. Hamid had himself opened it to the blare of drums and trumpets. He then left, after an hour, in the midst of an impassioned speech by an African delegate about super-power neo-colonialism. The Foreign Minister had taken over the chair, beamed indulgently at everyone, allowed each speaker to rattle on endlessly on themes of power, evil and poverty, and abruptly adjourned the conference, as instructed, at noon.

'I think your best tactic, Minister, is to speak towards the end of today's session. There will be a lot of unpleasant things said about the West. Of course we're used to that. We can provide you with speaking notes to refute the worst insults. The point of these things is, after all, to limit the damage as much as we can.'

They were bouncing and bumping again in the back of the Daimler. Edward was enjoying himself and the sensations of the dusty African city.

'I see this as a positive exercise,' he said. 'As I said last night, what happens here is important. If there's something we can do to help, I intend to do it.'

'Yes, of course, Minister. But I don't think this is the time or the occasion. What they want is money, and we don't have any to offer them today.'

The parliamentary assembly chamber was decked lavishly with bunting, banners and photographs. A hall not of leather and wood but of the metal and plastic of the new age. It was very large, following another principle of the new age – the size of the parliamentary chamber is in inverse proportion to the existence of democracy. The seats set aside for the United Kingdom were squeezed beside an enormous Soviet delegation. Sally counted twenty-five of them standing in silent but superior awkwardness around the leader of their delegation. Sandford-Smith murmured a name in Edward's ear, so he went up and shook hands with the Soviet Deputy Minister. But others had noted Edward's arrival. Ambassadors and ministers came up constantly to introduce themselves. He found it easier and much more flattering than the awkward shaking of hands at garden fêtes in Sussex villages.

A fanfare heralded Hamid's arrival. He had discarded his Western-style suit of the previous day for his full military uniform. Edward thought how impressive he looked – tall, black, shining, splendid. As he walked across an aisle between the delegations, Hamid grinned and inclined his head towards the neighbouring nameplates of Britain and

Russia. It was impossible to say which of the two his smile was intended for.

Yet another fanfare, and Hamid was re-opening the conference. He welcomed the 'distinguished ministers and delegates, the friends of Meridia'. Many names, he said, remained on the list of speakers. They would all be given the floor in turn. He hoped that everyone would be brief. He need hardly remind them that the conference was addressing Meridia's problems as they reflected on the world at large. The interests of rich and poor met in his country.

'The poor man never forgets his true friends when he throws off his rags. Meridia is a slave to no country. She knows her friends by their actions not their words. I ask you all now to come forward and declare yourselves.'

Speech after speech after speech followed. A few by Western officials representing their Governments, brief and perfunctory, listing the help they already gave, maybe promising a little more. But overwhelmingly, waves of rhetoric from the third world, picturesque figures mentioning no help at all, but loud in denunciation of the evils which afflicted Meridia and their own countries. Occasionally the fires were stoked by bulky technocrats from the Eastern bloc, who likewise mentioned no practical help, but backed up the rhetoric of denunciation with quotations and figures.

Edward abstracted himself. He had a speech typed fair in front of him, produced by Sally in a neat folder from the depths of her despatch case. At a certain moment, during a lull, he went up to the rostrum and delivered it word for word. He put nothing of himself into it, and it had no content of his own. A paragraph of sympathy

94

based on past friendship, three paragraphs on the existing aid programme, a final paragraph, much fought over in Whitehall, saying that Her Majesty's Government would take into account any recommendations of the conference in a positive spirit, but bearing in mind the limitations of their resources. A hopeless little fraud of a speech, but all that was possible under present policy. Sir Reginald Anson had been right in saying it was not an occasion for a minister.

Nevertheless Edward had a fruitful morning. He found it easy to think when others were talking. He spent two hours doodling, responding occasionally with monosyllables to Sandford-Smith, and thinking about Meridia. He had had a long talk with Sandford-Smith after dinner the night before. He had read his briefs thoroughly before breakfast.

The pattern was fairly clear. The conference was a farce, a manoeuvre of Hamid's to gain time, to take the temperature while he made up his mind. Hamid knew as well as anyone the danger of slipping into the Soviet orbit, how help became control almost overnight. The combination of Soviet advice with American oil money was of course a new one, but it did not alter the underlying rules. In that combination it would be the American oilmen and their clever lawyers who would be the dupes Hamid probably realised this, and this was one more reason for his hesitation.

Edward did not any longer doubt the reality of the plan in Annex F. The evidence was there. Whitehall doubted the evidence because if true it would lead to pressure for an expensive and unwelcome change of policy. In the conference hall at Mangara, watching

Hamid, watching the Soviet Deputy Minister and the American Ambassador slog it out, sipping sticky coffee from a small cup half-full of sugar, Edward decided to push for the change of policy.

It was intellectually right that Britain and the Europeans should jolt the American Government out of their lethargy and put together an initiative to frustrate the Russians. It was intellectually right that Britain should have to find more than pennies for the enterprise. It was the right sort of cause for Edward Dunsford to take up at this stage of his career.

The conference ended in confusion. Hamid summed up in much the same words as he had opened. Nothing had been achieved. Everyone talked of lunch. Edward was shepherded out into the bright sunshine. His mind was made up. All that was lacking was an emotional re-inforcement for the intellectual decision, and that was soon to come.

9

Nothing looked as if it had been there for five years. Nothing looked as if it would be there in five years. Much of it was being taken down at the moment when Neil Wainwright's plane landed from Moscow, much was being put up. He had come from drab grey communism to drab grey capitalism. Friends in New York had warned him that he would be disappointed in London, but nothing had quite prepared him for London Heathrow.

He had spent the flight up in the clouds with a bestseller about the Civil War. His psychiatrist had warned him against reading business papers on business trips.

'You're drying up, Mr Wainwright,' the man had said. 'You're only thirty-two, but you have the desiccation component of a man of sixty. I recommend a course of intellectual hydration, say a Harold Robbins or a Jeffrey Archer twice a month. When you've read them all, start again – you won't notice.'

Neil Wainwright had gone to the psychiatrist because

he felt tired. He had been relieved that the man had not talked about sex.

As he waited for his suitcase to lurch into the carousel, Neil wondered whether Guy Carlton would look like his voice. It had been civil of him to offer to meet Neil at the airport, or more probably he planned to discuss the Meridia deal privately with Neil before they lunched with Guy's partners at Speyer's. The two men had not met, so there was a problem of identification. Neil had liked the way in which Guy Carlton had dismissed the idea that either of them should wear any kind of tag or label.

'I usually wear a yellow rose,' he had said on the telephone.

And there he was beyond the customs, exactly as one would expect, dark, silent, with receding hair, steady grey eyes and a pink newspaper under his arm. As a New Yorker, Neil was quick to spot Jewish blood. Not much there, but certainly some, as shown by the line of the nose and perhaps by the civility. English politeness, in Neil's small experience, was defensive, designed to keep one at arm's length. Guy Carlton's went deeper. As they shook hands for the first time he smiled as if he had known and liked Neil for many years.

Nevertheless the ride into London was fairly silent. Guy drove his own Rover fast yet carefully, giving attention to the road and the traffic in a way which discouraged conversation. He had asked, 'How did you get on in Moscow?' as they walked to the short-term car park.

'It was very interesting. They're still definitely enthusiastic.'

'Ah – Meridia, you mean.'

A pause, as they stood by the lift.

'Any snow yet?'

'They expect it in a fortnight.'

Guy evidently wanted to postpone discussion of Meridia until lunch. It was another cold, heavy, grey day. Neil was dismayed by the motorway and the later approach to London. There was a mean ugliness of design about the bridges, the road signs, the petrol stations, the broken-down centre barrier which would dismay even a New Yorker. The high-rise buildings, whether factories or apartment blocks, were a stunted compromise, and it was not until he glimpsed Hammersmith Bridge that he saw anything built with confidence.

'Rather sleazy?'

'Harlem is worse.' Neil found himself blushing, as if he had been caught despising a woman who was supposed to be beautiful.

'Harlem is dramatic poverty.' Guy slowed down to just below the speed limit. 'London has many beautiful things in it, but very little that is dramatic. That is its point, per-haps its virtue.'

'I don't quite follow.'

'Look over there.'

Neil saw a bus stop surrounded by litter, a betting shop, an Indian restaurant.

'No, beyond.'

A street of suburban houses built in the 1930s, cut off from the main road by bollards, a few roses still in the front gardens, a scarlet virginia creeper, an even brighter pillar box, small gables and pediments in architectural confusion.

'Suburban living, that is England's gift to the twentieth

century. The Scots can't do it, nor the French, let alone the Italians. Miles and miles of houses like that. Moderate incomes, moderate opinions, moderate achievements. Pleasant, sensible people, with front and back gardens. They worry about their children, but their children end up like them. They vote Conservative, but constantly disappoint the Conservatives because they are not entrepreneurs. You can cut their taxes, but you can't get them to take risks. Forget the British upper class which hypnotises you Americans. Forget the media, the cloth-capped workers, forget the bankers we're going to meet. All these are minorities. It's the people up that road who count.'

'What do they feel about Meridia?'

Guy smiled.

'May I call you Neil? I'm beginning to think you have a one-track mind. But it's a good question.' He paused. 'Nothing, of course. They don't know or care about Meridia. They could be brought to take an interest, but only with great difficulty, and only for a few days, or weeks at most. The Falklands, the Poles, gallant little Belgium, Gordon at Khartoum – yes, there are precedents. Powerful when aroused, that kind of feeling for a distant place. But it doesn't last. You have to do quickly what needs to be done, before the mood fails.'

'I didn't know you were such a politician.'

'All bankers in Europe are politicians. We have to be. I only wish a few more politicians were bankers.'

They sat in silence through the Cromwell Road, past the museums and the Brompton Oratory. Gradually London became more like what London was supposed to be. Guy Carlton looked at the digital clock.

'Plenty of time. D'you mind if we call on a friend? It's her birthday.'

He jerked his head towards the back seat, on which sat an oblong package wrapped in paper with a pattern of shiny gold and purple balloons.

'You'd like to meet her. Rosemary Dunsford.'

'Dunsford?' The name was half-familiar.

'Her husband is the Minister at the Foreign Office who looks after Meridia. He's out there now.'

'At Hamid's conference?'

'Exactly.'

'That's just window-dressing. Hamid has made his decision, he knows where the real dollars are. They were saying in Moscow . . .'

'Here we are. She's rather beautiful and rather devastating.'

There was just room for the Rover in Eaton Close and Guy parked expertly. Three detached houses stood back and at an angle from the square, smaller than the houses of the square itself and for that reason still houses instead of flats. The central house was fresh-painted so white that it dazzled even under the present dull sky. Two bay trees in brisk black and white tubs pointed the eye to the dark green front door and polished brass knocker. To Guy it was one of a hundred London houses which he knew. To Neil it was style, the true, reticent, hard-headed style for which New Englanders yearn, which they glimpse in Boston but associate, often forlornly, with London.

'Oh, Guy, how sweet of you to remember. Come in, the coffee's still hot.'

Banal words in response to a ring on the door and a peck on the cheek. Nevertheless Rosemary, too, had style, indeed a style somewhat more flamboyant than her house. For her thirty-ninth birthday she wore tight black velvet trousers, a dark red sweater, and extravagantly at her throat, quite out of place, a cluster of diamonds in a brooch which Guy knew to be her best piece of jewellery.

'That oaf Edward forgot entirely.'

'Mangara's not the best city to . . .'

'Balls. There are a hundred ways he could have sent a message. Nor even a bunch of forget-me-nots.'

She marched through the narrow hall, a hunting tapestry on her left, two varnished ancestors of her own on the right. Through an open door a modern kitchen beckoned them back into the twentieth century. An old lady was washing dishes but Rosemary took no notice of her.

'We quarrelled before he left. At Garth's party, as you know. Then again in Sussex on Friday. But forgetting my birthday's not part of the quarrel. I know him better than that. He keeps no rancour. He'll have forgotten all about the quarrel by now. And of course that makes it worse. It means he's impregnable . . . I can't help him, I can't hurt him, so long as he forgets everything that isn't politics.'

'You're quite wrong. He loves you and depends on you.' Guy lowered his voice to thwart the daily lady, but neither he nor Rosemary made any effort to spare Neil's blushes. And blush he did. Guy had introduced him, perfunctorily in the English manner, at the front door, but it was only now that Rosemary turned to him.

'Sorry. This must be frightfully boring for you. Have some coffee. Guy knows he's allowed to talk nonsense. He's about the only friend Edward and I have in common. How well do you know Edward?'

'I haven't yet had the pleasure of . . .'

102

Rosemary laughed.

'Oh dear. In London we assume everyone knows everyone else. Edward is my husband. He's successful, pompous, and besotted about some God-forsaken dump in Africa. I don't know how long I'll stay with him.'

Neil stood helpless by the breakfast table. He felt her look him up and down. At Harvard he had known girls. He and his friends had discussed the ebb and flow of their relationships for hours in a solemn jargon which had served to keep both pleasure and pain at arm's length. He had first been to his psychiatrist after the first girl, a tall blonde from Virginia, had thrown a cup of coffee at him. Lately, in New York, he had been working too hard to have time for girls. He was in no way equipped to deal with Rosemary.

'I guess it's hard being married to politics.' It was the best he could manage.

'How do you know? Are you in politics?' she asked, looking him up and down again. Because of the lack of a laundry in his Moscow hotel, Neil's shirt was in its second day. He was conscious that it was more polyester than cotton. The four-hour flight had badly creased his light grey suit. It was of course several hours since he had shaved, and then he had cut himself on the right side of his chin.

'I'm just a New York corporation lawyer.'

'How old?'

'Thirty-two.'

'He looks younger,' she said to Guy. Neil felt that in the last half-minute she had taken off his grubby clothes and put them on again.

'That's one way you can tell Americans who are going

to succeed. They always look younger than their years.'
Guy sipped his coffee, then looked at his watch. 'We must
be off, or we shall be late for lunch and my fellow direc-
tors will complain. Rosemary, you are abominable, you
haven't opened your present.'

'I can see it's a book.'

'You'd have opened it long ago if it had been diamonds.'

'Diamonds I have. A book is a treat. Nowadays I only
read *Country Life* and *Interiors*, and Edward goes to sleep
with *Hansard* every night.

'He used to read a lot.'

'He used to be a human being.'

It was a luxurious book on Turner, copiously illus-
trated.

'You told me once that you liked him.'

'The late ones, with those great storms of light.' She
thumbed through it. Neil watched her long fingers and
the thick gold bracelet falling down the red sweater
towards her wrist.

'It's sweet of you,' she kissed Guy on the cheek.

They had been standing in the kitchen. It had never
settled into a leisurely call, with chairs or the offer of cigarettes, and now it was over. Guy moved towards the hall.
Rosemary followed, then turned and looked at Neil for
the third time.

'Do *you* like Turner?'

'Yes, particularly the early ones with the calm land-
scapes.'

Rosemary laughed.

'My God. I can see you need educating. What are you
doing after your ghastly banking lunch?'

'Catching a plane to New York.'

'No, you're not. I've got nothing to do this afternoon. I'll meet you at the Tate Gallery at four sharp. You can't go home leaving the Turner problem unsolved. By the postcards, don't be late.'

In the car, Guy said, 'Don't say I didn't warn you. They call her the "*belle dame sans merci*". It's trite but true.'

'Who calls her that?'

Guy glanced sideways and Neil was irritated to catch him suppressing a smile.

'Oh, people.'

They were in the Mall, nearing Admiralty Arch.

'That's the Foreign Office down there, where Edward Dunsford works.'

'Are they really on such bad terms?'

'They quarrel in public, and you heard how she talks about him. But that's been so for years. Like dozens of others they settled into that kind of co-existence. There are two daughters.' He paused. 'It can be quite a stable relationship. People get used to being irritated with each other. They even feel affection through the shouting, and stop noticing how awkward it is for everyone else. But with the Dunsfords I'm not sure.'

'What do you think will happen?'

'There's an edge to it now. On his side. It's helping to corrode him.' Guy stopped again, as if realising that he was talking to a relative stranger. 'I used to know Edward well when he was at the bank. Nowadays I rarely see him. I can't tell what will happen.' End of conversation.

Lunch at Speyer's was not at all what Neil had expected. He was used to working lunches in New York. Forty-five minutes from start to finish, open ryebread sandwiches from the delicatessen, fruit or milkshakes, some of the richest men in the world absorbing nursery food, talking business all the time, crumbs on the papers, not a minute lost, no alcohol, no tobacco.

On the eighth floor in Bishopsgate there were Pipers, Topolskis and a Hockney on the wall. There were twenty minutes for drinking, though Neil noticed that the more powerful men took tomato juice with a strong shake of Worcester sauce. Lunch was gazpacho, braised pheasant, and an array of cheeses, with a Loire wine first and a 1976 claret. Neil was set next to old Speyer, Guy's father-in-law, a shrunken man with a head like a frog and a clear, beautiful voice. He talked precisely, without any English slurring, because his grandfather had come from Heidelberg in the 1930s. There were eight at table, average age forty, eating, drinking and talking lustily, but not a word of banking. British politics, the next American presidential election, recent holidays, Ibiza versus Zante, future holidays, Marrakesh versus Barbados, grouse and pheasants, the Arc de Triomphe and the Newmarket sales.

Old Speyer was courteous, but determined to tell Neil of his campaign to buy back from the Metropolitan Museum in New York the dining-room of his country house in Wiltshire, a masterpiece in plasterwork which an impoverished earl had let slip around 1925. High principles and personages were involved, and the tale was not short.

'The Foreign Office ought to intervene before the Committee meets. I telephoned to Edward Dunsford yesterday to tell him so. Unfortunately he has gone to Meridia, though that is certainly a vain expedition.'

'You think so?' It was the first breath of business.

'Certainly, young man. Meridia is the country where tomorrow never comes. And in any case that conference is simply a blind.'

Neil was determined to talk to *some*one about Meridia. 'Hamid, as you know, is very close to settling with the Russians and with the Arkansas Consortium. The Soviets are still keen. I've just come back from Moscow. It's all going very well. We just need a few more European names.'

'Ah yes,' said Speyer, without expression.

'Can you tell me that Speyer's might reconsider?'

Speyer blinked his frog's eyes, and pushed a pheasant leg to the side of his plate.

'Mr Wainwright, I am no longer the Chairman, and I cannot possibly answer your question. I understand that Guy has been put in charge of the problem. You must discuss it with him.'

'But . . .' But it was useless. Guy was at the other end of the table. It was two o'clock. How could he explain to the partners in New York that he had spent most of a working day in London, lunched at Speyer's and not managed to have a serious word with anyone about a project worth five hundred million dollars as a start, and maybe double that in two years' time?

Defeated, Neil turned to the second subject of interest. 'Didn't Edward Dunsford work here at the bank?'

'That is so.'

'To an American it seems odd that a man should give up a banking career with good prospects for a life in politics.'

'For a German also.' Speyer finished his claret, and his courtesy returned. 'But you must understand that in

England, though politics is no longer a gentleman's profession, it is still possible for a gentleman to persuade himself otherwise. You know the Palace of Westminster?'

'You mean Big Ben?'

'Big Ben is for tourists. I do not mean Big Ben. Beyond is an amazing palace. Gothic in architecture and in spirit. The Gothic of the English nineteenth century – darkness, pinnacles, discomfort, too hot, too cold, poor food. But splendid, the splendour not of reality but of dreams. It is a palace of enchantments. Men like Edward Dunsford can deceive themselves there much more easily than in his banker's parlour.'

'So what's the secret of that deception?'

'It is not power over others, not the spirit of domination you would find in the Kremlin or indeed in Gracie Mansion – if that is where your Mayor lives?'

'It is. But . . .'

'Go one day to the House of Commons as an elector, a constituent. Be you high or low, rich or poor, the procedure is the same. You are told by a policeman to wait, in a gilded hall with soaring absurd arches, mythical patriotic saints, and an impolite post office. You wait, minutes, quarters of an hour. If you are importunate or self-important you will fill in a green card, and the policeman carries it away, but it makes no difference. Eventually the Member of Parliament arrives, trailing clouds of glory from some sanctum, some further Gothic hall which you cannot penetrate. He bustles towards you, apologises, shakes your hand, explains how he is busy, is pleasant with you. He radiates the superiority of the elected person. That is the superiority, that is the enchantment which Dunsford feels, they all feel and which you and I cannot feel.'

'But that's what I mean. Isn't that the pleasure of power?'

'No, no, you mistake. Only the foolish ones suppose that they have real power. No, the pleasure is more insidious. It is the pleasure of service, the pleasure of being elected to serve others. It is the dangerous pleasure of the priesthood, and of the Pope, the proud slave of the slaves of God, *servus servonm Dei*, but brought up to date. Today it is easier, Mr Wainwright, to deceive yourself if you are chosen by the people than if you are called by God. The service of the people, that is the real seduction.' He stopped, so definitely that it seemed for a moment that he did not mean to continue. It was seven years since Neil had taken part in such a conversation, and he was out of practice.

'You know Mrs Dunsford, too?' That was a fatuous question to ask. God, it was half past two, and the coffee had only just come. Where the hell was the Tate Gallery?

'And we accept the tyranny called service,' said Speyer, winding himself up again as if Neil had not tried to change the subject. 'The press are immensely, unfairly, continuously rude to Members of Parliament. But that is unreal. MPs read foul things about themselves at breakfast, and go to lunches and dinners where everyone gathers round and adores. Their salaries are appallingly low, but their washing machines get mended sooner, their rail warrants are first class, they catch the eye of the waiter in the restaurant. Do you read Trollope?'

'Barsetshire.' The old man was becoming a bore.

'Good, but not the best. Try the political ones. Trollope tried and failed to get into Parliament. He writes about it as if it was heaven.'

109

At the end of the table Guy at last gave a sign. He put out a half-smoked cigar, and pushed back his chair. Farewells were quick. After two hours of gossip each guest suddenly remembered that he was a busy man.

'It's been a real pleasure to make your acquaintance, Mr Speyer, and to hear you talk so interestingly.'

'Go to the Metropolitan as soon as you can.'

Neil confused this for a second with the Tate and Rosemary, and the confusion showed.

'To see my dining-room before I buy it back.'

'I certainly will, sir, I certainly will.'

Guy and Neil were in the car again.

'Where are we going?'

'Where is your rendezvous with Rosemary?'

'I didn't think you heard. You had left the kitchen.'

'I heard nothing. I looked back and saw. You forget that I know her quite well.'

'The Tate Gallery at four. Where is that?'

'I will show you. So we have plenty of time to talk.'

Guy parked the car and they walked in St James's Park, quickly because they were without coats, and the cold was keen. The air had cleared, to the extent that the surface of the lake reflected a faint yellow sun. The starlings congregated until there was a parliament in two or three neighbouring plane trees, then, dissolving in a spasm of energy, they swept noisily across the afternoon sky, jabbering like politicians on the eve of an election.

'I want to talk to you about the Meridia consortium,' said Guy.

'You mean MEECON. I've been trying to talk about it all day.' Though when it came to the point, Neil found himself less eager.

110

'Tell me then how you see it.'

Neil had worked out some patter in the plane that morning. He produced it without further thought.

'Professionally I can say it is the most exciting project I've ever been associated with. It breaks new ground in collaboration between the super powers. It deploys the main strengths of the United States, namely entrepreneurial and technological skills, and the main strength of the Soviet Union, namely political acceptability in the third world. The United States' oil companies could not have come in on their own because the United States is not acceptable as a dominant partner in a black African country. The Soviets could not have come in on their own, because its state oil enterprises are notoriously bureaucratic and backward. Of course, it's not as simple as that. We lawyers have had to tie together two completely different materials in such a way that neither tears nor breaks.'

Neil made to continue but Guy interrupted with his own analysis.

'Let me tell you how I see it. There are three ways in which your deal could be frustrated. Hamid could lose power. Or he could change his mind because he was made a better offer. Or your Administration could interfere to stop you going ahead.'

'So you have thought seriously about it.' Neil did not mean to be rude, but he had almost despaired of getting any serious talk out of the British.

Guy smiled. 'We do occasionally think in this city, between mouthfuls.'

'Hamid has asked for personal protection, and the Soviets are giving it. They told us this in confidence,

111

without details. They seem confident they can keep him at the top of the heap.

As regards the better offer, they discounted that absolutely until just before I went to Moscow. They seemed certain no one would come forward. They even encouraged Hamid to call this conference in Mangara to prove the point. They thought that would give him a chance to show off on the international stage, which he loves, and at the same time prove that MEECON was the only friend he had with a full purse. But the day before yesterday they began to ask us about Edward Dunsford.'

'Because they heard he was going to the conference?'

'Exactly.'

'They were worried that he was putting together a better offer?'

'Not that far. But they wondered why a British minister was going to a conference where all serious countries were represented by officials.'

'Because he had a row with his wife, and wanted a break. Because he is a stubborn man who is interested in Meridia because no one else is. Because he's smelt something about MEECON he didn't like. Some mixture of these, I should think, and other ingredients I don't know of.'

'None of those would make much sense to Moscow.'

'Because they have forgotten about human nature. They prefer coherent, well-thought-out plots and conspiracies. They are not an advanced society. In an advanced society there are usually mixed motives and half-measures. Edward Dunsford is a better-than-average example of our mixed-up political personage. But in any case he is not important. He counts for nothing in this.

His superiors care nothing about Meridia. Nor, as I said this morning, do the people who elect them. The wood is wet, he has no chance of lighting a fire, even if he wanted. So in Moscow they can relax.'

They had paused on the bridge across the lake. The ducks, still mindful of summer, swam furiously below them in search of bread which they had not dropped.

'See the nearest building, with the grey, elegant tower. That's the Foreign Office. See those stunted modern white towers beyond, that's the Ministry of Defence. The world and the British public believe that their diplomats are suave and devious men, weak in resolution but full of guile and tricks. Their soldiers, on the other hand, they believe to be bluff, honourable, verging on the stupid at the start of anything, but coming through in the end through sheer doggedness. The architecture, the novels, the press have made the myth. Perhaps it was so once. Now it's certainly the other way round – subtle soldiers, straightforward diplomats. No value judgements there – it's a matter of taste. I find both quite agreeable.'

Neil did not know what to make of this. He was not at home with paradox. Guy brought the conversation back on course. They left the bridge and began to walk alongside the lake towards Buckingham Palace.

'And what about my third point? What if your own Government were to step in and stop it all?'

'They're well into that. The Russians want all kinds of assurances. They told us they needed a guarantee from the White House, or at least the State Department. My senior partner Joe Bourton went to Washington twice. He got as far as the Deputy Secretary, but the file had

113

been on to the President's desk by then. Cautious neutrality, that was the response.'

'But I gather they have reserved the right to step in if in practice they didn't like the way it was going.'

'Exactly, that was the snag. Bourton worked hard on State, he called a couple of senators who used to work with the firm, but he couldn't budge them beyond that. So we had a tough time in Moscow on this point. But they gave up in the end. Or rather they substituted one demand for another.'

'Meaning?'

This was where Neil had most carefully rehearsed his argument. It was the crux of his visit to London. Yet somehow the words did not come out as practised half-aloud in the toilet of the Aeroflot plane.

'They concentrated instead on the non-American financial backing. We asked you this before, getting Speyer's and the Paris Rothschilds and Yokohama Finance to put up their names and quite small sums. But that was to be the icing on the cake; we wouldn't have pressed it if you'd stayed reluctant.'

'Now it's important because the Russians want us to be there to put pressure on *our* Government if Washington begins to waver.'

'Right. What was the icing on top has become the fruit in the cake itself.'

'I must tell you that Speyer's won't. You may take that as final.' For the first time that day there was an edge of hostility in Guy's voice. He quickened his pace. They had reached the quiet end of the lake, cloistered by the walls which bore the weight of the traffic rushing round the Victoria Memorial.

'We could give you a six per cent cut of the action instead of three.' But, as he spoke, Neil knew this was wrong.

'That's not the point. It's not the money.' For once Guy was at a loss for words. 'I find it deeply depressing.' He sat on a hard wooden bench, and motioned Neil to do the same. It was as if they were both to do penance for their profession.

'I'm not depressed by you, you're young and clever and enthusiastic about law and banking. But I am shocked by Joe Bourton, a man everyone knows and respects for his experience. Yet there he is, shuttling up and down to Washington, harrying senators and secretaries, begging to be allowed to hand Meridia over to the Russians.'

'It's a banking proposition, not political.'

'Banking for you, politics for the Russians. How many bodyguards have they provided for Hamid already? Of course you don't know, that's their business. You've given it to them before anything is signed. How many Russian advisers will MEECON bring to Meridia? You don't know. With your dollars how many doors are you opening to the Russians in every Ministry in Mangara? You don't know.'

Neil was irritated.

'You're much more negative than you were on the telephone.'

'I know more. We've talked it over.'

'I don't see why you in Speyer's have to take the world's burden on your shoulders. After all, that skyline down there you showed me just now, that's yesterday's power. It's a long time since Meridia was red on the map. I don't understand why you don't pocket a six-per-cent cut of the action, and leave the State Department to worry about the politics.'

Guy leant forward, elbows on knees, long hands joined in front. There was something of the schoolmaster about Guy.

'Because we here, yesterday's men, remember our yesterdays quite accurately. We don't have to repeat our old mistakes just because you've put a new label on them.'

There was a pause.

'I should report that as a final decision by Speyer's?'

'You should.'

For no particular reason, Neil asked, 'Would Edward Dunsford agree?'

Guy looked surprised. 'I really don't know. He'll be back tomorrow. Stay and ask him. He'd be interested to see you. Though, as I say, he has no real authority.'

Neil thought. 'No, I must get back. The senior partners are meeting tomorrow afternoon. They'll want my report.'

And so the walk ended.

'I'll drive you to the Tate. You've twenty minutes in hand.'

'Time to walk?' Neil did not mean to be rude, but he did not want Guy to be there when he met Rosemary again.

'Plenty of time if you step out.'

Guy gave directions, received a stilted thanks for lunch, shook hands, drove off.

Neil arrived at the Tate Gallery on the stroke of four, somewhat out of breath, thinking of Henry James. He had always despised the Americans in those stories, mostly girls, who let themselves be bewitched and overborne by European sophistication. The kind of Americans whom Neil knew were just as sophisticated and twice as tough as any Europeans. In fact, they ran the world. But had he held his own against Guy Carlton? Hardly. How would Bourton have handled him? Neil ran two at a time up the steps and switching his mind from one subject to another found the postcard counter. No Rosemary. He remembered how her hair tumbled over the red sweater. He waited there for ten minutes. Then he walked out again on to the steps and waited twenty minutes. Back to the postcards, in case there was a side door for people like Rosemary. He thought of telephoning, but fought the idea down as degrading. Even Henry James's milksops would not have stooped to that: By a quarter to five he knew she would not come. And it was time to find a taxi to take him back to Heathrow.

10

'What? This is intolerable. They can't cancel all of them.'

'They have, sir. I've been round to all three Ministries myself. They're seeing no one.'

'And what about the President? For heaven's sake, he can't refuse to see the Minister. It's unheard of.'

'I've talked to my friend at the palace. He couldn't have been more embarrassed about it.'

'He damn well should be.'

'Apparently the President is locked away with his Ministers. No explanation that makes sense. But they've gone out of their way to be apologetic.'

The Ambassador was pacing the room in a fluster, one hand twitching nervously at the knot of his tie. Even two walls lined with books could not conceal the tastelessness of the room. The architect had designed an outsize undergraduate room of a modern and not very well endowed Cambridge college – bare walls, cheap furnishings, a nasty feel. It only lacked an ill-made bed and a bottle of stale milk.

'Minister, there has been some very unfortunate news.' Edward had entered in search of a drink. 'I've just been told by my Second Secretary that the three calls we had arranged for you this afternoon have all been cancelled without any warning or explanation. I'm afraid that seems to go for the President as well. I can hardly believe it. It's all quite intolerable and inexcusable.'

Sally followed hard on Edward's heels, clutching a draft telegram in her neat writing. It summarised the morning's session, and suggested a form of words for London to use in handling questions from the press. It was agreed the Embassy would stay in touch with the Foreign Ministry during the afternoon. If a summons to the palace came before Edward left to catch the flight back to London at eleven that evening, well and good. Sally was surprised. There was no injured ministerial pride, no angry words or short-tempered exit from the study. There was a tolerance and lightness of spirit about Edward she had not seen before. With Sandford-Smith they went in to meet the twenty or so people who had come to the Ambassador's lunch.

It was the British community's turn to meet the Minister of State. A few businessmen, the parson from the Anglican Church, some new faces from the Embassy, the head of the British Council office, a handful of technical advisers supplied under London's limited aid programme. Among the guests were a middle-aged nurse, and the television reporter who had been at the airport. Between them that afternoon they decided Edward's future. Monica Hayward was the Sister at the El Sharif Hospital twenty miles outside Mangara. She had been in Meridia for years. She conformed to no ordinary National Health

119

standards: short, round and friendly, rather than tall, white and stern. Everyone in the small British community knew of her and her work. Because Mrs Sandford-Smith had quickly befriended her, an invitation to meet the Minister of State had naturally been sent to her. She was pleased to come, but feeling a little out of place. She showed it by laughing a little louder and more often than she should. By contrast, Anthony Warren of Herald Television showed by a practical, disdainful air how surprised he would have been not to be there. In fact he had been asked to fill a last-minute gap.

It was the nurse and the newsman who got Edward to the El Sharif Hospital that afternoon. Edward sat next to Monica Hayward at lunch. Mrs Sandford-Smith had pushed them together as they queued for their plates of meat and rice, and steered them dutifully to a sofa in a corner. He was interested by the modest story of her work, impressed by her dedication and intrigued by the little hospital she helped to run. Anthony Warren joined them with his coffee. He had already sent his report about the conference but had few hopes it would attract much notice in London. No family sprawled in front of their television set in Orpington would watch with any interest a squabble among foreigners over issues of which they were happily and disdainfully ignorant. But human suffering and misery always earned TV companies good marks. The El Sharif ought to have a bit of each and was worth a try. So when Sister Hayward tentatively suggested the Minister might come to see the hospital for himself, Warren seized his chance and pressed her case eagerly.

Edward suddenly found himself unhappily cornered.

120

He did not want to go. It would be hot, dusty, evil-smelling and disagreeable. He was squeamish about hospitals and medicine ever since he had once fainted in the dentist's chair. But in the TV man's hearing he had been praising Sister Hayward's work. In the TV man's hearing the Ambassador had dropped a comment to Edward about the sudden gap in his programme that afternoon. Perhaps he could have found an excuse to duck Monica Hayward's invitation. But in his heart Edward knew his choice was the sick or the swimming pool, and his conscience won. So, against his inclination but according to his conscience, he accepted the invitation to see the hospital.

They checked again with the Foreign Ministry without success. There was no word of an interview with President Hamid. The Ambassador excused himself: he was not a great hospital visitor, he said. A Third Secretary, just out from London on his first posting, was produced to accompany them. So, within an hour, Edward and Sally were bumping south out of Mangara with Sister Hayward in the Embassy Land Rover. In their dust followed a Japanese jeep containing Warren, a camera operator and a man with a satchel of batteries and a microphone. They took a brown dirt road through a brown dirt country, low hills, a few sun-baked dwellings here and there, goats, the odd woman walking home, a few aged Bedford lorries battling into the interior.

It took an hour to reach the little town and its hospital. They saw a low, battered building of cheap brick and peeling plaster sitting in a compound behind a mud wall. A pair of metal gates had lost their hinges and slouched against the wall. A faded red cross had been painted on one by a grateful patient. Yet this shabby place was bustling with life. Its courtyard was full of figures, shouting, silent, strolling, slumped, lame, beggared, healthy, grotesque, emaciated and dying. Only the colour, not the sickness and despair, could be sensed when they first jumped from the Land Rover once it parked beside the crazy gates. The television team were already filming. Sally began to fiddle with her own Instamatic. Then she realised that these were not masks at some fancy-dress party. The faces were real, and the suffering was real. Edward had no viewfinder to distract him. He had come, he thought, as the dispassionate outsider, the Minister who recognised his duty to grace simply by his presence. He had toured hospitals in Lewes and old folks' homes in Sussex villages. But he was not prepared for what he now saw in the little courtyard, the swollen limbs, horrible disfigurements, bleeding wounds, suppurating ulcers, the pallor of sickness. Half of them were children, dying of malnutrition, their stomachs swollen, their limbs little more than matchsticks. A shrunken woman, who looked sixty and was probably twenty, was hunched over a pile of rubbish, vomiting and choking. An orderly was running towards her.

Here and there, amidst it all, were little islands of hope. His eye was caught by a child, perhaps four or five years old, who sat in a brilliant multi-coloured dress in the middle of the yard. She held her hands beneath a tap, cupping one to catch the tiny stream of water, carefully pouring the precious liquid from hand to hand. It was a delicate ritual of washing. She might have been a young girl jealously but sparingly enjoying her first expensive perfume. But the scene gave Edward no comfort. He looked round and was appalled.

Monica Hayward had shed feelings like this many years before. She now shed the diffidence which she had shown at lunch and in the Land Rover. She did not mind the cameras which followed them about. She was far from callous. But her countrymen knew too little of real suffering. They passed through the courtyard and she took control. The sick Africans who surrounded them knew her as the woman who had cared for their families and their friends. Sometimes they were cured, but even the dying found a form of comfort in her care. So they came with trust to receive a little hope. She moved among the crowd easily and kindly. Edward saw a horribly deformed arm reach out to touch her, and Sister Hayward took the old man's hand in hers. Edward shuddered. He was shocked to realise how unnatural these things seemed to him.

It was much hotter. The TV camera followed them inside the building. Anthony Warren's nose had led him correctly. The scenes were just what he had hoped for as they toured the rooms and corridors. Patients lay in little rooms surrounded by anxious relatives chattering, cooking, crying, silent, waiting. Some were too ill or too stricken to notice the strange intrusion. Edward and Sally moved in a daze behind their guide. She would stop and explain the circumstances of a particular family. Edward would stand, hands clasped in front of him, or an arm across his chest and his chin cupped in his palm. From time to time he leant forward to shake a bony hand or murmur some useless encouragement to the sick. Once a little girl in a hot and noisy room shook with convulsions and fainted beside her father's bed. She fell dramatically and unexpectedly to the floor. On everything the TV lights cast an unhealthy glare, picking out with awful clarity the cracks in the white plaster and the lines on the sick faces.

It was hot, stuffy, squalid. There were flies, noise, the smells of disease and the sounds of suffering. Sister Hayward continued to bustle up and down corridors, her strange group of sightseers behind her. Round a dark corner she almost fell over an old man, a collection of bones heaped beneath the folds of his wrinkled skin. He crouched, whimpering, on the cool, dusty, black-and-cream-speckled tiles. The nurse pushed confidently through two swinging doors. She stopped abruptly, with a murmur of apology. Before them two surgeons in green were stitching up a man's stomach. They turned for an instant towards the intruders. Their hands and clothes were soaked in blood. Edward winced. Sally turned white and grabbed at his arm. The cameraman was fiddling with his equipment outside in the corridor.

'I'm sorry, I think I'm going to pass out.'

He led her out, she still clutching his arm. He found an open window and held her while she inhaled the tiny breeze that found its way through. A cockroach sat in a corner of the passage. The sick shuffled past the two figures by the window and ignored them.

'I'm terribly sorry. I'm not used to this sort of thing.'

'I'd be more surprised if you were. Are you all right?'

Her face was a mixture of grey and white.

'Better, yes, but still pretty awful. Perhaps we can find some water, and somewhere to sit down.'

Monica Hayward approached with yet another patient in tow. Edward realised he still held an arm protectively around Sally's shoulder. He decided to keep it there for the time being. Miss Hayward took no notice.

'We do what we can, Mr Dunsford. But it's a struggle. There are never enough drugs, you know. And we've hardly any equipment. If we order something one day we never know whether we'll have the money to pay for it the next.'

'What about skills?' asked Edward, as they threaded their way back through the hospital to the courtyard and their car. 'Money won't buy good people for you.'

'People can be found, Mr Dunsford. There are many like us here. But, you see, if we haven't got the resources we can't use the people anyway. So there's a limit to what we can do.'

Edward stood once again in the courtyard, surveying the crowd, arms crossed. It was a world remote from his own. He thought of Rosemary with her expensive clothes, worrying about her headache or whether there was ice enough for her gin and tonic.

'But you're a drop in the ocean, Sister Hayward. How much can you contribute here?'

'I hope a little, Mr Dunsford. I have a skill. I want to use it. These people need help desperately. I think I can do something for them which I couldn't do if I were in some large teaching hospital in England. So I stay. It's as simple as that, really.'

Anthony Warren was standing a few feet away in front of the camera, the life of the hospital courtyard busy behind his back. He was putting together the finishing touches to the visit, mixing in his journalist's palette a

125

handful of darker colours to etch the picture more clearly in the middle of that Orpington sitting-room. Edward had already said a few words to him in front of the camera. He was visibly moved, but he still chose his words with care.

'These people are clearly desperate,' Edward said. 'They need the care and the help which only the West has the resources – and I hope the will – to provide. We must do what we can to help.'

It was enough. The newsman always recognised the opportunity for interpretation.

'So, as Edward Dunsford told us earlier, there is hope for a people when one sees the effort and dedication of this tiny staff and their brave English Sister, who labour against incredible difficulties to help the sick and the appalling suffering which they find here. A Foreign Office Minister has said the El Sharif Hospital demonstrates the size of the task the world has to undertake. This afternoon he has pledged that the British Government will do all it can to help in that task. To anyone who has seen the misery and suffering we have today, those words will find an echo. Let us hope they find some sympathy, too, with the British Prime Minister and his Foreign Secretary. Because so far the British Government have made clear that there isn't much money available. Perhaps this Foreign Office Minister, Edward Dunsford, who has seen for himself the nightmares which poverty brings, can persuade them otherwise. This is Anthony Warren reporting to you from Meridia.'

The camera swung round to show Edward and Sally shaking hands with Monica Hayward, Edward and Sally climbing into their Land Rover and waving self-consciously goodbye.

Sally was still pale, but feeling better. She wanted to chatter. Edward did not. He sat silent and depressed. After a few false starts Sally decided she had better say nothing during the drive back.

Edward was wondering again how Rosemary would have reacted to it all. He suddenly remembered.

'Oh God, I've forgotten her birthday.' He stared gloomily through the bouncing window at a brown, dusty, evening sun.

They caught the overnight flight to London which left Mangara later that evening. There was no summons to the palace, and no Foreign Minister at the airport. Hamid was still in the middle of an endless stream of meetings. But the Foreign Minister did ring through to the VIP lounge as Edward and Sally waited to board the plane. He was friendly and apologetic. Edward spoke warmly in reply. They agreed that their friendship had made a very imperfect beginning. But they would make good the false start as soon as they could. Edward hoped that the Foreign Minister would take an early opportunity to stop off in London if he were coming that way. This was a standard courtesy between Foreign Ministers.

This time Edward gave Sally the window. They had large, comfortable seats in the first-class section of a new wide-bodied jet. Before they had sat down an air hostess was hanging up Edward's jacket and offering champagne. A menu card was produced, boasting how much their forthcoming dinner would justify the airline's reputation for its food. It was already eleven thirty. Nevertheless, the menu card promised that dinner would be preceded immediately after take-off by a selection of irresistible 'heavy snacks'. The other passengers began to trickle through into the economy section, like flotsam passing through a sluice-gate. Edward nodded in vague recognition at an unimpressive English columnist who formed part of the slow-moving chain.

Edward hated flying. It was partly the physical sensation, the noise which drummed relentlessly hour by hour into one's ears. It was partly the sense of physical abstraction whereby neither mind nor stomach could remember, as soon as the aircraft door was closed, whether the body should be working, resting, eating or sleeping. Nor was the victim given any choice: food, blankets, drink, headphones, slipperettes were pushed indiscriminately at him, brow-beating him into helpless prostration.

The jet climbed steeply away from the airport. It did not turn over the city to correct its course. Mangara slipped almost immediately into the night. But not out of the thoughts of either of them. Sally opened her office case. On the flight back from his short European trips, Edward had sometimes scribbled a short note of impressions and recommendations to the Foreign Secretary. He must surely want to do so on an occasion like this. She offered him some sheets of blue draft paper. He was staring at the glass of champagne in his hand, apparently intent on preventing the contents from spilling.

'Minister, I thought you might like to write something for the Secretary of State about the conference.'

'No. Later perhaps. I haven't yet got it clear in my mind.'

She was surprised. In her experience it was not like him to be uncertain. He made his decisions quickly and confidently. Occasionally he made a small pretext of discussing a submission with her first. She was always slightly flattered to be asked to give an opinion. But she knew he had always made up his mind before asking.

He had hardly spoken a word since their visit to the hospital. Until then she had thought they were coming closer together. Now she doubted herself again. She had been right in the car after all: four days would make no difference. She replaced the draft paper in her case.

'When you do write something, Minister, I don't think it should be only about the conference.'

'Why not?'

'I don't know how you feel about what we saw today. I thought it was awful, terrible.'

'So what do we do about it?' He put down the champagne on the armrest between them and looked at her.

'Well, something, surely?' She found her voice again, confidently as she had the previous day. 'I just find it awful that politics gets in the way all the time. The Russians are pouring in people, but they're not there to help. And we go around saying the right things knowing that those ghastly bureaucrats in the Treasury will never give a penny to any cause further than the end of their nose.'

'That's not the answer I'd expect from a young, aspiring diplomat.'

'Stuff the bloody office.' She stopped. Helped by the champagne she turned very red. 'I'm sorry, Minister. That was very rude of me.'

Edward waved away a votary offering a tray of heavy snacks. He was tired, but a little elated by the champagne. He liked this girl. She was turning out a good companion. He had stopped pretending in Mangara. And it was stupid to start again now.

'Sally. Two things. First, when it's just the two of us like this it would be very nice for me if for once you stopped calling me Minister. Otherwise it keeps everything so formal. You and I would never be able to talk properly.' He wondered whether he should add 'or get to know each other', but decided against it. She nodded, but did not know what she could say. And what on earth *was* she to call him?

'Second, I want you to know that I decided this morning, before the hospital, that we shouldn't treat this deal with the Russians and the oil companies as a foregone conclusion. Hamid's proud, but I don't think he's a fool. He's been too long where he is not to sniff the dangers of what he's flirting with. It seems to me that gives us a chance.'

She was trying to look hard both at him and the stewardess with the snack trolley.

'All right, a small one. But a chance that if we show that we care and will do what we can, roping in as much of the West as we can, he might drop the Russians.'

A bottle of champagne appeared at Edward's elbow. The air hostess filled their two glasses. Sally was not sure how she should treat this unexpected intimacy. She sipped at her champagne.

'You said that's how you felt before the hospital.'

'I found it exactly as you did. Awful. Sickening. Hopeless. People in need of real help. I expect our friend

Warren will have over-coloured my offer of help in his bit for the TV news. In some ways I hope he has. The hospital showed that the need is there – without all the politics behind it.'

'Yes. But the politics makes the need that much more pressing.'

'Exactly. But I don't think we shall easily persuade Patrick Reid of that. And that's why we need to think the thing through a bit before I write anything down.'

They continued to talk through their obligatory dinner, Edward toying with his *chateaubriand*, Sally eating her way ravenously through every course the acolytes piled on to the miniature Japanese china.

Two and a half hours out of Mangara the food and drink had been cleared away, blankets, eye-shades and nylon slippers produced out of plastic bags, the lights of the cabin dimmed. Sally, as exhausted as she had been hungry, fell quickly asleep. As she drifted away, Edward found her head come to rest innocently against his shoulder. He thought back to the absurd incident when their hands touched over the key to his red box nearly three days before. This time the contact between their two bodies lasted. He moved his arm almost without thinking to cradle her head and shoulders. He, too, was asleep ten minutes later, his head slumped against Sally's with the innocence and trust of a lover. It was then that the journalist to whom Edward had nodded before take-off walked through the first-class cabin in search of another drink. He retreated before he found a stewardess, his craving for a large whisky and soda suddenly forgotten. He returned with his camera and a smile, and quickly photographed them. The *Daily Express* would be greatly pleased. Perhaps they would even use it as their 'Phototake of the Month'. He tried to imagine a suitable caption. The long journey to Mangara had been worth it after all.

11

The Managing Director of Thames Television heard of it about tea time. The line from Mangara was bad, but he got the gist, and asked the necessary questions.

'The kid actually died on camera? . . .'

'Relapsed into a coma? Same thing.'

'Quality of picture?'

'How did Dunsford react?'

'Anyone else get it?'

The inward telephone call from Mangara bred two outward. The first to the Controller of Thames's evening programme, *This Night*.

'You've got the stuff from the Herald man in Mangara?'

'Yes, it's first class.'

'Where are you going to put it?'

'It's being cut to ten minutes. I'm putting it right at the end of the programme.'

'Instead of?'

'EC fisheries dispute, effect on Shetland fisheries. Routine stuff, will keep.'

'Okay. Make a thirty-second clip and get it trailed from now on the hour every hour until you transmit.'

'The others won't like it. It'll upset their timings.'

'I'll talk to them. No one'll notice except themselves. Too late to get it networked, unfortunately.' He paused. 'How would it take you if I sold it to ITN?'

The Managing Director had paused because his suggestion would mean that the huge London audience of Thames Television would see the film of Edward Dunsford's visit to the hospital twice within half an hour – once at the end of *This Night* programme, again during the Independent Television News bulletin which followed. But there was no other way of getting the film to the whole country outside Thames. It was his policy to buy for Thames exclusive rights to the work of small independents like Herald, and this would be a flamboyant justification.

'No hardship. The material will stand it. How much do you reckon ITN will take?'

'Three minutes, I should guess. Perhaps four. I'll let you know. They'll do their own cutting, of course. I'll ring you back.'

And so it happened that in prime time on the more popular channel eight million people followed Edward Dunsford and Sally round the hospital. And that was just the start.

The BBC first heard of it a few minutes later. Their representative was young, educated and earnest. He had puzzled over the figures of Meridia's external debt in his sweltering flat in Cairo. He had flown down to Mangara two days before the start of the conference to catch the

134

flavour of the financial situation. Having failed to persuade his employers to send out a camera team he had been authorised to collaborate with the American CBS team already there. He had recorded radio interviews of considerable dullness with Hamid's Minister of Finance and with Edward Dunsford in the VIP lounge at the airport. With the help of CBS he had sent home a shot of Edward entering the conference building, a shot of Edward leaving the conference building and a still of the conference in session. He thought he had done everything possible, but being principled and apt to worry, he telephoned about the activities of the Herald team and quickly found himself making excuses.

'No, it wasn't in the programme. Look, it was just a hospital visit, nothing to do with the conference. All pretty routine stuff. I thought it was more important to follow up the chance of an interview with Hamid – no, I didn't actually get one, but I'm going back to the Presidential Secretariat tomorrow . . .', and so on.

The BBC rang Herald, but Herald's contract with Thames was watertight. They cut all references to the Meridian economic conference out of the nine o'clock and later bulletins. 'If you can't compete, don't try' was a well-established slogan in British television. But tomorrow was another day, and twenty-four hours is a long time in television. They ordered their top political correspondent, Sir Barry Trent, and a full camera team to Heathrow for the next morning.

The Foreign and Commonwealth Office heard of it a few minutes later in an 'Immediate' telegram from the Embassy in Mangara.

The Minister of State's visit to the hospital contained some harrowing scenes, including some with badly undernourished children. These were photographed by an independent British camera team which gained access without following the proper procedures through the Embassy. My Information Officer was not able to hear in full the commentary, or indeed the Minister of State's answers to questions. I have however reason to believe that the story may be treated in an undesirably sensational manner and that the programme if shown may cause offence here by presenting Meridia and its medical services in an unfavourable light. I do not need to point out the potential damage which this could cause to our relations at a sensitive time. While I recognise the difficulties I hope that strenuous efforts can be made to prevent the programme being shown.

The Resident Clerk on duty in the flat at the top of the Foreign Office showed the telegram to another Resident Clerk who was leaving to take a girl to the theatre.

'You're on the Meridia desk. Spot the gap in this one.'

The second young man read it. They were both in their thirties, enjoying their trade, old enough not to be timid, too young to be tired or eccentric.

'There's nothing about Dunsford's own views.'

'Sent after he'd left.'

'An afterthought.'

'Too late to be of any use.'

'And silly anyway.'

'What's the drill in these things?'

'If he'd made a good case, and if we'd a day in hand, we'd ask the IBA to have a look at it. Very informally.

Their decision, not ours. As it is, I'd better just ring the Head of Department to be sure.'

He found the man's home number in his list, dialled, reported and listened.

'As we thought. Nothing to be done. You're to compose a soothing telegram to Sandford-Smith in the morning. Give my love to Jenny.'

Neil Wainwright saw the programme in the TWA Executive Lounge at Heathrow Airport. His plane had been half an hour late, an hour late, now two hours late. TWA were certain the delay would not be more than two hours. That would get him to New York in good time for the report to be typed and distributed in advance of the meeting. After the excessive lunch at Speyer's he would not need the TWA dinner. Bourton had told him when he started in the firm that a secret of success was to eat only one substantial meal a day. Bourton had also recommended the brand of sleeping tablets: two taken as soon as the engines started would be enough to give sleep without deadening his brain for tomorrow. Neil Wainwright had an orderly mind, and liked small physical matters to be tidily organised. At that moment, as he packed his report in his black almost-leather despatch case, and was in danger of thinking of Rosemary, someone at the end of the lounge turned up the volume of the television, saying, 'Look at that then, ain't that something?'

So Neil Wainwright saw all except the first two minutes of the hospital visit. He saw the little white-washed, tumbledown hospital, the round, ruddy English nurse whose virtues the reporter mentioned four or five times. The camera dwelt a long time in close-up on the faces of the sick, the hungry and the dying. It followed Dunsford into the hospital, saw him listening, questioning, shaking hands, giving a word probably of encouragement, amidst a pageant of horribly colourful sickness. The dirt, the dust, the blood were picked out by the camera in careful detail. There was one telling and disturbing shot of a little girl collapsing to the floor. It may have been anguish or illness. It hardly mattered which. The picture remained vividly in his mind. There was a short interview with Edward. He was grave, concerned, restrained. He said nothing of politics, he simply said what anyone would have said in the same circumstances: it was terrible, it was unnecessary, it needed help. The interviewer took up these words at the end of the film and twisted them cleverly into a jibe against the Government. It was over in four and a half minutes.

Really important people hardly ever watch television. Their evenings mark an extension, even an intensification of activity, not a sudden switch from work to leisure. So it was not surprising that the Prime Minister did not watch the Herald programme. He returned to 10 Downing Street at about 11.30 p.m. from a dinner of the Institute of Engineering at the Mansion House. His stiff collar chafed his neck where he had nicked himself shaving, he had noticed that the insignia hanging below the white tie needed polishing, and the speech he had read out was dull and five minutes too long. Civil servants who drafted speeches could never distinguish between the written and the spoken word. He never had time to sort them out. He wanted to go to bed, but wanted even more to loosen his collar and drink a weak reflective nightcap in the company of the first editions of next morning's papers. Luckily his wife had gone to bed, so this was possible. There were three red boxes of work, which he was prepared to ignore. But there was also a note asking him to ring Singer, the Chief Press Officer; and so the Prime Minister heard of the broadcast.

'It was very powerful indeed, Prime Minister.'

'Edward Dunsford or the circumstances?'

'The suffering. He said little, but was obviously moved. The commentary implied that something should be done. It did not say what.'

'Of course.' The Prime Minister grunted. He did not know Edward Dunsford well: a workaday, self-contained man with a beautiful wife, who had earned his present position and was now beginning to appear towards the bottom of the lists of Cabinet 'possibles' which the Chief Whip submitted on the eve of each Cabinet reshuffle. He would never get one of the two or three top jobs. The Prime Minister could not imagine Dunsford feeling really strongly about anything except his own career. He could not imagine why Singer should have bothered him with it.

'I can't imagine why you bothered me with it.'

Singer had an unimpressive manner. He gave the impression of being unsure and easily bullied. But he had a feel for the flow of politics which was rare in a government information officer.

'I'm sorry, Prime Minister. I know you've had a long day. I may be wrong, but I think that interview will stir up at the least a big mail for you, perhaps a lot of trouble. But, as I say, I may be wrong.'

'When's Dunsford back?'

'Tomorrow. I've just made sure that the head of the

FCO News Department goes to Heathrow himself. There'll be a crowd.'

'The important thing is that Dunsford shouldn't commit anyone to anything. There's no money for Meridia, and I won't have policy bred out of a sentimental television programme by a junior minister at the airport. He can say that he's reporting to me. When he's said that once he should say it again. And again, until they're bored.'

'That could mean a bad press the next day.'

'For him, Singer, for him. That's his fault for visiting hospitals when he's supposed to be at a financial conference. You'd better go out yourself.'

Rosemary did not see the programme because she had been watching *Lucia di Lammermoor* on BBC Two. It was her favourite opera, seen in New York, Rome, and at Covent Garden one evening when she and Edward were engaged. The mad scene had dragged a little, but the foyer had been full of friends, and the future had sparkled.

No such champagne excitement now, only indecisions and a little too much private alcohol. None of the legitimate ties, neither Edward, nor the girls, nor politics, nor the London nor Sussex homes held her interest and loyalty for more than a day or two at a time. Nor did she have anyone or anything illegitimate to enliven her, just a string of random temptations. That young American lawyer whom Guy had brought, for example. She liked his white skin, the light freckles, the turbulent reddish hair, his modest yet intelligent manners. Modesty with a limit, she supposed. Probably there would have been scurries in motels or in university dormitories.

But when it came to the point with Neil, Rosemary had drawn back. There was a lot to lose and, in her fortieth year, she was not so itchy that she need run after every presentable young man who presented himself. So she had not gone to the Tate. It had never occurred to her either to ring up Speyer's and let Neil know in advance that she was not coming, or indeed to go to the Tate and look at the Turners with him without bringing him back for a drink and bed. Neither would have been her style. But as the sombre last act of *Lucia* swelled around her she wondered, on the sofa with a glass, whether she would ring up Guy and find out what had become of the young man. Conceivably he might have changed plans and be staying in London overnight.

At that moment, Guy rang her. He had been to the same dinner as the Prime Minister but had, as usual, videoed the ten o'clock news. He told Rosemary what he had seen.

'I think it'll cause a stir.'

'Against Edward?'

'No, no. Indeed it'll put him in the news for a day or two. What he does with it after that is up to him.'

But her mind was on other things. She found it difficult to concentrate on Edward.

'Oh Guy, what became of that young man?'

'Neil Wainwright?'

'Yes.'

'You tell me. You were going to meet him this afternoon.'

'I couldn't manage it.'

'Then I suppose he's flown home with a broken heart and a pocketful of Tate Gallery postcards.'

141

'He told you then?'

'He was anxious not to be late.'

A pause.

'Did you sign up with him?'

'We did not.'

'That was Meridia too, wasn't it?'

'It was.'

'I wish I understood about Meridia.'

'That's balls, Rosemary.'

'Well, it's almost true.'

'I expect Edward will tell you all about it tomorrow.'

'God, I can't think of anything more tedious. I have a defence mechanism now, you know, Guy, I can't help it. I simply cannot remember anything Edward tells me.'

Another pause, then Guy changed his voice.

'Don't be so silly. Anyone would think you were stupid. I won't argue with you. I'll give you two pieces of advice. One, don't talk to journalists till Edward gets back. Two, I'm not sure, but I think Edward's winding himself up for a fight. If so, you must help him to win.'

'It'll be a sham. Political fights are always shams.'

'Don't you be so sure. Take those earplugs out, and for once try to listen.'

A final pause.

'Thank you for ringing, Guy. And for the book. And for being rather good to me.'

The opera was over. Rosemary stood for a moment in front of the empty screen. A real fight, yes, she and Edward against the odds and against the world, that might be fun. It would certainly have been fun years ago. It came as a new thought. At any rate, she would do her best.

The telephone rang. It was the *Daily Express*.

'No, I can't comment at all, I'm afraid . . . yes, I expect him back tomorrow . . . no comment . . . really nothing more to say. Good night.'

Heavens, it was difficult to be good. But she would try this time, she really would try.

12

Edward and Sally woke over the Mediterranean. They were not in each other's arms. They felt dirty and dehydrated. They were flying against the clock, and it was always breakfast time. Theirs had been cleared away over Elba. But it was after they crossed the coast of France that the radio message came. It was brought down the aisle by the captain himself.

'Good morning, Minister. Having a pleasant flight, I trust?'

'Yes, indeed, thank you.' Edward was glad that he had just shaved in the toilet, applied some British Airways Gentleman's Cologne and put on his tie.

'A head wind, but we should be on the ground just fifteen minutes late, at 0935.'

Edward fiddled with his watch, putting it back the necessary three hours.

'There's a message just come in from the British Airports Authority. A lot of press interest, apparently, in your arrival After consulting the Foreign Office and

Downing Street, they've laid on a press conference in the usual room. Radio and TV are expected.'

'Good, thank you very much.' Edward spoke as if this was all routine, but he and Sally knew that it was not. A Minister of State returning from a financial conference would normally be lucky to win a mention on page three of the *Financial Times*. Edward straightened his tie for the second time.

'D'you think they've disowned me? Or sacked me? You heard him mention Number Ten.'

'It is a bit surprising,' said Sally. She deliberately did not call him anything. She could not say 'Minister' after their conversation the previous night. Nor, somehow, could she yet call him anything else. She reacted, as a trained civil servant, burrowing instinctively in her briefcase for some bit of paper which could be presented to her Minister as a brief. A minister could not be expected, or indeed allowed, to do or say anything substantial without a brief.

'Stop doing that,' said Edward, not roughly but with a directness which he would not have attempted before his trip. 'You haven't the faintest idea what questions they will ask. And the main points are in my head anyway.' Also in his head was the worry that the excitement was to do with Rosemary. Perhaps she had run off with Guy, or with Charles Elliott, or said something outrageous. But surely they would have found some way of letting him know.

'It must be the hospital visit. Warren must have done something sensational after all,' said Sally, pulling a flushed face out of the brown pouch. She, too, had been left to achieve a rudimentary wash and brush, but she knew that her hair was sticky.

'I wonder. They'll hardly have had time to get anything shown,' said Edward. 'And anyway to them it was just routine. Dying blacks are two a penny to the media. I doubt if they'll sell what they took.' He paused, then put his hand on hers, and looked into her face. 'The hospital moved us, Sally, so we think it will move others. When we get back to the office we'll find that cynicism is still king.'

The official black Ambassador car was at the foot of the aircraft steps as usual, but unusually there was a man inside, as well as Jack. The blurred face took a recognised shape. It was Singer, the Number Ten press spokesman, a man who never said a disrespectful word to ministers but was disliked by most and feared by all. Unlike them, he knew the Prime Minister's mind, and doled out to the press such morsels of that mind as seemed to him right for their diet each day. Ministers never knew what the political correspondents invented and what Singer had fed them. Seeing him in the car, a grey face with a newspaper on his knee, Edward felt certain that Rosemary had done something awful.

It was not that. Relief rose within him. Sally, sticky-haired, white-bedroomed old Sally, had been right. Her petticoat was showing below her skirt, but she had been right. It was the hospital. Somehow, in a way which Edward did not understand, everyone was excited about the sights and sounds far away in Mangara which had excited him. His own emotion had subsided, indeed he had tried to subdue it because he was sure others would not share it. One person who was still immune from all emotion was certainly Singer, but his courtesy was copious.

'The Prime Minister is very pleased with the way

things have gone,' said Singer as they followed the Airports Authority car through the complicated slalom of Heathrow. 'Very pleased. In last night's programme you struck, if I may say so, Minister, exactly the right note of compassion. The Prime Minister is content that you should handle this press conference exactly as you judge right. But he supposes that you will want to avoid anything which might be misrepresented as a commitment.'

'A commitment?'

'Of public money to help Meridia. The PM thinks you may be under some pressure in view of your visit to the hospital.'

'I said nothing wrong then?'

'Not at all, not at all, but in the commentary there was a tendency to imply . . .'

'I'm not responsible for the commentary.'

'Of course not, of course not. But the PM is anxious that there should be no misunderstanding. The aid budget is totally committed already. He is clear that the Cabinet would in no circumstances approve extra from the contingency reserve for that purpose.' There was steel now in Singer's voice. The car stopped outside the newest VIP lounge, the entrance to which had been painted blue and orange by a mad young decorator on the public pay-roll.

Singer continued, 'The PM thought you could get out of the difficulty by stressing that of course junior ministers do not make policy, and your role would be limited to reporting to the Prime Minister. He authorises you to say that you will be reporting to him direct.'

Bloody little squirt. He had touched a spot which is

147

tender in all junior ministers. The second eleven explain and defend decisions which others have taken.

'Has the PM talked to the Foreign Secretary about all this?'

Singer was for a second nonplussed.

'I'm sure he will do so today.'

But it was a pointless point to score, for there was no chance of Patrick Reid backing anything for Meridia.

'I want to make a telephone call.'

'I think the journalists will all be assembled. Some of them will have deadlines . . .' Singer did not want Dunsford out of his sight. Junior ministers had been known to telephone journalists direct.

'I want to speak to my wife.'

'Of course, of course.' Singer knew a bit about that too, and allowed himself a half-smile.

Rosemary was in, and good humoured.

'I hear you may have a fight on your hands.'

'Who told you that?'

'Guy. He rang to tell me of the TV programme about the Congo.'

'Meridia.' It was an old joke between them that all African countries were the same to her.

'Are you all right, sweetheart?' He could not rid himself of the idea that she had done something dreadful.

'I'm fine. I had a lovely birthday yesterday.'

Damn.

'Meridia's not the best place for shopping. Or for greetings telegrams.'

'Don't worry. Guy brought me two presents to make up.'

'Two?'

'A coffee-table book, and a nice young American with freckles.'

Guy? A young American? Dangers? But there was no time to probe.

'I must go and take the press conference.'

'Goodness, how grand. Did you get any sleep?'

'Not much.' At least she hadn't said anything about Sally. And the best was to come.

'Do well then, Edward. And remember, I don't know the first thing about it, but I'm on your side.'

A surge of pleasure went right through him. That after all was what he wanted.

The bulbs of the photographers popped, the camera lights glared, the questions came fast. Edward ran his fingers through his hair. He felt excited, and at his best. This was what modern politics was about – the quick thrust of explanation, a mind trained to turn its store of information at a second's notice into sharp persuasive words which would be understood and accepted within hours by millions of listeners and readers. Sally, faithful to her profession, thrust some sheets of paper at him, but he rejected them.

The debts, Hamid's regime, the Russian presence, the American attitude – but above all the hospital visit, the hunger, the suffering. After ten minutes all the questions centred on that theme, and after his good start Edward began to find himself on the defensive. Singer in the chair began to call journalists who he thought would widen the discussion, but it did not work. A tall, white-haired man from the *Daily Telegraph*, who had been silent, unwound himself from his chair. He rarely came to press conferences, being the paper's resident cynic.

149

'You were deeply moved by what you saw, Minister. We none of us doubt that. Does the Government intend to do, I repeat *do*, anything about it? Or do you just intend to go on being deeply moved?'

Edward glanced sideways at Singer, but Singer looked at his fingernails.

'It's not for me to make policy,' he began. Singer nodded just a little too emphatically at his fingernails, and Edward revolted.

'I shall be reporting direct to the Prime Minister,' he said, and Singer nodded again. 'And I shall recommend a substantial Western effort to save those who are starving, suffering and dying in Meridia.'

There was a chorus of simultaneous questions, and Singer could do nothing to select.

'Will Britain take the lead?'

'How much will it cost?'

Those were the two which Edward caught.

'In my judgement, and I can only speak for myself, Britain should take the lead, and that means making a leading financial contribution.'

Singer was quickly on his feet. He did not look at Edward.

'I think that's as far as we can take it today. We're running a bit late, so there's no time for separate radio and TV interviews. The Minister has a number of engagements in London, and we must let him go.'

There was a murmur of dissent, and for two seconds it looked as if the ploy would not work. Singer opened the side door for Edward to leave. Edward hesitated for a moment, tempted by the excitement still in him to burn the last bridge, but thought better of it.

'Thank you, ladies and gentlemen. Good morning.'
And straight into his car, without Singer who had a car of
his own, but with Sally, silent and scared beside him.

'Too far?' he asked, as they reached the motorway.

'I don't know.' She shivered.

They drove straight to the Foreign Office but it took over
an hour through the mid-morning traffic. The car had
brought out a box full of new work, and Sally tried to
interest him in it. His own telegrams from Mangara on the
financial conference, Sandford-Smith's telegrams on the
hospital visit, invitations, MPs' letters, the minutiae of a
minister's life. Edward could not concentrate on them.

'Radio Three, Jack.'

No cricket at this time of year, thank God, and a decent
chance at that hour of Beethoven or Brahms. Edward
knew less about music than Rosemary, but the well-worn
classics could soothe his nerves. As Jack twiddled the
dial, Edward's own voice filled the car.

'. . . and that means making a leading financial contribution.' It still sounded good.

'Mr Dunsford refused to amplify that statement, and
the press conference came to a somewhat abrupt end.
Much remains to be learned, but one thing is clear. Faced
with the dramatic evidence of poverty in Meridia, Britain
has decided to cut through the complicated manoeuvres
of the super powers, and take the lead in a bold international initiative. In a specially extended version of *The
World at One* the BBC's diplomatic correspondent will
assess the implications of this unexpected move and seek
comments from experts around the world.'

In the ante-room of his office, James Harrison stood,

papers in both hands. He had brought in a girl to help answer the telephone, but the lights of unanswered calls blinked on the bank of switches beside the receiver.

'The Secretary of State asked to see you as soon as you came in.' He looked at Sally. 'It seemed very urgent.'

'What else?' Edward could see that James was flustered, and that would not do. He kept his own voice even.

'Just hundreds of messages. From the media, asking you to appear. They're bypassing News Department and ringing here direct. From the Chief Whip. From the public, lots of unknown people. Mrs Dunsford, too, she rang just now, she's had dozens of calls, she asked you to ring back. Then there's Mr Headley from Lewes, he . . .'

'We can deal with all that later. Sally, sort it out as best you can. I'll be back in a minute.'

And so to Patrick Reid. The Private Secretaries in his ante-room waved him through without a word. He forgot to notice the room's usual smell of musty authority. None of them came with him, which meant that the Foreign Secretary had said that the conversation was to be private. Edward knew how it would start, not how it would end.

Patrick Reid, too, was flustered, and angry. Edward had never seen him like this. Usually Reid, like many people empty of real character, knew how to keep up appearances. Indeed his whole life had been a study of that art.

'What the hell have you been saying?'

'It sounds as if you know.'

'I know because I happened to be with the PM when Singer rang from the airport.'

'You can't trust Singer.' That was feeble, because on that day at least Singer had done his job, and tried to persuade Edward to do the same.

'You committed us to something directly contrary to Cabinet policy.'

'The Cabinet has no policy. That's the trouble.'

They were both standing up, the Foreign Secretary behind his desk with his back to the park, Edward still only three paces into the room. There was a pause, and he could hear a band playing in Wellington Barracks, and the cistern filling in the little private lavatory from which Reid must just have emerged.

'I just managed to save your job. For today at least. But you don't deserve it.'

'Does the Prime Minister want my resignation? If so I will write it out at once.'

'Don't be even more of a damned fool. You can't resign with all this going on.'

Edward noticed for the first time on Reid's desk a heap of messages like those which young James had been clutching in his own office down the corridor.

'You should be pleased. We've got a real chance to . . .'

'Listen to me.' Dislike was there in every syllable, and the Foreign Secretary's native Edinburgh accent began to come through. But he had regained control of himself.

'Listen to me. I'll not argue with you, young man, on points of policy, which are my responsibility. I'll just tell you what is to happen. The Prime Minister is answering questions in the House at three fifteen. He will specifically say that you spoke without authority. At five he and I and the Chancellor of the Exchequer will meet in his room. We will review the situation. You will not be there.

Nor will you go to the House of Commons. Nor will you appear on radio or television. Nor will you stay here in the Foreign Office. You are to go home and remain there until I telephone you. Is that clear?'

'Clear, and thoroughly humiliating. I'd rather resign.'

'Then your political career will be at an end.'

Edward hesitated. The situation had galloped away with itself. He had been a fool to come in straight to Reid like that. He should have talked to Alan Boyle, talked to Sally, got advice, reflected. Instead, over-excited by the press conference, he had launched himself against a fortress, which had been hastily but thoroughly prepared.

He hesitated, tried to conciliate.

'Patrick, I enjoy working here. I know we don't get on, but surely together . . .'

'I've nothing more to say. Good day to you.'

Perhaps he had been wrong. Perhaps Reid had some character after all. Or was it the strength of office which he held?

Edward hesitated again, then turned and left the room.

Alan Boyle was outside in the corridor.

'What's going to happen?'

'Nothing, nothing.' Damn it, Edward felt tears start in his own eyes. For a moment he thought he was losing control. It was the lack of sleep in the plane, he was dog tired. He brushed past Boyle into his office.

'Get me my wife on the phone.' He blundered into his own room. Rosemary at least was on his side on this strange day.

'No reply from your house, Minister.' That was odd. But he would go there anyway. It was what Reid had told him to do, but funnily it was also what he wanted to do.

The excitement had left him. He wanted Rosemary to laugh at him, put her arms round his neck, pour him a drink, put him to bed. He wanted this topsy turvy day to end.

'I'll go home I think. Will you tell Jack?' He tried to sound casual. Sally seemed to understand the sudden change of mood.

'Not the park door, Minister.' Back in the office there was no strain in being formal again. 'There's a crowd of journalists waiting there.'

'Where then?'

'I'll tell Jack to park at the foot of Clive Steps.'

He slipped out of the side door into King Charles Street, down the steps, and so home.

He let himself into Eaton Close with his own key. Rosemary was not downstairs. Nor upstairs. Where was she? Had the warm feelings he had shared with her on the telephone just been a flicker from the dead past? He could think no more that day, and it would be a mistake to try.

Slowly and deliberately he took off his clothes, found some pyjamas, brushed his teeth, drew the curtains against the afternoon light, took the telephone off the hook, and lay down to sleep.

13

Extract from Hansard, *Tuesday, 22 October*

3.15 p.m. *Questions to the Prime Minister*
1. *Mr Spriggs* (Tonbridge) to ask the Prime Minister if he will list his official engagements for Monday, 21 *October*.
2. *Mr Charles Elliott* (West Hants) to ask the Prime Minister if he will list his official engagements for Monday, 21 *October*.
The Prime Minister (Mr Michael Berinsfield). With permission I will answer questions one and two together.
In the morning I held talks with the Executive Committee of the Confederation of British Cable Operators. At lunch I entertained the Prime Minister of Portugal, Senhor Pedro do Cunhal, and continued discussions with him in the afternoon. I conferred with various of my colleagues, and in the evening attended a dinner of the Institute of Engineers.
Mr Spriggs. Did the Prime Minister have the opportunity last night to see the remarkable television programme, in which my Hon. Friend the Member for East Sussex took part,

showing unspeakable suffering in Meridia? Will he confirm the undertaking given by my Hon. Friend that Britain will take the lead in an international initiative to put an end to a degree of suffering which is a disgrace to humanity?

The Prime Minister. I have had reports of that programme. My Hon. Friend the Minister of State has returned to this country in the last few hours and I look forward to hearing from him about his visit to Meridia and the financial conference at which he represented the United Kingdom.

Mr Charles Elliott. Did my Hon. Friend have authority from the Cabinet to pledge fresh expenditure? Regardless of the merits of the case, and I am second to none in my sympathy for the sufferings of the Meridian people, is it not important that junior ministers when travelling abroad or giving press conferences at Heathrow should stick to their brief and not become intoxicated with their own self-importance?

Hon. Members. Shame.

The Prime Minister. Without associating myself with my Hon. Friend's remarks I would simply say that we have taken no decision about additional aid to Meridia. We are already giving thirty million pounds this year. The House knows of the strain on the aid budget.

The Leader of the Opposition (Mr Treadware). Is the Prime Minister aware that this was a disgraceful reply? (Some Hon. Members: Hear hear.) Has not his telephone been ringing all morning, as mine has, with calls from ordinary British people insisting that something be done? There is a massive outcry, and quite right too, and yet the Prime Minister has the gall to stand there and repudiate a pledge given by one of his colleagues. We saw old people and children dying last night . . .

The Speaker. The Right Hon. gentleman must put a question.

Mr Treadware. Very well, Mr Speaker. Is the Prime Minister going to do the decent thing and act on the promise given or is he going to turn about and sack the Good Samaritan?

Hon. Members. Answer!

The Prime Minister. As I understand it, no promise has been given by the Minister of State. Certainly no decision has been taken by the Government.

The Leader of the Liberal Party (Mr Goodenough). Surely the Prime Minister realises that he cannot leave it there. Was he not aware of the agonies of human degradation which that television programme revealed? Has he not got by now the transcript of what his Hon. Friend said this morning at Heathrow about a major British contribution? He should hold a meeting with the Minister of State at once and announce a decision this evening

The Prime Minister. I have every sympathy for the cause which is being argued, but I cannot be expected to announce a decision of this magnitude off the cuff.

Sir Guy Winchilsea (South Kensington). Is the Prime Minister aware that many of us on his side of the House are deeply worried by the vagueness of his replies? Can I tell him that within hours of the broadcast an all-party delegation of my constituents came to press me hard for a British initiative? Meridia is a country with which Britain has long ties of friendship. We are worried by Russian intrigues there. When can he confirm that the Minister of State's response is fully endorsed by Her Majesty's Government?

One Hon. Member. Where is the Minister? Has he been sacked already?

The Prime Minister. I will reflect carefully on what has been said. (Hon. Members: Disgraceful.) I can assure the House that my Right Hon. Friend the Foreign Secretary will make a statement as soon as possible.

The Speaker. Question number three. Mr Jones.

The Leader of the Opposition. On a point of order, Mr Speaker. The Prime Minister can see now that he has the whole House against him, except for a sycophant or two . . .

The Speaker. Order. We must get on. The House will have many opportunities to discuss the matter which has just been raised.

Sir Guy Winchilsea. Further to that point of order, may I give notice that I will bring the matter up again at the earliest opportunity. We really cannot have this country exhibiting meanness and going back on its word.

The Speaker. As the Hon. Member knows, that is not a point of order. The Prime Minister has heard what was said. Question number three. Mr Jones.

Ten minutes later the Prime Minister seemed deep in paperwork in his office at the House of Commons. With a calm gold pencil he was side-lining passages in a long submission on his knee, as if there had never been a rowdy scene in the Chamber a few yards away. He ran a government with a small majority in the Commons, and the opinion polls seesawing dangerously. Before long he would have to choose a date for the next election. His colleagues in the Cabinet were getting edgy. So were the back-benchers with marginal seats. In these circumstances calm must be the first virtue. He rose courteously from the armchair when the Chancellor of the Exchequer came in. Gordon Leith-Ross was youngish, fresh-faced, bespectacled. He had been a surprise appointment as Chancellor, because nothing in his career at Transport and then at Agriculture had led anyone to suppose that he was the man to run the finances of the nation. But equally there had been no particular reason why not. He had been competent in a low-key way at the earlier jobs. Everyone trusted him, and he was one of the few people to whom the Prime Minister found it easy to open his mind. The Prime Minister motioned his Private Secretary out of the room.

'No Patrick?' asked the Chancellor, looking round.

'I asked him to come five minutes later.'

Leith-Ross digested this.

'Well, you got by.'

'Only just. And only thanks to the Speaker. I don't like it. We're in trouble.'

'Charles Elliott did his best.'

'Everyone knows he and Edward Dunsford can't stand each other. He wanted Dunsford's job. Even wrote to me asking for it.'

'Maybe you should have given it to him.'

'Maybe. But I have a mild preference for honest men.' He paused. 'Does Winchilsea still carry a lot of weight in the party?'

'You know better than I. But the answer's yes.'

'Sentimental old fool.'

'He's been on the Executive of the 1922 Committee for donkey's years. Always kind to everyone in private. Remembers wives' names, that sort of thing.'

'Could I shift him if I saw him privately?'

'Ask the Chief Whip. But I think not. He's got his

knighthood already. No, that's unjust. He believes in the third world. I had trouble with him on the Aid Sub-Committee.'

'How many votes would go with him and Dunsford?'

'If we held firm and they rebelled?'

'Precisely.'

'Say twenty-four. You'd need to do a Whip's exercise. But I'd guess twelve Conservative votes against us, and about as many abstentions.'

'Then we'd be beaten by ten.' They both knew by heart that the Government's natural majority over all parties in the Commons was only twenty-six.

'You could work on the Ulster Unionists.'

'A ludicrous notion. The price would be too high.'

There was another pause. The Prime Minister held out polished feet towards the gas fire. The light was failing outside, and the big Gothic room was only partly lit by old-fashioned desk and table lamps. The effect was cosy and traditional.

'So you want me to find some money?' asked the Chancellor.

'I don't want at all. But could you?'

'The aid budget is really stretched. There may be an underspend on that road in the Falklands, perhaps on the Bombay dock project, too. But it's too early to be sure. Six months still to go in the financial year.'

'Contingency reserve?'

'No, we really mustn't raid the reserve. The Health Service will gobble up a lot of it, the way we're going. And I really don't want to raise taxes next March. That would be an even bigger rebellion.'

'The Cabinet was weak on the Health Service.'

'But you won't want to start that argument all over again.'

'Certainly not.'

The door opened. 'The Foreign Secretary,' said a voice from the shadows.

'Ah, Foreign Secretary, come in and sit down.' The Prime Minister changed his tone completely, switching to formality. *Autres collègues, autres moeurs.*

'I'm sorry you had that difficulty just now, Prime Minister,' said Sir Patrick heavily, lowering himself into the empty armchair furthest from the fire. He wore a stiff white collar, and lawyers' garb of black coat and striped trousers. 'I've been thinking it over, and I am convinced that you should get rid of Dunsford. It's the only way to reassert your authority – and indeed mine.'

'What have you done with him?'

'Oh, he's gone home to his loving wife. I told him to stay there and say nothing, as we agreed.'

'Did you tell him you'd be pressing for his dismissal?'

'Certainly not, Prime Minister, certainly not. But I left him in no doubt that his hare-brained scheme would not work.'

'How much money does he want for Meridia?'

'I've no idea, Prime Minister. I would not dream of asking him. The whole idea is preposterous.' Sir Patrick looked sharply at the Chancellor. He did not know Leith-Ross well, and noted that he had been in the room for some time. 'Don't you agree, Chancellor?'

'I had lunch in the City,' said Leith-Ross, looking at the Prime Minister. 'They are not humanitarian by nature, of course. But Meridia has a lot of oil. The new discoveries in the south are said to be huge. They don't want the

162

Americans and Russians to snap them up. There seems little doubt that a deal is cooking. An American corporation lawyer was here this week trying to sign up Speyer's. He came direct from Moscow.'

'Do we know anything about that?' asked the Prime Minister.

'It's all hearsay,' said Sir Patrick, nettled. 'A wild intelligence story, some chattering among financiers, and Dunsford has been exaggerating it all for his own purposes.'

'Have you checked in Washington?'

'There was no need. No need at all. We checked in Mangara. President Hamid said there was nothing in it.'

A girl came in with tea, which she poured quietly into white cups with a gold rim. Milk for the Chancellor, lemon for the Prime Minister and Foreign Secretary. No need to ask. She had been at the job for years. The three men stared at the fire until she left.

The Prime Minister uncrossed his legs, and gave up the attempt to be civil to his Foreign Secretary.

'Let me recapitulate, then. There are two strands to the matter. First, there may be a carve-up of Meridia between American interests and the Soviet Union. The City knows about it, the Chancellor knows about it, even I have heard of it; but the Foreign Office knows nothing about it and so says there's nothing in it. Then there is the call for a humanitarian effort. The Foreign Office has no idea, no idea whatever, how much this would cost. Is that a fair summary of the position?'

'It's not a question of cost, Prime Minister, if you will forgive me saying so. It's a matter of your personal authority over a member of your Government. As Charles Elliott said . . .'

'Would it be ten million? Or a hundred? Or five hundred?'

'You're not seriously thinking of finding Dunsford the money?'

'No Patrick. I am simply trying to get at the facts. The Opposition have not got going yet. They have hardly found Meridia on the map. But they will. Much worse, we may be heading for a back-bench revolt and a public explosion, so there is perhaps a case for establishing the facts. At present they seem remarkably scanty.'

Sir Patrick looked sombrely at his own future. He did his best, God knows he did his best, but standards of public life were slipping. Dunsford was a nonentity. It was absurd to overturn government policy because of a junior minister's indiscretion. Yet as his car had turned into the outer gates of the Palace of Westminster, a group with crude placards had recognised him and a blowzy woman had banged on the car door and shouted at him, 'Back Dunsford now.' For a moment he had wished himself back in the Edinburgh law courts.

The Prime Minister summed up. His quick mastery of tactical situations had brought him to the top of the party.

'We need time. I reckon we can gain a week, but only if we show that we are genuinely looking at the options. Singer will make that clear to the press this afternoon. Patrick, you had better make a short statement to the House on Friday morning. A thin House on Friday, you should get by. But you will have to be ten degrees more sympathetic than I was just now.'

'And Dunsford?' Patrick Reid was somewhat mollified by being given a share of the action.

'You'd better ring Dunsford, and tell him to be back at

his desk tomorrow. Say that we will look at his ideas thoroughly, but meanwhile he is to keep out of the papers and off the box. I will see him, but only when we have got all the facts and studied them. And find out from Washington what they're really up to.'

Reid made as if to protest, but thought better of it.

'Gain time? How will you use that time?' asked Leith-Ross.

'To think, of course. That's what time is for.'

'You'll turn Dunsford into a national celebrity.'

'He's that already. These things happen quickly. Both ways. If we handle it right, he'll be famous for a week, forgotten in a fortnight.'

'How will you deal with him? Eventually, I mean?'

'There's one commodity we need for that, Gordon. Rope. Plenty of rope. Then we shall see.'

When Edward woke he knew that Rosemary was in the house. She was not in their room, and there was no sound elsewhere, and he did not know why he was sure. He noticed a light shining outside the half-open bedroom door. The lamp, a converted *sang-de-boeuf* jar, stood on the big mahogany chest at the top of the stairs, and he certainly had not switched it on earlier.

Edward lay quiet under the coverlet, collecting his thoughts, remembering the conversation with Reid, thinking of what he should have said. *Esprit d'escalier* the French called it, the brilliant retort devised only on the staircase going down. But there would be other opportunities. He was not going to give way. The Prime Minister would try to keep him in the Government, because Prime Ministers hated noisy resignations. But the Prime Minister would have to pay a price. A hundred million pounds minimum, thought Edward, watching the last edge of grey light fade where he had not drawn the heavy curtains tight. A hundred million pounds for the British contribution to Meridia was far more than anyone in the Foreign Office, even he himself or Alan Boyle, had imagined so far. But the stakes were higher now. Perhaps he would let them count the existing aid programme to Meridia as the first slice of the figure. Say seventy-five million pounds of new money. Without that, he would resign. He and Rosemary could live for a month or two on his parliamentary salary and on Rosemary's dividends. The girls were still too small for their education to be expensive. He could probably get a job in the City fairly soon. Guy Carlton would help him. He might even go back to Speyer's. In some ways, he would be sad to leave the Foreign Office if it came to that – his room, the portrait of George III, the great sombre staircase, James and Sally – particularly Sally. Then he had a thought which jerked him upright in bed. The Prime Minister would probably give his job to Charles Elliott. That would be hard to bear. He could not imagine Charles Elliott and Sally getting on together, they had nothing in common. He imagined Charles at the despatch box, answering questions – and himself rising from behind him with a scathing supplementary.

He closed his eyes for a minute more of luxury between sleep and waking, and when he opened them Rosemary was in the room. The blouse of parchment silk with full sleeves caught tight at the wrist was an old friend; so were the dark green velvet trousers. She came over and kissed him full on the lips. Then she put on the pillow a small bundle of letters.

'All delivered by hand,' she said. 'Am I to take it that at last I have a famous husband?'

He caught her by the arm and tried to pull her on to the bed, but she slipped away. He knew that she would never ask him about his trip, and would interrupt him if he tried to tell her.

'I don't mind him being away,' she had said at a dinner party soon after he became a Foreign Office minister. 'What I can't take are the travelogues when he gets back.' Everyone round the table had laughed. At that stage in their marriage she had often found it easier to give messages in public than in private. After that he had given up the attempt to explain his office life or even to make it sound amusing. He knew that in fact she followed it pretty closely, but her interest could not be forced. Over the next day or so she would find out anything that intrigued her about Meridia. What she would never have were the underlying facts and perspectives. These were masculine and boring.

He opened the envelopes. An invitation to appear on the late-night BBC news. A fulsome letter of congratulations from Guy Winchilsea enclosing an early day motion which had been tabled in the Commons, '. . . calls upon Her Majesty's Government to endorse the courageous initiative taken by the Honourable Member for East Sussex and pledge immediate and substantial assistance to the people of Meridia.' A pink envelope from an old lady in Chelsea enclosing a one pound note 'for those poor black children'. A note from Guy. 'This is getting interesting. I must talk to you soon. I'll ring you in a few days when the heat's off a bit.'

167

'Why have you taken the telephone off the hook?' asked Rosemary.

'I wanted to sleep.'

The telephone was her lifeline and she replaced the receiver briskly. It rang immediately and she answered it. With a hand over the mouthpiece she said:

'Oxfam and War on Want asking you to address a rally in Central Hall Westminster tomorrow lunchtime. Buses from all over England.'

'I can't. Tell them many thanks, perhaps later.'

'Later never comes. Hadn't you better do it? They say there'll be plenty of television.' Usually Rosemary fought hard against speaking engagements on principle, because they enlarged that dim masculine sector of Edward's life which he controlled himself.

'No, I really can't. I've been gagged.'

She made polite regrets down the telephone, and he told her what had happened with Reid. She laughed. The situation appealed to her appetite for a fight.

'Pompous old ass. We'll scupper him. I wondered what all this afternoon sleeping was about. You don't usually have jet-lag. I assumed you'd be hard at it in the office dictating lovely minutes to lovely Sally.'

'Come and join me.' He held out his arms, again.

Rosemary shook her head.

'Later perhaps.'

'I'll take you out to dinner.'

'No vote tonight?'

'Certainly there's a vote tonight. But they can't have it both ways. If I'm not allowed to practise politics, then I must certainly be allowed to take my wife out to dinner.'

Rosemary was pleased. She sat on the bed.

'We might try that new place near Victoria, the Cibanou. It has the new cuisine. Small helpings and high prices.'

'Tell me more about Guy's young American.'

'Why? Nothing to tell. I was wearing my chastity belt.'

'Don't be an ass. Why did Guy bring him?'

'Just passing. Something to do with your Meridia and all that. You know me, I listened and sent it right out of my mind.' She touched his knee under the coverlet. 'Now you tell me about Sally.'

'Sally Archer? Nothing to say. I think she enjoyed herself.'

There was nothing at all to feel guilty about, but he felt a small note of guilt creep into his voice.

'I expect she did. I don't suppose she's been beyond Dover in her life.'

'You're absurd about that girl. She's an experienced member of the Diplomatic Service and has travelled quite as much as you.'

'There's no need to be defensive about her. I'm talking metaphorically. She's got an insular mind.'

'How do you know? You've hardly ever bothered to say hello to her.'

'I don't have to. I can tell by looking at her hair.'

'You really are absurd.' But change the subject to firmer ground. 'I'll ring the restaurant.'

At that moment the front doorbell sounded, and Rosemary looked out of the window.

'My God, there's a small crowd. And your car with Jack and the young one,' she said.

'What on earth do you mean?'

'James, isn't it? The one who'll be quite good looking in five years' time.'

James Harrison was a bit out of his depth. Normally he worked hard at being jaunty and mischievous, but today was not normal. Today he felt just young and anxious. He had pushed his way through the group of journalists on the doorstep. He did not think he liked Edward Dunsford, but at this moment he desperately wanted him to survive, and everything to come back to normal.

'Sally's gone home to sleep. The Secretary of State wanted you to have this straight away. I gather he's been trying to ring you for two hours.'

Another envelope. A crisis consisted of ripping envelopes open.

Dear Edward,

It appears that your telephone is out of order. I have spoken again to the Prime Minister. I am to make a statement in the House. There has of course been no change in government policy, but I am setting in hand a thorough review of the whole Meridian situation. Your participation is naturally desirable, and I should be grateful if you would come to the Foreign Office as usual tomorrow morning. Meanwhile it is essential that you do not broadcast or see the press or take part in other manifestations.

Yours sincerely,

Patrick Reid

Rosemary read over his shoulder.

'They're on the run,' she said, her eyes bright.

'Maybe. Or it's a trap,' said Edward more slowly. Then he too brightened. 'Anyway, we'll make him sweat overnight. James, tell his Private Office that you caught me just as I was taking my wife out to dinner.'

'And the reply?'

'No reply. Just say I put the letter in my pocket and went out to dinner.'

'Darling, I think you're actually developing style.' She rang the restaurant while he shaved and dressed quickly. Rosemary took his arm, and together they stepped out of the front door and stood smiling for a moment between the two flanking bay trees. A dozen cameramen and journalists began their professional hubbub.

'Have you resigned?'

'Was that message the sack?'

'What is your comment on the Prime Minister's answer in the House?'

'I've nothing to add or take away from what I said this morning. And now, if you'll excuse us, it's early supper and a good night's rest. I wish you the same, gentlemen.'

At the Cibanou she took a tiny cucumber and prawn mousse, and then a *mignon* of beef in two mouthfuls. He took soup and duck, and they shared a bottle of champagne. They dealt with the meal swiftly, and pleasantly, speaking little, because they knew that there was more important business ahead.

Back at home, the pillow and coverlet were still crumpled on Edward's side of the bed. He stood for a minute by the window while Rosemary undressed. The journalists had gone, and the old-fashioned street light shed a friendly glow over their corner of the little square. A young man and a pretty girl in a long dress laughed together below him on their way to some dance or night club. Perhaps, after all, there was a life to be enjoyed here. Perhaps it could still work.

She stayed in command, even in bed. Not since before

171

the arrival of their two daughters had he felt her lose herself to him. But in those days his own mind had not wandered elsewhere while they were making love.

Her body still excited him as he pushed aside the nightdress from her breasts. She was strong and still beautiful. He smiled selfishly at the thought that others would still want her. He buried his head in her soft, warm flesh.

'Gently, gently,' said Rosemary, as in old days. But his clumsiness excited her, and her hands moved quickly over his body as they had not done for a year at least. Their lovemaking was not marvellous, and it was too soon over. She lay silent, and in the darkness he could not tell how she had fared in the absurd flurry which he had created. Sometimes in the past she had torn away from him at that moment, furious and hopeless. Now she gently pushed him away and kissed him on the side of his cheek.

'Good night, darling,' she murmured.

He was back lying at her side now. He wanted something more.

'You'll help me, then? If you help me, I think I can win.'

She switched on her bedside lamp unexpectedly and sat up in bed. She was naked, and he noticed that her shoulders were losing their plumpness.

'If I promise too much, I'll let you down. You know that.'

'I don't ask for a promise.'

'What then?'

'A sign.'

'You've had your sign.'

'Was it a good sign?'

'It was a good sign. Now go to sleep.'

He lay quiet after she had gone to sleep, recovering the solitude and possession of himself which were so important to him. He thought of a word of thanks and a prayer, but that habit had long gone. He was dead tired. Because of some small fault with the cord, the curtains were again not tightly drawn, and the friendly street light just reached the foot of the bed. For a minute or two before he slept, Edward was at peace.

By habit Edward woke early, Rosemary late. It had not always been so, but it was a convenient arrangement for a creaking marriage, because it meant they were not forced into each other's company at breakfast. When things were going well between them Edward brought Rosemary a tray. It was easily done, for she liked just an orange, a single slice of brown toast and honey and a pot of coffee from which she could then pour at least three cups to stimulate her leisurely entry into the day. And of course the papers.

Edward thought ahead to this ritual as he shaved. He was careful today not to let either the shaving brush, or later the toothbrush, discharge a splash or speck on to the mirror above the basin, for that was an accident of which Rosemary particularly disapproved. She was haphazardly houseproud, caring passionately about a few such matters, yet careless about the muddle of garments inside her own chest of drawers. The drawing-room must always be spotless with the cushions plumped, whereas in the kitchen, though it was equally open to visitors, dirty plates and glasses would accumulate until either Edward or the daily lady washed them up. Today Edward mused quite cheerfully on these contradictions, which on black days roused him to fury. Then it was time to switch on the radio which lived in the bathroom, and listen to the BBC's summary of the morning press.

'Most of the papers lead today with the news from Meridia and the exchange in Parliament yesterday following Mr Edward Dunsford's return from that country. In a leading article *The Times* says, "Thanks to an amazing but understandable outburst of popular emotion following a television film from a Meridia hospital, the Prime Minister now has a major political problem on his hands in the unlikely form of Mr Edward Dunsford." Other papers carry their own harrowing pictures from Meridia. The *Sun* is alone in relegating the subject to its inside pages, concentrating instead on the Chelmsford rape case. With the exception of the *Daily Telegraph* all the papers carry editorials urging increased British aid . . .'

Excellent. Edward looked at himself in the spotless mirror. He was naked to the waist, and if he pulled in his stomach he could persuade himself that he had a boyish figure. He had slept well, for at the moment his wife loved him, and for the first time in his life most people in England had heard of him. It was a stimulating mixture, and he felt eager for the fight ahead. He passed back through the bedroom into his little dressing-room. Rosemary still slept. She had not taken her make-up off the night before, and her face was slightly smudged. In the dressing-room she had herded all the objects of Edward's bachelor life which she had allowed to survive – two small prints of his Cambridge college, a Wedgwood medallion of the Younger Pitt, a photograph of his parents in their porch at Cobham. The window gave on to their tiny paved garden, and Edward saw that the first frost had touched the roses. That gave him an idea a few minutes later as he operated the toaster and the percolator for Rosemary's breakfast. He hurried out into the garden and picked two dark red rosebuds, which would come to nothing now that winter was here. He put them on the tray with their stems crossed, laying them carefully so that the shrivelling effect of the slight frost did not show. Then, as usual, he piled beside the orange all the popular papers, reserving for himself *The Times*, *Telegraph*, *Guardian* and *Financial Times*.

Rosemary still slept. He put the tray quietly on the bed where he had slept and drew the curtains. Then he touched her bare shoulder gently.

'Breakfast, darling.'

She stirred, and opened her eyes. He kissed her and then left. She would wake now because she liked her coffee hot. Better to leave her alone to sort out her feelings for the day. He did not want to push his luck. And anyway he wanted to read the proper papers quietly in the comfortable armchair in the drawing-room.

He had hardly settled before there was a knock on the front door. The postman was carrying a bundle of letters far too bulky for the letter-box. He was a young West Indian with a smile and a Cockney accent.

'Bad news for me, sir, your getting famous all of a sudden.'

'It won't last, you'll see.' But at the moment Edward saw no reason why it should not last for ever. Fame was such fun, it had to endure.

At that moment he heard a crash upstairs and a loud angry indistinct noise which must be Rosemary swearing.

He ran up the stairs two at a time, happiness dissolving at each stride. The bedroom was empty, and as he entered he heard the bathroom door noisily locked.

'What is it?' He twisted the door handle.

'Sod off, you bastard.' He could hear her turn on the taps, and then a stifled sob against the noise of running water.

Edward turned back to the bed. The coffee pot still stood upright on the tray, but the centre of the bed was soaked in coffee, which Rosemary had poured over the inside page of the *Daily Express*. Under the still spreading brown stain Edward could see the gossip column, the headline 'Cuddle before the Storm' and the photograph, remarkably clear, of himself in the plane with his arm round Sally, and Sally with her head on his shoulder. Damn. He tried the bathroom door once more, but not hopefully. It was never any use pleading, least of all through a locked door.

'I never want to see you again.' When Rosemary was upset she lapsed into clichés.

Sadly, this time slowly, Edward went down the stairs, summoning up the courage to fight alone.

14

Neil did not sleep on the flight back from London. He tossed and turned in his bed when he finally reached it after dropping off at the office the manuscript of his report for typing early the next morning. In his waking and in his fitful dreams his mind went back constantly to his walk that previous afternoon with Guy Carlton, to Rosemary, to the real Meridia, to MEECON, to Russian threats, to himself. The flickering of these images across his mind always brought him back to the same nagging doubt. Did he really know what he was up to? Had he accepted too much of MEECON at its face value? Once sucked into the job the pressure to do well had pushed aside any serious questioning of the job itself. He had a job to do like everybody else, he argued to himself. He just wanted to do it well. It was for other people with higher salaries to worry about questions of right or wrong.

When he reached the Wall Street office at nine thirty

the next morning his report was typed and ready on his desk. He checked it, had sixteen copies made, and walked the original in to Bourton. At ten thirty Bourton's secretary rang him and summoned him to a meeting in the Conference Room at eleven thirty. Two other senior partners would be present. A total of eight. The meeting was likely to last until one.

Neil was worried. Speyer's refusal to take part in MEECON was much more significant for the package as a whole than the tiresome technical details he had sorted out with Viktor Radomsky in Moscow. Neil sat at his desk and toyed with a heavy ball of Murano glass. It was ironic that the incidental part of his trip to Europe had turned out to be the most important. That must be why Bourton had called his meeting, he supposed. But why summon half the firm as well? He had heard of the Star Chamber. Or perhaps it was all over already and they simply wanted to gloat at his failure.

And so the eight of them assembled round the long mahogany table, each of them with a copy of Neil's report in front of him. Bourton spoke for ten minutes. And silence fell. Bourton liked to think he possessed a sense of theatre.

Neil sat facing the window. He did not see the glass towers outside. All he felt was humiliation and the certainty that his ears were turning red.

Bourton spoke again. 'I tell you this cake won't bake without Speyer's and the rest of them bringing their Governments in on their backs. The Soviets want guarantees. Christ knows why. It's not even their money. But real, bankable guarantees we must give them.' He looked hard at Neil. 'Are you sure Speyer's can't be persuaded? What if we sidestep Carlton and try the old man?'

'I asked him at lunch yesterday. He's not in on any of this. Or, if he is, he's accepted the bank's decision and isn't prepared to change it.' Bourton was glaring at Neil, and opening his mouth to challenge that opinion. Neil pressed on. 'No, I'm absolutely sure it's Guy Carlton who decides, and he won't budge now.'

Bourton never swore in the office, however great the temptation. He felt it was great at this moment.

'And why? Because he has some crazy idea that we're all part of a great conspiracy to sell Africa off in little parcels to the Soviets?'

Neil looked up. He was not sure how much he had liked Guy Carlton, but he had respected him. 'That's about it. But it's not a frivolous view. He's thought a lot about the project. He's genuine.'

'Crap! We'll buy him out. Or rather in. All he wants is a bigger share. Why didn't you offer it to him?'

Neil glanced round the table. Bourton was gross and unreasonable. The two other partners had said nothing. But inquisitors did not have to speak. They merely went silently and efficiently about their work of preparing the bonfire.

'You misjudge them. For Speyer's it's not money, it's principle.'

Bourton exploded. 'Their principles stink. Their so-called politics stink. We're simply in the business of putting together a large financial arrangement. That's all they'd be in it for. Everyone stands to benefit.' He turned to Neil again. 'You should have argued that politics needn't come into it from their point of view. You've let the timid men in London screw this up. And you've given us a hell of a lot more work if we're to find a package of governments the Soviets will accept.'

Neil's ears felt very red, and he had an empty sickness in his stomach. The room seemed unbearably hot. But he felt stung, too, and unfairly humiliated. In the back of his mind was an awareness that if he just let Bourton's comments pass and knuckle down to Bourton's orders he would lose something he would not regain. Unexpectedly he found himself thinking that an Edward Dunsford or a Guy Carlton would not have let this pass.

'But of course politics come into it. We all know that the Russians are demanding a political guarantee for this project for political reasons. That's why you went down to Washington to lobby the State Department. That's why we want Speyer's in.' He felt very red now, but the sickness in his stomach was turning into excitement and he pressed on. 'I don't see why Speyer's shouldn't look carefully at the background to the arrangement. It's fair enough. Not because of the money. But the wider stakes are enormous. Sometimes I wonder whether we've really looked hard enough at it ourselves.'

'And what does that mean?' Bourton asked sharply.

'Have we asked ourselves why the Russians are so keen to press on and sign? Everyone knows how difficult it usually is to do business with them. They're cautious. They're suspicious. They negotiate hard. They throw up difficulties when there aren't any just to wring another concession from you.'

Bourton was leaning back in his chair and lighting a cigar. Was he listening?

'But there's been none of that. It's they who've been anxious and impatient. They're the ones who want the whole thing finalised tomorrow. Why? What's the rush for them? What are they really up to over there?'

The two non-speaking partners had leant forward on the table. They were joined by Bourton.

'Just what are you trying to say, Mr Wainwright?' he asked.

Neil did not know. He had come to no conclusion. There was only a sense of growing unease implanted – blast him! by Guy Carlton. But he had to answer.

'So what's your point?' Bourton asked again.

'Er. I'm not sure.'

'What the hell does that mean?'

'I mean I don't think we should let Moscow rush us. They want this thing to go ahead. That gives us some leverage, surely? I think we should look rather more carefully at each stage before we fall in with everything they want.'

The partner who sat on Bourton's left spoke for the first time.

'Are you suggesting this hasn't all been thought through already?'

'No, sir. Of course I'm not.'

'Do you imagine we haven't gone into this carefully with the American principals of MEECON? Or with Washington?'

'Er, well, it just seemed to me that . . .'

The partner turned to Bourton. 'The important thing, Joe, is to get on and find alternatives to Speyer's who can provide some similar political guarantee. But let's get on with it.'

'Sure. I'm with you, Chester. We must get on,' said Bourton.

And so they got on. They identified four other banks in the hope of finding two to give adequate company to the Paris Rothschilds and Yokohama Finance. Two German names, one French and one Italian were at last supplied by the other experts round the table. They and Neil were instructed to work out their approaches quickly. Bourton concluded by saying that he wanted the package tied up before the end of October.

'Stay behind, will you Neil?'

It was ludicrous how long the others took to tie up their papers, empty their coffee cups and get out of the room. Neil felt sure that he was about to be sacked. Or at least taken off MEECON, put somewhere safe and second-rate, informed that his future with the firm was tarnished. His sense of excitement deserted him, leaving him naked to what was coming.

When the room at last was clear except for Neil and Bourton and a haze of cigar smoke Bourton said:

'I want you to go back to London. And stay there till MEECON sinks or swims.'

'But . . .'

'But, you've got cold feet. You took off your little shoes and socks just now, and we saw them, blue with cold. But that means you understand European cold feet as well.'

Neil continued to gape.

'Don't be so dumb, man. The rest of us are just plain warm-blooded Americans, working for an honest profit. You understand the connection with politics. You struck up some understanding with that cold fish Carlton. Europe is full of Guy Carltons. They've stopped creating anything, but sure as hell they can foul up other people's creations. I want you over there as the firm's ambassador

182

for the duration. I want you to call me every morning at nine a.m. New York time precisely. Talk to Mrs Harris about your expenses. Are you on?'

'I'm on,' said Neil, still dazed, thinking of St James's Park, and Rosemary Dunsford, and the late Turners and the postcard rack at the Tate Gallery.

15

They were not late, but Jack was driving too fast. He had brought Edward to Lewes on this narrow twisting A road a dozen times, so he knew quite well when to expect a blind corner and where he could anticipate a straight stretch to overtake. Jack was a good driver, but unpredictable. On days when they were late he would drive like a snail, beckoning every schoolgirl and pensioner who hovered on the edge of zebra crossings, slowing at every green traffic light as if willing it to change in time to stop them. On days like this, when they had hours to spare, he would jab his foot to the floor of the car and drive like fury.

They were travelling at about sixty miles an hour seven or eight miles north of Lewes. The following Sunday the clocks would be put back to Greenwich Mean Time. But that Thursday afternoon there was just enough light to admire what was left of the autumn colours as they pulled round the bend. Half a mile of straight tarmac appeared to greet them, dipping gently down towards a level crossing and a distant red light winking at the approach of a London train. Two hundred yards and three cars in front a narrow lane met the main road at a shallow angle. A pub, built a hundred years before in the angle of the junction, obscured all but the first twenty feet of the country road. Edward had finished reading the papers in his red box. He had open on his lap the details of that night's half-yearly meeting of the Executive Council. Edward had pinned to them the letter he had read that morning from Derek Headley and a scrap of paper in Sally's handwriting: 'Minister. Major Peacock rang to say that he very much wants to have five minutes alone with you before tonight's meeting. He will be in the bar at 6.30 p.m.' Edward knew what it would be about. His agent had not seen Headley's letter but he would probably have guessed something like it had been sent. How petty local people could be. Just one meeting about a wretched motorway, that was all he had missed. Even junior ministers sometimes had better things to do than wag their tails every time their constituents whistled.

Two hundred yards in front, a green sportscar shot without warning from the side road. The driver had hardly braked, relying on his daring and his speed to see him on to the main road. The sportscar hit the van travelling south broadside. It bounced off, hit the kerb, rolled over twice, crumpled, and came to rest against a hedge. An arm dangled limply from the open window. Cars braked all around. Jack had been accelerating, and was suddenly confronted by the boot of the car in front. He stamped on the brake and swerved across the road. The Austin Ambassador bounced on a kerb and came to rest on the verge undamaged, but passenger and driver shaken. Other drivers were already crowding round the sportscar, trying to wrench open the door and drag out the man inside. A trickle of blood was running down the green paint. Jack had recovered himself and opened his door.

'Blimey, that was close. Better go and take a look. Might be able to help. Looks pretty bad to me.'

Edward was exhausted by the pressure and excitement of the last few days. For the second time that week he felt tears start in his eyes without warning. Another moment as part of that savage scene and he would have completely lost control. Like a bird which finds itself trapped inside a building, its grace and beauty dissolving into panic, Edward knew he had to escape.

'No,' he said sharply. 'Drive on. There's nothing we can do. Drive on, for God's sake.'

Jack had never heard the Minister speak like that. The door of the sportscar had been forced open now. The man trapped inside was not moving. Jack turned towards Edward, hesitated, then got back into the car and started the engine. A large white Jaguar which had stopped behind them flashed its lights and hooted furiously. Jack drove off.

Ten minutes later they were descending the hill into the back streets of Lewes. It was dark now, but the night was clear and bracing. A quarter moon hung over the town. Edward's head had cleared, and he felt ashamed. Rosemary would not yet have come down for the weekend, but that hardly mattered. He wanted to walk. He took his papers for the meeting, left Jack at the bottom of School Hill and sent him home to London.

'Meet me off the nine twenty-five train. Usual place

by the steps to the Tube.' Jack grunted and wished him good night.

Edward walked slowly up the hill. There was little purpose in his stride. He tried hard to focus his mind on the evening's meeting. He wanted to try to keep off local issues and focus it on the Government's record. He might even try to interest them in Meridia. There were bound to be questions about it. They would all have seen or read about his visit to the hospital. He had scribbled a few notes for his speech in the back of the car. But his mind kept wandering. To Rosemary, Sally, the damned picture and story in the paper, Patrick Reid, the hospital, the swimming pool in Mangara, the man in the green sportscar. This was not a jumble of unconnected threads. There was a clear line – or there would be, provided he unravelled it. He had seen the problem. He had been given a chance, despite old Reid, to show just how important the thread was. If only there weren't so many distractions. Yesterday he had thought that Rosemary and he might be finding some new bond in the fight which lay ahead. But one photograph and much accumulated resentment had quickly smashed the new affection.

He liked Lewes. It had a civilised feel, a sense of being close to its past that he had never had as a boy in a London suburb. He sensed the gatehouse of the castle, lurking somewhere in the darkness of a side street. He rounded a curve in the road, and passed three noble Georgian flint-faced houses. The windows of two were disfigured by large orange posters which screamed, 'STOP the motorway – before it's too late'. Edward started up St Anne's Hill towards the hotel. Pools of light on his left

187

marked the little lanes which dropped steeply to the plain lying at the foot of the town. During daylight, these streets gave a momentary glimpse towards the coast.

He turned into the old Elizabethan hotel which had once played host to Dr Johnson. He had to squeeze past a large white Jaguar which nuzzled ostentatiously up to the entrance. He found Richard Peacock, as he expected, chatting to the barman, his large red fist clutching a brandy and water.

'Edward! Nice to see you. What will you have?'

'Hello, Richard. Tom.' He nodded at the barman. The Major handed him a gin and tonic and steered him by the arm into a quiet corner of the room.

'Glad you were able to make it a bit early. One or two things on my mind I wanted to warn you about before the meeting gets going.'

Edward scooped up some peanuts. One escaped and fell to the floor, leaving flecks of salt down his silk tie.

'I know. Some of them like old Headley resent my absence last Saturday, resent all the fuss about my trip to Meridia, and want to make a thing of it. Right?'

The Major peered into his briefcase and removed a collection of cuttings from that week's local newspapers and five or six letters from conservationists, all very uncomplimentary about Edward's distraction from people's real worries.

'There are these. And there are mutterings. More than mutterings. Some of the officers have had some pretty nasty conversations the last few days.' He leaned forward. The barman was polishing glasses vigorously, glancing occasionally towards the face which his television screen and evening paper had made so familiar to his three young children that week. 'All this publicity about you and Africa really hasn't helped. It makes those who resent your absence last Saturday even more angry. They don't like it. So they mutter.'

'So you keep saying. What exactly do they mutter?'

'That you should be here, giving our problems a bit of your time. That while you're having unkind photos taken of yourself in aeroplanes, there's a real campaign to fight . . .'

Edward slammed his glass on to the table. Some of the contents spilled out.

'For God's sake, Richard. It was one meeting. Just one, that's all. Didn't old Councillor Antrobus chair it as well as anyone? Certainly as well as I could have done. I've read the minutes. It didn't seem to go too badly.' He sat back in his chair, now more resentful than angry. 'I've spent a lot of time on this bloody motorway. What the hell do these people want?'

The Major cleared his throat and looked down at the splash of gin on the table. These conversations were becoming more and more difficult. Much as he liked Dunsford, the fellow was sometimes conceited.

'Now listen to me. I've been around here a few years now. I wash my ears and my eyesight's still pretty good. I know you've done as much as any reasonable man could. But feelings run high with some people. And these people get annoyed seeing you on TV rushing around as a minister. They think you should be rushing around here, looking after them.'

'I know. Look at this.' Edward handed his agent Derek Headley's letter. The Major nodded. He had been told about it.

'He's gunning for you, Edward. You've got on the

wrong side of him. Don't know how. But you must watch him. If he can put you in a bad light on this one big issue he could make our lives pretty unpleasant.'

'Headley's a fool.' Edward looked at his watch and finished his drink. 'Better go and greet the faithful.'

The hotel room was filling up with Edward's party organisers, local branch chairmen, town and parish councillors, constituency officers, Young Conservatives, men, women, old, young, eager, cynical, interfering, conscientious. Worn tweed jackets, pin-stripe suits, silk scarves, shapeless cardigans. He knew half of them by name, most by sight. Fifty hard, metal, folding chairs were arranged in front of a low stage, a table and three wooden chairs. Geoffrey Dubarry, Chairman of Edward's Conservative Association for two years, ample, comfortable, good-natured, unctuous, as befitted the owner of Sussex's largest departmental store, had already arrived. He wore a waistcoat, whatever the season. His small darting eyes made him look perpetually surprised. He was bending over little Miss Simpson, the white-haired lady who ran the antique shop by the railway station. She was delicate and fragile like her china. She sat in a cloud of spinsterish lilac in her mauve scarf, mauve cardigan, mauve skirt and mauve shoes. Dubarry beamed when he saw Edward entering the room.

'My dear Edward,' chimed the Chairman's sing-song voice as if welcoming a valued customer at the shop door. 'Well, here we are. Another six months gone. I can hardly believe the time goes so quickly. You must be exhausted.' The sing-song voice rose alarmingly with the emphasis it placed on the middle syllable. 'We're so very glad to see you. So very glad.' Miss Simpson nodded vigorously.

Dubarry made this same pretty speech every six months, and a more formal version every time he chaired a party meeting. The lines to which he treated Edward as they shook hands he repeated from the stage when he opened the meeting ten minutes later. Edward sat on his right, Major Peacock on his left, nursing the pad of paper which was to receive the minutes. There were twelve empty seats facing the stage: Edward counted them while the Chairman launched into his speech.

'And now, ladies and gentlemen, I turn to some of the highlights of our last six months. Our summer fête, held by the very kind permission of Lady Denton in the gardens of Hamsey Hall, was an outstanding success – thanks to the efforts of many of you here – and that goes especially for the YCs, whose donkey polo tournament was an enormous attraction – together, of course, with *all* the sideshows that were organised – and the raffle for the colour television, which alone raised a profit of two hundred and fourteen pounds –' He paused, dramatically in danger of losing the thread of his sentence, darted his eyes alarmingly over his audience, and eventually found the thread again among the figures listed on the piece of paper which he clutched in his hands.

'– and produced our second-largest-ever profit of nine hundred pounds. Well done! Thank you all very much for all your hard work.' A self-conscious pause. 'And let's all do even better next year.'

The ladies in the audience smiled. One elderly man was dozing. A man in a pin-striped suit was slyly filling in *The Times* crossword. The Chairman spoke for another ten minutes, listing coffee mornings, the Young Conservatives' summer dance, nominations for new

Association officers. Edward looked round the faces before him and wondered whether they cared any more for the real world of power, pain, suffering and death than they did for this world of tombolas and House of Commons teas.

He lifted his head like the commuter in his train who wakes instinctively at the approach of his own station. Dubarry was coming to the end. He was daring to hint obliquely at the existence of another world.

'He has done sterling work as usual for the constituency these last six months. Of course, we're used to it now. It goes without saying we have a good, an effective and a conscientious Member of Parliament to represent our interests. In the midst of all his weighty responsibilities as a Foreign Office minister travelling the world and representing his Government he remains a reliable and solid Sussex representative. He knows our problems. He understands our worries. I for one am confident he will continue to fight for us.'

Edward looked across the faces. Someone said, 'Hear, hear.' Ladies were clapping politely. He noticed Derek Headley in the middle of the room; his face was set firm, and his arms tightly folded.

Edward got to his feet. He still felt tired and irritated. He had mentally thrown away the few words he had jotted on the back of an envelope. But he had better begin by playing safe – show Richard Peacock he respected his judgement and that warning. So he paddled into the prevailing shallows of mutual congratulations before contemplating colder and deeper waters.

'Having congratulated you, let me share a few worries with you as well. Because our local problems, here in this

192

part of Sussex, often have a bearing on larger, national problems. We want more money for our hospital, our old people's homes, our university down the road. We want our roads re-surfaced this year rather than next. We want a swimming pool in Lewes for our children. But none of us wants higher rates or taxes. We would all like the benefits without the costs. But let's be realistic. We voted into power a government pledged to cut spending at the centre, spending over which you yourselves otherwise have no control. Now there is a price to pay for such policies. There is a price to pay in a parliamentary democracy. And it is the job of ministers, meeting every Thursday in the Cabinet Room in Number Ten, to balance out the costs and the interests. To reconcile local and particular demands with the priorities of the country as a whole.'

He paused. This was all much too abstract. Those who sat before him had been converted years before to the general policies on which the Government had narrowly been elected the previous year. The coughing and the shifting of bottoms on the hard, metal chairs warned him he was losing their attention.

'So there is often a tension between what we would like here in this part of England and what a government with national responsibilities can do. Sometimes we must face the fact, however hard we agitate or organise, that our local voice cannot speak for the wider concerns or interests on which ministers must often, in the end, base their decisions. That is why I want to talk briefly about the M27.'

There was a stillness. They were all paying attention now. *The Times* crossword had been laid aside. Derek Headley, with his long, gaunt face and his unsmiling, grey eyes crouched behind his aggressive, rimless glasses, was looking fixedly at Edward. His arms were still tightly crossed, as if keeping in his store of venom.

'Most of you passionately don't want the motorway built. At least, not near your house or through your countryside. You are putting a tremendous effort into the campaign built around Sir John Huntley's public enquiry. Everywhere I go there are posters, petitions, leaflets, articles, letters setting out the arguments and the objections. That's as it should be. And I have responsibilities, too. I am doing what I can to help. I pester my colleagues in the Department of Transport. I represent your views to them. I have written again to Sir John Huntley to put the case against the northern route as I see it. Ten weeks ago I took a delegation, with Mr Dubarry here, to call on the Secretary of State. And I shall continue to do what I can to protect local interests. The strength of feeling about this issue is widespread. It has a strong voice and it must use it. But let's be under no illusion.'

He paused again. Dare he do it? Dare he plunge into this pool tonight? Could he be confident of coming back to the surface and swimming? He knew already he did not like putting his head under water. But it must be said by someone.

'We have to be realistic. That road will be built, I have no doubt of it. And it may be built where you don't want it. Why? Because there are national issues at stake here too. Ministers will have to make their decision after looking at the problem as a whole. Local feeling will be a factor. But you know as well as I that it will only count as one factor among many. There will be others which will conflict with your own strong views. So amidst our efforts let's not lose sight of national perspectives. They're inescapable. They affect us too.'

He spoke slowly and clearly. Not demonstratively. The demagogue's style had never been his. Occasionally he would emphasise a point with his thumb and forefinger conducting in time to the rhythm of his words. Otherwise, there were no distractions from the cadence of his sentences.

The room was very quiet. Edward saw out of the corner of his eye that the Major had stopped taking the record of the meeting. He saw no sympathy in the forty pairs of eyes before him. His own eyes danced haphazardly from face to face. Dammit, could they all be so blinkered? His impatience grew inside him. He walked to the edge of the diving-board and plunged off.

'There is a wider point, too. We cannot always let our hearts and lives be ruled by local issues. They are important. They have their place.' He swallowed his pride for a moment and looked up to the diving-board as he plunged towards the pool. 'I was elected to represent and do my best for local concerns.' Then he turned back to meet the water. 'But in Westminster and as a minister I have to face the other side. As a government we have responsibilities to the country as a whole. We have national aims. We cannot afford to lose sight of them. And each day, as a minister, I come to realise more forcefully that we have to look wider still. If we want to preserve the values we hold dearest, we can't turn our back on the wider dimension. Even a far-away African country – even Meridia where I was earlier this week – demands our attention, our efforts, sometimes our money.'

Edward stopped. He felt he had tumbled rather

ungracefully into the water and had not yet returned to the surface. Derek Headley had stood up. Dubarry stirred beside Edward and coughed.

'Questions at the end please, Derek. I don't think Mr Dunsford has quite finished.'

Headley glared at the three men on the stage, two sitting, one standing, like himself.

'I'm not sitting here listening to this rubbish any longer. This is damned intolerable.'

Miss Simpson looked round nervously out of her mauve cloud. Headley appealed to his audience.

'Disgraceful and intolerable, that's what it is. For a man who we voted into Parliament, who we've worked for and supported these last few years, to have the nerve to tell us that he doesn't actually give a damn for the biggest and most sensitive issue in these parts.'

Edward leant forward, his hands on the table.

'Perhaps you didn't quite hear what I was saying, Mr Headley .'

'Oh yes I did. I heard every condescending, arrogant little word. And I couldn't believe my ears.' He looked round. 'I wondered if he knew what he was saying. But I heard it all, Mr Chairman. Oh yes, very plainly indeed.' He looked round again, sweeping up support from his audience. 'It's clear to me that Mr Dunsford doesn't give a fig for the motorway or the strength of people's feelings in his own constituency. If he did, where was he last Saturday, may I ask? Doesn't he care that people regarded that as a vital meeting where the public support of our MP for the campaign was crucial? Fantastic, isn't it? As if that wasn't insult enough, Mr Chairman.' Edward sat down. 'Then, on top of that, Mr Dunsford comes here tonight. He makes no apology. He insults us again – with a long rambling lecture in which he suggests that these are all petty little worries much too unimportant for a grand government minister to worry about.

'Mr Chairman,' he cast a baleful look round the room. 'Mr Dunsford has lost touch with us here, and with his constituents. He's not just neglecting us. He's doing us real harm in the constituency. He's too concerned scampering around the world getting his picture on the television – and in the newspapers – to worry about the problems which we here have to grapple with.'

He paused again. Perhaps he realised that his next assault might go too far. But to hell with it. He didn't like Dunsford anyway.

'It seems to me he's also lost any sense of common decency, judging from what I saw of his behaviour at a road accident up beyond Cooksbridge a couple of hours ago.'

The Chairman's eyes were darting furiously around the room in search of a rescuer. Edward sprang to his feet.

'And what do you mean by that, Mr Headley?'

Headley realised his shaft had found its mark. His voice softened to a satisfied and almost apologetic tone.

'I meant only that I found it rather odd to see you driving off when the rest of us who happened to be there were doing what we could to help. That poor devil in the sportscar was in a very bad state.'

He sat down.

Edward sat down, too. He was flushed and angry. He had not expected the biscuit manufacturer's venom. Had this been a public meeting in an election campaign he would have lashed back, giving as good – no, better –

197

than he got. But here he was not sure of his ground. He had leapt too eagerly into the pool and left them standing splashed and indignant around it. He must win back some ground. If the feeling around him now persisted there would be more trouble. He was glad Rosemary was not sitting in the front row, in an expensive tweed suit, glaring at him with her blackest look.

There was a series of questions about the road. Was Edward suggesting that a decision had been taken, that the campaign had no point now? Was it true that draft orders for the northern route were already circulating among Whitehall officials? Would a petition to the Prime Minister help? What about some of the local farmers selling off tiny parcels of land along the route to hundreds of protesters? After all, it had been tried before in the Midlands, and it had almost done the trick. Edward answered. He was positive, reassuring, back in command. But a doubt still lingered about his own position. Was he committed? Would he really make the effort which was needed of him?

Next to the owner of *The Times* crossword, a hand was waved in the fourth row.

'Yes, Mrs Stephenson. You have a question on this point, or can we move on?' asked the Chairman.

Violet Stephenson, a large lady in an ample blue dress rose to her feet. 'Mr Headley raised a crucial point, it seems to me. Could Mr Dunsford tell us plainly where we all stand? Does he support the campaign or doesn't he?'

Edward stood up again. Bless you, he thought.

'Let me make my position absolutely clear. I support the campaign. I will do my best to help at the public enquiry. I shall continue to represent your views to the

Secretary of State for Transport. But in doing so I want to raise no false hopes. I want no one to believe that effort and energy guarantee success. But we must all do what we can.'

Dubarry, the Chairman, rose to his feet.

'I think that takes care of that item, ladies and gentlemen. I should like now to move to the Treasurer's six-monthly report.'

Miss Simpson from the antique shop by the railway station smiled with relief and approval. *The Times* crossword was re-folded to the contours of its owner's thigh, and a ball-point resumed its task of blackening the white squares. Derek Headley continued to glower and mutter.

The meeting ended at ten fifteen. Some left quickly and made for the bar to have a last drink while there was time. The ladies – Violet Stephenson inevitably prominent among them – tended to stay behind, form little groups and chatter. Headley gathered some friends into a corner. Edward felt exhausted and begged a lift home from Major Peacock.

They drove without speaking in the Major's ageing Land Rover until they joined the main road just above the prison. The roar of the engine and the rattle of the car made a subtle conversation impossible. Richard Peacock spoke first.

'Headley's got the bit between his teeth, hasn't he?' he shouted. 'What was all that about a car accident?'

'Near the pub beyond Cooksbridge. Sportscar collided with a van. Pretty nasty. But there was nothing I could do. Lots of other people around helping.'

'That bugger's always in the right place at the wrong time.'

The Major swerved to avoid a rabbit which suddenly

confronted them in the middle of the road, staring into the car's headlights with flashing startled eyes. 'Suppose that's why he's made such a packet with his wretched biscuits.' He laughed. 'My father would turn in his grave if he thought a biscuit-maker was bidding for the chairmanship of his old Association.' There was a crash of gears as they slowed to turn on to the road which took them along the foot of the Downs. There was no moon now. The night was dark and threatening. A streak or two of rain began to appear on the windscreen.

Edward's eyelids had been closing. Now he was awake.

'What? He wants to be Chairman?'

'It's only gossip. He wants to push out Dubarry. Thought you might have picked that one up already.'

'But why try and get at old Dubarry through me?'

'Why not? Geoffrey's too nice to see off on his own merits. No one would stand for that. But a real upheaval in the constituency, fox and chicken stuff, and who knows what a frightened Association might not be stampeded into.' They crawled carefully round the churchyard at Westmeston, gears crashing again.

Major Peacock glanced round at Edward as he picked up speed along the narrow twisting lane.

'That's why you must be careful about him. And about this bloody motorway.'

When they turned into the carefully raked pea-grit drive of Long Meadow it was raining hard.

16

Edward pushed his hand through his hair and leant back in the red leather worn smooth by generations of ministerial trousers. He threw the papers back on to his desk.

'This won't do.'

The red chair balanced precariously on its back legs. An inch or two more and he would topple back into the pile of *Hansards* stacked on a table in the corner of the room. He breathed out hard in a fit of exasperation. He was annoyed again. He seemed to have been annoyed a great deal in the last month.

Sally was standing by his desk, her hands clasped in front of her. It was her stance of Private Secretarial deference.

'I know it won't do. I told the Head of the Department as soon as I'd read it that you wouldn't accept the recommendation.'

The chair continued to balance precariously on its back legs.

'And what did he say?'

'I'd rather not tell you. But the gist of it was that that was the way things were and that it was about time ministers faced up to them.'

Edward turned towards the window. It seemed to have been raining constantly ever since his Thursday evening meeting in Lewes. The window rattled and the cold air outside blew through the gaps in the ageing Victorian casement. The gas fire in his room gave off an unpleasant smell. It was a thoroughly foul day.

'Has he read Alan Boyle's covering minute?'

'I don't think so. Alan hasn't copied it round the office yet.'

'Why not?'

'He rang to say that he wanted to wait until after your meeting. He doesn't want to provoke any comments from Sir Reginald until afterwards.'

Edward brought the two suspended legs of his chair back to the ground. He kept his eyes on the neatly typed blue papers on his desk. A red tag tied them to a card submission folder in which six flags marked the background papers which had been attached for the Minister's 'ease of reference'. He read Alan Boyle's dissenting minute again as though Sally was not there.

Even though he seemed to ignore her he did not want her to go.

'Alan Boyle's right. Let's keep all this away from the Permanent Under-Secretary for a bit.' He leant back again and looked up at the distant ceiling. It was as high as a squash court, Rosemary had once said, though heaven knows how she would know about such things. 'If anything is certain in this building, Sally, Sir Reginald would dearly love to line up the entire Office against a new policy on Meridia before these papers get to the Secretary of State.'

James Harrison put his head round the door.

'They're all here, Minister.'

'They can wait,' Edward said abruptly. James retreated behind the door, not before he had smirked an instant at Sally. The *Daily Express* photograph had been a great success with him and he had pulled her leg mercilessly. So had half the Foreign Office. The diary pages of *The Times* and the *Evening Standard* had rung a number of times and tried unsuccessfully to speak to her. She had been embarrassed – though less than she might have expected. But it had provoked a fierce argument when she had seen Charles Elliott that same evening. They had had a blazing row. He had stormed out of her flat saying that he wasn't going to sleep with some minister's call-girl, thank you. She had stayed up most of the night, first in tears, then in a haze of unexpected cheerfulness as she drank her way through most of the bottle of white burgundy he had brought for her. She crawled to the office the next morning feeling terrible but somehow better. Blast Charles Elliott. She might sleep with him but he didn't own her like a four-acre field over which he had exclusive grazing rights. The more she thought about the photo in the *Express* the more pleased she became. Even so, the prickings of her conscience were not far away.

She and Edward had said little about the photograph. He had brought the newspaper to her desk on that Wednesday morning and smiled apologetically at her. Her face had reddened for a few minutes. James Harrison, sitting across from her, had been beside himself with amusement. He swayed in his chair, once Edward had retreated to his room, in howls of laughter. Sally was annoyed with him.

'But it's just so funny,' he had gasped. 'Just what I guessed all along.

'Don't talk rubbish, James.'

Sally had guessed the effect it might have had on Rosemary and felt sorry for Edward. And Edward, as he had sat at his desk still cursing the photographer, had imagined Sally having her leg pulled by the secretly envious junior solicitor or trainee accountant who probably took her out to Festival Hall concerts from time to time.

Edward was pacing round his room, reluctant to let his meeting on Meridia begin. He picked up a newspaper from the long mahogany table. A week after his return Meridia was still being given good space on the foreign news page and in the background commentaries. He glanced idly down the columns. This was the issue on which a new step in his career might be built. Even a small success in changing government policy would be his success. His voice would carry a little more weight in the House. There would be invitations to speak at meetings and to the right London dinner parties. He hoped Rosemary would play along. Perhaps she could be bribed. At present she was still in a total sulk. Even Charles Elliott might have to swallow his pride and invite him to address the back-bench Foreign Affairs Committee more often. And Patrick Reid would have to listen in his black jacket and striped trousers when Edward spoke. But his sudden notoriety was two-edged. Yes, it would be satisfying to chalk up a success over Meridia. Yes, it would certainly put his name on the map for a time. Yes, it could be a point in his favour when the Prime Minister next sat by a late-night fire in the little flat at the top of Number Ten reckoning his ministerial arithmetic. But he might still not succeed. By the sudden chance which public life sometimes brings he had staked out a position on the political battlefield. But success in the first skirmish might not breed success in the main engagement. And having set himself up in the public gaze failure now would bring its humiliation. Patrick Reid would be looking for his chance to strike back. He already saw the whole business as a gesture of personal affront. All his instincts were against the novel or the imaginative. It was instinct, not vindictiveness, which would drive him on against Edward, to slap him down when he could, as a schoolmaster might an unpleasantly precocious pupil. So the pupil must tread carefully.

Nevertheless, the Prime Minister's mandate remained from that Tuesday afternoon meeting with his Foreign Secretary and his Chancellor. He wanted to look at the options. And that was exactly what Edward was determined should go to him. Not the lame and half-baked justification for doing nothing contained in the submission folder on his desk.

He turned to Sally. Unexpectedly she had sat down in one of the green armchairs. She was watching him closely.

'I won't put that submission to the Secretary of State. You can understand that, can't you?'

'Yes. I can. Those papers don't put the case fairly at all.'

'No, of course not. But it's more than that. It's not just pride on my part. The fact is the Office doesn't even understand what the case is. It doesn't even know the facts.' He went back to his desk and leafed through the

205

submission folder until he found paragraph nine. He stabbed at the thick, blue-crested paper.

'The little it says about the financial consortium is hopelessly wrong.'

'But we have no proof yet.'

He interrupted her. 'Listen to this bit.' He quoted from the page in front of him. '"The economic and financial future of Meridia remains uncertain. The country's greatest potential natural resource lies in the very substantial oil deposits in the south of the country. But they are located far from any viable point of export and even further from potential markets. At today's oil prices, and given the partnership terms so far offered by the Meridian Government, exploitation would be totally unprofitable for the foreseeable future. There have been recent rumours of a possible exploitation arrangement involving Soviet and American interests. We have checked these stories carefully. There has been no recent intelligence to corroborate an earlier report. Our Ambassador in Washington reports that there has been recent interest shown by a group of US oil companies but that this has produced no concrete results."' He threw the papers aside. 'It's rubbish. It's all hopelessly wrong.'

'How can you be so sure?' Sally had begun to feel uncomfortable sitting while he was standing reading. She had felt more relaxed with him since their journey. She could even begin to imagine what it might be like to spend time with him in London outside the office. But in the office the conventions held and were not so easy to shrug aside. So she pushed herself up from the uncomfortably low armchair. She lost a shoe doing so and a crimson-stockinged foot searched the red carpet self-consciously to retrieve it. She looked up and caught him smiling at her.

'Shouldn't I bring them in so that you can start the meeting?'

'No. I'm not ready. They can wait a minute or two longer.' He paused. 'I take it Alan Boyle's coming?'

She nodded.

'Go and bring him in, Sally. On his own.'

She found her shoe and slipped round the door into the outer office. There was a babble of voices outside.

Edward stared across to the enormous full-length portrait of George III. Alan Boyle was the only senior official in the Office who clearly shared his sympathies and suspicions about Meridia. Perhaps he just wanted to make his mark. His dissenting minute on the department's submission was his first public commitment. But whatever his motive Edward wanted to keep him as an ally. He must fasten him a little more firmly on the hook.

'Morning, Minister.'

'Alan, draw up a chair. I wanted a word in private. Sally, you stay too.' She closed the door. They sat in a triangle: Edward back behind his desk, Sally at the side by the gas fire and Alan Boyle, not completely at his ease, opposite Edward peering at his Minister across the pile of paper in the battered wooden in-tray. Occasionally the window creaked in the wind, or in the tiled corridor outside there was the muffled rattle of a messenger's trolley. Otherwise they were cocooned from the rest of the Foreign Office.

'I'm sorry these papers have come out like this,' Alan Boyle said. 'I went through the issues carefully with the various departments before anything was drafted. If there had been time I would have had the whole thing re-done. I feel quite strongly that there is a very good humanitarian case to be made – as you yourself said at your press conference last week. And that's my judgement as a bureaucrat, not – with respect – as a politician.'

'Sally and I saw the humanitarian case for ourselves. It goes without saying.'

'I agree, Minister. As my minute says, we can't afford to ignore the increasing Soviet presence either. Aid is a weapon against them. Of limited power, I accept. But we have to use it before it's too late. I believe Hamid is still looking both ways. If we do nothing he will pretty soon turn his back on us.'

Edward was again performing a circus act with his chair. He reached out to drag his new ally further into the plot.

'That's the point, Alan. It's a point neither you, nor these papers, nor the entire Foreign Office has grasped. The Russians are already making the offer which will turn Hamid's back on us. But it's bigger, sexier, than any of us is ready to believe. Because the Russians have, or will have soon, that oil deal everyone's trying to claim doesn't exist.'

There was a distant buzz of a telephone next door, and the low murmur of voices. The Under-Secretary opened his mouth to speak, but Edward continued.

'A week or two ago I suppose it was just a feeling. A nagging worry. Now it's a certainty.'

He had met Guy Carlton the night before at Guy's club for a swim before dinner, something they had not done for months. But for an elderly man wearing goggles who crawled slowly and deliberately up and down the pool they had had the great watery cavern to themselves. They swam twenty lengths, two and a half times across the Thames at Westminster Bridge Guy told him. As they had always done, they talked as they swam side by side. Breast stroke was for sociable swimming. Their voices sounded flat and hollow against the water, the blue and grey tiles and the glass roof. Edward was out of practice and breathless after twelve lengths. But after the first two lengths there was no reason to speak. Guy talked of Meridia. He talked about the approach made to Speyer's. He explained why they had turned it down, and would go on turning it down. But the Russians were ready to pounce and Meridia needed help. He encouraged Edward to stick to his guns. Edward listened with alarm to the story of MEECON and Neil Wainwright and the walk in St James's Park. Under the shower as he rubbed shampoo into his dark hair he digested Guy's story in silence.

Now he told it in abbreviated form to Alan Boyle and Sally. The Under-Secretary did not look at Edward when his account was finished.

'I fear we've failed you rather badly, Minister. We should have known all that long ago.'

Sally interrupted. 'But it strengthens our case conclusively.'

Perhaps she did not notice the possessive pronoun she used. Edward did.

'Let's get them in here.'

Sally disappeared into the outer office. Ten officials returned with her, the heads of four departments and six assorted desk officers and experts. There was an incoherent mumbling of 'Morning, Minister' as they gathered round the long Victorian table where meetings took place.

Edward sat at the head of the table, Alan Boyle at his right, Sally at the far end near the door to the outer world. Edward glanced at the faces before him. He hoped he looked as fierce as he felt.

'I've read this submission. It fails entirely to deal with the oil exploration consortium being put together by the Americans and the Russians with Washington's knowledge and tacit approval. I consider that a key element of the problem. It must be covered properly if the Secretary of State is to be able to assess the arguments for increasing our aid to Meridia properly.'

He paused. The head of a department who sat three places away spoke.

'But, with respect, we have covered that aspect, Minister.' He shuffled through his photocopy of the submission and pointed to paragraph nine. 'Here. We've been into it all quite fully. We've consulted the Embassy in Washington and in Moscow. The stories that have been floating around have been quite clearly enormously exaggerated.'

Alan Boyle shut his eyes. Sally looked hard at the polished table. One of the desk officers tried to stifle a yawn. There was an explosion.

'Rubbish. Absolute rubbish. That shows exactly why none of you understands the problems we are trying to find an answer to.' He glared at the awe-struck faces round the table. One of them suddenly looked very white. Edward continued to spit out angry words. 'We're not dealing with the whim of a junior minister who returns from some little jaunt overseas anxious to do his bit for a country by which he's been charmed out of his senses. We're dealing with a real and a serious problem. There's immense public interest. We're dealing with the political future of a country in Africa with immense strategic importance for us. We're dealing with a country which the Soviet Union is going to turn against the West while we all just sit here chattering. If it succeeds, Meridia will be lost to the West as a friendly country for a long time. If we do what we can to prevent that happening now, then there's a chance – just a chance perhaps – that we might succeed. Why the hell doesn't anyone here know all this? If you don't know it you damn well ought to know it. What the hell is all this so-called intelligence for? We're dealing with some simple, obvious facts, and it's about time someone did some constructive thinking about them.'

There was silence in the room. Somewhere in a distant part of Horse Guards a pneumatic drill started up. Alan Boyle coughed.

'I am not prepared to put these papers to the Foreign Secretary. They are hopelessly inadequate. Hopelessly.' He turned to the Under-Secretary. 'We've discussed the background, Alan. Today is Tuesday. I want a fresh submission on the proper lines which takes into account the facts of this problem, and I want it for my box tomorrow night.'

'Yes, Minister.'

Somebody round the table began a sentence but Edward was already getting up. So far as he was concerned, the meeting was over.

When they had all filed out of the room Edward called Sally back and motioned her to shut the door.

'Do you think I was a bit harsh?'

Before their time in Mangara she would have blushed and not known what to say.

'I thought you were terrific.'

Edward grinned and leant back again in the red leather chair. One day he would lean an inch too far and send the *Hansards* crashing.

17

It was just seven on Wednesday morning and almost time for Sally to be out of bed. As she left the office the evening before Edward had told her to get a good night's rest. It was unlike him to be thoughtful, though Sally had noticed that he was more considerate when he himself was under stress. However much she thought Edward might secretly have been enjoying himself at his meeting, yesterday had certainly been bloody. She had a pretty clear idea of how he saw her – dependable, nice, dull to the point of irritation, orthodox and respectable – and now somewhat tired and washed out. Yet here she sat in bed, propped against the pillows, her white nightgown lying in a heap on the floor, with Charles Elliott asleep beside her. Charles was naked and she noticed the neatness and sparseness of his neck and shoulders. There was no superfluous flesh, and none of the ungainliness of middle age. She had only once seen Edward without his shirt, when he had swum in the Embassy pool in Mangara; he was not fat but she had seen that his shoulders and his

213

waist were thickening. He took sixteen and a half shirt collars; Charles only fifteen. The skin colour was different too, Charles olive against the sheets, Edward white with the occasional freckle. It was amazing that here she sat, Sally Archer, staid, middle-class and slightly feminist, comparing the physique of one naked Member of Parliament beside her with that of another who was her employer and a minister to boot. For a moment she sighed for the simpler, sillier days not long ago when she had worn no make-up, went to bed alone after the Channel Four film and insisted on being called 'Ms'.

The evening before, Charles had hammered on the front door of her flat about ten o'clock, just as Sally was hoping that after all he would not come. An omelette had been eaten, a chapter of Proust consumed to bring on drowsiness. She had been tired rather than sleepy, thoughts whirling far too fast through her brain. She had deliberately refrained from the television news which had seemed to carry an item almost every day for the last week about Meridia, the aid programme, the row in Parliament, the implications for the Government – and about Edward Dunsford. She just did not want to hear anything more about Meridia or about Edward Dunsford. But she would have been cross to find that either had faded from the news altogether. What an inconsistent, feeble person she was.

On cue as she reached that point, Charles Elliott had started hammering on the door. There was a two-tone bell, there was a brass knocker in the shape of the campanile of St Mark's in Venice, but only Charles used his fists on the varnished wood. He had been in a furious temper, poured a neat whisky for himself without thinking of Sally and started at once denouncing Edward, thus waking her up thoroughly. She had not seen Charles since an angry scene the week before over the photograph, though they had twice spoken tersely on the telephone.

'He's gone to ground now, back down a hole with that bitch Rosemary. But she'll kick him out, the PM and Reid will kick him out, from what I hear his constituency will kick him out. No hole left to go in. He's made the biggest mistake of his life.' He sipped savagely.

'If you really believed that you wouldn't be so cross.'

Charles had laughed at her shrewdness. One of the interesting things about him was the way he appreciated intelligence for its own sake. Because he was a scheming, intolerant, disappointed man, he was usually pretty miserable. But she had noticed before now one intelligent comment from her could change his mood. Indeed at that moment he had kissed her.

'I shall never take a stupid mistress.'

'Well, then?'

'You're quite right. The House of Commons is a den of cowards nowadays. They all watch the television in those horrible holes upstairs and then come downstairs to the smoking-room and dining-rooms with their silly little minds programmed for them. Tonight they were all saying the Government would have to give way to Dunsford, find huge sums for Meridia, call a new international conference, that sort of garbage. And all because our constituents are bleating louder than usual.'

'They really are?' How fickle people were. Meridia mattered to her a great deal now, but a week ago she would have bet Charles – had they been on speaking terms – that the fuss would not last to the weekend.

'They certainly are. You and Dunsford really set something off when you went to that hospital. Do you know, the other night I was actually cut at dinner at the House. First time it's ever happened. Three young dimwits would not let me join their table because I had been the only one at question time with the guts to back the Government. "Before you join us we think we should let you know that we are all friends of Edward Dunsford." This from that spotty little Tory reformer from Norfolk, who's probably never spoken to Dunsford in his life, and will throw him over in a week or so as soon as the Whips get round to him. He's got a voice like a choirboy. So I sat down to a cold salad by myself, and dammit if they didn't come in with an urgent telephone message from the Chairman of my Association asking me to reconsider my line.'

'Is that the garage proprietor?'

'It certainly is. A racist, if ever you saw one. We've only a few blacks in the constituency, but he wants to ship them all home. Yet now he's urging me to support a huge new programme for the blacks in Africa, just because he's seen you and Dunsford blubbing on television. Did they issue you with glycerine beforehand?'

'You're revolting.'

Then he had taken his whisky into the bathroom, noisily locked the door, turned on the taps, and soaked himself for ten minutes. Sally, not knowing what to expect, went to bed. Except for that last thrust he had not asked her a single question since she returned from Mangara about what she had done or how she had felt.

When he reappeared, clean but still apparently angry, with a white towel round his waist, he had slipped into bed and made love to her. Not roughly but mechanically, thinking of her pleasure as well as his, but not giving more of himself than was necessary. His bad temper made no difference to his technique. Competence without commitment. It had always been so, ever since that weekend conference two years ago on Middle East policy organised by the Church of England in the middle of Windsor Great Park. Simple food, a simple bedroom at the end of a long corridor, a simple weekend, until Charles Elliott had knocked on her door at 2 a.m., talked for an hour sitting on the brown blanket on her bed, then for the first time persuaded her into sleeping with him, and had shown her a new dimension in her life. She could still remember the plain dark brown curtains at the window of that bedroom, the washbasin in the corner and the *Annunciation* in oils above the bed.

This time, after a pause in her arms, Charles Elliott had begun at last to ask her questions. How had she enjoyed herself? How had the conference gone? Had she liked the Ambassador and had he looked after her well? Had it been very hot, and was it true that even diplomats had to queue for petrol? How had Edward done at the conference? How had the visit to the hospital come about? Had it been suggested by the Meridians? – by the Embassy? – by Herald TV? Had Edward known that Herald TV would be there? Was it really as horrible as it appeared, or had it to some extent been staged? What had been happening at the FO since they got back? Charles put his questions in a softer voice than he had used so far that evening. He turned her on to her stomach and with one hand he caressed her back between the gawky shoulder-blades. He interspersed questions about her own feelings with questions about Edward, but not skilfully enough to deceive Sally for long. She stiffened, then relaxed and continued to give truthful answers. He was pumping her, trying to forge a weapon against Edward. Sally had long since shed illusions about her lover. He was a selfish, awful man, clever but without ideas, perceptive but without feelings, censorious but without scruples. At first she had had nothing but herself to offer. Now she knew, whatever his feelings, that her usefulness to him went beyond the warmth she gave him in bed. He was using her. The different strands which might have held them together had snapped or indeed never been tied, with the one first and important exception. He still gave her physical pleasure, as he had just proved once again. This had never been important to her until she discovered it, and, lying by Charles's side and answering his questions, she wondered why something so fundamentally silly now mattered so much to her. Perhaps she exaggerated. Perhaps she could go free and after a week or so of pangs revert to her old self-sufficient life in the nunnery of Whitehall.

Meanwhile, there was no real problem in giving truthful answers to Charles's questions. He was trying to incriminate Edward, but there was no crime, and therefore nothing to fear from the truth. Everything in Meridia, everything at the hospital, everything at Edward's press conference at Heathrow, everything at the Foreign Office since had happened naturally and without guile. There was no weapon to be turned against Edward.

After a time Charles fell silent. His thin, strong hand continued to massage her back. Then suddenly he pulled it away as a final thought struck him. He sat up in the bed beside her.

'Did Edward say anything to Hamid about Speyer's?'

'About Speyer's?' Both his abruptness and the question surprised her.

'His old bank. They've done business with Meridia for years. From what I hear that's all over. Unless Edward talked them back into favour.'

'I told you he didn't see Hamid. And there was no brief on Speyer's.'

'Sometimes you're still amazingly naïve.'

'And I'm sure he never said anything about Speyer's to any of the Meridians.'

'Why so sure?' He was bolt upright now.

'Come on, Charles. He's not like that. He's absolutely straight in money matters. And in any case he's cut all connection with the bank. He had to when he was made a minister.'

'Naïve again. Indeed, absurd. He was chatting hard to Guy Carlton only the other night at a dinner party.'

'That's not a crime.'

'Nor is doing a favour to a bank which used to employ him, and might do so again. Indeed perhaps the whole commotion . . .' He broke off, pleased.

'Don't talk such gibberish.' She wanted to wipe the pleasure from his face. It was crazy. Edward was not doing Speyer's a favour, it was the other way round. Guy Carlton and Speyer's were giving Edward the information he needed. She felt like hitting Charles for getting it wrong, and he sensed her anger.

'Relax, Sally. And thank you, Sally. You've done me the usual good turn, and perhaps thrown in another for good measure.' He kissed her on the forehead, turned away from her, and settled to sleep. For a second she wanted to throw him out or at least scratch the olive skin of his back from the nape of his neck to the bottom of his prominent spine. But her weariness crowded suddenly in on her, and she too slept, thinking of Edward at the press conference last week at the airport, standing there saying too much, beyond the reach of her precious briefs.

Now it was morning, and Sally gathered her thoughts and tried to decide whether yesterday had ended well or ill. Charles slipped out of bed. She had nothing ready to say to him. She could hear him whistling through the open bathroom door as he shaved. It was a habit which did not fit his self-contained, calculating character, but it usually meant that he was in good humour. He dressed quickly, and soon was once again Charles Elliott, second-rank politician, sharp of face, conventional of dress, a public man making his own breakfast in a hurry. The whistling stopped, and he appeared carrying his black leather wallet in one hand.

'I'd forgotten one item in our agenda,' he said. 'Cuddle before the storm.' He produced the cutting from his wallet. 'I've cooled down a bit since last week. Not least because so far as I can remember from Cambridge days, Edward isn't much good in bed.' He dropped the cutting on the bed. Sally glanced at the well-known photograph, but was too angry to blush.

'What the hell do you mean?'

'I don't mean that you've yet gone to bed with Edward. That's not in your character, probably not in his. But you may be getting fond of him. You spent all our conversation last night protecting him. So I'm forewarning you — so as to avoid any disappointment.'

'Would you mind?'

'I'd mind for you,' said Charles. He finished a cup of coffee. 'He is going to be destroyed. You must realise that. Edward has flown too near the sun, and the sun will destroy him. It would be a pity if your wings melt at the same time. I promise you one thing. I won't be there to pick you from the ocean. I must go now. Goodbye. Have a good day.'

She had noticed before that Charles had a good range of exit lines. The outside door of the flat closed emphatically, not quite a slam. For ten minutes, most unusually, Sally sat in bed without a book or papers, and thought. Sometimes she actually hated Charles Elliott.

18

Oblivious to the magnificence of the office around
him, the Foreign Secretary smelt the danger in the
papers on the table. But he thought he had found a way
through. The submission had been re-written in the thirty
hours as Edward had stipulated and the recommendation
on aid to Meridia had changed from 'unnecessary' to
'highly desirable'. A figure of seventy million pounds, to
be found by diverting other monies from existing commitments in the aid budget, was mentioned. Edward had
marked the papers with a terse, strong endorsement. But
the submission now bore two dissenting minutes, one
from the Head of the Overseas Aid Branch, and one from
Sir Reginald Anson on two sides of typescript which dismissed the evidence as flimsy and the political objective
as impractical. Patrick Reid had read his Permanent
Under-Secretary's minute with deep relief. With Anson
on his side his chosen tactic was likely to succeed.

The Foreign Secretary wore a heavy, country, tweed
suit, symbolic of the approaching weekend. He wanted to

keep this meeting short so that by lunch time he could be speeding west along the M40 in his brown official Rover to his house in Gloucestershire. If they made good time there might just be enough daylight to spend a couple of hours chopping wood in the orchard. But time was already passing. He took out a heavy gold watch from his waistcoat pocket. They had been at it for forty minutes. And they had got nowhere, except to define more clearly the numerical strength of each side. Edward had support from Alan Boyle and – a surprising change from two days before – the Head of the North Africa Department. Boyle had bravely spoken first, and powerfully. But Sir Reginald carried the rest with him. The Foreign Secretary's manner throughout had been one of profound scepticism.

Edward was speaking again.

'We simply must move quickly. We cannot underestimate the dangers for Western interests which the MEECON oil consortium represents. Nor can we doubt any longer the seriousness and speed with which the project is going ahead. We all agree that Hamid sees himself controlling events around him and choosing his friends as it suits him. And that is still how things are – just. But once MEECON is finally put together and the political arrangements in place, the door to Meridia will be slammed in our faces.'

A pair of St James's Park pigeons cooed unseasonally and insistently on the balcony outside one of the windows. The Foreign Secretary fiddled with the papers in front of him. Damn the man! First it was all a question of suffering humanity. Now it was all a wicked plot by Kremlin officials and Texas oilmen. When he spoke he addressed his Private Secretary.

'Andrew, would you please deal with those wretched pigeons.'

The Private Secretary walked self-consciously to the window and began waving his arms.

Sir Reginald Anson, his back erect in his chair, swivelled his head slowly towards the Foreign Secretary, unclasped his hands and laid them palm downwards on the table.

'With your permission, Secretary of State, I think it may help if I try to recapitulate the main arguments before us.'

'Please do, Sir Reginald.'

Edward slouched back in his chair, thrust his hands in his trouser pockets and stared moodily up at the gilded ceiling. Every so often he would glance down at his lapels, remove a hand from a pocket and flick a piece of dandruff into space.

'If I am not mistaken, the case laid before us by the Minister of State rests essentially on four considerations. First, the imminence of the MEECON exploration arrangement. Second, the intimate link between MEECON and the Soviet arrangements for consolidating their hold over Meridia. Third, the readiness and ability of President Hamid to take assistance and political friendship from the highest bidder. And fourth, the assumption that the President's traditional ties with Britain and Europe would incline him to switch his allegiances from their present trend if HMG were able to offer a sufficiently large inducement.'

The Foreign Secretary looked at his watch again.

'That's my understanding of the recommendation, certainly.'

224

Edward opened his mouth and drew in his breath to speak, but held back under a glare from Patrick Reid.

'Thank you, Secretary of State. And I would go on to summarise the objections to these assumptions as follows. First, the evidence about the position of MEECON and the intentions behind it is, to say the least, conflicting.' Sir Reginald paused and looked pointedly in Edward's direction before he resumed. 'Even if – and I repeat I myself am profoundly sceptical – even if the arrangements to establish MEECON have gone so far as some claim, we must allow that the position of the United States Government is crucial. They may not have been as candid with us about this matter as they might have been. If that is so, it is to be regretted. And if they have given tacit agreement to these arrangements, then we must keep in mind the present constraints of their policy.'

He paused impressively. This point had been covered in none of the papers but his own minute. He was proud of that, and it made it worth putting his point again.

'Secretary of State, the disarmament talks in Geneva are at a critical stage. The United States Government is under great domestic pressure to reach an arms agreement. They have tabled new proposals at the negotiations which they are most anxious the Soviet Government should accept. Yet we all know that under the rules of diplomacy one must pay a price to reach an agreement. Gentlemen, it is not impossible that that price could be a temporary Soviet presence in Meridia. If that is their sober and settled calculation then any intervention by us would be rash and . . .' he groped for the conclusive words, 'utterly inappropriate.'

The Permanent Under-Secretary was speaking with

maddening punctiliousness. Edward leant across the table.

'But Sir Reginald, you fail to appreciate . . .'

'Please let the PUS finish,' Patrick Reid snapped.

Sir Reginald paused, magisterially. That was a good sign. It should be plain sailing now. He continued.

'Second, past experience shows equally that the Soviet Union never commits its strategy to one set of tactics only. Whatever plans it has for Meridia will be pushed forward on many fronts simultaneously. MEECON might be one facet. But only one.'

In his precise way Sir Reginald realised the danger of beginning to mix his metaphors But his dismissal of Edward's ideas was now in full flood and he could not stop to choose his words more carefully.

'Third, all the evidence shows President Hamid to be, let us say, a little mercurial in his character. He picks from here and there according to his whim. He is not consistent in his choice of friends or allies. There is nothing to prevent him from holding out his hands in two contrary directions simultaneously.'

Edward sat back in his chair fuming.

'That's one view only. Others might think differently.'

'But it is, Secretary of State,' and Sir Reginald looked pointedly in Edward's direction, 'a view based on the assessment of people who, unlike Mr Dunsford, have actually had the opportunity of meeting the President and seeing him at close quarters.' He moved sedately on. 'And, lastly, there is no necessary reason why the enormous social and economic problems of a country like this could be so improved by the modest assistance HMG could give as to make any difference to the political allegiances of its

Government. No matter how genuine our intentions –' this time he did not look at Edward '– I fail utterly to see how they could make any real difference.'

Edward broke in. 'For heaven's sake, Foreign Secretary, this is too serious a matter for diplomatic figure-skating.'

The meeting seemed to be approaching its climax, but Patrick Reid's reply surprised them all.

'Thank you all very much. This has been a most useful discussion.' He paused. 'I shall be going through the problem thoroughly with the Prime Minister on Sunday.'

He began to collect together his papers. His Private Secretary rose to open the door.

Edward stayed in his seat.

'But we have to reach some conclusion. It's up in the air as it stands.'

The Foreign Secretary had tucked his papers under his arm like a lawyer's brief and was on his feet.

'Thank you all very much.'

All except Edward filed out to the hectic bustle of the Private Secretaries' room.

'Patrick, this is absurd. We reached no decision.'

The Foreign Secretary was behind the fortress of his desk, safe and in command.

'I think you must be mistaken. This meeting was not called to reach a decision.'

'What on earth do you mean?' Edward was on his feet too. 'The PM asked us to re-examine the facts. We have to reach some sort of conclusion.'

There was clear dislike in the tone of Patrick Reid's reply.

'We have gone over the arguments this morning so that I am clear in my own mind when I lunch at Chequers on Sunday. That was the purpose of our meeting. Nothing more.'

'For God's sake, Patrick, do you mean you're just going to chat about all this with the Prime Minister over your port? Is this what you call looking carefully at all the options?'

'I consider it a perfectly proper way to discuss difficult policy decisions,' he said icily. 'Now, if you don't mind, I have other things to do.'

Dunsford could not believe what he heard. His temper broke.

'I bloody well do mind. You can't possibly consider this a proper way to behave.'

There was a silence. Patrick Reid then spoke very slowly. He knew what he was doing. He had his temper under control.

'May I remind you which of the two of us is Foreign Secretary.'

Edward's mind was racing. The man was impossible, but he would gain nothing by abusing him.

'Patrick, you must understand that this issue is not important to me for any personal reason.'

'Is that so? Perhaps I have underestimated you?'

'I believe very strongly that we have to act to keep the Russians out. And what we do can make a difference.'

'You're entitled to your views. I'm grateful for them. But I happen to disagree. So does the Permanent Under-Secretary.'

'All right. But you can't just ignore the immense public interest. Or the pressure we have been under in the House – rightly, in my view. You must in all fairness put the facts . . .'

'Now listen, young man. I'll have no more of you trying to tell me what my job is.' He could control his temper no longer and his voice slipped quickly back into its native Edinburgh. 'I'll give the Prime Minister such advice as I find fitting.'

He turned and moved to gaze out of the tall windows behind his desk, his hands clasped behind his back, shoulders stooping slightly. The interview was over.

'But it's not enough.' Edward grabbed at the only piece of Whitehall wreckage left in these stormy seas. 'It must at least go before Cabinet.' His words were rapid and full of imperatives. 'The Government must have a proper chance to decide. We can't afford to get this wrong.' He saw his chance slipping away. 'If you're not prepared to take this to Cabinet, then I'm prepared to make trouble.'

Silhouetted against the window the Foreign Secretary thrust his hands into his pockets and turned to face the room. He was digesting this foolish threat slowly.

'If you do, young man, I warn you now that your career will be finished.' His tone could not have betrayed more fervently how very much he hoped that his prophecy would come to pass.

19

'Oh! Mrs Dunsford. How nice to see you.'

Rosemary was met as she entered the shop by a cloud of lilac topped by silvery hair. Miss Simpson, dressed as she had been at Edward's Association meeting the week before, chirped as she always did when Rosemary came to browse. Rosemary usually bought something.

'Hello.'

Rosemary gave her best garden-fête smile. She wore the conspicuous clothes of a Londoner who dressed deliberately for the country – well-cut tweed skirt, shoes suitable for fields and cart-tracks only if they never meet a splash of mud, green anorak, and a silk scarf tied luxuriously round the neck. She could never quite remember the lilac lady's name, but she was always friendly, and so presumably did not mind.

'I haven't seen you for such a long time.'

Rosemary smiled again, her eyes searching the shop to see if she wanted to buy. The conversations in the antique shop were usually one-sided.

'May I look at the tiny Victorian chair over there? It looks perfect for the girls.' Rosemary was well-organised in some things. November had come and she was looking for her first Christmas presents.

'Yes, yes, of course, Mrs Dunsford. Do, please.' The old lady resumed the thread of her earlier comment. 'We miss seeing you, you know, Mrs Dunsford. Of course you're very busy. But I'm glad you didn't come to our last Committee meeting.'

She was moving a collection of fire-screens and old brass so that Rosemary could see the chair.

'Your husband had such a difficult time, poor man. I'm afraid we have a few members who simply don't know how to behave like gentlemen. It really was too bad. I felt ashamed.'

She paused, a brass poker in one hand and a large iron door-stop in the form of a King Charles spaniel in the other.

'And over such a tedious thing, too.'

'Perhaps some people thought it was important.' Rosemary took a closer look at the chair.

'Oh yes, I dare say, Mrs Dunsford. I dare say. But all over a motorway, Mrs Dunsford. Some people feel just too strongly about it in my opinion.' She peered out of the shop window, through a collection of odd wine-glasses, copper bedpans and Victorian jewellery, down towards the station. 'You know, it's hardly going to affect many of us all that much.' She glanced back at Rosemary. 'Not enough to excuse all this fuss about Mr Dunsford, you know.'

She twitched her nose nervously like a squirrel about to dart to safety up a nearby tree.

'I'm sorry. What . . . ?' Rosemary began to ask when the bell on the shop door gave a jangle and a powerfully built middle-aged galleon sailed in.

'Well, well, Mrs Dunsford. How very nice to see you, my dear.'

Mrs Violet Stephenson was one of the few local ladies whose name Rosemary always remembered. She was a JP and a capable and active member of the Executive Committee, busy with charities, fêtes, the local children's home, organiser of Christmas parcels to old people and the local prison. She enjoyed to the full the gossip and excitements of local politics. She worked hard for the public good as she saw it. But she carried an unsafe pair of ears. She liked to talk and share her knowledge.

Rosemary had decided against the chair. The upholstery was badly stained, and one leg had woodworm. She would have liked to escape. Mrs Stephenson blocked her exit.

'So nice to catch you on your own, Mrs Dunsford. There's never a chance for a proper talk at all those public functions.'

Rosemary's mind was suddenly empty of a convincing excuse.

'Mrs Stephenson, I'd love to have a talk. But I was really on my way back to the High Street.'

'But so was I, my dear, so was I. Let me come with you. I'd so like a little chat. I've got something rather important to say about Edward. There's a coffee shop just up the road.'

Captor and captive left together and walked back up the hill. Rosemary was already wondering what the antiques lady had been going to say about Edward.

232

Now Violet Stephenson. She had not asked after his meeting in Lewes. What had he done? Edward had been behaving like an ass in the past fortnight. He would not shut up about Africa. He seemed to think some fearful principle was involved. All right, so he had found a cause and if it got him noticed by the right people, so much the better. But to her Meridia now meant only that stupid photograph. She had wanted to help at first. She had promised Guy she would do her best – but the photograph in the *Express* had ruined that good intention. It still irritated her. Yet she knew there was nothing behind it. Edward was not the type to leap into bed with other women. And that Sally What's-her-name seemed too demure to sleep with a teddy-bear. How dreary it made Edward seem sometimes. He might be more attractive if he did have an occasional self-indulgence. That would make him a prize really worth fighting to keep. He would not even quarrel about the stupid picture. Ever since she had thrown her breakfast over the bed and stormed into the bathroom that morning she had wanted a proper argument about it.

However that was between her and Edward. Any scoring against Edward should be done by her, not by others. If Violet Stephenson was out to make trouble, she would listen as long as necessary, and then put her in her place.

They perched on miniature wooden stools in the coffee shop. Mrs Stephenson took ten minutes to work round to Edward.

'Such a nuisance for our dear Edward. But this has now become a serious issue. People in the constituency are looking for a lead, you know. Never underestimate the force of public opinion when it feels itself threatened. Like a stag at bay.' Mrs Stephenson was pleased with this pretty picture.

Rosemary eyed her across her cup of machine-made coffee. It tasted like wet cigarette ash. She longed to get home and pour herself a drink.

'The motorway?' she asked non-committally.

The large woman pressed herself conspiratorially over the table.

'In the beginning, my dear. But more now, I fear. Much more.' She eased herself with difficulty back into an upright position. 'Derek Headley's formed a little committee. It's really a matter of taking one's responsibilities seriously. You know, looking to the worries of local people.'

Rosemary put down her cup and decided she would definitely not finish the revolting coffee.

'I don't follow you, Mrs Stephenson.'

'I forget what Derek calls it. The Policy Committee I think. Something like that. I only agreed to take part because I thought it would help Edward. Provide another channel for the expression of local views. That sort of thing.'

Her staccato delivery was caused by her attempts to drag her handbag from the floor to the table.

'A new committee, you mean?'

'Oh yes. Quite new. Quite small too. But representative.'

'So it's chaired by Major Peacock?'

The handbag was squeezed at last on to the table.

'Oh, Good Lord no, Mrs Dunsford, no, no. It's Derek Headley's own idea. I don't think it would be at all right

234

for Richard Peacock to be there. I mean, he's a little too close to Edward, isn't he? Could be rather embarrassing for him, I should think. No, no. But all this does have the blessing of the Chairman, of course.'

Rosemary looked hard at Mrs Stephenson, but her face was buried in her large handbag. She was self-consciously turning over the contents.

'And has it been meeting long, this policy group?'

'Heavens, no. It's all very recent. Obviously,' Mrs Stephenson added with meaning. Her head emerged at last from her scrutiny of her handbag. 'We all got together for the first time after Communion last Sunday. Over sherry at Derek's.'

Rosemary had met the biscuit manufacturer three or four times. He had always been disagreeable. She remembered his snide remarks at Garth Andrew's dinner party a month before.

'And what is this committee going to do, exactly?'

'Oh, you know what committees are like. Write a report. Rope in some poor suffering wife to type it for them in spare time she doesn't have. That sort of thing.'

Mrs Stephenson returned briefly to her handbag. Her last piece of news was still to come.

'Of course, I think Derek's sometimes a bit too personal about all this. He wants the committee to produce a rather hostile report. Insists on writing it himself, too. That's where I think I can help. In keeping the whole thing, you know, balanced.' With a man's handkerchief finally produced in triumph from her handbag, she paused to brush away the remnants of coffee from the corners of her mouth.

'It's all being done in too much haste to my mind,' she

235

said slightly crossly. 'You see, they want to have it discussed at the next meeting of the Association. And that's only in a week or so, you know. It seems rather underhand to me. Derek and some of the others wanted to keep it all from Edward until the last moment. You know, put him on his mettle. That sort of thing. Well, I suppose it's all politics, isn't it? But I thought you ought to know.'

She leant forward again in genuine kindness. For a moment Rosemary feared she might be wanting to squeeze her hand.

'You know, Mrs Dunsford, we all think Edward is an awfully good man. He's done terribly well for us. Really. But, well, I suppose there are times when we all have to make sure that we're all going about the right things in the right way.' She drew herself up and looked impressively at Rosemary. 'After all, that's what it's all about, isn't it?'

Rosemary decided it was time Edward stopped crashing on about Africa and turned his mind to his real problems. But she put on her coldest voice to reply to Mrs Stephenson.

'I'm sure my husband would be the first to agree with you, Mrs Stephenson. He wouldn't be in Parliament otherwise.'

'No. That's right. Of course not. Yes. We all think that.'

Rebuffed, Mrs Stephenson ordered a cake. Rosemary slipped off her stool and into the street, leaving Mrs Stephenson with the bill and only a mutter of thanks.

20

Looking back later on the whole story, trying to tidy up his memories, Edward thought of Saturday, 2 November as the worst of the bad days. Not that anything in particular happened on that day spent at Long Meadow with his family; indeed that was the trouble. Rosemary was there but not there. She drove her red Metro fast up and down the drive on various errands, checking brusquely with him each time whether he would be there to look after the girls, as if his movements were in all other respects of no interest to her. She served and ate meals in virtual silence, then retired to conduct long telephone conversations behind closed doors. On the Friday evening she had asked in a rehearsed monotone, without looking at him, that he should sleep in his dressing-room. This had happened before and would happen again. He did not argue, not wishing to be further embroiled or humiliated.

The Saturday morning was crisp and fine. Sussex tried to be Massachusetts. The trees stood still in the bright sunshine, occasionally letting fall a single red or yellow leaf. The outline of the Downs was sharp, the noise of a ploughing tractor carried far, and at breakfast time there was still a shimmer of frost on the lawn. It was the right day for picking the cooking apples from the big tree behind the house. Last year he had done this with the two girls, and it had been great fun, almost a festival. A ladder, two baskets, a rake to claw off the big apples at the end of the branches, small hands clasped to catch them below, a good deal of shouting and squeaky laughter. They had spread the apples out carefully on newspaper on the shelves of an old dresser in the garage, making sure that no apple touched another, taking the bruised ones in at once to the kitchen.

'Shall we make it Apple Day, Katie?' he said to Catherine at the end of silent Saturday breakfast. She turned the page of her magazine, and looked up at him with Rosemary's eyes.

'Sorry. Jane and I have to do homework.'

For a moment he wanted to brush this aside, and drag his two pale girls out into the cold sunshine. But the moment passed. Perhaps Rosemary had talked to them. Perhaps they really did have homework which had to be done on Saturday. He knew too little about their schooling. There was so little time to know about anything except the Foreign Office, the House of Commons, and Rosemary. Rosemary, having more time, had made these her children. He had drifted away from them. Now they did not want to pick apples with their father.

He took a cap and jacket from the downstairs cloak-room and went out of doors alone. He wished that he had overruled Rosemary's dislike and bought a dog. With a dog and the energy a dog brings he would by now on such a morning as this be half-way up the Downs, blowing away the cobwebs, as his mother used to say. Without a dog, without the girls, there was no incentive. Edward pottered, thought of finding the apple ladder himself, decided against it, opened the gate into the pasture where there were sometimes mushrooms, found no mushrooms.

If he were a real politician on top of his form he would now be ringing up his friends and allies in the Government, in the Commons, in the press and television, briefing them about the awfulness of Reid, forcing the issue into the open, keeping up the pressure. As it was, the pressure was relaxing fast. The Meridian question had retreated to page four of *The Times* that morning. No journalist or broadcaster had rung him up for forty-eight hours. The two awful old men meeting at Chequers tomorrow might be able to sweep the whole thing under the carpet. A week ago that would have been inconceivable. Edward, hanging up his jacket again in the cloakroom, felt that he had missed his chance. It was not loyalty to the Government which was holding him back, but exhaustion. There was some defect, some fatal lack of energy, in his own system. For the moment the savour had gone out of everything which had been the salt of his life – marriage, children, house and garden, Foreign Office, even the political struggle. The perfect autumn sunshine was mocking: it should have been a day of mist and rain.

In his study on the desk beside the four-year-old photograph of Rosemary and the girls sat the draft of a talk which he was to give to a small seminar at Sussex University the next morning. It was a dull talk on aid policy, prepared for experts by experts. He had accepted the invitation months ago, even though it was for a Sunday morning, because the Professor in charge of the seminar had buttonholed him pleasantly at the Vice-Chancellor's party, and because as a Sussex member he liked to keep in touch with the University.

The opportunity was there, of course. It would take about a quarter of an hour to work into the talk a blistering three paragraphs in favour of a new aid package for Meridia, another ten minutes to give it to the BBC and the Press Association by telephone with an embargo for the following morning. He would be deliberately reviving the crisis. He would be daring the Prime Minister to sack him. Although he did not know the Prime Minister well, he guessed that this time the bluff would be called.

He thought again of life without a ministerial job. He could replace the salary quite quickly, he thought, and of course he would stay as a back-bench MP. But how would he fill the hours now spent at the Foreign Office? Before he had become a minister there had been no such problem. He had been on the way up, he had relished time with his wife and children, the telephone rang constantly, life was exciting. But if he were sacked he would henceforward be on the way down. The world would forget him, and there would be plenty of time for fearful rows with Rosemary and boredom in the company of these pale, thin girls. No doubt he would still be asked to speak at second-rank party meetings, and his air fare (tourist) would be paid to second-rank international get-togethers; but such events, acceptable as steps on the upward path, would be dreary indeed on the way down. And he would certainly miss the Foreign Office itself, and Sally Archer. His mind paused there, and he thought of ringing Sally up and asking her advice. He found her home number from a Foreign Office circular which lived in the top drawer of the desk, and dialled it. In his present mood he expected no reply, and he was right.

Later on, sitting at the desk, Edward went through the seminar draft, making minor deletions and small changes of phrase. At one point a project in Meridia was mentioned as an example of a successful intervention in agricultural marketing. He crossed out the reference altogether, sadly and slowly, believing that he was turning his back on an effort which could have changed his life. The odds had just been too great.

'Edward.'

Rosemary stood in the doorway toying with the silk scarf at her neck.

'Can we talk?'

Edward glanced up from his clutter of papers. She had not spoken with such a voice since their last night of harmony.

'Is this a truce?'

'That depends on you.'

She sat down on a sofa opposite him. It was late afternoon. A dying sun threw a red glow across the room, picking out little patches of dust on the furniture.

'How?'

'I had a frightful conversation with Violet Stephenson in Lewes yesterday. I think you ought to know about it.

But you don't get this for nothing. I want a promise out of you first.'

He put down his pen.

'No promises before I know the demands. I'm a politician, remember.'

'Don't be tiresome, Edward. I'm trying to help.' Her voice was not warm, but no longer glacial.

'My dear Rosemary, no matter how many years you and I are married, I'll never fathom you.'

'You haven't promised.'

'You haven't told me what I've got to promise.'

'I want you to give up this bloody African thing. Today. Now.'

Edward picked up his pen and began shuffling the papers of his speech. He sighed self-righteously.

'Please don't start all that again. I'm sorry, I must finish going through this speech for tomorrow.'

He expected Rosemary to sweep angrily out of the room. She sat forward on the sofa but she did not get up.

'Stuff your speech. This is important.'

He stopped playing with his papers.

'All right. What is?'

'Something serious is going on round here right under your nose and you're so tied up with this ridiculous tiff with Patrick Reid that you don't even know about it. Or care, I suppose.'

'Are you talking about Violet Stephenson now?'

'Yes. She trapped me for half an hour in the town yesterday and told me all about Derek Headley's little gunpowder plot. I suppose that is news to you?'

'I haven't a clue what you're talking about.'

'The fact is, Mr Edward Dunsford, Headley's got

242

together some committee or other which he wants to use to push you out.'

'That's ridiculous.'

'Will you listen? Headley's got it in for you so he's formed what old Ma Stephenson called a policy group. They're writing a report in which you get slammed to kingdom come, and which Headley's going to get voted on at some party meeting or other in a fortnight's time.'

'Oh, come on, Rosemary. She was talking balls. He can't. Not even old Dubarry would let Headley get into that sort of game.'

Edward thought of the good-natured face of the Association's Chairman, benign and bumbling. But no fool.

'Well then, you can think again, because he's part of it all, too.'

Edward walked across to the window, stuffing his hands into the pockets of his old brown corduroys. Down in the orchard one of the girls was chasing the cat in and out of the apple trees. But his thoughts were no longer on apple-picking. One part of him wanted to believe that Rosemary had made it all up. She wanted to frighten him out of something which he knew was important and which she found boring and irritating. She had spent the whole day working out her story. Why else had she not mentioned it the night before?

The other part of him was not so sure that she had made it up. It was a story whose details did not bear her imprint. Headley disliked him, apparently a great deal. The biscuit-maker had made his feelings quite clear at that meeting on the day of the car accident. And Edward

243

had not forgotten the gossip which Richard Peacock had shouted above the roar of his Land Rover later that same night.

He turned round. Rosemary was sprawled on the sofa, a soft hand brushing flecks of cigarette ash from her black velvet trousers.

'Well?'

'I'm not sure. There's a simple way to check.'

'Come off it. Old Violet likes you, God knows why. Anyway she couldn't have been making it up, she's too thick.'

He went over to the telephone and began to dial a number,

'If you're trying Richard Peacock I shouldn't bother. I spoke to his wife yesterday. He's away till Wednesday fishing in Wales.'

'So what? They have telephones in Wales.'

'Not where he's gone, Edward dear. That's the whole point of his going.'

He put down the receiver.

'Well then, that settles it.'

'Thank heaven. So at last you're going to do something about this mess.'

'On the contrary. I trust Richard. If there were the faintest chance of Headley getting together a group of the discontented he would know. Richard would not be in Wales if Headley was plotting to call a vote against me at the Association meeting.'

She began to speak but he interrupted her.

'Okay, I'll grant you some of the story. Namely that Headley hates me, and that the Association meets on 13 November. But I don't accept the bits in between.'

This time Rosemary did move. There was no attempt to argue with him.

'Suit yourself. I'm trying to help you.' She looked at him coldly. 'Just try and ram that into your thick head, will you? But if you're too bloody proud to believe me that's your lookout.'

Edward tried to intercept her departure, wanting to explain himself.

'Please, Rosemary. Don't . . .'

She swept past him and out of the room.

'You're impossible.'

He wanted to explain. But not now, he told himself. Later. Soon.

The seminar was quiet, almost sleepy. The bare room looked out on to bare brickwork and stained concrete. Wherever one looked the buildings seemed only straight lines and sharp angles. Where there were curves in the brickwork, they were ugly and unsubtle, carved by a computer rather than a pair of hands. The downland which began to rise a hundred yards behind the University might have been fifty miles away.

These were students earnest in pursuit of world development, about fifteen of them, early twenties, long limbs comfortable in jeans or corduroys, shaggy sweaters and plimsolls, clutching plastic cups of weak coffee. None of them would ever vote Conservative, apart from one fair-haired boy who looked out of place in a tie and blazer but who had hopes of joining the Diplomatic Service and had been told that dress counted. Otherwise the rest of them were concerned with the content of the Government's aid policy – and, that morning, with mastering rather than challenging it. How about the technique of cutting off aid to countries which became objectionable dictatorships? How was that handled in the European Community context under the Lome Conventions? How about the proportion of bilateral to multilateral aid? Was it true that the FAO had a far worse ratio of administrative to field costs than WHO or UNDP? It was not Edward's field, but the briefing had been competent, and he rather enjoyed the intellectual exercise. These were pleasant, worthwhile people. Outside it was still cold and sunny; the coffee and the talking combined to produce a fug on the window-panes. Edward was not an academic, and put no value on discussion for its own sake; but he preferred this outing to spending another silent, frustrated day at Long Meadow. He decided that he would lunch at a pub in Brighton with the Sunday papers and afterwards take a brisk walk along the beach.

The seminar ended, with thanks and the scraping of chairs. There had been one question about Meridia, which Edward had turned politely aside. But one of the students, younger than the rest, clean shaven with a sharp nose, lingered.

'Radio Brighton asked me to do a short interview. I freelance for them on university things. I've got my tape-recorder next door. It's a room I'm allowed to use as a studio.'

'Okay. Just on the seminar?'

The sharp nose quivered slightly, and the boy blushed. He was some way yet from being a hardened newsman. In his nervousness he betrayed a public-school education.

'Actually, I wanted to ask you about this, too. But only of course if it's all right by you.'

And so, from the *Sunday Express* which the boy produced from his folder, Edward learned of Charles Elliott's little bit of venom.

What Lies Behind the Phoney Meridia Crusade?
by Charles Elliott,
Tory MP for West Hampshire
Chairman of the influential back-bench Tory
Foreign Affairs Committee

The Meridia crisis is fading. The Government has wisely refused to be flustered. Indeed we can now see that there was no crisis at all. Just a phoney call to a phoney crusade, dreamed up by excited television men and an ambitious second-rank politician called Edward Dunsford.

At the very moment when you read these words the Prime Minister and Foreign Secretary will be pacing the rose garden at Chequers discussing their next moves. I guess that once round the roses will be enough to settle the matter. The PM, under momentary pressure in the House of Commons, promised to review all the options, and the Foreign Secretary repeated the pledge in more detail a day or so later. But that was ten days ago. Now the panic has subsided. Now they can afford to come to the House of Commons and tell us what the country needs to be told – that they have no intention of being stampeded into squandering hard-earned taxpayers' money to prop up a corrupt military dictatorship in Meridia.

This Government has a record second to none when it comes to standing up to the Communists. But that doesn't mean that we have to shell out millions every time there is an unverified scare of a Soviet takeover.

And as for the dying black babies, we can see now that this is a matter of mismanagement by the Meridians themselves. Contraceptives don't cost much, President Hamid. Spend more on them and less on luxury cars and shiny uniforms for your own bodyguard, and the British people might give you greater respect. And you'd have fewer babies dying in your streets and hospital wards.

Where does that leave Edward Dunsford? As he looks in his shaving mirror this morning down on his Sussex estate, Edward Dunsford will see a sorry sight – a humiliated second-rank politician on the way downhill. Last Sunday he was on the crest of a wave, by this Sunday he is struggling and spluttering in the trough. The humiliation is not quite complete. For he knows that as they pace the rose garden at Chequers the Prime Minister and the Foreign Secretary will be asking themselves a question about his future. Not whether he will force his way into the Cabinet, but why he was appointed a junior minister at all. Not whether they need to do a deal with him, but how to be rid of him without further fuss.

Why did he do it? Why did he exploit a dull visit to a dismal country to create a phoney crisis for the Government to which he still belongs? Not certainly out of idealism. The only subject which brings out idealism in Edward Dunsford is the career of Edward Dunsford. He has spent five years in politics, and during that time he has not shown the slightest interest in poverty or disease or the other problems of the third world. So it's a bit late to persuade some of us that he is really concerned about sick babies.

What then was Edward Dunsford's motive? There is one point which he should clear up straight away. Dunsford used to work for Speyer's, the London merchant bank which specialises in African affairs. Nothing wrong with that. Of course under the rules he had to give up his formal connections with Speyer's when he became a minister. I do not doubt that the rules were scrupulously obeyed. But there is still some explaining to be done. For note what has been happening. Edward Dunsford when appointed to the Foreign Office insisted on concerning himself with Meridian affairs. He insisted against official advice on going to a financial conference called by President Hamid. He used that visit to mobilise support for an international aid package which would, we are told, put paid to a deal between the Russians and some American oil companies to bail out Meridia.

But who did the Russians and American oil men displace as Hamid's chief banker? Speyer's, the bank which launched Dunsford on his career.

Who stands most to lose if the Soviet deal goes ahead? Speyer's, the bank with which Dunsford still has close informal and personal connections.

Who stands to gain most if instead of the Soviet deal there is a British-led aid package backed by the traditional friends of Meridia? Why, Speyer's, the bank to which Dunsford might naturally and easily return one day when politics holds no more attraction.

Now all this is speculation, and may be mere coincidence. Dunsford has a quiet day ahead of him, for no one has asked him to the Chequers meeting. He should spend today drawing up a clear denial of any continuing connection with Speyer's and of any conversations with Speyer's about Meridia. He can clear away the fog of suspicion with a word. It is time that word was spoken.

Edward carefully folded the *Sunday Express* and put it down on a low, stained, coffee-table. Libellous? Probably not, for the newspaper's lawyer would have crawled over it, replacing accusations by insinuation. Tolerable? Certainly not. And here was a young man with a microphone into which Edward could explode. Even in his anger he knew what he was doing. An interview with BBC Radio Brighton would not stay that way if it contained anything juicy. It would be on the national news within an hour, on the Press Association tapes within two, on every front page tomorrow morning. But his anger was for the moment in control. It is a moment which most intelligent politicians long for but rarely experience – the moment when they are so certain they are right that the usual reservations and qualifications fall away like unwanted paraphernalia from a soaring rocket.

He sat beside the boy, who was fiddling with his tape-recorder.

'They always need something for voice levels first. I ought to ask you what you had for breakfast.'

'Luckily for you, I did not have the *Sunday Express*.'

'You mean you . . .?'

'I mean I wouldn't be here. I'd be scorching the road to London.' But what would have been the point of that?

'Can we begin?'

'Of course.'

The boy changed to a voice which was meant to be harsh and challenging but had a quaver in it.

'Have you any comment on the suggestion in one of the Sunday newspapers that there are motives of personal interest behind your support for Meridia?'

'Yes, I have a comment.' Edward was deliberately slow. 'The suggestion is false, wholly false, and I intend to ignore it. I do not stand to gain a penny out of Meridia, either now or in the future.'

'Then you will . . . ?'

'Please allow me to add something further. The article to which you refer is typical of the weary and futile cynicism which is steadily dragging this country down. There is no attempt to argue the merits of the case. It is assumed that the public will not stomach anything so serious. We find instead of argument a personal attack – instead of analysis a slimy piece of gossip. For some days after my return from Mangara I thought there was a chance of sensible debate leading to the right decision. I am much less optimistic today. But there is a heavy price to pay for such cynicism, and the day of payment may not be far off.'

The interviewer was well out of his depth.

'Do you mean to resign then?'

'My friends and I are waiting for the Prime Minister and Cabinet to make up their minds. Then we can take stock. My personal position is not important one way or the other. We are a parliamentary democracy and it is in the House of Commons that this matter will be decided. What we cannot accept any longer is this lethal mixture of unjustified delay and silly cynicism.'

The interviewer searched for a telling final question, and failed. Edward wondered why he had referred to friends when he had none. The interview ended untidily with much snapping of knobs.

'Tell them not to cut it about.'

'I'll tell them, certainly I'll tell them.'

On the way out Edward was given a message that Sir Guy Winchilsea would be grateful if Mr Dunsford would telephone him as soon as possible. Edward returned the call twenty minutes later after ordering a rather expensive lunch at Wheelers. He felt better already. A good interview, like a good play, could purge you of pity and terror.

When lunch was over and the coffee had been served, the Prime Minister said:

'It is rather cold outside. I hope that nobody will notice if we omit the tour of the rose garden.'

Two of his three guests smiled. Being more experienced politicians than Edward Dunsford, both the Foreign Secretary and the Chancellor of the Exchequer had read the *Sunday Express* before leaving for Chequers. They recognised the allusion to Charles Elliott's article. The third guest did not smile, being the Permanent Secretary to the Treasury.

Patrick Reid was as usual ill at ease in the Prime Minister's presence. The Prime Minister's mind worked more quickly than his own and contained an element of irony which the Foreign Secretary found alien. He was also cross because, summoned to Chequers for eleven o'clock, he had found the Prime Minister embedded in a discussion on exchange-rate policy with the Chancellor of the Exchequer and Treasury officials. Chequers had been presented to the nation by Lord Lee of Fareham as a haven of rest, but that was seventy years ago. The house still looked restful, the lawns and roses were superb in summer, the logs burned splendidly in the big hall in winter; but the appearance was deceptive and Chequers had become an outpost of Whitehall. One office meeting succeeded another, even on Sunday. The Foreign Secretary knew that the ruler of Abu Dhabi had been invited to take tea. He did not know whether the discussion on the exchange rate had finished or merely been interrupted for lunch. He was irritated that, once again, the Chancellor was there before him and showed no sign of going away. Gordon Leith-Ross's co-operation with the Prime Minister obviously stretched across the whole range of politics and departments, and was thus of an entirely different character from his own.

'Shall we turn now for a few minutes to your matter, Patrick?' said the Prime Minister.

The Permanent Secretary to the Treasury made as if to go.

'No, no, Roger, stay. We politicians have no secrets from you.'

'I think, Prime Minister, that I have carried matters to the point where today we can take the necessary decisions without great difficulty.' Patrick Reid did not know how to cope with an informal gathering. He always spoke as if to a committee or a courtroom. 'My office has kept yours informed of the various steps which I have taken and I need not reiterate them here. Suffice it to say that Dunsford has been outmanoeuvred both inside the Foreign Office and with public opinion outside. The unseemly tumult of ten days ago has subsided. I conclude that the way is open for you to announce that, having reviewed all the options, you propose to maintain the aid programme for Meridia at the present level. Sir Reginald Anson agrees.'

'Patrick, you've left out the House of Commons,' said the Chancellor.

'No, I have *not* left out the House of Commons. I have arranged to address the Foreign Affairs Committee on Tuesday. I . . .'

'Francis is anxious,' said the Prime Minister. Francis Peretz was the Chief Whip. 'He feels the Opposition is bound to try something very soon. They will create an occasion to force our rebels out into the open. The dangerous news is that Winchilsea is organising the rebels.'

'Not Dunsford?' asked the Chancellor.

'Not Dunsford. You've kept him busy in the Foreign Office, Patrick, for which I thank you. I'm told he has constituency trouble. And we can all guess that being married to Rosemary Dunsford is not a spare-time occupation. Anyway, whatever the reason, Dunsford has not been cultivating the backbenchers. But Winchilsea has formed a group, and will table an early day motion as soon as he can get twenty Tory names to it.'

'Guy Winchilsea has no public appeal,' said Patrick Reid. 'He can hardly string three words together.'

'He has an old Etonian accent you could cut with a knife,' added the Chancellor.

'But Dunsford will do the speaking and handle the media. Unfortunately he's got the knack of that. Winchilsea will do the organising, and he's an old hand at that.'

'You mean they're conspiring together?'

'I don't know that. Francis has no evidence. But if they're not they soon will be. Events will force them together. Unless Dunsford drops the whole thing in a fit of weariness.'

'He'll not do that,' said Patrick Reid. 'He's a man stubborn beyond belief. His other troubles will simply stiffen him. I'm confirmed in my previous opinion that we'll have to be rid of him.'

'That is certainly an opinion to which you have held through thick and thin.' The faint sneer in the Prime Minister's voice related to the Foreign Secretary's general reputation in the Cabinet as a weathercock.

A Private Secretary came into the dining-room quietly, without knocking, and handed the Prime Minister a piece of paper.

'The Foreign Secretary is right again,' he said, having read it .

They all in turn looked at the telex excerpt from the Press Association's news service.

Now Dunsford turns on PM

In a slashing attack at Brighton, Foreign Office Minister of State Edward Dunsford today denounced 'the weary and futile cynicism which is dragging this country down'. Without mentioning the Prime Minister by name Dunsford, speaking to BBC Radio Brighton, launched an amazing outburst at the Prime Minister's handling of the Meridia aid issue. 'For some days after my return from Mangara I thought there was a chance of sensible debate leading to the right decision. I am much less optimistic today.' Dunsford thus reopened the whole Meridia question as the current burning issue in British politics and went on to hint strongly that the final decision would be taken by the House of Commons against the wishes of the Government. Using exceptionally strong language he concluded, 'what we cannot accept any longer is this lethal mixture of unjustified delay and silly cynicism'.

'That's it, then,' said Patrick Reid. 'You've given that young man enough rope, Prime Minister, and he's hanged himself. He'll have to go.'

'But remember the Commons. We can't afford a defeat there. We must be sure we have the votes.' The Chancellor spoke without much conviction, as if he merely felt that every proposition coming from Patrick Reid needed a counter.

They were still sitting at the lunch table though the WRAF orderlies had cleared everything except the coffee cups from the glowing surface.

The Prime Minister sitting opposite the window looked out for a minute at the grey flagged terrace and the tidy rose beds beyond. A policeman slowly paced the terrace where it ran on the right towards the covered swimming pool.

'Palmerston lost a big vote in the Commons on foreign policy. Dissolved, and won an election handsomely. The Arrow War, 1857.'

The others stared at him, then spoke at once. Even the Permanent Secretary broke silence.

'You're hardly thinking, Prime Minister . . .'

'The exchange-rate position, Prime Minister, is not conducive . . .'

'You can't call a general election in December . . .'

'Don't let's get over-excited.' The Prime Minister enjoyed their bewilderment. 'I'm not suggesting anything. Except that the Commons isn't the only place where votes can be held.' He looked at his watch, and rose. 'And now, I think . . .'

'But we haven't decided anything,' said Patrick Reid.

'I know the one decision you want from me. You shall have it, you shall have it.'

'You mean Dunsford . . .'

'He's left me no choice. I do not sack people on Sundays. He will be out by tea-time tomorrow.'

21

It was an artificial Monday morning. Edward felt as if he were walking through treacle. After his drive up from Brighton he had taken the telephone off the hook, drawn the curtains, and sat for four hours in Rosemary's drawing-room, thinking and reading, drinking, reading and thinking. He loved the London house, perhaps even more than Long Meadow, because he had lived there longer. But the house nowadays only gave him pleasure when he was alone in it. Once or twice he went to the garden door, and peered out. The moon was full, and he could sense the frost once more settling on the garden. He wondered idly what Rosemary had done with the roses which he had picked for her breakfast tray; it seemed a long time ago. He read *In Memoriam*, then picked up Trollope's *Phineas Finn*. Another junior minister in trouble, with women and with his career, abandoning it all, going back to marry some dim little girl in Ireland. Once there was a loud knock on the door, louder than Rosemary could possibly make, so he did not answer; almost certainly a journalist. He boiled himself two eggs and poured some more whisky. He tried not to think of his own problems, and succeeded. It was dark in the drawing-room; light came just from his reading lamp and from the gas flames in the grate. His cheeks were pleasantly rough from his cold walk on the Brighton beach, and soon his eyes began to droop. He took Tennyson and a last tumbler of whisky up to bed. 'Old age hath yet his honour and his toil . . .' Propped on two pillows Edward doubted it. But unexpectedly he had found pleasure in his private evening.

But that had been an act of self-isolation which could hardly be sustained. On Monday morning Edward made a feeble effort to sustain it. He did not turn on either radio or television at eight o'clock. He threw the newspapers into the wastepaper basket without a glance. He spoke so curtly to Jack in the car that no conversation could come to birth. But of course there was no escape.

Once he had climbed into the Ambassador it carried him inexorably back into the ruins of his career. Edward had no real doubt what would happen. The Prime Minister had tolerated his first indiscretion out of a calculation that the storm would blow itself out more quickly if there were no resignation or dismissal. But the second act of defiance, the momentary explosion yesterday in that makeshift studio, called into play an even more fundamental rule of politics, that rulers, if they wish to survive, must be seen to rule.

Edward knew this. It was the logical next step which had frightened him. It was to keep that thought away that he had gone back to Tennyson and Trollope, to boiled eggs, toast and whisky, and the telephone off the hook. For the logical thought was that Edward should resign of his own initiative, should jump before he was pushed. The thought could no longer be held at bay. In the official car he began drafting in his head his letter of voluntary resignation. Terse, polite yet scathing, ending with thanks for the privilege of serving under the Prime Minister.

But it was a letter which he would never send of his own free will. Edward had already shown courage, and had a reserve of courage still in hand. But he was a natural minister, not a natural rebel. He had his moments of excitement, but there was nothing of the Jacobite in his nature, no love of a lost cause or of romantic victory against the odds. For Edward success in his profession was an official car, plenty of hard work genuinely tackled, and the reasonable respect of his peers. He knew in his heart that he had thrown away success, and yet for the moment its trappings still surrounded him. That was why Monday morning was artificial.

It was ten when Edward and Jack drove across Horse Guards. The attendant guarding the park door looked at him strangely. Or perhaps that was imagination. On the big staircase just before it divided he met a girl coming down with a tray of glasses. She was pretty, he had met her before, and he said, 'Good morning,' not knowing her name. She stopped, the glasses tinkled while she blushed, 'Good morning, Minister,' and on they went, he up, she down. Sally and James sat at their desks, bowed over files. They hardly looked up as he hung his coat. On their mantelpiece was a squat South Seas idol in polished wood, a gift of some visiting minister, which Edward had banished from his own office on grounds of excessive ugliness.

'Not got rid of that yet?'

'Not yet, Minister.' James spoke as if from the tomb.

On his own desk the telegrams and other incoming work were ranged as tidily as ever. A little upright wooden holder held the diary card for the day. Two calls by Ambassadors before lunch, a white blank in the afternoon. That was not what he remembered. He rang for Sally.

'The Secretary of State was holding a meeting on trade with South Africa this afternoon. Has it been cancelled?'

She hesitated. He noticed her dress, plain and dark blue, with a white collar rather too large, so that her neck looked slightly scraggy. She looked white and nervous.

'It's been postponed. The Secretary of State's been called over to Number Ten.'

'Do you know why?'

She shook her head.

'Is there another time fixed for that meeting? It was important.'

She paused, looking down on to his desk.

'It's going to be later this afternoon. But, er, we had a message from the Private Office.' Her hesitation meant that she was wondering whether to tell the truth. He guessed that she would, and she did. 'They said you need not bother to come.'

'I see.' Then he noticed how pale she was. 'Are you all right?'

'Oh yes, I'm fine,' she said quickly.

He was about to say more when James interrupted them.

'The Algerian Ambassador's here. Shall I bring him in?'

He nodded. There was no reason not to live out the rest of the day as though it were normal. And yet he knew his fate hung over him that day, as certain as death. Somewhere in the dust the moment had been marked by someone. But the mark could not be seen from a distance so the traveller merely plodded on, aware that somewhere along his path a hand would reach out and stop him.

The two calls by Ambassadors were for form's sake only, one a new arrival and the other on the point of departure. Edward sat through them in a daze. Yet the objects in his room seemed more real to him than ever before. He noticed little details which he had never seen when his life in the Foreign Office had been taken for granted.

James sat in on routine meetings, so Edward did not see Sally again for an hour. He thought he might invite her to share her sandwiches with him. But when the last Ambassador had left, she was not at her desk next door. So Edward sat in his room alone, munching mechanically through two dry sandwiches bought for him at the office canteen by one of the typists, and sipping a strong Bloody Mary mixed for him by James. Edward read through and signed off the submissions in his in-tray. He buried himself in them, finding inconsistencies of detail, writing long comments on the covering minutes. The telephone was silent. His mind wandered occasionally back to his conversation with Rosemary in the study on that Saturday before. The germ of a doubt was growing in his mind about her story. Perhaps Headley was up to something. Twice the doubt was strong enough to persuade him to dial his agent's number. There was no reply. Once he tried to ring Geoffrey Dubarry at his department store. When he gave his name, Edward was told Mr Dubarry was away for the day and not expected back for some time. But once the effort was made Edward sank back into the artificial world of the desk on which he rested his elbows. He must merely wait. It seemed point-less to act. He merely plodded on waiting for the hand to stop him and point to his mark, traced in the dust at his feet.

His door opened and Sally came in. She shut it behind her. It was a deliberate act, reserved for private conversa-tions. He noticed she was carrying the *Sunday Express*.

'You saw this?' she asked abruptly.

'You know I did. That was what sparked me off on the radio.'

'I know. But there was something I wanted to tell you about it. It's not very easy . . .' Sally turned away from him and walked to the other end of the room. She stood by the television set in the far corner, searching for words, gath-ering strength. He had never seen her like this before. He had a premonition that he would rather not hear what she was about to say. There were enough scenes in his life already. Sally had represented the absence of storm, the simplicity of an ordinary existence, and more recently friendship as well.

James came in without knocking.

'A message from Number Ten, Minister.'

'Yes, James?' Edward felt the frost settling on his life, as on the little London garden last night.

'The Prime Minister asked if it would be convenient if he telephoned you in five minutes.'

'Of course.'

James left. Delayed execution, that was a characteris-tic refinement. Edward shuffled the telegrams on his desk, working out what he would say. Defiance, apology, something in between? He must be cool, non-committal, that was the answer. He felt hot and bothered.

He suddenly noticed that Sally was crying, real sobs, tears blotching her face.

'I told him it was bloody nonsense, I tried to ride him off it. . .' She sat suddenly on the sofa, awkwardly with knees together and feet apart. He went quickly over, and sat beside her, dimly pleased that someone was suffering as well as himself, but unable to understand why.

'What on earth are you talking about, Sally? Who? You spoke to the Prime Minister?' He touched her arm.

'No, of course not. Not the Prime Minister.' She pulled her arm away. 'Charles Elliott.'

He looked at her without understanding.

'Charles Elliott. Don't you understand?' She put her head in her hands. Edward noticed for the first time her nails were short and bitten. Had they always been so?

'I've been sleeping with him for the past two years. But it's always been separate from all this. From you. Until last week, last Thursday night, when he asked me a lot of questions about you and Meridia. I told him nothing. I promise you, nothing.' She rubbed a tear away from her eye. Edward was silent. There seemed nothing to say. 'You must believe me. I've always been loyal to you.' She jerked herself away from him, shaking, tears running down her cheeks. She found a handkerchief in her sleeve and began to blow.

Edward sat very still. He simply did not believe what she had said. Sally and Charles. Charles and Sally. It wasn't possible. They lived in completely different segments of his own life. They could not have come together. For an awful moment he had a picture of Charles lying by

264

her side, Charles on top of her. He banished the image. What was it to him, anyway? He encouraged that line of thinking, staring across the room, oblivious for the moment of the girl beside him. He tried to think of it as an office problem. The Private Secretary to the Minister of State was sleeping with the Chairman of the Conservative Foreign Affairs Committee. A matter for Personnel Department certainly. For Security Department as well? Perhaps, but only if there was a suggestion that confidential information had been compromised. How pompous all that sounded. Rosemary would laugh – did Rosemary know? The thoughts and images tumbled incoherently through his brain. The girl snivelling beside him on the sofa was nothing to him. Yet how dare she behave like a slut. And with Charles, the friend turned enemy, that was the poison on the arrow.

Then the telephone rang. The conversation was brief and banal. Edward had assembled no fine phrases, and even if he had there would have been little chance to use them. There was something about this Prime Minister, perhaps any Prime Minister, which induced monosyllables from his juniors.

'Good morning. You know what you said, you've seen how it was reported.'

'Yes, Prime Minister.'

'I imagine this means that you no longer wish to serve in my Government.'

'Well, Prime Minister . . .'

'That is certainly my conclusion. It is a pity.'

'It might be simplest if I put out a short statement. At four o'clock, if that is convenient to you. There will be nothing hurtful in it.'

Nothing to be said, nothing to be done. The frost had descended. He had reached the line traced in the dust.

'That will be convenient.'

A pause.

'Thank you, Edward, for all that you did before this trouble.'

'Thank you, Prime Minister.'

'Goodbye.'

A click.

Sally had stopped mopping. She already knew.

'I don't believe any of this. It's all so awful.'

He had forgotten about her, but now remembered. What she had told him had hurt. But somehow less so now that there was a greater hurt.

'It doesn't matter. It's your life. Nothing to do with me.'

'I really didn't tell Charles anything. Only the truth. Nothing else. He invented that *Sunday Express* stuff out of his own head.'

Edward said nothing, not out of rudeness, but because there was too much else to think about.

'Look, please, can't we talk about all this?' Sally said, still on the sofa. She had her feet together now, and looked less awkward. She was trying to be sensible. He had not yet reached that stage. 'I feel . . .'

'What about?' He was putting the telegrams into his out-tray. 'I'm sorry. It's no good. I must be off now.'

Edward had sometimes thought of how he would eventually leave the Foreign Office. There would be a big party in his room, with champagne or at least sparkling wine, given him as a surprise. He would make a witty, generous speech. At a certain stage, not too late, he would leave, taking with him the distinguished battered old red box which a minister was allowed to keep. Sally and James would accompany him down the great staircase, and out to the park door. There would be a photographer or two, bulbs flashing. He would shake hands with James and kiss Sally lightly on one cheek, thanking them gracefully for their help, promising to keep in touch. Jack would drive him away, and he would wave out of the back window, full of a pleasant sadness.

It was not to be like that. He felt brutal towards himself and others, and not far from tears. He must be quick, that was all he knew. Already he was out in the anteroom, scorning a backward glance.

'I must be off,' he said again.

They did not know what to do, and did nothing. Sally said foolishly, 'Jack will take you home.'

Of course even that was in doubt. If his resignation dated from the telephone call then the car was no longer his.

'I'll take a cab.'

Sally's face was red and blotchy. She felt sick and frightened as though she was standing on a cliff and watching a man drowning, unable to help him. It was important that she should see Edward leave wrapped in a last small act of kindness.

'No, you can't. It's still your car as far as we're concerned. You must take it. Please. Jack's at the park door.'

He snatched his coat.

'Thank you both very much.' He paused with his hand on the door. But Edward could not say any more. He blundered along the corridor and down the stairs, his eyes seeing no one, not even the blue-coated messenger whose trolley he had to skirt as he rounded the corner on

267

the ground floor. The image of Lord Mountbatten astride Foreign Office Green turned its back on Edward as he emerged from the building. He slumped into the car. He did not look round to wave as they drove off.

22

The silence in the black official car was more deliberate than usual. They swept down the length of the park, past a few winter tourists, past a few early commuters hurrying home via Victoria. Edward stared out of the window, seeing nothing. He was angry and humiliated. The Prime Minister, Charles Elliott, Sally Sally What should he be feeling? Betrayed? Sorry? Jealous? He could not think clearly about the future. He had no idea how he would cope with Rosemary's fury or with the public excitement which his dismissal was bound to provoke.

He asked Jack to drop him on the edge of the square before they reached Eaton Close. His pride would not let him remark on their parting or offer a word of thanks. Jack would know anyway. As would all the Foreign Office drivers by now. He would write later. A paragraph or two then would be easier than a short sentence now. Edward got out of the car.

'Best of luck, Mr Dunsford, sir. Terrible thing to happen. All of us are very sorry.'

Jack was out of the car, too. He shook Edward's hand. Edward opened his mouth, half-smiled, and then strode off down the street. He found kindness more difficult to bear than hostility.

As he unlocked the door and entered the house he heard Rosemary laughing and an American voice he did not know. It was Rosemary's after-dinner laugh, loud and sexy. Edward hung his coat in the hall.

'Bloody hell,' he muttered. He felt his stomach tighten.

He went into the sitting-room. Rosemary's back was towards him. A young, slim, red-haired figure was getting hurriedly to his feet. Rosemary turned, her smile vanishing. She looked expensively casual.

'Good God! What brings you back so early? Don't Ministers of State have any work to keep them from their homes these days?'

'Hello, Rosemary.' Edward looked blankly at the tall young man in front of him.

'How do you do, Mr Dunsford. My name's Neil Wainwright.'

Rosemary intervened, taking charge.

'This is Guy's nice young American friend I told you about.'

Edward looked at Neil for a moment.

'You remember. He was here with Guy a couple of weeks ago when you were on your famous "help the starving multitudes" trip.'

Edward shook the hand which was offered him.

'Yes. Of course. Edward Dunsford. How do you do?'

Rosemary had sat down and was busying herself with a tray lying on the table in front of her.

'We were just having tea.' She was pouring tea from the silver pot kept for special visitors.

'I'll join you.' His voice seemed to echo in his head. It was unusually subdued. Rosemary gave him a look as she gave him his tea.

She offered a cup to the American. 'Lemon, I suppose?' She made sure that their hands touched.

'Isn't that how you have tea here?' Neil was feeling uncomfortable again, with Rosemary's overpowering self-assurance and with Edward's unexpected arrival.

'Oh no, Neil. Only if we're trying to put Americans at their ease, or impress our neighbours.' Rosemary laughed again. Teasing was always the first stage in her flirting. Edward was silent. For a moment no one spoke.

Neil turned apprehensively to the man he had silently envied on the airport television screen that night at Heathrow.

'I know Guy Carlton, sir. I guess you and he are old friends.'

Edward sipped his tea. There was another short silence before he replied.

'Yes. Guy told me about your visit.'

Rosemary was on her feet, brandishing the teapot.

'Sorry. Forgot the hot water.'

She made for the tiny kitchen. Edward excused himself and followed. She turned on him, still with the teapot.

'Well, you're a ball of fire, I must say. And you look awful.'

Edward stood in the doorway, his hands in his pockets.

'What on earth is he doing here?'

'Neil just dropped in out of the blue. He's been sent to Europe again, something to do with Meridia. He's staying

271

at Brown's Hotel.' She turned to fill the kettle. 'Do you mind?'

'Look, I want to talk to you for a moment. But I can't with him here.' He looked over his shoulder. Rosemary was the most difficult of all to tell. 'It's happened.'

She turned off the tap. 'What's happened?'

'For Christ's sake, you can guess, can't you. The PM rang me at the office just now. I'm out.'

'You're what?'

'I'm fired. Dropped. Kicked out. Call it what you like.'

Edward had shut the sitting-room door behind him so that until now Neil could hear only a murmur of voices across the passageway. Now he heard Rosemary's hysterical shout as plainly as if he had been standing next to her.

'What?' Rosemary screamed. 'You idiot. You bloody idiot.'

'And what in hell's name did you expect me to do? Apologise? Grovel? Hold out the palm of my hand so I could be smacked? What do you think I am?'

She spat out her words at him.

'I don't believe it. What about me? And the girls? What about your so-called career you keep saying is so important to you? You've just chucked the whole bloody lot away.' She was still holding the kettle.

'Listen, Rosemary, you're not being reasonable. We've been through this before.'

'Through what? What's important enough to throw away your entire future? And humiliate me in the bargain?' She looked at him with hatred. 'You're mad.'

'Look, it's a matter of principle. Honour, if you like. Meridia's important. I've made my position plain. I can't

272

go back on it. What's more, I'm right. And I intend to keep at it until they have to agree.'

Rosemary did not hear his last sentence.

'Fuck your sodding principles.'

The kettle narrowly missed him but smashed the glass door of the kitchen. The glass fell outwards. She burst into tears and pushed past him out into the corridor. He tried to stop her and grab her arm. She pushed him away and ran up the stairs wailing. Water and broken glass lay all over the kitchen floor. The bedroom door slammed and there was silence.

Edward leant against a cupboard, hunched his shoulders and ran his hands through his hair. He felt sick and frightened as though he had committed murder. It was no use running upstairs after Rosemary. She would have locked the door. What on earth was he going to do? He had left his public self-assurance hanging with his coat in the hall. He put his head in his hands.

The sitting-room door creaked and opened. Edward looked up. He had forgotten they were not alone. Neil stood there with a red face, deeply embarrassed.

'Look, Mr Dunsford. I think I'd better go. I'm really very sorry about all this.'

Edward ignored the comment and walked back into the sitting-room. He made for the tray of decanters which stood on a red-lacquered cabinet by the window.

'I'm going to have a drink. I suggest you do the same.'

He poured out two large whiskies. He noticed his hand was trembling. Neil took the glass wishing he had not come. He should, if he was doing the job for which he was paid so highly, now be sitting in the stuffy executive lounge at Heathrow waiting for a flight to Frankfurt,

273

studying the arguments for a last attempt to drum up European support for MEECON. It served him right to land stupidly in this awe-inspiring domestic disaster.

'I couldn't help hearing your conversation just now.'

Edward gave a thin smile.

'I really think I ought to leave you and Mrs Dunsford alone.'

Edward suddenly felt irritated.

'For heaven's sake, sit down man,' he said sharply. 'I don't know what you're doing here but you haven't finished your drink and don't think you're embarrassing me. We shan't see Rosemary again tonight.' He finished his drink, went over to the red cabinet and poured himself another whisky. He noticed the gin decanter was almost empty again. He stood gazing out of the window, his back to Neil. Funny that he should meet Rosemary's American now of all times. Why had he come? Was Rosemary really up to something? No, it wasn't possible. Not now. Rosemary had always been pure bluff.

'Do you mind my asking what, uh, happened? I mean why? Rosemary, er, I mean Mrs Dunsford, was saying that everyone was backing you up.'

'Not quite everyone. Not, for example, the Foreign Secretary. Nor the Prime Minister.' Edward sat down wearily. 'They count, you see. They expect their ministers to stop rocking the boat once they've had their wrists slapped. Well, I was slapped. I got angry. Too angry, I suppose. I spoke out. Nothing very much. A tin-pot radio station at the weekend. But everyone got excited. And that was that.'

He sat slumped in his chair, eyeing wearily his second whisky. Neil's stomach was fluttering again.

'Er, you know I've been involved in the Meridian thing too, Mr Dunsford?'

'Yes. Guy told me. Very depressing. And very dangerous.' He sat up. 'You see I really don't think you know what the hell you're doing.'

'A watching brief in London. And we're still trying to get the Germans to join. I'm on the way there now.'

'We'll all have to pay for it eventually.' Edward stretched out his legs and sprawled back in his chair. The second whisky had calmed him. He did not know what on earth he was going to do. But he felt warm and better.

'Be a good chap and get us both another one of these.'

'Sure. Er, do you have any soda?'

It was nearly six o'clock. The press were bound to start ringing him soon. They would want a comment, a statement. He ought to prepare something. The first reaction, the first words, were the most important of all. He needed to make an impact now. It would be tomorow's story. To wait would be too late. Yet it seemed such an effort at the moment. He wished he did not feel so lonely.

They sat for another hour talking. About Neil, about the new investors he was chasing in West Germany, the technicalities of the scheme. Edward was half-interested. He wanted to talk. It helped to keep reality at bay.

At seven thirty Neil got up for a third time to go, feeling slightly unsteady and flushed – but from the whisky rather than the awkwardness of being in the Dunsfords' house.

'Sorry, Mr Dunsford. It's been really nice talking to you. I'd better head off to the airport now I guess. My flight to Frankfurt, you see. I must be on it.'

Edward did not get up to say goodbye. He stayed

sprawled in his chair and squinted at his watch. 'When does it leave?'

'Seven thirty or so.'

'Well, you've missed it now.'

And so began an evening which both men later wanted to forget. After a time Edward succeeded, Neil never, for the American had the thinner skin.

He asked himself afterwards why he ever agreed to go out with Edward, who was clearly intending to make himself drunk. Curiosity was at the heart of it – how did a sacked British minister of the upper-middle classes behave in the last quarter of the twentieth century? Then, professional zeal, for after all Neil had to keep Bourton supplied on the telephone with all he could pick up about the politics behind MEECON. But it was more complicated than that. This was the husband of a woman whom Neil found fascinating and sexually attractive. He remembered the dry touch of her hands as she gave him the teacup. Edward had a special interest for Neil because Edward had married Rosemary, made love to Rosemary, had kettles thrown at him by Rosemary.

A taxi took them to the first pub, brightly lit off Gloucester Square. They sat at an iron table, ornately Victorian in design, but modernised with bright yellow paint. A full-scale copy of the Apollo *Belvedere*, also bright yellow except for a band of black across his loins, stood on a plinth beside them. Two things were at once clear even to inexperienced Neil: Edward had never been there before, and it was a pub for gays. Edward took no notice of his surroundings. He ordered two whiskies, and went on talking about the Foreign Office, about MEECON and

Meridia, about being sacked. Fascinating stuff, but Neil was not absorbing it. This was partly because his head and stomach were giving warning signals, mainly because what he wanted at this stage from Edward was personal, not political.

A waiter approached. 'Excuse me, sir, but the gentlemen over at table six wondered if you would like to join them . . .'

For the first time Edward seemed to notice his surroundings, the smiles of welcome at table six, the lipstick on the mouth *of Apollo Belvedere*. He gave a five pound note to the waiter, and they left.

In the second taxi he said, 'That wasn't a real pub. There are no real pubs in London.'

'I thought the right thing in an English pub was to drink bitters,' said Neil.

Edward laughed.

'Bitters is what my wife puts into cocktails. Bitter in the singular is what they drink in English pubs. Now, my dear Neil, I'm going to show you a real English pub.'

But it turned out to be full of Irishmen, in Pimlico. Neil went to the lavatory and the cold air made his head swirl. He could walk out now, and in ten minutes could be in his room at Brown's Hotel, drinking an Alka-Seltzer and ordering scrambled egg for his supper from room service. Twenty-five minutes, if he walked. But what would happen to Edward? He found him half-way through a big Guinness.

It was a dirty and dark pub, and Edward had slopped Guinness on the floor. For the next quarter of an hour, he said nothing at all to Neil. He glowered into his first glass, then into his second. The barman plucked up courage.

277

'Seen you on the bloody box, haven't I?'

'This is no damned good,' said Edward. He took Neil by the arm, just above the elbow. 'I want to talk to you about you. Can't do it here.'

'We could go to my hotel. It's . . .'

'Take you to the Beefsteak. Sound English dinner. Back to the nursery. Sausages and mash. Honest vegetables.'

So the third taxi of the evening took them towards Leicester Square. But Edward had another thought.

'No dinner at the Beefsteak on Mondays. I forgot.'

A pause. He found himself thinking of Garth Andrew and then of Garth's smart Mayfair club.

'Nightingales. Come on, Neil. I'm taking you to Nightingales.'

Inside the club Edward's memory became hopelessly jumbled. He brazened it out past the man on the door into a softly lit hall, warm and reassuring after the chilling wind. A murmur of voices came from a room beyond. A smooth young man in a dinner-jacket apologised for not recalling Edward as one of the club's members. Edward's voice rose but at that stage had not slipped out of control. What was the man implying? Of course he ought to recognise Edward's face from before. Good God, did a Minister of the Crown have to prove his identity everywhere he went? Didn't the man read a newspaper occasionally? He'd better ring his very good friend Mr Garth Andrew if he had any doubts. Edward paused, and decided to sound friendly.

'Now look, it's been an enormous pleasure to meet you but my friend here has come a very long way for the pleasure of sharing a bottle of champagne with me. So kindly find us a table, won't you?'

A well-dressed man about Edward's age materialised softly and whispered in the receptionist's ear. Edward and Neil were led across a room, warm and low-ceilinged, to a corner table. There were four chairs. A waiter produced a wine-cooler, some outrageously expensive non-vintage champagne and four glasses. The manager appeared at their side.

'Good evening, Mr Dunsford. What a pleasure to see you here, sir.'

Edward nodded. Dimly he realised how quickly his face was likely to fade from people's minds.

'Do you wish to be private, sir? May we offer you and your guest some company to share your champagne?'

Edward grew more civil by the minute.

'It's kind of you. Perhaps later. For the moment I want to ask Mr Wainwright if he intends to sleep with my wife. It might be better if I did this without assistance from your ladies.'

The manager vanished, no doubt accustomed to such West End chit-chat. Neil was not. There was a silence.

'Well, I asked you a question.'

Edward's voice was not hostile.

Neil spoke part of the truth.

'I would like to be friends with you both.'

'How often have you met Rosemary?'

'Today was the second time. You know that.'

'Are you a virgin?'

'I really don't see . . .' Hell, if this was a game, he was not going to chicken out. 'No. I'm not.' It was just about true. He tried his champagne.

'Good. Rosemary hasn't the patience for a good teacher.'

'Mr Dunsford . . .'

'Edward.'

'Edward, I don't know. the nature of your standards and beliefs in this matter, or those of your wife . . .'

'Rosemary.'

'Rosemary. But let me assure you that I would never . . .'

'Crap. Isn't that what you call it? Crap.'

Neil did not persist, knowing that he had been about to tell a lie. He was thinking seriously about his stomach. The room was hot. The combination of recently taken drinks made it certain that he would be sick. His Harvard education told him that. The question was simply how soon.

Edward still seemed in control both of stomach and brain, though he had taken three glasses to every two of Neil's. He spoke with pedantic slowness, as if to someone ignorant of the English language.

'A final word about Rosemary. I haven't lost her yet. Forget the shouting and broken glass, they are not significant in marriage. You have red hair, but you're not the sort of man to take on a husband in open fight. Today's been a bloody day, but there are other days. I tell you . . .'

But he never did, because two girls appeared, propelled by the manager. Julia and Caroline, Caroline and Julia. Neil never knew which was which. Both were blonde and big and, so far as Neil could tell, well-bred, well-educated and very English. With them came a second bottle of champagne. Neil decided with relief that the champagne was their *raison d'être*. They were not the sort of girls who would expect to be taken upstairs. The band appeared on the dais and began to tune instruments.

He reckoned without Edward, who had had a worse day and was much more drunk.

'Charming,' he said, once the girls were seated. 'Charming, but my friend and I are tired, so let us skip the preliminaries. '

He stood up, just as the band launched into something loud and Latin American. Neil was never quite sure what happened next. Either Edward pulled at the girl's blue dress (Caroline, probably) or trod on it while clumsily suggesting a dance. She stood there, gaping above the neck to show large white teeth, and below the neck to show one large white breast from which the dress had beat a forced retreat. Then she squeaked, an absurd noise from a statuesque girl, but loud enough to bring the manager and a much bigger hunk of muscle who answered to the name of Manuel.

'I'm sorry, sir,' said the manager. 'You don't seem to be feeling very well. I think it would be best if I helped you to a taxi.'

The blonde was adjusting her dress. Edward lunged past the manager as if to unveil her other breast. Afterwards Neil decided that Edward had no such precise intention; but at the time he seized Edward by the shoulder and pushed him back towards his own chair. Edward looked about him like a bull at the end of the fight, and said quite gently:

'You don't understand. The bastard's sacked me.'

Then he hit Neil on the chin, drew back his fist and tried again at the manager who, however, was not born yesterday.

'Manuel.'

And so it was that Edward and Neil were out on the

281

pavement in Berkeley Square, Edward perforce, Neil by way of companionship.

'We'll send the bill to the House of Commons,' shouted the manager from the lighted doorway.

Neil was very sick into the gutter. Edward stood under a lamp-post for a moment or two, swaying uncertainly. Then silently, in slow motion, the Member for East Sussex sank unconscious on to the pavement.

Neil eventually began to look for the fourth taxi.

23

The train gathered speed after slowing down through Reading. Edward put down the last of the pile of newspapers he had bought at Paddington half an hour before. His head still reeled whenever he moved too quickly. Unless he sat absolutely still his stomach would embark on a progression of emotions which would make a sprint necessary towards the little room at the end of the carriage.

He had bought a first-class ticket hoping it might buy him greater privacy. This was expensive, because Cornwall was a long journey, not covered by his MP's vouchers for constituency travel. But the last thing he wanted was to be recognised or spoken to. The open-plan carriage was barely a third full. No one sat opposite him. The young guard who had checked his ticket as they careered through Maidenhead had not even glanced at him.

It was all just as well, as the pile of newspapers at Edward's side testified. He was front-page news in every

one. Most had old photographs from his press conference at Heathrow. He leafed through them again. The
thickness of the black headlines gave him a perverse pleasure, like a flagellant who beats himself harder with his
chain to draw more blood from his back. *The Times*'s main
headline was: 'FOREIGN OFFICE MINISTER DIS-
MISSED IN POLICY ROW OVER MERIDIA'. The *Daily
Telegraph*: 'DUNSFORD SACKED FOLLOWING MERIDIA
OUTBURST: PM takes tough stand against challenge to
his authority'. The *Guardian*: 'MERIDIA AID POLICY
FALLS VICTIM TO GOVERNMENT ANGER'. The *Daily
Mail*: 'DUNSFORD SACKED AFTER NUMBER TEN
ROW'. The *Sun* was the most lacking in sentiment: 'OUT
YOU GO! Dunsford gets the boot in PM fury'. The state-
ment from Downing Street had been short and factual. *The
Times* printed it in full:

> The Prime Minister this afternoon requested the resigna-
> tion of Mr Edward Dunsford, Minister of State at the
> Foreign and Commonwealth Office. The Prime Minister
> explained to Mr Dunsford that he greatly regretted taking
> this step, but that Mr Dunsford's recent statements criti-
> cal of the policy of a government of which he himself was
> a member left no alternative. The Prime Minister
> expressed his appreciation for the contribution which Mr
> Dunsford had made as a Minister of the Government.

The press concentrated on three aspects of the story. Who
would replace Edward? Charles Elliott's name was mentioned more than once; Edward was surprised that an
announcement had not been made already. Would
Edward continue his Meridian campaign? Some papers

stressed the support he had among government back-benchers and thought that he would. But most were sceptical and thought he would not. Outside the Government they said his voice would carry no weight. There were plenty of ministers who had suffered a similar fate before. In the end not one had succeeded in changing his party's policy. And what would the Opposition make of it? *The Times*, in its editorial, warned the Government to tread carefully. Its narrow majority was under continual threat from any cause which could unite the opposition parties and attract a handful of rebels from its own side. There was strong public sympathy for a more forthcoming policy towards Meridia. The Prime Minister might think he had plucked out a thorn from his side by sacking Edward Dunsford. But the former Minister of State had caught the country's mood, and no government operating with a narrow margin in Parliament could keep safely out of step with a change in the political atmosphere. 'Britain can only be governed with the consent of people of widely different opinions,' it warned. 'A government such as Mr Berinsfield's today which ignores the opinions of those who disagree with it is going to come to grief.'

All the papers commented on the mystery of Edward's disappearance. Where was he? Why had he made no statement? Was there no strength after all in the convictions he claimed? Only the *Daily Mail* had the story which Edward dreaded finding. He had bought the late edition at the bookstand on Paddington Station. The news must have come in too late to influence the other papers or to change the headlines and the main part of the story. But there, tucked away in the last three paragraphs on page two was mention of a fight in a London nightclub the previous evening 'in which we believe Edward Dunsford was himself involved. The owner of this exclusive club refused to comment to our reporter late last night. But nor would he deny that Dunsford had visited the club very recently. An eye-witness has confirmed that a man looking remarkably like Dunsford started an ugly scene in the club last night and had to be forcibly thrown out. If so, it is hardly surprising the ex-Minister is lying low and playing hard to get.'

He had been right to come away.

Trying to read the name of the station as they sped through Newbury sent his head spinning again. What he could remember of the previous night left a sick void in his stomach. He closed his eyes.

His alarm had been set for a normal day and had woken him at six. He had turned on the light by his bed, and for a moment, but for a gentle swaying of the room around him, his world had seemed normal. Then he remembered and it came crashing in on him. There was no red box to finish over his breakfast. Jack would not be waiting outside in his car at eight thirty. Sally would not be breezing into his room asking if he could face a cup of the girls' instant coffee. It was gone. Merely a part of his past. Sally, too. No longer dear, loyal old Sally. Merely the Sally who shared her bed and body with Charles Elliott. Yet in his confused and dizzy state he was not sure whether he despised the girl's choice or envied Charles his.

But his thoughts of Sally did not last long. They kept coming back to himself. What was he going to do? And what about Rosemary? What on earth would she say?

Then he remembered Rosemary. And the tea. And Neil. The terrible argument in the kitchen. The flying glass. And later. He put his hand to his left eye, which was throbbing. It felt badly bruised. He had got up and examined himself carefully in a bathroom mirror. It was true. There was no doubt he had been punched.

For a few minutes he had panicked. He searched the house for any sign of Rosemary. She had not slept in her bed. Despite the early hour he rang the number at Long Meadow, noticing as he picked up the receiver that it had been left off the hook. By Rosemary, he had no doubt. All night? And perhaps all the previous evening? He counted forty rings before he put the telephone down. He rushed into the kitchen, scattering fragments of glass which still lay there from the aftermath of their quarrel. The hook which they always used was empty of keys. Wherever Rosemary had gone she had taken his car. He stood for a moment, trying to order his thoughts as the kitchen spun round him. Then the telephone rang.

'Hello? Rosemary?'

There was an unfamiliar voice at the other end.

'Good morning, Mr Dunsford. This is Jim Henry of the *Daily* . . .'

Edward slammed the telephone down. He was shaking. The telephone rang again almost immediately. He cut off the call and laid the receiver on the table. One reporter ringing up meant more close behind him. But he did not want to talk yet.

He made himself some strong coffee and a piece of toast and, swaying gently, carried them upstairs. Uppermost in his mind were the events of the previous evening, not the afternoon. He remembered the girls at the club. He remembered Neil's frightened face. He remembered now being punched. He prodded gingerly at his eye. He did not know how he had come home or who had put him to bed. He supposed it was Neil. That made it even more humiliating.

He needed time to think and he needed to be where no one could reach him. But how?

Garth Andrew crept into his mind as he toyed with his piece of toast. Nightingales was Garth's club. Garth would be appalled – and amused. He would understand. He could be trusted. He was discreet, despite appearances.

Edward put down the piece of toast. Of course. The cottage.

He picked up the telephone. It was still only six forty-five. But he would understand. A sleepy voice answered the call.

'Garth. It's Edward. Edward Dunsford.'

A pause. Then a sleepy voice jerking wide awake.

'My dear boy. What a mess this all is. Where on earth are you?'

'Garth, I'm sorry. I know it's terribly early. But I need your help.'

'Wish I could, dear boy. Nothing would please me more. But even I couldn't make Berinsfield change his mind now.'

'No, no. I'm in a greater mess than anyone knows yet. Not at all what you think. I have to get away for a few days where no one can get at me: And I mean absolutely no one. So I was wondering if the cottage was free?'

'No one in their right mind spends November in Cornwall. But of course. It's yours, dear boy. No problem.

288

I'll ring Mrs T and ask her to open it up and get in some food. When do you want it?'

'Today. I want to go down today.'

'Today? Is that wise?'

Edward said nothing.

'Well, naturally, if you're sure . . .' Another silence. 'Don't worry. It's done. I'll ring her this morning.'

'Garth, bless you. Look, one more thing. Please don't tell anyone I'm there. Anyone. And that goes for Rosemary, too.'

'Steady on. The famous can't escape for long. The hounds are out. Everyone was desperate to speak to you last night. For all I know the police might start looking soon.' There was a pause. Edward held his breath. 'All right. I'll say nothing for three days. But no more. People will start to worry.'

Without the car there had been no choice but the train. For most of the journey Edward found he could not think properly. He let sensations of despair, anger, humiliation and tiredness drift over him. He slept from before Exeter until the train jolted to a halt at Plymouth. Gradually his body righted itself. When he woke he found he was hungry and the world no longer spinning. Crossing the Tamar cheered him, for it was a boundary he knew, and he could pretend that all recent horrors lay to the east of it. Westward, look, and so forth. He bought ham sandwiches and a can of lager from an attendant pushing a trolley through the swaying train. With each station they passed he felt better.

He had been twice with Rosemary and the girls to Garth's cottage. Never by train. He wondered whether he should hire a car, but he did not want to identify himself

289

by filling in a form. So when he left the train at Truro he found a taxi. The driver, middle-aged and pear-shaped, and wearing an ancient battered green cap, got out to open the door. Edward gave him his destination.

'I don't know so well about that. That's St Just way, isn't

Edward nodded. The taxi-driver adjusted his cap in a good-humoured way.

'Cost you a bit, sir.' He named a sum.

'All right,' said Edward, getting into the car. 'But not by the main road. We'll drive out towards Falmouth and take the ferry.'

The man was a slow, deliberate driver. It took them half an hour to reach the steep-sided little valley which harboured the Harry Ferry. They were in time. The ferry was chugging slowly on its chain across the river towards them. So many times Edward and Rosemary had driven furiously round those last corners to avoid the half-hour wait, only to find ten feet of water lapping against the slipway, and the ferry moving inexorably on its way to the opposite bank. But even Rosemary agreed it didn't matter. This was the genuine route to take. The main road was for the lorries and the trippers.

Edward stood outside as they crossed the river, enjoying the chilling breeze which met them on its way up from the estuary. Back in the warm car on the other side he soon dozed off, his head nodding against the window. The driver had mistaken his directions, and they were descending towards the church at Roseland before Edward woke and realised where they were. They turned back to the St Mawes road and found the turning a few minutes later. The driver took the narrow lane cautiously.

A mile further on, having dropped down to the river and glimpsed a handful of boats languishing on their winter moorings, they doubled back, turned a corner shrouded by high hedges and reached the cottage. It stood in its little valley by a sluggish stream. The house was really two white-washed stone farmworkers' cottages, two hundred or so years old, which had been knocked genteelly into one by a previous owner. Green painted sash windows, a heavy grey slate roof which was bearing a good crop of moss, a fat chimney-stack at each end, a little too much ivy, a low wall topped by a hedge of escalonia, and a garden running on one side down to the stream and on the other ending in a wood which rambled on up the hillside.

Edward got out. Nothing stirred. No sign of life. It was perfect. The pastoral illusion. He knew it would not last; three days at most. When he had paid his fare and the taxi had driven off, Edward stayed for a moment outside with the silence. He remembered the first time he and Rosemary had come. The cottage had seemed unlike anything else they knew of Garth. He was a man for large houses and grand entrances, not low doorways and awkward corners. The cottage was a picture out of Dornford Yates rather than a late twentieth-century Londoner's retreat. On that November afternoon Edward felt a moment of peace. He picked up his bag and went inside.

24

It was Wednesday morning. Through the double doors of the empty ministerial office came the faint sound of the ornate French clock on the mantelpiece striking nine. Sally sat at her desk gazing past unwashed windows at the skeletons of the trees which bordered St James's Park. She felt miserable. James Harrison had turned his own dismay against her. She looked like a lap-dog without a master, he had said. His brilliant ties had, in the last two days, become more preposterous. But he, like Sally, could not believe how suddenly their two lives had changed. Whenever Sally wandered aimlessly into Edward's room she felt a sense of bereavement. Table, sofas, desk and chairs kept the familiar smell but to touch them was to rifle through a dead man's belongings. Soon someone new would inherit them and make them his own. They did not yet know who. But the thought made her shiver. She also felt guilty. It had been Charles Elliott's dagger, but she had placed the weapon in his hand. On Monday evening she had written a long letter to Edward on her best notepaper, apologising, asking for the chance to explain. She had torn up three versions and the fourth lay unfinished on her desk.

The telephone buzzed at her side. Perhaps, after all, it might be Edward.

'Mr Dun . . . er, Sally Archer.' She had not yet shrugged off the habit.

'Sally, hi, it's John.' Another Private Secretary to another Foreign Office minister. 'Still no sign? Where on earth's he got to? Has he been in touch?'

'No, nothing. Not a word. Not yet, anyway.'

She put the phone down. Where was he? She had tried the Eaton Close number a dozen times the day before. There was no reply from the house in Sussex. Seven or eight MPs had telephoned, including Sir Guy Winchilsea. When he had rung on Tuesday demanding to know where he might find Edward he had hung up abruptly, muttering about Edward keeping in touch, as soon as she said she did not know where he was. Major Peacock, who had rung her from a call-box somewhere in Wales on Monday evening, had rushed back to Lewes the next day. But he, too, was baffled. They had talked of calling the police but had backed off. There was no need. Half the London press corps was trying to track him down. Journalists kept telephoning. Surely she knew how to find him? What were Personal Secretaries for? She tried to be polite at first. The effort soon became too much. Last night a man from the *Star* with a whining voice had rung her up for the third time, and she had told him to get lost. The newspapers were more excited by the mystery of the disappearance than by the politics of Edward's sacking. A pile of that morning's papers was strewn on the floor by

Sally's chair. No longer were they carefully annotated each day and laid out neatly on the mahogany table next door.

She was frightened by what his disappearance might signify. Sally had no idea whether Edward was the type to commit suicide. She had seen so little of his emotions. He seemed too resilient, too much in control of himself to try anything so desperate. Even so it was a worry, nagging at the back of her mind. The *Daily Mail* story about the London nightclub, strangely, had not run. But she had read it carefully as she had read every newspaper story about Edward for the past two weeks, and had wondered.

As she sat pretending to read some papers on her desk she wondered again. Abroad? Ill? Hiding? On holiday? Politicians who came to a bad end often seemed to take a holiday. She stopped. No, it wasn't in her office telephone book. She had looked through that a hundred times for an odd number which he might once have given her when he had been away at a weekend. She thought hard. It was August. He had gone down to Cornwall with Mrs Dunsford and the two girls. She remembered now. No one can get at us down there, he had said. So please don't ring. But she had taken down the number anyway, just in case.

She grabbed her handbag and found her diary. Somewhere in those pages at the back which always get used for the garbage of one's annual life she had buried the number. For five minutes she thought she must have been wrong. But eventually, tucked away on a page full of book titles, addresses, shopping lists, and notes of odd requests made by Edward in cars and corridors, she found it.

She hesitated. James was leafing idly through the early-morning telegrams.

'James, what about some coffee?'

'My turn as always, I suppose.' He threw the telegram folder into an out-tray and wandered grumbling into the secretaries' room, now silent for two days, to find the kettle.

She hurriedly punched out the St Mawes number. As she waited for it to click through she felt a void opening in her stomach. If he were there, what would she say? Why was she ringing him? Probably he would say nothing, or bark at her and put the phone down.

She counted. The number rang fifteen times. Then a voice, far away, suspicious. But his.

'Hello?'

'It's Sally.' She was half-whispering into the telephone. 'Look, I'm awfully sorry to . . .'

'How did you know I was here?'

'I guessed. I didn't know. No one seems to know where you are.'

There was a long silence at the other end of the line. She noticed her palms were wet.

'Look, I'm terribly sorry. But I was worried.'

His voice sounded irritated and unfriendly.

'Why? Why now? I've had my reward and that's that.'

'No. It's not that. It's just that . . .'

'Look, Sally, it was clever of you to find me. But I came here because I wanted to think things out without other people trying to barge their way into my life.'

She suddenly felt angry. Why was he so damned conceited? Why could he not understand that she had private feelings, too?

'I'm sorry that's the way you see it. I think you're being bloody unreasonable.' She was almost shouting now.

'What?'

She slammed the phone down, furious at the rebuff. Her eyes pricked with tears of frustration. James was standing by her desk, holding mugs of coffee. Balls of powdered milk were floating on them.

'Good God, Sally. Not another lover thrown to the lions, I hope?'

'Shut up.' She took her coffee from him and went back to the papers on her desk.

She ignored the winking light which showed a call on her line. James picked it up.

'James Harrison speaking.'

There was a pause. 'Er, yes. Yes. Of course.' He flicked up the button to put the caller on 'hold'.

'It's him.' There was a look of awe on his face.

Sally grabbed her phone. 'I'm terribly sorry. I . . .'

Edward's voice, still distant, but noticeably warmer.

'Sally, please stop saying you're sorry. Every time we have spoken this week you've been apologising.'

'You see, I was worried. I wanted to explain.'

'You're very sweet. I know. I was beastly to you.' Words like that came to him only with difficulty. 'Look, I don't suppose. I mean . . .' His sentences, though clipped and pointed, began to falter. It was always a sign of a personal question, of a small embarrassment. On the rare occasions it had happened in the past she had thought how awkward he was.

'I really don't want to burden you with my problems. But it would be good to see you down here. We could have that talk you're so desperate for.'

296

Sally hoped she had heard him right.

'If you really think so.'

'Good. Hang on.' He returned after a pause. 'There's a train to Truro which leaves Paddington at twelve. Will that give you enough time to throw a few things into a case? There's lots of room down here. I'll send a taxi to pick you up.'

'I'll make it.'

She put down the phone. James was giving her a long meaningful look over the rim of his coffee mug.

'Something you'd like to tell me, perhaps?'

Half a mile from the lighthouse was a beach sheltered on three sides by cliffs. No road led to it, but on a hot summer day it would be crowded with people, those who had walked down from the National Trust car park further along the cliff, and those who had sailed to the beach across the estuary from Falmouth and St Mawes. On a gusty, grey November morning Edward, a piece of driftwood in his hand, had the beach to himself. Out to sea he could pick out little dots of humanity. But the two or three fishing boats dipping their way through the white horses of the Carrick Roads on their way back to warm fires and comfortable wives seemed as far from his reach on that morning as did Westminster, Whitehall, Rosemary and the girls. He threw the piece of driftwood into the grey sea. Edward wished he might jettison his own past so easily.

After an hour the incoming tide drove him off the beach and back up the cliff. Even though it was a three-mile walk back to Garth's cottage he relished the exercise. He had thought at first that coming down to the cottage would give him the freedom to analyse and to plan, carefully, objectively and coolly. But it all seemed an enormous effort. Better to concentrate on the turf at his feet or on the hedgerows and brambles which plucked at his coarse old jacket.

Most of the time he felt desperately tired. He found he could exercise no choice over his thoughts, and could concentrate his mind no more than a novice at a chessboard who can barely see one move ahead. Rosemary, their terrible argument, his wretched career, Patrick Reid and the Prime Minister, the growing doubt over his position in the constituency – all washed over him, like the waves on the beach rolling Edward's piece of driftwood up and down the shingle. The scouring of these uncontrolled thoughts across his mind hurt him. He wanted to cut himself off from them. He had kept away from the newspapers which he might have bought in the village, and had refused to turn on the radio and the television. Sometimes he had sat in the cottage staring at nothing, feeling drained and weak. If his world really were crumbling he would rather delay the full knowledge of it.

He stopped to prod with his toe the black velvet body of a mole which lay by the side of the narrow lane he had now joined. It was not always so bad. Occasionally he felt stronger and his mind clearer. But when he did try to think it came out for the most part only in images of Meridia – the white flowing robes, the figures gazing at him in the hospital, the dust and the hopelessness. He was surprised that the obsession seemed to have grown. He wondered he should not resent the whole business for having proved the cudgel which had broken his body. Yet he felt only more determined to follow it through. It was as though he had entered a race, and every time the end ought to be in sight the distance to cover grew longer. He did not know how far he would have to run, only that the greater the pain the greater was his determination to keep going. What worried him were the next steps. Without his place in the Foreign Office he had little left with which to strike at Patrick Reid and the Government.

As the lane dipped down from the hill top and he came in sight of the stream which led to the cottage, Sally crept into his mind again. She and Meridia were his only deliberate thoughts. He still wondered if he had been right to ring her back and ask her to come. What did he want from her? What, after all, could she give? He no longer felt hurt by her confession about Charles. He missed her steady, undemanding company – like a comfortable old jacket which is never properly appreciated until one day it has to be thrown away. Or maybe, just maybe, he wanted through her to hit back at Charles Elliott. He could steal Sally from him. He put the idea out of his head and told himself he was a fool. Anyway, he decided he could not work out the answer by thought. He was numb, and since yesterday morning when he had woken to tragedy breaking over his head he had not known what he felt. He would only know when he saw her.

Sally arrived out of the rain and the Cornish darkness at eight o'clock.

'Hello, Sally.'

They met almost as strangers. She looked cold and awkward. She wore a tweed suit he had not seen before, beneath it a cream silk shirt with a large collar. They eyed each other rather nervously in the little hall of the cottage. There was a strong smell of unexpectedly expensive perfume. Perhaps a gift once from Charles? She must have put it on in the taxi. Yet it was still good to see her.

'I hope you're not ratting already on your new Minister?'

As he spoke he realised it might be Charles Elliott. Sally reddened.

'No. No chance of that. No one's been chosen yet. The gossip round the office is that the PM's going to wait for a bit. Don't know why.'

She eyed him mischieviously. 'But the Secretary of State's hopping mad.'

He smiled for a moment. Her anxious look cleared.

'Oh Edward. I . . .'

Sally was reminding him of another world. He felt defeated and useless.

'Let me fix you a drink.'

He led her, his shoulders drooping, into the sitting-room and made two gins and tonic. They sat down together on a narrow sofa.

'You look awful, Edward.'

He sat forward, hunched his shoulders even more and stared at his glass. She put her hand on his arm.

'I've been worried about you.'

He smiled grimly but did not look at her.

'I saw a story in the *Mail* suggesting you might have been involved in something ghastly on Monday night. I was sure it wasn't true. But I was just worried that if something had happened, on top of everything else, well . . .' She trailed off. 'Are you sure you're all right?'

He turned towards her, though his eyes seemed to stare elsewhere.

'Did anyone else take up that story?'

300

She shook her head. 'Don't think so.'

'Then I've been lucky.'

He sipped at his drink. A hissing log on the fire burst into flame and spat angrily at them. She tried to jolly him along, her voice unnaturally cheerful and rather silly.

'You know, I'm amazed no one has found you yet. I think you're terribly clever. The press haven't stopped ringing up. And lots of other people, too.'

'Oh?' Edward continued to stare down at the carpet.

'Oh yes. Mainly MPs.' She named them. 'Including that extremely pompous Sir Guy Winchilsea. Said you'd promised to be in touch.'

Edward thought back to the conversation he had had with Winchilsea on Sunday, between the radio interview and his lunch. Then he had thought it worth going on, with Winchilsea and his friends ready to give some support.

'Mind you, he can't be so awful. I noticed this morning he's put his name to an early day motion on Meridia. With about a dozen others. Strong language, too.' She warmed to the subject, hoping he might be interested. 'The Opposition are on to it. They've forced a debate on Meridia one day next week.'

Edward looked up, as though he had not been listening. He had not yet taken in the possibilities of her news.

'Has Major Peacock spoken to you?'

'Mm, often. He came back from Wales specially. He's been in a bit of a state about you.'

Sally had almost finished her drink and it was cheering her up.

'Did he say anything?'

'What? About you, about Monday?'

'No, about things in Lewes.'

Sally thought. Edward was not looking at her, but he could imagine the frown and the slight puckering of her nose as she did.

'There was something. Something about the next meeting of the Association, I think. How important it was for you to be there.'

'Did he mention a man called Headley?'

'No, I don't think so.'

Edward realised it had been a mistake to ask Sally after all. With her came flooding back everything he had wanted to blot out for even a few days. He had known ever since Sunday when he had spent the evening alone at Eaton Close that Rosemary had been trying to help with her gossip from Violet Stephenson. He hated himself for not having believed her. Perhaps it would be too late now. Tucked away in Cornwall, he did not yet have the strength to fight more than one battle at a time. The debate. He must concentrate on that first.

'Edward, I've spoken to someone else, too.'

He turned round now. Did she mean Rosemary? He remembered he had not even asked.

Sally looked hard into the fire. 'I must tell you this.'

No, not Rosemary.

'I tracked Charles down in the House. In the Lobby actually. We had the most fearful row, with lots of people watching us. I told him he was a liar and a bastard and that I never wanted to see him again. I wanted to hurt him so much. Though I know I can't. He's not that type. And I'd only hurt his wife even more.'

'Why worry about his wife now? Isn't it a bit late for that?'

'Of course. But I just wanted to show him up, even for a moment. So I chose the most public place I could.'

'Be careful, Sally. He'll do you more damage than you can do him.'

Sally put down her glass and was fumbling in her handbag. Her eyes glistened.

'I hate him. And myself Look what's happened to you. Why? What had you done to him?'

She began to cry furiously. Somehow she did not seem to find her handkerchief

'Come on, Sally. You know as well as I do that I'd dug my grave already. Politicians have to have thick skins, that's all. And mine isn't thick enough. I don't hold that against him. Charles doesn't really upset me. It's something worse.'

'I don't believe you.' Tears were running down her cheeks now. 'What?'

'Fear. A sort of fear which will come to you one day. The fear that you've reached that point in your life where you know you're not going to become what you'd always secretly dreamed of. Failing. Realising that it's only a pathetic little dream. An illusion. A joke. Nothing more to come. That's what frightens me.'

'Then don't let it. You don't have to. You don't.'

She was shouting. Edward feared she might become hysterical.

'Sally, don't.'

He put his arm round her to try to comfort her, forgetting as he did his own problems. It was not clear to either of them later what happened next. As he drew her to him he kissed her tentatively on the forehead, as he might have kissed little Katie had she woken in the night

303

screaming from a nightmare. But Sally's reaction took him by surprise. She returned his kiss with passion, searching for his lips. Sally was not hysterical. Yet her mind was suddenly clear and she hoped desperately that he felt as she now did. She wanted to atone for some tremendous sin, to prostrate herself, to show him how much he really meant. She wanted to show him a great future still within reach. She could feel his body against hers. Her long fingers clutched at his shirt, pulling him against her, plucking at buttons.

Edward pushed his mouth hard against Sally's. Without reaching any decision his hands began to explore the rather thin and unexciting body which he had first wondered about in the dusty swimming pool in Mangara.

'Please, Edward, I want you so much.'

He began to fumble awkwardly at her clothes, pulling a button off her shirt as he did so. His mouth searched her neck and a smooth white shoulder. Edward was responding mechanically to her wish and now to some promptings from his body. His mind remained aloof and disapproving. How, with his world collapsing about his ears, could he be engaged in this absurd and humiliating flurry with his Private Secretary? Faces kept rushing across his eyes, Rosemary, Garth Andrew, the pear-shaped taxi-driver, the blonde at Nightingales. He managed at last to detach Sally from her tweed suit. He could feel her losing control. She lay on the sofa with her arms around his neck, clothes, shoes, tights all strewn in a heap on the floor. He could see her body very dearly, every detail of her skin, just as he had once tried to imagine it. His body was excited now and he broke away to undress, keeping only his shirt. There was just room for

304

them both on the sofa, if they stayed close. She took the lead, timing her caresses, pulling him on top of her. He was amazed and thought of Charles Elliott; did she lead him with the same intensity? His mind, still detached, let his body have its way. At the moment of climax Sally sighed a great sigh, as if the ills of the world were cured and it only remained to sleep. Edward, his eyes shut, thought of Rosemary. For three minutes afterwards, the two bodies lay embraced. Edward felt increasingly uncomfortable, rather cold, and deeply ashamed. His mind and body came together again and disliked what they found and remembered.

'No, Sally,' he said. 'No, not possibly,' as if it were not too late. He was out of the sitting-room, taking his clothes with him before, understandably, she began to cry.

25

The same time that evening, in a large house about three miles from what might one day be the northerly route of the M27, six men and one woman sat in a modern drawing-room sipping gins, whiskies and some of Derek Headley's best dry sherry. An intruder to the Headley 'estate' (as the biscuit-maker liked to call it) happening to peer at that moment through the leaded windows might have guessed he had come upon a group of friends enjoying a cosy evening. But they were not all friends.

'I think this is going too far, if you want my opinion. I don't like all this stuff about his criticism of the Government bringing discredit on the constituency. We're not here to comment on all that business.'

An elderly man, a white fringe of hair still clinging to an otherwise balding head, was looking through a set of badly typed papers. Violet Stephenson was right – the draft of the Policy Committee's report had been typed by Headley's wife. Years before she had been a far-from-efficient secretary.

Derek Headley adjusted his spectacles and rested an arm on the neo Georgian mantelpiece, a tumbler of malt in his hand.

'Sorry, Arthur. You're wrong there. It's very relevant. It's all part of the same pattern. There's no difference to my way of thinking between Dunsford ignoring his responsibilities to the Government and ignoring his responsibilities to us.' He took a gulp from the tumbler. 'No difference at all. The man just can't be trusted. We have to show why. It's as simple as that.'

A short young man with a green tie and a belligerently high voice spoke up.

'That's right. And I think he's gone over the top this time. Why else has he just disappeared? I suppose he's ashamed to show his face. Well, that doesn't say very much about him. He's still got a job to do here, hasn't he?' He smiled. 'Well, maybe not for too long, eh Derek?' He threw a meaningful glance towards the fireplace.

Violet Stephenson sat foursquare on the sofa like a battleship in dry dock. She felt uncomfortable about the direction the group was taking in Headley's hands. She disliked Headley's so-called report and was beginning to distrust, and dislike, Derek Headley.

'I agree with Arthur,' she said. 'Edward Dunsford's a good man and he's done a lot for us over the last five years. A damn sight more than his predecessor. I agree, he could have been more active over the motorway.' She looked at her host. 'But it's that we're here to consider, Derek. Nothing else. The job of this report is to offer some constructive criticism.' She shook her copy of Headley's draft. 'This is as good as getting him to resign.'

Headley removed his arm from the mantelpiece and put down his tumbler.

'Look, Violet,' Headley said. 'We're simply putting down the facts and making a few recommendations. Nothing more than that. No one's trying to decide anything. That's for the Association to do.'

'They're not facts,' retorted Violet. 'They're all prejudice and innuendo. I can't accept this paper. It's malicious. All this business towards the end about deliberately working behind his Prime Minister's back to further his own interests. It's libellous. He's not that kind of man. We'll have to re-write it.'

'There isn't time. The Association meeting is only next Wednesday,' a man in a tweed suit contributed. 'And this report's got to go through Dubarry.'

'Yes, and he'll need a bit of time for it. The Chairman's mind doesn't always work too quickly.' Headley smiled grimly. The short young man with the high voice sniggered.

'So you see there isn't time, I'm afraid, Violet.' Headley went on. 'Now I'm happy to accept a few minor changes from anyone – if there are any.' He looked round the room, daring someone to speak. 'But this paper's not being rewritten.'

Violet hauled herself up, clumsily but not without dignity.

'In that case . . .'

'Look,' said Headley, trying to sound friendly for once. 'I want this report agreed unanimously as much as anyone. Let's have a vote on it, shall we?'

Six hands went up, including Headley's. Violet Stephenson looked angrily around her. She thought of her confidence over the High Street coffee cups with Rosemary Dunsford and was sad she had after all been able to do nothing to restrain Derek's nasty little group.

'That seems to do it nicely.' Headley smiled. 'Hope you're happy, Violet. Now perhaps we can get on. More drinks anyone, before we put this business to bed?'

Violet Stephenson looked at the six men for a moment, gathered her capacious handbag to her capacious bosom, and left. As she crossed the hall she caught a high-pitched snigger from behind her.

26

There was a change of mood in Meridia, and in Meridia that meant a change of mood in one man. A sense of irritation. A suspicion that he was being led by the nose. The signs were small at first. A phrase hidden in a conversation, a hesitation or two where before there was enthusiasm and praise. Changes only perceptible to some of those who were closest to President Hamid . Not all of them would have read the signs aright. It was like the appearance of a little crack in the plasterwork of a room. It had not been there the day before. It might signify nothing. It might be only plaster deep. Or it might end in the house falling down.

The cracks in Julian Sandford-Smith's life that same Wednesday evening were all old ones, so far as he was concerned. It was almost eight o'clock as his car bounced up to the jetty. Even then, when it had been dark for nearly three hours, he still felt desperately hot. He had given himself plenty of time in which to change slowly for his dinner on the river. He had felt fine when he left the house. But already a large area of his shirt was sticking uncomfortably to the seat of the car, his face had reddened again, and a brightly-coloured handkerchief had been produced three or four times to pat at his glistening forehead. He brushed a fly off the thick woollen cloth of his unsuitable trousers. Pity his wife was not feeling up to coming. He was rather looking forward to his evening. It should be cooler on the river. It was a worry about his wife though. The third time this week she had backed out of something. Must be the heat too, he supposed. Bit rough on a big woman, this climate. He dug out his handkerchief again.

The Ambassador told himself that Edward's dismissal – the news irritatingly given to him by his Second Secretary since he had decided to give the World Service a miss that Tuesday morning – had not been a complete surprise. Rather an impetuous chap. Look at the way he had rushed off to that hospital. And he had hardly made the Ambassador's own life easy since, with constant demands from London for more reporting on everything under the sun. It was not surprising that he had developed little affection for Edward. But, strangely, the Ambassador felt rather sorry for him now. He had read extracts from Edward's press conference at Heathrow. In retrospect he had thought it rather good. Some nice phrases. A bit overdone of course, but then all politicians were given to exaggeration. That was their job, after all. It was true that Sandford-Smith had not liked Edward. But even so, it must be rough to be given the push like that.

The car lurched forward into a particularly large pothole and sent a fresh wave of petrol fumes over its occupant. Immediately his throat dried and his stomach tightened. he would never get used to this place.

Twice a year the German Ambassador hired an aged, rusting river-boat and gave a party on the river which ran through the city. Twice each year he filled it with an impressive collection of ministers, government officials and diplomats, filling them with vast quantities of food and German wines as the boat steamed sedately up and down. Cocktails lasted down to the bridge. Dinner began once the boat had turned round and begun to lumber back upstream. On this evening there was an inexperienced man at the wheel, and for a tense moment the boat, hitting a post in the shallows, almost ran aground. As the boat jarred against the bank Sandford-Smith sent half of his gin and tonic down the shirt of the Deputy Minister of Telecommunications, and the wife of the Indonesian Chargé d'Affaires grazed her knee against a railing. But three drinks into the evening no one much minded.

'Ambassador, come and eat with me.'

Sandford-Smith looked up from the buffet table where he was assessing a large dish of fish stew to see the Foreign Minister beaming at him. The Foreign Minister was dressed in a Western-style suit. This was a surprise. Usually he insisted on his flowing white robes as a symbol of national pride. They found chairs in a quiet corner of the deck. The Foreign Minister had helped himself only to a spoonful of rice and a chicken leg. Sandford-Smith looked guiltily at his own plate, piled high with shrimps, fish, chicken, various stews, rice and salads, and a number of things he had not recognised but had found impossible to resist.

'I hope you're enjoying yourself in Mangara, Ambassador?'

The Ambassador wished he had not been so greedy.

'Oh, very much so. Very much indeed. Mangara's a remarkable city. Yes. Fascinating.'

He prodded gingerly at the mountain of food on his plate. A large piece of chicken rolled off and fell to the deck.

'I always make a point of coming to the German Ambassador's parties.'

'Good show he's put on, I must say. Especially coming out like this on the river.'

'It gives you quite a different picture of the city, don't you think, Ambassador?'

'Yes. Yes, I do. Very much so.'

He wondered why he felt so ill at ease. It was not just the greedy pile of food on his knees. Then he remembered. He had not spoken officially to any of Hamid's ministers about the sacking of Edward Dunsford. It would be difficult to explain.

The Foreign Minister had already finished his supper.

'I was very sorry to learn about Mr Dunsford. I was looking forward very much to making his acquaintance. I'm so sad that we didn't meet when he came to Mangara.'

'Yes. Er, indeed. He was very sad too not to have had the chance to meet you, Minister.'

'Tell me, Ambassador. Why did your Prime Minister sack him? Was it really to do with Meridia? But why all this fuss in England about Meridia? It's all very difficult to understand.'

Sandford-Smith cleared his throat and put a large spoonful of fish stew back on to his plate.

'Er, yes, it is, isn't it? But these things happen in politics. It's a very unpredictable profession in any country, don't you agree, Minister?'

The Ambassador laughed, a little too loudly. The black shadow of a narrow iron bridge passed slowly across the deck. They must already have passed the President's palace. Sandford-Smith had intended to look out for it.

'Ambassador, I studied in your country. You know as well as I that it's only when criticism of his Government touches a really raw nerve that a minister loses his job.'

Their conversation was drifting dangerously towards the rapids. Sandford-Smith did his best to block its course.

'I don't think there was a raw nerve in this case, you know.'

'I have been wondering about that. But, on reflection, I think there was. You see, so far as I understand it, Mr Dunsford seems only to have wanted to help our country, and the Prime Minister did not agree. Why, Ambassador? I don't understand. Why shouldn't the British Government want to help Meridia?'

The Ambassador put down his plate now and wiped the corners of his mouth desperately. Why couldn't someone come and interrupt them?

'But we do, we do. Look at the aid we're giving this year. It's really . . .'

'But Mr Dunsford wanted to give us more. Much more.'

'Yes, I know. He did. And with my support, of course,' he added in parenthesis. 'But unfortunately it's just not possible. There are too many conflicting demands. I mean, we have our economic problems too, Minister. Big ones. I mean . . .'

'What I simply don't understand, Ambassador, is why people in Britain seem to be so worried about who our friends are. All this talk in your papers about the "Soviet menace" and so on.' He held up his hand as Sandford-Smith opened his mouth. 'Oh yes, I see them all you know. But what I want to make clear is that you really mustn't be misled by appearances. Times are changing in Meridia. Really. Believe me.'

The Ambassador's mind was becoming confused. He longed for a simple conversation with the wife of an obscure envoy about the heat of the tropics, the beauty of the river at night, the dust of the city, the absence of sky-scrapers ruining the view, anything. He had not come properly prepared. He had drunk too much, trying to quench his thirst in this constant heat. He gulped down the remaining wine in his glass. What was the man trying to say?

'Well, Minister. You see, er, these changes aren't always easy for us. I mean, er, some of your new friends. Quite a lot of them, really. Especially recently. These things are signs, you know. Of how you feel. And so on.'

He came to a halt.

The Foreign Minister called over a waiter and had him fill their glasses. He nudged Sandford-Smith good-naturedly.

'Things aren't always what they seem, Ambassador. Let me reassure you, you will be seeing more changes very soon. Changes which will reassure you of who our real friends are. Come. Let's drink to old friends getting to know each other again.'

He laughed knowingly and raised his glass.

'I'm sorry. I mean I don't . . .'

'You are confused, Ambassador. You must trust us. Let me just say that the President has looked at the river, the Eastern river, I mean, tested the water, and decided he doesn't like its temperature.'

He drank Sandford-Smith's health generously. The Ambassador sipped at his wine uncertainly. It was a waste. Good German red wine is difficult to find outside Germany.

The Foreign Minister moved on soon afterwards in the company of the Roumanian Ambassador whom he had encountered at the pudding table. Sandford-Smith spent some time gazing out on the river wondering what it all meant. It had been a signal, definitely a diplomatic signal. A bit long-range for his own taste. But that's what it must be. He was a straight-talking man himself. All this hinting and nudging was really most confusing.

The black water drifted past as his mind grappled with this new perplexity. He must talk to the American Ambassador. He would know. But later. This was a social occasion first.

The American was much younger than Sandford-Smith, still on the way up rather than, as the Englishman, having now arrived. This always gave him an irritatingly well-informed air. I'm one step ahead and don't I know it, was probably his family motto. Still, he was a valuable source of some of Sandford-Smith's reporting. Later that evening they met on the deck at the front of the steamer, below the wheelhouse. They leaned nonchalantly over the rail together. The light breeze off the river was almost cooling now, and a pleasant buzz in his head told Sandford-Smith that he had drunk just enough for comfort.

'Did you have the chance to say much to the Foreign Minister tonight?'

'Nope. Reckon we talked ourselves into the ground at the Foreign Ministry this morning. Phew. I reckon an hour and a half is a bit more than I'm paid for.'

'Oh.' How typical of the man. As he looked out to the bank he could just see shadowy figures running up and down the jetty, waving. Children, always children, wherever you went, day or night. Still, thought Sandford-Smith, he may not know what was divulged to me this evening.

'I had a long chat with him over supper earlier.'

'So I noticed. Giving you the new line, I suppose?'

'Well, I'm not sure it . . .'

'Damn good news. Our oil companies will start spitting blood if they lose this nice fat deal. But, as I told Washington in my cable this afternoon, if Hamid really is serious about chucking the Sovs this time round there must be a chance – just a chance, mind you – that the oil companies might be able to come back later under the stars and stripes.'

Sandford-Smith's mind was reaching back furiously to his conversation over the chicken legs.

'Yes. He said much the same to me. A bit vague, of course. More a preparing of the ground than anything else, I should think. But then that's very much what I would expect.'

The American looked away and laughed. 'Don't underestimate him, Julian. I think maybe this time Hamid's for real. He's on the turn.'

Sandford-Smith found the American's complacent self-assurance irritating. He decided to sound statesmanlike.

'Really? On the turn? Well, I'm very sceptical myself. After all, it's not as easy as that. Once they've got a foot in the door the Russians don't leave that quickly.'

The American was shaking his head. Sandford-Smith pressed on.

'I mean, in any case, why should the President change his mind now? From his point of view things aren't going too badly. If you want my opinion, I should say he is still very much hedging his bets.'

There was much shouting on the shore. The boat shuddered as the screws changed tempo. They should now have been in reverse, but for some reason the speed seemed to quicken. There were raised voices in the wheelhouse above them. They were approaching the jetty faster than they should, Sandford-Smith thought. The American Ambassador seemed oblivious.

'I tried to pin the Foreign Minister down this morning, but he wasn't giving anything with me either. But the reasons are obvious. You talk to the head of Hamid's office. He'll tell you.'

'What exactly?' My God, this man could be infuriating.

'Promises and guns. That's all Hamid's got out of them so far. And he's pissed off with it.'

Sandford-Smith winced. 'But . . .'

'Really pissed off, Julian. I mean, whatever we might think of Hamid he really, genuinely, wants to do something for this place. Money, experts, technical assistance. You name it, he wants it. But it's got to be for real. And what have the Soviets done? Nothing. They haven't given him anything except a lot of crap. Okay. So what's new in that, you're asking?'

He lowered his voice and bent confidentially towards

Sandford-Smith. To an outsider it would have been the classic pose between two conspiring diplomats. In the background the shouting in the wheelhouse was getting louder.

'What really got to him was this. Last Thursday night Hamid discovered they'd been using some of their flights to bring in massive quantities of small arms and ammo.' He held up a hand. 'Oh no. Not for Hamid's army. That's the point. The Soviets have been stashing it in a ware-house off the airport which they'd persuaded Hamid to let them have months ago as a sort of bonded store. That's why he's hopping mad. And this time he's really doing something about it, Julian. Yes, sir. We got a report from one of our funnies this morning. Hamid's talking about kicking out sixty-three Soviet dips. And soon. Sixty-three out of eighty.'

'They're what? Surely he . . . Hey! Watch out . . . !'

Sandford-Smith gasped. He would have said much more, but at that moment the boat hit the jetty, almost sending them both over the rail on to the lower foredeck. The impact staved in part of the wooden jetty, sending timbers cascading into the river. Behind the two Ambassadors people still clutching glasses and coffee cups were sent sprawling over the deck. There was shout-ing and cursing, and the sound of smashing glass. Tables and bottles went flying. The Italian Ambassador was trapped beneath the bar as it collapsed on top of him. The Soviet Defence Attaché ended up in the river and had to swim ashore, though he was so drunk that this might have happened anyway.

In his bed later that evening a rather bruised German Ambassador decided that next time it might be safer to

319

stick to dry land. Sandford-Smith had no such regrets. He returned home and terrified his wife with a highly coloured account of his adventure, so highly coloured that she did not fall asleep until long after midnight for the worry of it all. Sandford-Smith, on the other hand, pleasantly full of German wine, slept soundly. It was not until the next morning that he remembered the other reason for his confusion and excitement the night before. He sat for a long time in silence behind the battered postwar desk in his office and then began to compose yet another telegram.

27

After breaking away from Sally, Edward stumbled int his clothes and out into the murk of a Cornish night. The weather had abruptly changed. A sea mist blotted out moon and stars. The tiny garden was dripping and silent. He had humiliated the only nice woman he knew. He wanted Rosemary, but Rosemary would never do him any good. She had helped in the past, but that was over. He tried to shut all thought from his mind. Everything was wrong, so it must be best to think about nothing. In the darkness he blundered into a rose bush and the thorns caught his hand. The pain forced his mind to some sort of coherence and he found his way back into the cottage. Those few minutes had restored Sally to her tidy tweed suit and her normal self. She put down the telephone as he entered. Her voice was matter-of-fact. She had read the situation correctly. The second round of tears would come later.

'I'll just catch the sleeper from Penzance. I've ordered a taxi.'

'That's absurd. Penzance is miles away in the wrong direction. And the sleepers will all be booked.'

'I've checked. There are plenty free tonight. I must be in the office first thing.'

They paused, neither wanting the evening to end in such banality, neither knowing a better way.

'Coffee? Garth has some from the Yemen.'

'No thanks.'

They stood together in the tiny entrance hall, constrained almost beyond endurance.

'This is ludicrous,' said Edward after a long silence. 'The cab will be at least fifteen minutes.'

'I'll go out into the garden and wait for it there.'

'It's wet.'

'It was a fine evening.'

'It's wet now.'

Sally walked back into the sitting-room, picked up an ancient copy of the *Spectator* and pretended to read. Edward had poured them both a cognac but Sally did not touch hers. He tried once to storm the *Spectator*.

'Look, this is absurd. We've just made love. We must talk.'

She hardly lowered the paper.

'It doesn't follow. There's nothing more to be said.'

'We can't part just like this.'

'That's a cliché from a bad film.' It was only the second time Sally had ever criticised anything he had done or said. The Private Secretary had vanished for good. He felt cross, and his natural selfishness in private matters asserted itself. The girl had thrown herself at him, he had taken her, not very enthusiastically it was true, but if she did not want it that way, she was welcome to silence and the *Spectator*.

322

At last the taxi grumbled up the lane and its lights shone through the thin curtains.

'I'll go, then . . .'

'When shall I see you again?'

'I don't know. There doesn't seem much point.'

'Look, Sally, thank you for coming down. Thank you for . . . I'm sorry . . .'

'You said that before. I'm not a tart, you know.'

The taxi hooted, a bad-tempered, wheezy summons. Edward found a torch and an old umbrella of oiled paper, trophy of some oriental tour. He opened the door and escorted Sally into the darkness.

'Goodbye, then. You've plenty of time.'

'Goodbye.'

A kiss, a formal farewell, and a touch of hands. Hers were thin, warm and dry. Edward went back into the cottage and filled his glass to the rim with a fierce Soviet cognac. He wondered if he should have given Sally money for her ticket and the taxi. There were no precedents. But, as he had been told, she was not a tart.

What, however, was he? The materials being to hand, Edward found it easy within an hour or two to get drunk.

He woke with a hangover so fierce that it confused his sense of time, and he believed that he was still recovering from his evening at Nightingales. He lay in the narrow bed, listening to the trickle of rain in the gutters. Garth, whose London house was ornate to the point of absurdity, carried simplicity to an equal extreme in his Cornish cottage. The bedroom walls were white, and there were no pictures. The bed was hard, and if you raised your head abruptly it banged against an inward bulge of the ancient wall. Edward felt no temptation to do this. His head suffered enough already from the Soviet cognac which he had found in the cupboard downstairs. In London Garth served admirable wines. In Cornwall he kept the strange liquids presented by grateful foreign clients, the Algerian red, the Egyptian pink and a lethal array of East European brandies and liqueurs.

Sparrows were chattering in the grey light outside the bedroom window. One cock sparrow fluffed out his feathers on the window sill, delighting in the rain. Edward could not think what he was going to do, in the next hour, week, month, year, decade. He seemed himself to have blocked every avenue of action. The Minister had destroyed his ministerial career, the constituency MP was in trouble with his constituency. The husband and father was estranged from his wife and children. And now he had chased away a girl who could have been a steadfast friend, and perhaps much more. Her deferential Private Secretary attitude towards him had stunted their relationship; he now argued to himself as if that were all her fault. He tried to imagine their bodies embracing again, this time wholeheartedly and in comfort, Rosemary and Charles banished. But his imagination stumbled and would not oblige.

The cottage shook as the boiler next to the kitchen obeyed its clock and roared into life. Garth, while believing that country life should be simple, held even more firmly that water should be hot. Edward had found only thin summer pyjamas in his hurried packing, and on the bed there was one blanket too few even for a Cornish November. So a hot bath – that at least was a definite objective. But after that? He could perhaps spend a day or two more at the cottage, solitary, living out of tins, made gloomy by Balkan drinks, suspended above real life, waiting for the trapdoor to open beneath him.

This would give him time to thin}, but Edward did not at that moment put much value on the power of thought. Earlier, yes; there were many, many occasions in the last few weeks when a little more time for thought might have saved him from trouble. He had been over-confident, full of himself, anxious for action. At the decisive moments of the last month, at Heathrow, at the Foreign Office, with Rosemary, at Sussex University, at Nightingales, and certainly last night, there had never seemed time for thought because of the rush of events, because action had been imperative. There was plenty of time for thought now that thought would do no good. To avert thought, he switched on the tiny radio by the bedside, finding at once the seven o'clock news.

'. . . and now, to assess the significance of this unexpected development, here is our political editor, Jeremy Coleridge. Good morning, Jeremy.'

'Good morning, Brian.'

'Jeremy, tell us honestly, were you surprised to find the Meridia debate brought forward to today?'

Edward forced his mind to concentrate.

'Well, Brian, the signs were there all right. It was clear that the Government wanted to get this awkward debate over and done with. It's a shrewd move, bringing it forward. We had all supposed it would be on an opposition supply day next week. Now, as you say, it's to be in government time today. The Opposition could hardly object, as they now have their supply day next week free for any other subject they like to choose. The people hardest hit are the Tory rebels.'

'We hope to have Sir Guy Winchilsea later in the programme, Jeremy. We tried Edward Dunsford, but he's still evidently playing hard to get. But why should the Tory rebels be upset? There's no logic in clamouring for a debate and then complaining when you get your way.'

'But you've put your finger on it, Brian. Like you, they can get no answer from Edward Dunsford. He's gone to ground. No one can find him. I can't remember anything like it before. More than half of Fleet Street is in search of him, and getting nowhere.'

'Why is that so important? It's only one vote.'

'Edward Dunsford is much more than one vote. He's the symbol of this cause. To coin a phrase, the debate without him is *Hamlet* without the Prince. Sir Guy Winchilsea is a good organiser and well-respected, but no one could call him an orator.'

'You mean, a bit too like Polonius to be a real winner?'

'Polonius, Brian?'

'Forget it, Jeremy. One last question. Is the Government going to be beaten?'

'If Dunsford stays away, they'll be safe. If Dunsford turns up and makes a good speech, touch and go.'

'Well, by this time tomorrow we shall know. And we shall certainly do our damnedest to get Edward Dunsford on the programme. Thank you, Jeremy.'

'Thank you, Brian.'

Edward switched off the radio abruptly, and lay back on the pillow, listening to the sparrows. The call of destiny relayed by the *Today* programme. Or a siren singing him to shipwreck on yet another rock?

For about half a minute the optimistic and pessimistic elements of his nature fought each other, but there was little doubt which would win. Even a tired and buffeted politician has to be an optimist at heart. And few things could be gloomier than sitting alone and purposeless in the cottage, now that the weather had turned and Sally had come and gone.

Edward swung out of bed, and found the railway timetable in the pocket of his overcoat, flung untidily over the bed. The early morning train from Penzance would get him into Paddington just before three. No Jack to meet him of course, but a taxi would get him to the Commons just as the debate started at three-thirty. No, there were questions on Thursday about the business for next week, so the debate would not start till four. Even better. And he would have plenty of time to write his speech on the train. Next he found the telephone number of the St Maws taxi service. At least they would be getting rich.

28

The Government Whips met at ten every morning when the House was sitting, in a room without windows, just off the Members' Lobby. In the evening the room was pleasant, comfortable with dark green leather chairs, oak panelling and a cupboard full of whisky. In the morning it was dark and frowzy. There was no one to make coffee. It was not clear whose job it was to empty the cigar ash from the big brass pedestal ashtrays. The Whips met there because they had always met there. Most days the meeting was short, gossipy, short on substance. But today's would be earnest.

'Did you hear Guy Winchilsea on the radio?' asked the youngest Whip.

'Thick as mud,' said his nearest colleague. They all listened to BBC Radio Four at breakfast. Rarely did they hear any radio or television for the rest of the day.

'We've cooked his goose. No Dunsford, no time to organise. I doubt he'll get a dozen in the lobby with him.'

It was meant to be an optimistic remark, but they fell

silent. If Winchilsea took a dozen with him to vote against the Government, and the Opposition voted in full strength in the same lobby, then the result would be a tie. Fortunately the Opposition had been slack lately, but then there were three government back-benchers ill, and several more abroad.

'To work,' said the Chief Whip.

Five in addition to Winchilsea had already told the Whips they would vote against the Government. Three were hopeless cases. Two needed speaking to again: one might be a junior minister soon if he behaved, the other was already in trouble with his constituency.

'Any chance of getting Winchilsea to make them all abstain?

They thought about this. They liked Winchilsea. He was a decent, wordy man, and there was no bitterness or dishonesty in him, and those were the qualities which the Whips distrusted most.

Reluctantly they discarded the idea. Winchilsea had gone too far in public. But those with him should certainly be leaned on to abstain.

There were six who had refused to give the Whips a straight answer, and five who had evaded the Whips altogether. Half of these were disappointed men, whom the Prime Minister had discarded or refused to promote. Three were keen aid men, devoted to the cause of world development.

'Surely the PM could put something in his speech to bring them round? It needn't be much. Send out a couple of British doctors to that hospital Edward Dunsford went to. That would do it.'

'No chance.' Francis Peretz, the Chief Whip, usually

shared his thoughts with his colleagues. Short, Jewish, bespectacled, he had been an unusual choice and had done extremely well. Today he was troubled.

'No chance because the PM won't do it, or because it wouldn't bring them round?'

'He won't do it.'

What troubled Peretz was the knowledge that the Foreign Office had put a proposal on these lines into the draft of the PM's speech. Foreign Office officials had managed to smuggle past Reid the idea of a small field hospital, with Britain taking the lead in organising and financing it. They had thought it would appeal to the Prime Minister as a manoeuvre if not as a field hospital. Only one million pounds in the aid budget. Peanuts as the price of saving the Government, but the PM had crossed it out at once and refused to discuss it. The draft speech when the Prime Minister went to bed had been notably unconciliatory. Peretz had told him so, and been thanked with a smile. Either the old man was losing his grip or he had some lurking thought to hide from his Chief Whip. Neither thought was comfortable.

Next to be reviewed came the invalids. They more or less cancelled out. Two Conservatives seriously ill in hospital, one elderly knight convalescing from a heart attack. They *could* have called in the elderly knight, who had been rash enough to convalesce at the Westminster Hospital nearby. But a telephone call to the Labour Whips showed that they had four sick whom they did not intend to bring in. That was a relief.

They turned with relish to those abroad. This was a familiar game, which they called 'cat and mouse'. The Whips did not care for foreign countries, being insular by profession, but they knew of their strong attractions for Members of Parliament. Indeed one of the favourite perquisites of parliamentary life was foreign travel. Many a select committee investigating pensions, or the curriculum in secondary schools, discovered the need to look in depth at parallel experiences in China or Peru. The Whips let them go, having little choice but, when they had the chance, delighted to claw them back.

'Too late I suppose to call back that lot from Pakistan?'

' 'Fraid so.'

They remembered how they had called back the Foreign Secretary himself from an official visit to Nepal some three months earlier. Patrick Reid had fussed, pulled every string, telephoned the Prime Minister, argued that he would miss his all-important audience with the King in Kathmandu. In vain: 'the Government in danger,' said the Whips, and back he had come, spending Monday in a plane, Monday night voting, Tuesday in a plane back to the sub-continent. The Government's majority that night had been twenty-nine, and Reid's double journey clearly unnecessary. A vintage occasion, and they had opened a bottle of champagne in the Whips' room when it was all over.

'There are the observers at the Disarmament Conference in Geneva. Three of ours, two of theirs.'

'How would our three vote?'

'Rock solid, though angry.'

'Have them back.'

'All three, or shall we pair the senior two with the Labour men?'

'All three. The Labour system is slacker. They may not get their two into the lobby.' And so it went on. As the arithmetic refined itself, it seemed almost certain that the Government would squeak home.

'No news of Edward Dunsford, I assume?' said Peretz, as they came towards the end.

'Rosemary genuinely doesn't know where he is. I'm sure of that. Nor does the Foreign Office. I tried Speyer's. I tried his agent. I even tried that nightclub where he had the bust up. Nothing.'

'*If, if* he turned up . . .'

'We'd have to do the sums again. At least a dozen more could stray.'

'Let me know at once if anyone hears anything.'

'What do we do if he rings in? Stranger things have happened.'

Peretz thought for a moment.

'Put him on to me.'

But he was not sure how he would handle that situation. Most men, in his experience, had their price. Sometimes a threat was enough. Sometimes a minor promise. Surprisingly often it was enough for Peretz to show that he understood the dissident's point of view for the dissident to abandon it. In those cases the price was a half-hour conversation. But that day, with all his experience, he could not imagine what Edward Dunsford's price might be.

Rosemary sat looking at the rain tumble into the little garden at Eaton Close. She had come up to London because she could not keep the girls any longer out of the Pembroke Square school where they were weekly boarders without exciting comment. It was a dull reason, and it had been a dull week. She had half-hoped, half-feared to find Edward. There were indeed signs of Edward. He had made the bed in a masculine sort of way which was easily detectable. Likewise he had washed his breakfast plate, cup and saucer, but had left them conspicuously to drain. The evidence suggested a one-night stay, presumably Monday. Now it was Thursday. Rosemary did not know whether her marriage was over. She itched for a good old-fashioned row, without knowing what would come out of it.

Where the hell was he? She had glanced at *The Times* and absorbed the news that the Meridia debate had been brought forward to that day and that Fleet Street knew no more than she about Edward's whereabouts. If he had really hidden himself he might not have heard about the debate. That really would be unfair. Combative by nature, over-dosed with a sense of the dramatic, fond of Edward though unable to live peaceably with him, Rosemary felt deeply for half an hour or so that it would be ludicrous and wrong for that debate to take place without Edward. She searched her mind yet again for some due to his whereabouts – and found it. Next she found Garth's number in the red and white Paperchase book by the telephone. It was worth a try.

Edward had caught the train with three minutes in hand. Crossing the Tamar, brushing the south coast of Devon, watching the rain against the soft hillsides, he was happier than for some time past. Going to the cottage had not been a success, coming away from it was better. He liked the solitude of his first-class compartment, the strong taste of the coffee on the ledge before him, the swift old-fashioned motion of the train, and the smooth flow of the pen which transferred the thoughts from his brain to the notebook on his knee. After several days of chaos he was faced again with a specific challenge. He had to make a successful speech in the Commons that evening. This was an end in itself. None of the long-term questions had been answered, but a short-term objective had been interposed, and that was something. The Speaker was bound to call him, as a Privy Councillor and as the prime mover of the Meridia question. The House would tolerate twenty minutes from him, so he must do it in fifteen. The effective speeches were always somewhat shorter than the audience expected; long-windedness was the mark of the second-rate politician. To speak for fifteen minutes required notes for twelve minutes, for three to five minutes would certainly be needed to deal with interjections. His notes would have to include at least a couple of passages to be kept in or left out by last-minute decision. Warming to a familiar task of his profession, Edward scribbled contentedly.

Mrs Treyarnon was not best pleased. Monday was her day to go to Mr Andrew's cottage and check that all was in order. Thursday was quite a different day, with different duties and pleasures allotted to it, including the taking of tea with her married daughter in Truro. But Mr Andrew had been very definite on the telephone, very worried about Mr Dunsford, almost fierce in his insistence that Mrs Treyarnon, regardless of the days of the week, should go up and see what if anything was happening.

Obliging Mr Andrew was not exacting. Ten pounds a week was not bad just for hobbling down the lane and once round the cottage to make sure nothing was amiss.

Thirty pounds a week was not bad for the little bit of cleaning and washing-up involved when Mr Andrew or his friends were down for a long weekend. So it was worth hanging on to the job, even though today it meant putting herself out. Moreover, to Mrs Treyarnon, nurtured on soap operas and romantic women's magazines, there was the chance of a bit of excitement. After all, Mr Dunsford had become a personality now, and she would recognise his face from the television.

But it turned out to be only a matter of dirty glasses and an unmade bed, slept in by one person only so far as she could tell. Mrs Treyarnon had half-expected the corpse of a prominent politician or at least a suicide note. As she rinsed the glasses, she felt a mild sense of grievance. Mrs Merritt next door had received a cheque for fifty pounds from the *Daily Express* simply for reporting on a village argument about the smell of pig effluent from a nearby farm. Mr Dunsford lying dead in his bed would have been worth a lot more.

But that was the wrong way to look at it. Mrs Treyarnon sat down rather hard on the kitchen stool. Someone had certainly been at the cottage. Someone with a woman, because there had been a trace of lipstick on one of the glasses. Mr Andrew had certainly thought it was Mr Dunsford. Everyone, certainly including the *Daily Express*, was looking for Mr Dunsford. She, Mrs Treyarnon, had found Edward Dunsford, or at least his coffee cup and brandy glass. She could ask at least one hundred pounds, perhaps two hundred, perhaps even have her photograph in the papers. She decided to use the telephone in the cottage to save her bill at home. And after all, she might have been mistaken, there might have been two in that bed if they had lain close enough together. That sort probably did snuggle close. Mrs Treyarnon dialled directory enquiries, as her port of entry to the *Daily Express*, wealth and fame.

It was not an easy day at 10 Downing Street. As usual the staff were in turmoil, and the Prime Minister calm. Michael Berinsfield had specialised in calm throughout his term of office, and it had served him well. But he liked a certain agitation in his staff, and was not above stirring it up himself if necessary.

Thursday was always active because of Prime Minister's question time in the Commons between three fifteen and three thirty. Not that Berinsfield had much trouble with the Opposition nowadays. It was a matter of technique. The procedure of the House gave the Prime Minister the last word, the art was to use that advantage to please your supporters and gain a headline in the next day's press. The careful briefing on every issue of the day would take place in the Prime Minister's upstairs flat over cold meat and salad at one o'clock.

Today there was the much greater excitement of the Meridia debate, which the Prime Minister would open at four. He had worked at the text of the speech overnight, and it was being retyped by a relay of Garden-Room girls, skilled in deciphering the tiny twisted scrawls with which the Prime Minister amended the text drafted for him. Several besides Peretz had noticed how hard in tone the speech had become as a result of those scrawls.

Now the Prime Minister, alone in his study, was reading a second text, the draft of the speech with which the Foreign Secretary was to wind up the debate immediately

336

before the crucial vote at 10 p.m. that evening. He read calmly, making no notes, smiled to himself, and rang the bell. By the time his Principal Private Secretary presented himself, however, he was in ill humour.

'This won't do. Has the Foreign Secretary seen it himself?'

'I understand he made some changes yesterday, and is working on it again now.'

'It won't do at all. A lot of rubbishy platitudes. Typical Foreign Office bran. It's quite out of line with my opening speech.'

'Certainly, as your speech is now . . .'

'I'll do it myself.'

'Do it yourself, Prime Minister?'

'Yes I'll wind up as well as open. There are plenty of precedents.'

'Sir Patrick won't be pleased.'

'Then the sooner you tell his office the better. The Prime Minister's compliments to the Foreign Secretary, and since his speech for this evening is not up to scratch, there will be no need for him to make it.'

Robin Monteith, Principal Private Secretary, looked at his master, gauging his mood. Usually when they were alone together he could penetrate these moods of arrogance, which were essentially artificial, an attempt by the Prime Minister to conceal the real direction in which his mind was moving. The draft speech for Sir Patrick Reid, though certainly platitudinous, in no way strayed from the agreed government line, and both men knew it. Berinsfield wanted to control the end of the debate personally, and Monteith could only guess why. But guessing of this kind was something he was trained to be good at.

It was sometimes convenient to both minister and civil servant that the motives of the former should be understood by the latter without any word being spoken.

'If you persevere with this, Prime Minister,' said Monteith, 'I am sure that you should tell the Foreign and Commonwealth Secretary yourself.'

The Prime Minister thought for a few seconds. Then, 'Very well.' He lifted the receiver on his desk. 'Please call the Foreign Secretary. I would like to speak to him whatever he is doing.' Monteith had noticed before that there was something in poor Reid's character which brought out the bully in the character of his colleagues; perhaps it was the fact that he was a bully himself when he could manage it.

There was a pause.

'Ah, Patrick, good morning. All well with the world and the Foreign Office, I trust? . . . Excellent. I have been thinking of our debate this afternoon. You have heard that the latest Whips' report is really very optimistic? No sign of your friend Edward, and Winchilsea has failed to muster more than a handful . . . Yes, considerably better than we supposed yesterday, so I think we can relax about the debate, and concentrate on more important things. So much so that rather than trouble you I think I shall wind up myself, a few minutes will be enough, low key, perfunctory almost . . . Yes, of course I know, it's a perfectly adequate speech though I think it would have needed a good deal more work from you personally. Officials rarely have much idea about a wind-up speech . . . I realise that, but of course what the press have been told the press can be untold. There will be no difficulty whatever about that. I shall instruct Singer to tell them that I have asked you to concentrate on the international aspects, on the contacts with the Americans and with Hamid, and that it is really more sensible, in view of the highly sensitive nature of the subject, that you should stay out of the hurly-burly of today's debate . . . On the contrary, I undertake that it will be presented in a way which enhances your authority as the architect of our diplomacy . . . Yes, I really would prefer it that way. I have thought about it earnestly. I am most grateful for your understanding. I will let your officials know what supplementary briefing I need . . . That is most kind. Goodbye.'

Monteith grinned. He had been listening on the extension. It was that grin which had got him the job over three other applicants of equal ability.

'What are you grinning at?' said the Prime Minister.

'He was outmanoeuvred rather than convinced.'

'Of course, but that is sufficient.'

There was a pause. Monteith was reluctant to leave the room.

'Is there anything more I should do?'

'You mean, is there anything more I can tell you?'

'If you put it that way, Prime Minister.'

'There *is* just one more thing. It is possible, not probable mark you, but just possible, that I might want to see the Queen tonight, rather late and rather urgently. Could you very informally find out if that would be feasible?'

Monteith grinned again.

'I guessed right.'

'I do not know what you mean. You are not paid to guess.'

But they both knew that was untrue.

29

The train, having started briskly in Cornwall and Devon, had begun to slow down, stop between stations, lurch forward again, and in general show signs of hesitation and unease. During one of these greenfield stops Edward asked the ticket-collector, a dignified Sikh, what was amiss.

'Potential industrial trouble at Paddington, sir.'

'What on earth does that mean?'

'I am unfortunately not in a position, sir, to give further clarification.'

Eventually, at about two thirty, the train came to a halt at Newbury racecourse, about an hour out of London. There were no races, no one about. By this time Edward's sense of contentment had long vanished. In the House of Commons, sixty odd miles away, the Speaker would be at prayers. For two minutes he and a handful of members in the Chamber of the House of Commons would join with the incumbent of St Margaret's Westminster in praying for the health of the Queen and the tranquillity of her realm.

Then an hour of questions, then half an hour discussing next week's business, then the Meridia debate. Edward's speech notes lay tidily on the ledge on front of him. It would be a good speech, if he ever got to make it.

The Sikh reappeared. His beard was grave.

'I am sorry to have to inform you, sir, that this train terminates here.'

'What's happened?'

'Operational reasons, sir.'

'What the bloody hell does that mean?' Even in normal circumstances it was a phrase calculated to enrage. The Sikh remained calm.

'It means that Paddington Station is closed, sir, on account of industrial action. No train may enter, no train may leave. Our train is instructed to terminate here, thus avoiding any increase in the current congestion.'

'What's the cause of the strike?' But that was a useless question and Edward abandoned it. 'What are your passengers supposed to do?'

'I understand, sir, that taxis have been telephoned for, there is a bus service to Newbury town, and I am authorised to refund you the portion of your ticket which covers the journey Newbury to Paddington, sir.'

He began laboriously to fill in a credit note, but Edward had no time for this. After hours of sitting still he felt full of physical energy. There would only be one or two taxis at best. He pushed the speech notes into his case, jerked the carriage door open, and sprinted down the platform.

They both felt in their bones that it was a story which must not be allowed to get away from the *Daily Express*.

One of them was paid to doubt, but he did so perfunctorily.

'You're a frustrated politician holed up in a cottage in Cornwall, and you suddenly hear on the radio that the debate you're passionately interested in is being held that day. You have no car. What do you do?'

'We know Dunsford was at the cottage, the bit about the radio is guesswork.'

'We know he was there, we know he left in a hurry. No paper by that hour. Anyway, what does he do next?'

'Train?'

'Right. Look 'em up. Don't bother, I've done it. Eight fifty Truro. Paddington three. He'd just catch the train. He'll just make the debate.'

'He might hire a car.'

'They don't have the kind of hire-car at St Mawes that you can just dump in London. And he'll want to work on his speech. You can't do that in a car. And you can't hire a car without giving your name. He's still trying to cover his tracks. He wants to make a dramatic entrance to the Commons, remember. A train's the thing.'

'So he just makes the debate.'

'No, he doesn't. Look at this.' It was a slice from the agency tapes. 'No trains entering or leaving Paddington. Incoming trains stopped outside London. Rail chaos, thousands stranded, etc., etc.'

'So?'

'So, find out where the eight fifty from Truro got washed up. Get our local lad into action. And a photographer. Ring the stationmaster, all the taxi firms, car hire, the lot. It's an *Express* exclusive and it could be big.'

'If it exists.'

'Correction. It's *got* to be big. Otherwise it won't run till tomorrow. And don't spare the cottage in Cornwall either. Did the daily lady say lipstick on the glasses?'

'And Russian brandy on the table.'

'Russian, you say? Jesus Christ, what are we waiting for?'

Sir Guy Winchilsea, sitting in the library of the Travellers' Club, patted first his stomach and then the speech notes by the cup of coffee in front of him. He was satisfied with both. He had lunched alone off the cold table and a small carafe of club claret. Soon it would be time to go down to the House. It had stopped raining, and he would walk across the park, not forgetting his umbrella. He had written that morning a short note to the Speaker saying that he hoped to catch his eye during the Meridia debate. Sir Guy was not a Privy Councillor and therefore had no priority on the list. But he was reasonably confident that he would be called. The Speaker would have read the press, listened to the radio; he would know that Sir Guy had put himself at the head of the small group of Conservative rebels.

Sir Guy had been vexed yesterday, but was serene again today. He had been vexed because he disliked the sharp tactics of the Government in bringing forward the debate. With Dunsford present there would have been a chance of defeating the Government and getting more help for Meridia. That was what Sir Guy wanted, for he was not personally ambitious. He would rather have served under Dunsford in a successful enterprise than led the sedate but unsuccessful rebellion of which he was now in charge. He had no illusion about his own speaking ability.

No votes would be swayed by his plummy voice. But there it was, he had no choice. Dunsford had behaved bravely over Meridia, but now discourteously in going to ground and not returning any of Sir Guy's calls. There must be something unstable about the fellow.

Sir Guy gathered together his notes, and the assorted press cuttings and White Papers which his research assistant had collated for him. Perhaps there were too many statistics in his speech, but it was too late to alter now. Sir Guy was never one to improvise. He finished his coffee and slowly descended the staircase, using the handrail installed for Talleyrand.

'Good afternoon, Sir Guy. Going to speak today?' This from a Permanent Secretary of progressive tendencies on the way upstairs.

'I hope so. I hope so.'

And so, with a touch of self-satisfaction, out into Pall Mall. Sir Guy, aged sixty-two, had achieved a way of life which, though dull and often mocked, was pleasant to himself and mildly useful to others.

'The Foreign Office thought you should see this, sir.'

They were under pressure of time. The Prime Minister, having answered questions in a somewhat restive House, had come out for a few minutes to his office down the corridor from the Chamber to read his speech for the last time. He would have to be back in the Chamber in ten minutes. The last moments before a major speech were often snappy.

Sandford-Smith's latest telegram was put in front of him. It was too long to read.

'What does it say?'

'The Ambassador has talked separately to the Meridian Foreign Minister and to his American colleague. He thinks things are changing again.'

'He's a fool, of course they are changing. A country like that is never still. What does he mean?'

'It's not very clear, Prime Minister. But conceivably Hamid may be coming back to the West, and the Americans may be preparing to receive him.'

'And the MEECON plan?'

'Too soon to say, sir, but if this is right the Americans would obviously want to scupper it.'

'And we will be asked to contribute to the alternative.' Berinsfield saw it all clearly. The calf would be fatted for the return of the prodigal. More aid would be needed for Meridia. He never ceased to marvel at the precise ironies of political life. Dunsford was going to be ruined, and Dunsford was going to be proved right. But strictly in that order. It was no good trying to alter the natural sequence of things. And these were emphatically not thoughts for the staff.

'Let's get it straight. All of this is surmise?'

'Yes'

'As of this afternoon, neither the Opposition, nor Dunsford wherever he is, nor Winchilsea knows of any change in the position?'

'There is no definite change to know of.'

'There is nothing inaccurate in this speech I'm about to make?'

'Nothing at all inaccurate.'

'The Americans are still hopeful of agreement with the Russians at Geneva?'

'So far as we are aware.' They all knew the connection,

for they had often discussed it. So long as there was hope of a strategic arms reduction agreement at Geneva the US Administration would not want a major row with the Russians over Meridia.

'Fine. I must go back. Put the Mangara telegram in my overnight box.'

Edward Dunsford had just passed the most frustrating ninety minutes of his life. Newbury was a deeply incompetent and unhelpful place. He had found a taxi at the race-course station, but a taxi mean and parochial in spirit which refused to take him to London, and dropped him merely at the nearest local car-hire firm. All their cars were out on hire. A businessman on the same train as Edward had just taken the last one. By the time this had been established and confirmed the taxi had disappeared. There was some telephoning. Edward walked up Northbrook Street to the clock and then right along the Old London Road towards another garage which had said it had a Maestro available. The rain had stopped, but there was a keen wind and Edward had no coat. The garage was substantially further along the road than Edward had been led to believe.

But there at last, round a corner, the inane little flags fluttered, the used cars paraded more blatantly than the local planners had allowed, the petrol pumps shaved a penny off all nearby competitors, and the proprietor Mr Ernest Hodson was ready with a Maestro. There were two other men on the forecourt, but Mr Hodson was evidently ready to deal with Edward first. Edward looked at his watch – five to four. He would be in the House of Commons well before six. Normally someone who wanted to speak in a debate was expected to be there throughout, and certainly to listen to the opening speeches from the front benches. But the Speaker could make exceptions, and no circumstances could be more exceptional than these.

He wrote his cheque as requested, and produced his bank card. Mr Hodson either did not notice or was not surprised at the name. He would arrange to have the car picked up at Eaton Close the next morning.

'Driving licence?'

Driving licence. Edward looked in the inner pocket of his wallet, but he knew it was not there. He had needed it the other day to fill in a registration form; it was in the third left-hand drawer of his desk in London.

'Haven't got it, I'm afraid.'

Silently Mr Hodson, large in a pale grey flannel suit, handed Edward back his cheque.

Edward could almost hear his self-control snap. All day he had managed to dominate his anxiety, tiredness, sense of defeat by concentrating on the debate. He had rallied his remaining energy and concentrated it on getting to Westminster and making there the speech of his life. He was not going to be thwarted now by a silly rule about a driving licence.

He shouted at Mr Hodson, at his bald head, bulbous nose, self-righteous expression, at Newbury, at British Rail, at Rosemary, at Sally, at the Prime Minister. He behaved entirely out of character.

'My name is Edward Dunsford, and I've bloody well got to get to London this afternoon to speak in the House of Commons. My driving licence is in London, you can see it for yourself tomorrow. Now, get out of my fucking way.'

A big hand restrained him.

'Not so fast. I know who you are, Mr Dunsford, and I know what you're about, and I don't like either. I don't hold with dishing out our money to black dictators. But that's neither here nor there. The point is, no driving licence, no car hire. It's the law of the land.'

The two men already on the forecourt had joined them. One of them now muttered to Mr Hodson and touched his arm. The other made Edward a tiny gesture towards the Maestro, parked ten yards away, front door open, key in the ignition.

Edward hesitated, but only for a second. His inhibitions had temporarily vanished. Grabbing his despatch case, he ran to the car and jumped in. She started at once. As he revved he heard Mr Hodson shout, saw in the mirror Mr Hodson break away from the two men and move towards him. Luckily there was a pause in the London-bound traffic on the main road, so Edward did not have to wait. As he swung out from the garage on to the tarmac he saw the flash of the camera behind him.

The House was full when at four precisely the Prime Minister opened the debate on Meridia. He began deliberately in a tone of arid authority which the House knew well, and which helped to keep it quiet. He set out in detail the aid projects financed by Britain in Meridia in recent years, the main commercial contracts run by British firms, the visits paid by ministers in both directions. This was dull stuff, most of it irrelevant, designed to portray in uncontroversial terms a close and solid relationship between the two countries.

'Now my Right Honourable Friend, the Member for

East Sussex – whose absence—' he glanced round inter-
rogatively – 'yes, whose absence from this debate we all
regret – developed the conviction that all this was not
enough, and that we should do more. His conviction was
formed during a brief visit to Meridia, and quickly
became a raging torrent of enthusiasm. Now, Mr Speaker,
enthusiasm is an admirable quality in any member of this
House. But a junior minister in particular needs to be
sure that his enthusiasms are in harmony with the strategy of the Government which he has agreed to join –
strategy worked out painstakingly at meetings which he
has not attended and based on reasoning with which he
cannot be fully familiar. This precaution my Right
Honourable Friend neglected, with the consequences
which the House knows, and which he was the first to
accept were inevitable.'

The House was listening attentively, without interruption, as it usually does when a speaker is at the kernel of
his argument.

'But of course this present controversy did not arise
simply because of views held by my Right Honourable
Friend. The views of a junior minister, however distinguished his record, are not in themselves usually
explosive material. The present controversy arose because
my Right Honourable Friend visited a hospital which was
at the same time host to a British television team, because
he was met on his return by an inordinate number of
journalists, and because last Sunday he gave an intem-
perate interview to a local BBC radio station. I would
certainly not accuse my Right Honourable Friend of seek-
ing publicity – any more than the fly seeks the flypaper –
but the result is even so a rather sticky mess.'

He had thought of this metaphor five minutes earlier and had jotted it at the edge of the typed text without deciding whether to use it. Perhaps it was a mistake, for Dunsford had personal as well as political friends, and there was a small murmur of dissent from behind him.

Sir Guy Winchilsea chose the moment to rise, and the Prime Minister at once gave way, sitting back on the front bench and cupping his ear, creating the impression that Sir Guy was so old and indistinct that every effort was required to catch his words.

'Would the Prime Minister, rather than making gibes against a respected colleague who is not here, turn his attention to the strong case which has been made out on strategic grounds for additional help for our old friends in Meridia to prevent them falling under Soviet domination?'

The Prime Minister had no difficulty with this.

'My Honourable Friend leads me neatly into the next part of my argument. But first I would say that my Honourable Friend is in one respect inaccurate. My Right Honourable Friend the Member for East Sussex *was* a colleague of mine in Government, but is no longer so. Regrettably he ceased to be a colleague precisely because he used against the Foreign Secretary and myself the kind of gibes which my Honourable Friend finds objectionable.'

Berinsfield drew to his close. The short, neat figure in the dapper suit, the dry voice, the stiff white collar, the careful logic, the occasional brutal thrust combined to create a formidable parliamentary technique.

There were three reasons, he concluded, for challenging the Government's policy. There was the purely factious reason. He expected the Opposition to vote against government policy tonight simply because it was government policy. There was the sentimental reason, but a government should take its decisions on the basis of sense not sensibility. We lived in a world containing millions of diseased and underfed human beings, some of them much nearer home than those with whom the debate was concerned. A government could not shift its aid policies each time a television crew, or even a junior minister, visited an African hospital. Third, there was the strategic argument. The House of Commons contained many armchair strategists who would doubtless have their say. No one in the Government underestimated the strategic importance of Meridia. What they did doubt was the argument that the only way of sustaining the West's interests in that part of Africa was to pump in more aid.

The Prime Minister sat down without attempting a peroration and without making a serious attempt to woo the rebels behind him. The cheer was respectful, not enthusiastic. There was a buzz of whispered comment.

'A hard speech,' said the Chancellor of the Exchequer, leaning across Patrick Reid on the front bench to congratulate the Prime Minister.

'I want to win the hard way, without any concessions.'

At that moment as grey old Walter Treadware, Leader of the Opposition, launched into his speech, a written note was passed to the Prime Minister from the box at the site of the Chamber which contained Monteith, Singer, and other staff from Number Ten and the Foreign Office. The Prime Minister reacted with irritation and showed the note to Reid. It was from Monteith.

'There has been an urgent new development. Grateful if you could come out for two minutes. R.M. 7/xi.'

Reid, easily flustered nowadays, assumed that some criticism of him was intended. 'I know nothing of this. I am aware of no new developments.'

'They ought to know by now that I can't leave the bench. Treadware is good for half an hour, and I expect the Speaker will call Winchilsea next. I must stay for that.'

The Prime Minister was not particularly deferential to the House of Commons, but no event, short of the cataclysmic, would have induced him to breach one of its basic rules of etiquette. A speaker must stay to hear the following speaker, and even after that it would be wrong to walk out as Winchilsea stood up.

So Monteith, cursing the strange sense of priorities which enveloped ministers once they were in the Palace of Westminster, had to scribble a full note.

Prime Minister,

I apologise for distracting you from the debate, but you should be aware of a strange telephone call which I received on your behalf at 4.10 p.m. from Mr Trenchard, editor of the *Daily Express*. The *Express* have succeeded in tracing Mr Dunsford, who is travelling to London to take part in this debate. His journey has not been without difficulty because of industrial action on British Rail Western Region. The sequence of events is not entirely clear, but it appears that Mr Dunsford is approaching London in a car which he drove away from a garage in Newbury half an hour ago without the authority of its owner and without completing the necessary contract. It is alleged that Mr Dunsford is thus technically guilty of stealing the vehicle. Its owner, a Mr Hodson, has told the representatives of the *Daily Express* that he wishes the decision whether or not he notifies the police of this incident to be referred to you. The implication in Mr Trenchard's mind is evidently that by notifying the police without further delay Mr Hodson could ensure that Mr Dunsford is stopped before he reaches Westminster.

R.M. 7/xi.

The Prime Minister at once scribbled on top.

'No games. Do not return Mr Trenchard's call. Do not approach the police. If the *Express* pursue the matter, tell them I am grateful, but it is not a decision for me.'

30

There was nothing for Sally to do in the office. No new minister had yet been appointed to succeed Edward. The blotter on his desk was virgin, outside on the window ledge the pigeons made their messes without interruption. The filing was in order, the last of the letters of sympathy acknowledged. James had taken a new girl-friend to race at Newmarket. One secretary was attending to her nails in the further office; the two other desks were empty. There was nothing for Sally to do except brood.

But this she refused to do. She had offered herself to Edward, they had made love, and he had abandoned her. The oldest story in the world, usually lasting months or years had been amazingly telescoped into a few minutes. Useless to ask herself if she was really in love with him, useless to wonder why he had finally rejected her, whether they could have lived together or how long it would have lasted. The idea had been killed at birth. Sally had a strong English instinct against brooding over dead emotions.

But what to do? She wanted to go to the Meridian debate. A young American had just telephoned asking for help in getting a ticket to the Commons. The name, Neil Wainwright, meant nothing to her, nor his claim to know both Edward and Rosemary. She had been short with him, but he had planted the idea in her mind. Edward would not be at the debate, but the arguments with which she had lived for the last few weeks would be marshalled on their last and conclusive parade. The Foreign Office would not let her have one of the few and treasured seats in the civil servants' box, for she was not involved in the briefing of the Prime Minister or the Foreign Secretary. She had asked, and been rebuffed. So instead she queued, unofficially, anonymously, outside St Stephen's entrance, beginning alongside the statue of Cromwell, shuffling forward through the discarded sweet wrappers and soft-drink tins to the door itself. Her bag was searched by security men. Then she queued again, sitting for a while where the old Commons Chamber had been before the fire of 1834, watching important unqueuing people, Members of Parliament, her own colleagues in the Foreign Office, constituents with an appointment, bustle unimpeded towards the scene of action. Then, when Prime Minister's Questions were over, some sated citizens left the public gallery and there was room for Sally. Up steep stairs, up more stairs, leave the handbag, receive the order paper, through a final door and there she was, above and opposite the Speaker, looking down on the two front benches of the House of Commons. The gallery was crowded and to reach the one empty seat she had to scramble past several spectators, Neil Wainwright whom of course she did not know, and finally a plump bespectacled man who looked like an intellectual monkey.

'Sorry.'

'Not at all . . . Aren't you, weren't you Edward Dunsford's Private Secretary?'

'Yes.' Damn, her anonymity was gone. 'How did you know?'

'It's going to be a funeral party without the corpse, don't you think?'

An usher descended upon them, tall, thin and pompous in a white tie.

'Quiet there, please. No talking allowed.'

The plump man giggled slightly when the usher had gone.

'Silence in church. How do you do?' They shook hands, pressed close together. 'My name is Garth Andrew.'

Edward Dunsford had intended to take a taxi from Paddington to Eaton Close, to change into a dark suit while the taxi ticked over. But at the wheel of the Maestro passing between Slough and Windsor he decided to go straight to the Commons in his frayed tweed jacket, check shirt and pullover. A travel-stained entry would, he admitted to himself, certainly be dramatic.

BBC Radio Three was carrying the debate live from the Commons. The Prime Minister's speech made Edward angry and brought his foot down hard on the accelerator. No one could be angry at the Leader of the Opposition's speech, which he had made many times before. Not for the first time, Treadware totally ignored a tactical opportunity. He spoke for forty minutes about our responsibilities to the third world. His peroration was deeply old-fashioned. He used to the full the resources of his deep Yorkshire voice as for the umpteenth time he summoned the nation to its imperial duty as defined by Labour: '. . . a duty based now not on regiments and district commissioners and governors in their plumes, not on the might and panoply of imperial power, based now on service, on mutual respect, on the goodwill of young men and young women helping each other regardless of racial, religious or political differences. That is our ideal. It is because the Government has fallen pitifully short of that ideal that we condemn them tonight.' The Labour benches cheered because they liked the old fellow and his peroration. But he had failed to put any of the awkward questions, failed to exploit the resignation of Edward Dunsford, failed to use the hammer of his voice to tap a wedge deeper into the split in the Tory Party.

Edward heard Treadware's peroration on the radio as he drove into New Palace Yard. The policeman stopped him, not knowing the Maestro, but Edward had his pass and was soon parked in the underground car park. The lift and then the moving staircase brought him quickly to the Members' Entrance. Up the stairs, and along the corridor into the Members' Lobby, where certain privileged journalists are allowed to lie in wait. Edward hoped that the lobby would be empty because the debate had begun, but there under the statue of Churchill, as if expecting him, was the Political Correspondent of the *Daily Express*.

'What about the car, then?'

'The car?' Edward had expected a question about his speech, now folded neatly in the inside pocket of the sports jacket.

'The car you pinched – the car you drove away in Newbury?'

'I didn't pinch it. It's in the car park below. I shall return it and pay for it tomorrow. Everything's in order.'

He brushed the man aside and went through the arch into the Chamber. Damn, that was something else to worry about. Trust the press to go for the trivial irrelevance. Calm, cool, cool, calm – he must concentrate on the essential.

Edward Dunsford went forward to stand with two or three other members at the bar of the House, at the other end of the Chamber to the Speaker, government benches on his left, opposition on his right. Sir Guy Winchilsea was on his feet, making a statistical comparison which he found compelling.

'. . . and so, Mr Speaker, we find in real terms a reduction in bilateral aid to Meridia of no less than 4.7 per cent . . .'

Although he knew it to be a dramatic figure Sir Guy was slightly surprised at the rising murmur of interest, indeed excitement, which it aroused. Glancing up from his notes, he saw Edward, hair slightly dishevelled, tie less than tightly tied, in clothes more suitable to the garden than to the House of Commons. Edward was at that moment profoundly different from the smooth Minister of State who had so often answered questions in the Chamber. But it was not a matter of his appearance. Edward was charged, for the moment only, with the electricity, the special energy, which comes to people faced in public with either signal success or deep failure.

'I interrupt my remarks, Mr Speaker, to welcome the

arrival of my Right Honourable Friend, the Member for East Sussex, whose energy . . .'

'Where's he been then?' from one Conservative. A cheer of approval from several parts of the House, though whether for Edward or for the rude question was unclear. Edward, having resigned, was of course not entitled to sit with other ministers on the front bench. He saw a space in the second row below the gangway and crossed to sit in it. He was squashed rather tight between two colleagues, one of whom welcomed him warmly while the other stared blankly to his front.

'On a point of order, Mr Speaker . . .' It was Charles Elliott from a back bench, well-groomed, dark-suited and evidently in a fury.

'Point of order, Mr Elliott?' said the Speaker. Poor Sir Guy Winchilsea, speech in tatters, resumed his seat.

'My point of order, Mr Speaker, concerns the procedure of the debate. It is a long-standing convention of this House that only those may speak in a debate who have been here in the Chamber for the opening speeches. For the guidance of the House, Mr Speaker, can you say whether the Chair intends to respect that convention fully and in every instance today?'

There was a murmur of approval from around Charles Elliott, and of dissent from the Labour side. The Speaker stilled both when he stood up.

'The Chair, while of course aware of the conventions of the House, has unfettered discretion in the choice of speakers.'

Charles Elliott again.

'Mr Speaker, further to that point of order, with all respect, that leaves us in the dark and I wonder . . .'

The Speaker was up again.

'No, we cannot go further into this. I have made the position clear. Sir Guy Winchilsea.'

Charles Elliott subsided. Edward marvelled, as often before, at the authority conferred by the actual chair, the breeches and buckles, and above all the great long wig of the Speaker, which effectively concealed any passing doubts or frailties which the human face within might otherwise have revealed.

But Edward was in a tactical difficulty. The Speaker had kept his options open, but the act of calling Edward to speak would now be controversial. Edward left the Chamber the way he had come in, apologising to the knees which he brushed past. He went round through the Aye voting lobby until he was behind the Speaker's chair, then alongside the Speaker, who bent expressionless towards him.

Hastily, and not very well, Edward explained why he had been delayed. The Speaker said nothing, but showed him a long list. It was 6 p.m. The front benches would begin the wind-up speeches at nine. That left three more hours for back-bench debate. On the Speaker's list were twenty names, that is a total of five hours' debate. This meant that many members would simply not be called. Only three of those on the list had, like Edward, the rank of Privy Councillor, which gave them a certain priority. But all of them had presumably attended the debate from the beginning.

'I would very much like to speak,' was all Edward could say.

The Speaker inclined head and wig again, still in silence, and the interview was over.

Back in his seat, the drama ebbed out of Edward. He could not hear the radio and television bulletins pumping out across the world the news of his dash across England and sensational arrival at the bar of the House. He was out of range of the feverish speculation of the pundits as to whether he would be called to speak, and what the effect might be. The world was excluded; for the next four hours the only reality was the House of Commons.

Speech followed speech, and each time a speech ended Edward stood up to catch the Speaker's eye.

'Better sit down,' said the stout man on his right, barely known to Edward.

'What?'

'Elliott was right. Bad form to come in here like that, and expect to speak.'

'I've got to speak.'

The man grunted.

The arguments became stale and repetitive. The House began to empty. The quality of speeches went downhill. Edward was hungry. He had had nothing since a hurried breakfast, but did not dare to leave the Chamber. He felt alone with his speech, but when he looked at it he saw it would not do. It had been fine that morning, as he scribbled alone in his first-class compartment, the hot strong coffee beside him. Now it seemed false and artificial, quite wrong for this uniquely frightening audience. Edward began to scratch passages out.

Seven thirty, and Charles Elliott was called. He went straight for Edward. It was the *Sunday Express* article all over again, this time with no fear of the libel lawyers. Everything said in the House was privileged. People trickled back into the Chamber to listen. Remembering a picture of Peel being attacked by Disraeli, Edward wished he had a hat to pull down over his brows. Charles was doing himself no good, for the House did not like this kind of personal attack. But he was also harming Edward, for some mud always stuck. From his angle of vision Edward watched the sharp, classical profile, and saw the colour mount in the sallow cheeks. He remembered Charles's room at Cambridge, how the roses below his window smelt fresh after rain, how he and Charles had developed the affectation of a glass of very dry sherry together each evening before crossing the court to dine in hall. He had not thought of that for many years. Politics had coarsened Charles: what had they done to him?

'. . . no hesitation in describing the whole episode as a shoddy manoeuvre by a minister hungry for advancement and publicity, eager also to help the bank with which he was and may again be connected. Although it is impertinent for the Right-Honourable Member to present himself as he has in this House today, and although I hope very much that he will not in view of that impertinence succeed in catching your eye, Mr Speaker, nevertheless I am glad that he is here. He will be able to see for himself that the House is not deceived. He will be able to measure the extent of his own failure, and the justice of the decision to exclude him from office.'

This went too far, and Charles Elliott sat down amid silence. A Labour member was called. The digital clock flicked onwards. It was past eight. Edward was now sunk in gloom. The Labour member began to defend him against Charles's attack, and his gloom deepened. The speech on his knee was too clever, too trite, and yet there was no time to rewrite it, and if he left the Chamber to do so, he would certainly lose his chance to speak. The House emptied fast, for the Labour member was a great bore and it was dinner time. Soon there were only a dozen on the opposition benches and two dozen on the government side, several of them only there because they too wanted to speak.

What was the point? For twelve hours now he had concentrated all his effort on preparing the speech and getting to Westminster to deliver it. Despite the many frustrations, he had enjoyed the day, precisely because it had been a day of action with a clear objective. But after all what was the point? To swing the vote against the Government? Even that now seemed beyond his reach, but even if he could bring it off, what then? Would it help Meridia? Would it help those black babies? Would it reconcile him with Rosemary, undo his resignation, sweep him to a political success? Hard to imagine any such things. He thought about Rosemary, but the thought gave no help.

Then he saw Sally and Garth Andrew in the public gallery, high above him to the right. He could make neither head nor tail of that. So far as he knew, Sally had no connection or even acquaintance with Garth. But then he had thought the same about Sally and Charles. He gave her a little signal of friendship, a tiny wave and lift of the head, and she at once responded. Edward reflected that in a novel the sight of his girl would have chased away the hero's doubts and inspired him to the speech of his life. But this was not a novel, Sally was not his girl, and the speech he held in his hand was a mess, which her presence would make even more embarrassing. Edward Dunsford decided not to speak.

At that moment the Labour MP sat down, having spoken for twenty-two minutes. A dozen members in all parts of the House stood up. The huge wig of the Speaker revolved as he assessed the situation. Edward felt as if caught in a radar beam. As if under the impulse of rays emanating from the wig, without any conscious reversal of the decision he had just taken, he half-rose.

'Mr Dunsford.'

He had caught the Speaker's eye. It was nearly half past eight. Charles was on his feet at once.

'Point of order, Mr Speaker.'

'Point of order, Mr Elliott.'

'Reverting to the point I raised earlier, Mr Speaker, about members who try to speak without . . .'

'I have dealt with that point already. The choice of speakers is entirely a matter for the Chair. It cannot be discussed here. Mr Dunsford.'

Charles was on his feet again. The Speaker warned him down and for a moment Charles stood in rebellion. But he realised the point was lost, and subsided on to the green leather.

Edward began by apologising for his late arrival. That was easy enough, for the House always likes apologies. Members began to come back into the Chamber, some still wiping wine or food from round their lips. The trickle grew into a stream; the press gallery too began to fill.

But for what? Edward began to speak from his notes, beginning with an analysis of the strategic importance of Meridia and the story of the MEECON project. He had worked this out carefully so as to avoid any mention of the intelligence reports, but had just crossed half of it out as unconvincing. The remaining half certainly failed to convince. With part of his mind, Edward wrestled to turn his notes into speech; with the other half he watched the House, as if from the gallery. He heard a rising buzz from the members standing at the bar of the House, who turned to conversation among themselves as his words failed to grip them. The Prime Minister came in and sat by the Foreign Secretary on the front bench. Edward saw but could not catch the short, no doubt contemptuous, remark with which Patrick Reid brought him up to date. He saw Charles Elliott give an ostentatious yawn, arms outstretched along the back of the bench to his left.

This was no bloody good. Edward let his notes fall on to the seat beside him. Here goes, he thought. I shall probably never speak here again.

'I can't explain my actions without explaining what it is like to be a minister, a junior minister, in this or any other Government. It is hard work, it takes a lot out of you, and most of it is just not worth while.' There was a stir of interest. Members at the bar of the House stopped chatting among themselves. The Opposition front-bench spokesman with the longest legs took them off the table in front of him. Journalists from the superior papers in the press gallery scribbled languidly in long hand. The Prime Minister looked up from the letters he was signing.

'Most of the decisions you take could go the other way without disaster. They are sixty-forty decisions, or fifty-five-forty-five, or fifty-fifty. You coast along from day to day, enjoying yourself, treated on the whole as rather more important than you are, knowing privately that the Government and the country could rub along very well without you.'

'Hear, hear,' muttered a few of Edward's enemies; but he was not listening now to anyone but himself.

'But every now and then, out of your in-tray, out of some despatch or telegram or conversation, comes a question of quite a different order. The ordinary compromises of Whitehall and Westminster are no longer adequate. The answer comes not from some Cabinet committee, not from splitting the difference with the Treasury, not from a negotiation with the Opposition through the usual channels. It suddenly becomes clear that the ordinary processes of government and Parliament will not do, and that you can only be content with the answer which springs from your own intelligence and your own judgement. So it was with myself and the question of Meridia.'

The Prime Minister was on his feet, amused but wary and anxious to deflate. Edward at once gave way and sat down.

'I am grateful to my Right Honourable Friend who is giving us a fascinating analysis, not of Meridia, but of his own state of mind. I can assure him that such dreams of infallibility and absolute power are not confined to Ministers of State. They also occasionally afflict Prime Ministers. But is this not a doctrine wholly destructive of Cabinet government, indeed of parliamentary government? Surely it is not enough for my Right Honourable Friend to tell us that he was sure he was right? He has to persuade us of the reasons for this, and so far he has hardly attempted to do so.'

'The reasons are clear enough, they are well known to every member of the House.' Edward was in full flight now, finding his words easily, putting them forcefully.

'Meridia is a country important in its own right, doubly important to us because of our long connection and friendship. It is desperately poor, and its people need help. It has turned for help to a combination of Soviet power and American money in the project MEECON, which would be dangerous to our interests and fatal to Meridia. We can and should reverse our policy. All that has been said already. As for myself, I could have argued the case more discreetly. I could have contented myself with a few hundred thousand pounds of extra aid which would no doubt have been thrown to me under the Cabinet system to which the Prime Minister refers. Instead I behaved in a quixotic, some would say, self-indulgent way. I spoke out. I argued the case in public, and in the end I resigned.'

'Sacked,' said Charles Elliott loudly. Edward swung round on him.

'I accept the correction. Technically I resigned, in fact I was sacked. But I could have stayed on if I had kept my mouth shut and concentrated on my in-tray.

'Mr Speaker, the world is run not unlike the Prime Minister's Cabinet. Governments rub along together, speaking half their minds, preferring half-measures, half-hearted about everything. And I must tell the House that Britain is the expert, the acknowledged leader, in this manner of proceeding. We do not have the armed might, the financial resources, the technical skill of others. But when it comes to fudging an argument, perfecting a plat-itude, dressing up inaction as action – in all the arts of compromise we are acknowledged supreme. And these arts have their place in this humdrum world. I do not contest that. But sometimes, just occasionally, it is right to speak out, to abandon the middle position, to prefer courage to caution, to take the lead. Because I am absolutely and utterly convinced that Britain should take the lead over Meridia, I take my place on these benches tonight and appeal to the House to give ministers by their vote tonight an impulse to the act of leadership which is now so clearly needed.'

Well, thank God it was over. That was Edward's first reaction. There was a friendly cheer of approval as he sat down. It had certainly not been the speech of his life. The attendant tried to pass him an empty brown envelope, as was the habit, into which he could put his notes as an aid to the verbatim reporters of *Hansard*, but Edward had to shrug it away. There were no notes. There had been almost no argument. Simply an egotistical repetition of his own conviction. A young member passed him a note – 'Many congratulations. Just the job.' An older member, on his way back to the dining-table, muttered in his ear, 'Congratulations.' Sir Guy Winchilsea, who had no vanity, smiled kindly across the benches. So, within limits, it had been a success. Or, more likely, they were really congratulating him not on the speech but on the last four weeks. Either way, it was encouraging.

But the main thing was that it was over. He had forgotten Sally, and now when he looked up at the gallery he could not catch her eye. He looked along the rows. No sign of Rosemary anywhere, of course. He hardly listened to the two wind-up speeches. Nor indeed was there much to listen to. The Opposition front-bencher repeated Treadware's speech without the same eloquence. The Prime Minister was terse, unyielding, and cutting about Edward's speech. 'It is a new doctrine that the vote of the House should depend not on the merit of the argument but on the strength of the emotions of a retired junior minister.' There was some ritual noise as the clock approached ten, but the Prime Minister shrugged it off. '. . . the truth is that we are doing and shall continue to do our best for Meridia. We do not intend to be pushed by a temporary and ill-considered emotional spasm into new commitments which this country cannot afford.'

'The motion is that this House do now adjourn. Those in favour say "Aye".'

A strong shout of 'Aye' from the Government benches.

'Those against "No".'

Loud Noes from the Opposition, and from Edward and Guy Winchilsea.

'I think the Ayes have it.'

'No.'

'Clear the lobbies.'

The bells rang. And the policemen passed the cry in three long syllables from officer to officer through the Palace of Westminster. 'Dee – vee – shun'.

In the No Lobby, Edward could tell at once that it would be close. He spotted, self-conscious among the Labour and Alliance members, at least eight Conservatives. Everything would depend on how many abstained.

As the four tellers formed up after the vote there was a great roar of excitement from the Labour side. Their two tellers were forming on the right, and one of them held the crucial piece of paper. This meant that the Government had lost. The four men marched more or less in step from the bar to the mace in front of the Speaker's chair, and the senior Labour teller read the result in stentorian voice.

'The Ayes to the right 296.

'The Noes to the left 301.'

The Speaker, standing in majesty, repeated the figures: 'So the Noes have it.'

So he had done it. Would Rosemary count that as success or failure?

Cheering and counter-cheering, and waving of order papers on the Labour benches. Edward calculated that there must have been at least twenty Conservative abstentions.

'You did it,' said the fat colleague at his side.

'I think not.'

'Yes, you did. Winchilsea hadn't a hope without you. Disloyalty sometimes does produce results. But only in the short term. You'll see.' He would have continued in this vein, but the Prime Minister was on his feet.

'It might be convenient for the House to have a statement of the Government's intentions tonight. I ask the indulgence of the House for a delay of about twenty minutes . . .'

There was some pointless scoring of points by either side, and the Speaker suspended the sitting until ten forty-five.

As Edward left the Chamber past the Speaker's chair to his surprise he found the Prime Minister waiting for him. The two men stood aside from the stream of loudly talking members.

'Well done. A good speech. It made the difference.'

'It wasn't really a good speech.'

'No, it wasn't really. You can make a speech like that once in a career, and win with it. Not more.'

'I shan't make it again,' said Edward.

'No, I somehow don't think you will. But there's something else I wanted to say. Fix up that car business quickly, won't you?'

'Car?' Edward had genuinely forgotten. 'How on earth do you know about that?'

The Prime Minister smiled.

'When you think harshly of me, just remember that I *did* know about it. And I held my hand.'

There was nothing obvious for Edward to do. There would be a flood of requests for television and radio interviews, but they could not reach him where he stood behind the Speaker's chair, and he was not ready for them. So he might as well sort out the business of the car.

On the telephone Mr Hodson was only slightly rude. They fixed up a time and place for handing back the Maestro in London the next day. Edward agreed to pay an extra twenty pounds 'just to cover the annoyance'.

'Pity, in a way.'

'Pity?'

'You beat the Government just now, didn't you?'

'They lost, yes.'

'And we'll all have to pay more taxes to feed those blacks. The point is, you did it in my Maestro, and I could have stopped you.'

'I got away too fast.'

'Not then, later. The police could have stopped you long before you got to London. But he wouldn't let me tell them.'

'Who?'

'The Prime Minister, of course. Or rather, his office, when I asked them what I should do.'

Edward put down the receiver slowly.

The Prime Minister intercepted Monteith, his Principal Private Secretary, as the civil servants came down the narrow steps from the row of uncomfortable seats called 'the box' in which they had spent the last six hours. They had been locked in during the division itself, presumably lest, maddened by silence, they should break out and begin haranguing the legislators on their way into the voting lobbies.

'All the members of the Cabinet you can find. And the Chairman of the party. At once in my room.'

And so they gathered, in dribs and drabs, gossiping on their way through the ante-room about the debate.

'Jack would never have called him in his day. He was a real Speaker.'

'Not much choice, I'd say.'

'Technically it's only a vote on the adjournment.'

'Extraordinary old sports jacket he was wearing.'

'I'm told he rammed a lamp-post and drove into the car park at eighty miles an hour.'

The chatter died away as they came into the main room and saw the Prime Minister standing in front of the fireplace. The fire was unlit, the room bleak and unwelcoming. The Prime Minister motioned them to armchairs, then to small upright chairs in dark green leather, but himself remained standing.

'A good speech, Prime Minister,' ventured the Minister of Transport, young, chubby and ambitious, not quite up to it.

'No,' said the Prime Minister simply.

He waited until they were all in the room. Monteith hovered in the doorway, uncertain whether to go or stay.

'Prime Minister, the Secretary of State for Scotland has flu, and I can't find the Chancellor of the Duchy or the Chief Secretary.'

'Stay, will you? There'll be action afterwards.'

Then the Prime Minister turned to his colleagues, backing the authority of his office with the authority of a man standing speaking to men seated.

'Gentlemen, we were beaten, but I do not intend to preside over a change of policy.'

There was a pause, broken by the Minister of Transport.

'You can't resign, Prime Minister. After all, Meridia isn't . . .'

'Thank you. I have no intention of resigning. I intend to advise the Queen to dissolve Parliament.'

An election. No one in the room except the Prime Minister had thought of it. No newspaper had speculated on it. The Opposition had not even asked for it. And for a good reason.

'You can't hold an election in December,' said Patrick Reid, jolted out of his ordinary pomposity of speech. He disliked any interruption of routine, and his seat was not safe.

'I have considered that point, and we can discuss it. But first I must make the constitutional position dear. The Queen dissolves Parliament on the advice of the Prime Minister acting alone, not on the collective advice of the Cabinet. There is no doubt that the responsibility is mine alone. This is an informal meeting, the Secretary of the

Cabinet is not here, there will be no minutes. I am of course ready to listen to your views.'

No one spoke. In the corner a grandfather clock ticked portentously. The heavy gold curtains were drawn and behind them they heard a spurt of rain against the windows. Most of them had worked together for eight or ten years now, first in opposition, now in government, under this man. At the beginning he had been first among equals, but the office of Prime Minister had distanced him from them. The workings of his mind had never been easy to follow. Now he was proposing to plunge all their futures into uncertainty. No one, not even Leith-Ross, Chancellor of the Exchequer, at that moment wanted him to do it. Not one of them knew how to stop him.

'How long since there was an election in December?'

Peretz, the Chief Whip, knew the answer to his own question.

'Not since 1918. Obviously I have thought that through. There was an election in February 1950. The weather in February is worse than in December. In any case the convention against a winter election is out of date. Now we have helicopters, snowploughs, motorways. There's no question of polling stations being cut off or candidates stranded. And we never have snow in December anyway.'

'Bad for the Christmas trade,' said Leith-Ross.

'That's nearer the truth. But we will tidy up the parliamentary business next week, dissolve next Tuesday, that's 12 November, polling day 12 December and, after we've won, ten prosperous shopping days till Christmas. The shopkeepers will grumble at the beginning and do quite well at the end.'

He had thought it all out. There were many other possible questions, but no doubt he had answers to them all. Except the biggest question of all.

'Would we win?' It was Leith-Ross again. As the Prime Minister's closest friend in the Cabinet (which was not saying very much) he found it easiest to ask.

'Chairman of the party?'

So there had been collusion. Above his stiff white collar Lord Redburn glowed with the self-importance which inside knowledge brings. He tended to favour a snap election precisely because he alone had been consulted about it. And of course, being a Lord, he did not have to fight a seat. He fished a piece of paper from his pocket.

'In a collation of the published polls of the last fortnight we are two points ahead. In our own private polls that widens to four. The Meridian issue is against us at present, in favour of Dunsford. I doubt if that will last till polling day.'

'We don't want Dunsford campaigning in Sussex or anywhere else on the Meridian issue,' said Peretz.

'You are right. We do not,' said the Prime Minister. 'Please see to it.'

It seemed to be a joke. Peretz opened his mouth to ask how, but thought better of it.

The Prime Minister unbent, and appeared to take them into his confidence.

'Success in politics goes to those who turn bad news into good. It's an alchemy. Dunsford beat us today but Dunsford is of no account, as you will see. Nor is Meridia. That simply won't run as an issue. I know the precedents. The Bulgarian atrocities, Chinese labour on the Rand –

but both times that was the British middle class voting Liberal to ease its conscience. Nowadays we have a different electorate, and it votes on its stomach. The economic indicators are good, and getting better. Right, Chancellor?'

'Quite right, Prime Minister,' said Leith-Ross. 'We've got a small lead in the polls already, which is very rare for a mid-term government. We should have good new inflation and employment figures during the campaign. The incumbent usually picks up during the campaign. I do not believe we shall have a better chance to snatch another five years.'

Snatch, that was the trouble. It was a manoeuvre which might be resented. Most of them disliked it. They had their jobs, not just the cars and the dinners, which were peripheral, but the hard, satisfying, daily grind of Cabinet work. That was what they enjoyed, and the Prime Minister was putting it at risk. Since he had given it to them in the first place, it was not easy to complain. But Patrick Reid had a reason. He had recovered his normal polysyllabic habit.

'There is one consideration, Prime Minister, which I feel bound to draw to your attention since it falls within my responsibilities. Your opinion is that Meridia will not figure largely in an election campaign, and I would not hazard a guess upon that point. But you also said that you did not intend to preside over a change of policy. The difficulty is that the Americans have begun to contemplate exactly that.'

'What do you mean?'

'Well, Prime Minister, you will remember Sandford-Smith's last telegram suggesting that Hamid was shifting

376

his stance in the direction of the West. The disarmament talks in Geneva are apparently on the verge of collapse. If they do collapse our Ambassador in Washington has heard that the Americans may after all act to frustrate MEECON and prevent the Soviets installing themselves in Meridia. This would be the first signal of a new and tougher policy towards the Soviet Union.'

'How could they frustrate MEECON?' The Prime Minister was attending closely.

'They could put together a consortium to give massive aid to Meridia.'

'You are serious?'

'I gather it's being seriously considered.'

The Minister of Transport chipped in.

'But that's the Dunsford policy. We couldn't possibly go along with that.'

No one took the slightest notice. The Prime Minister laughed.

'What would politics be without its ironies?' He paused to reflect.

'Foreign Secretary, I suggest that you should speak at once on the telephone to the Secretary of State in Washington. Tell him as much as you think fit. As much as you need to persuade him.'

'Persuade him?'

'If necessary we will go along with whatever they want. But on no account must there by any breath or hint of it until after 12 December; 12 December, you recall, will be Polling Day.'

So that was that. They had come into the room as Cabinet ministers, fresh from the Meridian debate, but essentially thinking of next week's meetings in Whitehall, debates in Westminster, journeys to Brussels, red boxes by the fireside at home. They left the room still Cabinet ministers in name, but thinking ahead to quite a different future, to their next few weeks as mere candidates, in market places and village greens, up garden paths, at bus stops and school entrances, campaigning for their careers in the cold and wet. It was a humbling prospect, yet also exciting, for they were after all politicians, and elections are the core of politics. It is the excitement of being an elected person which reconciles politicians to their amazing and often disagreeable way of life.

Leith-Ross lingered in the doorway till the others had gone.

'Just out of curiosity . . .'

'Yes?'

'Did you *want* Edward to get here in time? Did you *want* him to win? Have you planned it this way all along? Planning to get us our next five years?'

The Prime Minister had not stirred from the empty fireplace. He did not reply for half a minute.

'No,' he said. 'I thought it might happen and I made plans in case it did. That's all, but don't tell the others. They will work it out just as you have. I'm not as subtle as all that. But it's not a bad thing that in their eyes I should be half-demon and half-magician. A Prime Minister needs a good disguise. Now off you go, and write your election address.'

31

Friday morning passed in a whirl of questions and interviews. Edward hauled himself with difficulty from his bed to do both breakfast televisions and three radio programmes. Five newspapermen came to the house, each with a photographer. He was in the limelight once more and this time he was doing the talking. Excitement and disbelief were running through him, happily confused with each other. He was fêted over lunch at the Beefsteak Club as the man of the hour. Quite out of character, for he hated shopping, he bought four expensive shirts in Jermyn Street. On the pavement, whether they smiled or glared, people recognised him. But it was short-term excitement. He knew it would not last. He knew more important matters lay ahead after the Prime Minister's announcement the night before. He should be thinking of Lewes and his own re-election campaign. But somehow he could not bring himself to that yet. He had no idea what the future would bring, no more idea than when he had woken the previous morning in the little bed in Cornwall. But the difference between Thursday morning and Friday was that now, whatever the future, he seemed part of it once more.

Depression fell on him again on Friday evening. Rosemary lurched back into his thoughts. He had still heard nothing from her. He knew that she had been back to Eaton Close. Dirty plates and glasses were scattered around the kitchen, her bed had been slept in. The sitting-room was a mess. When had she been back? The broken glass of the kitchen door still lay where it had fallen on Monday night. Why had the cleaning lady not been? What was going on? There had been no telephone calls, no messages passed on through friends, not even a letter – not that it was Rosemary's nature to write letters. He had no idea where she might be or what she was thinking. As the hours passed, the interviews finished and the telephone stopped ringing, he began to worry. He found the telephone book in the bedroom and began to leaf through it. She must be somewhere. In Sussex? With friends? He dialled the number of Long Meadow a dozen times during Saturday. Where could she be if she was not in Sussex with the girls? He tried their school, but they were no help. He rang those friends of hers whom he knew well. But it was awkward. He did not want to tout among them all for news of her. It would sound sordid. There was still no reply from Long Meadow.

Sitting alone at his desk in Eaton Close on Saturday afternoon Edward suddenly became frightened that she might have begun something stupid. She had once told him exactly how she would go about it if ever she wanted a divorce. In a panic he rang his solicitor.

'No, I haven't heard from Rosemary for weeks. In fact

not since we had dinner with you in September. Why? Is anything wrong? I mean, I don't like to . . .'

'No Colin, it's nothing. Nothing at all. I just thought she might have. No problem. Let's arrange something after the election. Thanks a lot,' and Edward rang off.

His first news of her came from Guy Carlton, with whom he had dinner on Saturday. Guy had rung up to congratulate him on his speech and discovered that he had no plan for Saturday evening. They dined at the Savoy, not at Guy's house in Roehampton, for Guy wanted to talk seriously in a way which neither he nor Edward would have thought right in the presence of women. Guy began cheerful over the whitebait, gossiping about the City and the coming election, but Edward was miserable, often silent, and rather sour. He spoke grudgingly about the last few days. He even found Guy's yellow rose irritating. Guy was nonplussed. What was the matter? He could not be upset at the events of the last week which had thrust him once more to the front of the stage. Was it something domestic? Was it Rosemary? Edward nodded reluctantly. But she had telephoned briefly the day before, Guy said.

'What on earth for?'

'We do speak occasionally when you've got other things on your mind, you know,' Guy laughed.

'What did she say?'

'Not much. She was in one of her cryptic, staccato moods. You know them better than I do.'

'Did she say where she was? It's important. You see, I . . . Well, I haven't seen her since Monday.'

'No, she didn't say. But I didn't ask. There was no reason to.'

Edward toyed with his glass of Vouvray.

'She said that she had tried very hard and that it hadn't worked.'

'You can say that again.'

'And that she was sorry.'

'To who? You or me?' Edward was feeling bitter.

'Look, I'm sorry Edward. I wish there was something I could do to help. Sometimes Rosemary and I seem able to talk.'

After that the meal never prospered.

Edward took the train down to Lewes on Sunday afternoon. He had not been totally negligent over the weekend. He had already spoken on the telephone to Richard Peacock about the election campaign. They needed to start work on the details, the posters, the handouts and Edward's speaking programme in the constituency over the next few weeks. The Major was already drawing up lists of helpers. It would not be difficult. The party was well supported in that part of the world. But Richard Peacock was in a fuss about the Headley problem and the constituency meeting on Wednesday. They agreed to meet in Lewes on Monday. The House of Commons was still sitting, but Edward decided to give it a miss.

Edward got out of the taxi at Long Meadow to find his car in the drive. Rosemary was back. She stood in the doorway, dressed for London.

'Rosemary, where on earth have you been? I've been trying all over the place. I must have rung here a dozen times since Friday.'

'I knew you'd be here before long. So I haven't been answering the phone.'

' Why not? I've been worried.'

He began to feel angry with her.

'You should have thought of that before. I did warn you.'

'What the hell does that mean?'

She laughed at him. 'You've got a short memory. Or have I just dreamt what's happened over the last week?'

'Rosemary, I have just had the most bloody and confused week in my whole life. I've been worried sick about you. I've spent half the weekend trying to find you. And as soon as I do you behave like this.'

'That's balls. You've spent the whole week losing your job, making a fool of yourself all over the place and bringing down your own sodding Government. Just tell me where in the middle of all that you found time to think about me for a change?' She turned back into the house.

Edward stood helplessly outside. The taxi-driver, who had still to be paid, coughed with some embarrassment behind.

' 'Scuse me, gov, that'll be four pounds fifty.'

Edward reached for his wallet. Damn Rosemary and her theatricals. He followed her inside with sinking spirits.

They had another frightful row. It lasted longer than on the previous Monday, half an hour at least, and covered much more ground. It was a good satisfying row, the kind Rosemary had been wanting ever since Edward's infatuation with Meridia had begun. Though the air was not cleared and there were no apologies or explanations on Rosemary's side, they reached a truce of sorts, enough to keep them together at Long Meadow for a few days. But not enough for Edward to broach the subject of next Wednesday's constituency meeting.

It was the politician's job to leave behind self-doubt, to live, breathe and speak with confidence. Pessimism and foreboding were for prophets, not parliamentarians. But Edward was not confident about Wednesday evening. From what Richard Peacock had told him on the telephone, Headley was out for his blood. Edward's colleagues would have laughed at him. He was the sitting member of a safe seat – one of the safest in southern England. He had been the subject of almost continual publicity for a month before the election was called. His part in forcing an election at this unusual time had made his face well-known to the public and guaranteed him a place in the history books. That gave him a good enough start. Most people in Sussex approved of the Government in very general terms, but they would be flattered rather than otherwise that their member had brought it down. And as for the local issues, general elections were about governments, not about motorways or local play centres for working mothers.

But there remained a vital fence before the race began. Edward had still to be nominated by his own party supporters. He doubted that he could take it for granted, no matter what some round him might think. Dubarry, the Association Chairman, was bullish but unconvincing at the long meeting Edward had with him and Major Peacock on Tuesday afternoon.

'Don't even think about it, my dear Edward. A formality. Merely a formality. Same as it always is.'

But the Major was not so optimistic. He tried to get Dubarry to focus on the difficulty of the report of Derek Headley's Policy Committee. The Chairman brushed this aside also.

'It's been overtaken, Richard. Simple as that. We can look at it later if Derek and his committee wish. But they won't. It'll die a death. You'll see. We've an election on our hands now. First things first, surely.'

The Major said no. Derek Headley had been intending to table his report at the original Association meeting planned for 13 November. The Chairman remained unmovable.

'I've been Chairman of this Association for quite a time now and I do know a thing or two about procedure, Richard, you'll grant me that. With the calling of an election the Association and all its bits and pieces go into hibernation.' He smiled at Edward. 'For heaven's sake, you're our chap, Edward. You've been the member for five years. That's that. Tomorrow's meeting isn't a meeting of the Association at all as such. It isn't open to Derek to raise points that properly belong to the Association's business. It isn't the time or the place for Derek's committee. Tomorrow is simply to allow Edward here to make his pre-election address so that we can have him re-adopted and get on with the important job of fighting the election. Simple as that. And that's just what I've told Derek,' he added.

Richard Peacock did not agree it was as easy as this. Headley would find a way. He could raise it under 'Any other business'.

'Nonsense,' said Dubarry. 'It's all sorted out. Plain sailing.'

Edward caught the infection from Richard Peacock. He knew he had to make a special effort at the meeting. That was why he was so anxious that Rosemary should accompany him to the meeting. He knew there were stories circulating about them. It would confound those who might want to think his marriage was in trouble. To the women that could be important. And it might be a way of bringing Rosemary back into his life.

He tried her out on Monday. Rosemary flatly refused. They spent the rest of that day in their own little worlds. Tuesday was the same, Rosemary busying herself about the house of which she was so proud, weeding an untidy border by the drive, mixing herself more drinks than were good for her; Edward on the telephone, in Lewes with Dubarry and Richard Peacock, working on his speech.

He raised the subject for the last time at supper on Tuesday evening. The two of them were in the kitchen, confronting each other over a dish of lasagne which Rosemary had found buried in the deep freeze. Edward was pushing a piece of pasta around his plate.

'You were right after all, you know.'

Rosemary sipped at the remnants of her gin. 'Really?'

'About Headley and his group of friends. I'm sorry I was so pig-headed about it. I don't know why.'

'It's a bit late now, isn't it?'

'For what?'

'Come off it, Edward. Look at the pathetic bloody little mess we're both sitting in just because you get a big idea in your head.'

Edward got up and walked stiffly over to the sink.

'Please don't start another post-mortem. I couldn't bear it.'

'Well, what do you expect?'

He thought back to the night after his return from Mangara. She had been kind then. 'It wasn't so long ago that you said you would help.'

Rosemary toyed with her lasagne. 'I meant it once. At the beginning. Believe me, I really did. But your trouble is that you always know better. That's what gets in the way.'

'My . . .'

· 'Listen, Edward.' She looked up. 'This is the last time I plan to tell you this. I don't want our life destroyed. I don't want you ruined. You could still have a fantastic career in front of you. For God's sake don't throw it all away.' She paused and looked at him coldly. 'I don't want to stay married to a failure. And I still count, don't I? So play your cards right and politics might just give you a second chance. But I won't.'

She finished her drink.

Edward did not reply for a moment. This was a threat Rosemary had not made before and he wanted time to absorb it. In the sink at his elbow was that day's dirty crockery which he knew he would have to deal with later. He would like to use detergent on their own lives.

'Is this an ultimatum of some kind?'

'If you like. You don't seem able to listen to anything else.'

'And the terms?'

'I want you back in politics. But not this village-green sort down here. The sort that matters. The sort I enjoy. The Cabinet.'

'There's small chance of that now.'

'For Christ's sake, stop feeling sorry for yourself. I thought you had some fight in you. You're good. Even I can see that. And there aren't all that many of you around. So Berinsfield is going to have to have you back one day. He'll have no choice if you play your cards right. Especially once he's rid of that fool Patrick Reid. You've just got to be around when the PM starts looking for talent again.'

'And if not?'

'I've had a week to think about it. And I've thought hard. It's quite simple, Edward. If you kick me in the teeth again by making us all look fools I'll leave you.' She looked around the kitchen. 'And I'll take what's mine with me.'

'Rosemary, this is absurd. After all these years you don't understand the first thing about politics. I can't possibly get back in by putting on a pretty face and just looking available. It doesn't work like that.'

He sat down again at the table. He was exasperated. He did not know where to begin.

'Do you want to stay in politics or don't you?'

'Of course I do. But . . .'

'Well just listen then. I'm not willing to spend the rest of my life with a nonentity. I want more than that. And I intend to get it.'

Edward's shoulders slumped forward. 'For God's sake, Rosemary. You have no idea what you're asking.'

'I've idea enough. So how do you choose?'

He thought of the events of the last month. What had it all been for? Pure self-indulgence? A dream? An illusion that he might do some good for once? That politicians did sometimes have principles they were ready to stand up for? He'd shown that they did. He wanted to go on proving it. Charles Elliott had been wrong at that dinner party at Garth's in Warwick Square. He had taken a stand, and he wanted to stick to it. But with Rosemary in this impossible mood, could he?

'You really have become the most frightful bore over

388

this Meridia business,' Rosemary was saying. 'I don't understand you. It's not been like you at all.'

'All right, I'll promise you one thing.'

'I'm offering you a straight yes or no.'

'There isn't a yes or no. Not yet there isn't. I don't want to give up this life and I certainly don't want to give up you. Especially you.'

'Thanks.' Rosemary got up from the table and began searching the kitchen for her cigarettes.

'But I can't promise you what you want. Getting back into the Government depends on the terms. I'm not wrong about Africa and I'm not going to say that I have been.'

'That sounds like no.' She found her cigarettes and sat down again.

'I've told you. It isn't yes or no. Look, neither of us has the chance of getting what we want unless I'm re-elected here. Let's get that over, you and me together, and then we can plan what happens next.'

'That sounds like a truce, not a decision.'

'I'm being practical. I need your help to get re-elected. Once I am we can start again.'

'You mean you'll give up this pathetic Meridian business?'

'I mean I don't want to lose what I still have. And I told you, I don't want to lose you.'

He put his arm across the table to take her hand. She pulled it back. 'But I need your help. Not the whole campaign. But parts of it. The difficult parts.'

'If you mean this meeting of yours tomorrow, I'm not going to . . .'

'Please. It's important. Especially tomorrow. Headley

389

will cause problems. You told me so, you were right. Please come.'

Rosemary lit a cigarette, in her slow, irritatingly dramatic style.

'All right, I'll come. But don't forget my terms, Edward. I'm not taking any more failures from you at my expense.'

There was another glorious November sunset on Wednesday afternoon. It cast briefly a pale pink glow along the line of the Downs, silhouetting the thorn trees which straggled the top of Blackcap in the distance, and picking out the evening shadows of old footpaths and boundaries on the hilltop opposite the house. Along the ridge two tiny figures were hurrying in the direction of Ditchling. It would be dark long before they reached home. From the window of the study at Long Meadow Edward stood to watch the day dying. He had never been superstitious, but at home, if nowhere else, he had always been sensitive to atmosphere, and the unexpected pleasure of that sunset gave him hope. The stillness and peace of the countryside around him found their way inside him. He pushed away the speech he had gone through half a dozen times and gazed at the view before him. How beautiful Sussex was. Unlike his own life it was unmarked by human folly or stupidity. In the most old-fashioned sense of the word, he had wronged Rosemary. Perhaps in another sense he had wronged Sally, too. Certainly he should feel guilt, as well as fear for the future. But for a few minutes, alone in the room, he put aside his doubts and felt that no evil could touch him.

Three hours later it was raining again and Edward's mood had changed. He sat in the car in gloom and silence. Rosemary was driving. She had come. Just. Edward was not sure whether he had paid a price or not. Where did his truce with Rosemary leave Meridia and the man of principle he had convinced himself he had become? He told himself he did not have to choose yet. He could put off the moment during the campaign, and put off Rosemary and the need to sort things out until after the election. With a postponement like that they would have a breathing space in which they might start to rebuild parts of their marriage.

Edward gazed vacantly at the wipers brushing away the rain from the windscreen. Rosemary had insisted on taking her car. The steering-wheel was the one place where her temper never got the better of her. She drove coolly and expertly. Just as she makes love, Edward thought, but quickly put the picture out of his mind.

The school car park was already two-thirds full when they arrived. The school, bare and echoing, was brightly lit. Its wood-block flooring had been swept and polished for the occasion, a broken window repaired. Two hundred people at least had crowded into the hall, squeezing on to metal-framed chairs with canvas seats. They had been individually invited as the party faithfuls for the regular six-monthly meeting of the full Association. But from the moment of the Prime Minister's announcement of the election the Association lay technically in abeyance, unable to raise money, unable to spend it for fear of breaching the strict rules governing electioneering expenses. Dubarry's decision as Chairman of the Association to retain the meeting but change its name was logical and sensible. A notice appeared in the local press. It was hoped that those previously invited would now attend a Special General Meeting to adopt Mr Edward Dunsford as parliamentary candidate for the constituency of East Sussex. 8 p.m., Wednesday, 13 November, in the hall at Southfields Comprehensive School.

It was a private evening. The press were not invited. But in fact the local papers were there, thanks to a quiet word on the telephone between Derek Headley and the editors of the *Evening Argus* and the *Mid-Sussex Times*. Headley and the remnants of his little committee hat carefully prepared the ground. The meeting would be their last opportunity. Headley now sat in the second row in the hall, his conspirators scattered behind him. In the first row was Major Peacock and his wife. On the platform of the school stage was a long metal table and six chairs, for the Chairman and his wife, Edward and Rosemary, the Deputy Chairman and the Treasurer.

Edward and Rosemary had to pick their way slowly through the noisy hall, shaking hands, smiling, waving, nodding at faces they recognised or which recognised them. There was excitement in the air which even Rosemary felt. It made her back tingle. She had forgotten in the last few months that politics could actually be fun. As they reached the stage she squeezed Edward's arm and whispered to him. He turned and smiled, the gloom lifting once more from his shoulders. He felt his own excitement mingle with a renewed sense of the calm he had felt as he had watched the setting sun earlier that afternoon. Perhaps it would be all right after all.

At ten past eight Dubarry rose to his feet and the meeting began. The audience came to attention easily and willingly. This was not a campaign meeting, more a family gathering. That is what Geoffrey Dubarry spent ten minutes telling them. Edward could have recited Dubarry's speech standing on his head. Delighted you could all be here. An impressive turnout. Only to be expected on such an important occasion. Edward Dunsford needs no introduction. Well known to us all. Sterling work over the years. A man of wide experience and the highest integrity. An effective Member of Parliament. Held in the highest respect by his colleagues. A man of determination and principle, as recent events have shown. None better could continue to represent us. But no more of this. Let him speak for himself. The Chairman felt pleasantly in control. He was listened to in silence. There were no murmurs of dissent. Some coughing here and there, but no more than to be expected in mid-November.

Edward got to his feet. He spoke for twenty minutes. There was no microphone. He had to speak slowly and loudly. He had decided he would not try to defend the past. He spoke of the future. It was dull, decent, obvious stuff. Nothing objectionable and nothing controversial. A rallying-call to the party flock. Only Major Peacock and a few others knew how carefully Edward was treading. He spoke of the national issues at stake in the election – the economy, defence, unemployment, inflation, the nuclear deterrent. He spoke of the work for which the party needed a fresh mandate to continue; he spoke of the determination of the electorate to give itself once and for all a strong and effective government.

'And that means Members of Parliament with minds of their own, and the courage to back their convictions.'

There was a ripple of applause, but he left the point.

'Ladies and gentlemen, the last election was a close-run

393

affair. That will not be repeated. Why? Because this country will not be fooled by empty promises. It will not be fooled by impossible expectations. Because we are not children to be taken in by parties who, over the next four weeks, set up a Christmas tree at every street corner, dress up as Santa Claus and grab at each passer-by saying, "Here's a gift for you", "Here's a present for you", "Look at our pretty tree", "What would you like?" Ladies and gentlemen, we will not be fooled by their pathetic glitter, their pretty wrapping paper and their coloured ribbon. This country wants sensible policies and sound government. That is what the Conservatives will continue to provide.'

No mention of foreign affairs. No specific mention of Meridia. It was an uninspiring but solid performance.

There was loyal applause when he sat down, muted because they had hoped for something more sensational. But something more sensational might have divided them. Rosemary nudged him and gave him a brief smile. Clever woman, she saw the point. How quickly her mood changed. Then there were questions. The Chairman took a dozen or so. None came from any recognisable member of the Headley crowd. For the most part the questions were about national issues. Two middle-aged ladies asked about the motorway. Edward answered with ease, making clear his concern, giving no promises. A young man in a pink woollen tie asked how Edward reconciled his election address with his recent criticism of the Prime Minister. Edward spoke of the distinction between shared beliefs and particular issues. No one took up the theme. Derek Headley had still said nothing. Edward glanced at him a few times, expecting a hostile stare. But Headley sat with his arms crossed and a self-satisfied smile. Dubarry now had only to close the meeting with a formal statement endorsing Edward's selection as candidate, and it would all be over. Edward brushed his hand through his hair and sat back in his chair. But he was not entirely happy. He had not carried them with him in some of his answers. Perhaps his main speech had been too matter of fact. His political instincts told him that he faced a deeply divided audience. Could the meeting really end without that fact emerging?

At nine fifteen Geoffrey Dubarry, impeccable in his three-piece suit, rose to his feet.

'If there are no more questions, ladies and gentlemen? Well then, since I am sure we have no other business this evening it only remains for me to conclude our meeting with a formal statement . . .'

He stopped. Derek Headley was on his feet. Four or five journalists in the audience produced their notebooks from their coat pockets.

'Excuse me, Mr Chairman, but I do have something to raise under "Any other business".'

Dubarry's little eyes darted in Headley's direction. 'I'm sorry, Mr Headley, I was not aware that . . .'

'Mr Chairman, there is a matter of the utmost urgency and importance which I wish to put before the meeting. I would not trouble you if it were not.'

Edward felt confidence draining from him.

'. . . something of crucial relevance to our meeting this evening,' Derek Headley was saying.

'Very well. But please be brief.' The Chairman thrust his hands into his waistcoat pockets and sat down. He had turned slightly pale.

'Thank you, Mr Chairman.' Headley pulled out a sheet of paper from beneath the loud check of his tweed suit and began.

'Ladies and gentlemen. I raise this matter only with the greatest reluctance. But since it concerns closely the position of Mr Dunsford and his suitability as our candidate at this election, I and a number of members within the constituency regard it as vital that we inform this meeting of certain matters before events go any further and before any decisions are taken which we would certainly regret later.'

Edward gazed over the two hundred faces in front of him. He had tried to keep his confident expression, but it was fading now.

'Some three weeks ago, Mr Chairman, with your agreement as Chairman of the Association, I and a number of concerned officers met together to consider the widespread disquiet which had been expressed within the constituency over the effectiveness with which Mr Edward Dunsford had represented the interests of this area. We did not take on this task lightly but only as a response to a degree of complaint, extraordinary – and probably unprecedented – in a constituency of this kind.'

The audience was still, no coughs, no shuffling.

'With your agreement, Mr Chairman, our group produced a report on Mr Dunsford's recent record as our Member of Parliament. We concluded unanimously' – Headley did not even blink – 'that Mr Dunsford had completely disregarded the strong feelings in the constituency over a number of major local issues. Above all, Mr Dunsford had done nothing to represent the acute hostility felt in these parts to the so-called northern route

396

proposed by the Government for the East Sussex section of the M27. And, more than that, both in public statements and in his excessively casual attitude towards important public meetings on this subject, he had made it clear that he had little interest in the issue, that there was nothing he could do to help, and that people with a legitimate grievance over this matter would just have to put up with whatever decision the Department of Transport eventually decided to force upon us.'

There was a murmur among the audience and a muffled cry of 'Shame' from the back of the hall. Few would have been at the executive meeting in Lewes three weeks before when Edward had tried unsuccessfully to preach a sense of realism to his audience. Edward felt his face reddening. He caught a glimpse of Rosemary. Her smile had gone. Instead he saw only a jaw set firm and flashing eyes. Geoffrey Dubarry was toying uncomfortably with his watch-chain.

'Mr Chairman, my committee regarded this attitude as unjustified, reprehensible and totally unacceptable. We looked further into Mr Dunsford's record on this matter and found his interest unaccountably wanting. We concluded, Mr Chairman,' – he bent down to his chair and picked up a folder – 'in a report which we have already submitted to you, but which unfortunately has not yet been properly considered, that Mr Dunsford's conduct as an MP has been lamentably lacking and, contrary to your own remarks this evening, deeply unsatisfactory.'

The members of the Policy Committee had been well spread among the audience. 'Shame', three more voices shouted more loudly from different parts of the hall.

'In addition,' Derek Headley continued, 'our report

concluded that Mr Dunsford's recent conduct as a former Minister of State in the Foreign Office could not go unremarked, throwing as it does grave doubts on his integrity as a member of the last Government and as a loyal member of his party. We should not forget that Mr Dunsford was sacked by the Prime Minister, I repeat sacked, for his outrageously disloyal outburst against the Government of which he was a member. Just because the Cabinet would not agree with his views of a remote and not very important part of the world which he wished to throw taxpayers' money at for highly questionable reasons. That, in the view of my committee, cast serious doubt on the good sense and judgement of Mr Dunsford, and on his ability to represent this constituency in Parliament properly.'

There was a hostile murmur of comment throughout the hall. The Chairman's eyes were darting over the audience, not sure what he should do. Rosemary was hissing at Edward.

'For God's sake, shut him up. Quickly.'

Edward sat rooted to his chair. He was mesmerised, like the mouse beneath the cat's paw. He could say and do nothing. Nothing would stop the man continuing to the end. He saw a curtain falling on his future.

'Finally, Mr Chairman, our concern was made even more acute when it became clear that the only reason why the Prime Minister was forced into this wholly unnecessary and damaging election was because of a parliamentary revolt within his own party which was led by Mr Dunsford himself. Was led, that is to say, by our elected representative against a government formed by the party of which we are members, and which we helped vote into office. Mr Chairman, I regard this as utterly scandalous.'

'Hear, hear.' It was a low anonymous mutter of approval, like the growl of approaching thunder. The audience was turning against him.

'I therefore find it unacceptable, Mr Chairman, that in these circumstances you should not only ignore these facts completely in your opening address, but be prepared to suggest that this meeting agree to adopt Mr Dunsford unopposed' – he almost shrieked this word – 'unopposed as our parliamentary candidate. Mr Chairman, that would be wrong. Indeed it would be a scandal.'

The Chairman half-rose to his feet and tried to interject.

'Derek, for heaven's sake. Please. This really is most inappropriate.' But Headley was not to be stopped.

'I insist that this meeting be permitted to vote on a proposal that we take no decision on a candidate this evening, and that a Committee of Selection be set up immediately with the urgent task of finding a suitable candidate to stand for election. Of course there is no reason why Mr Dunsford should not ask to be considered, if he wants to. But I can hardly believe even he will dare to, given his disgraceful record.'

Headley finally sat down. Geoffrey Dubarry leapt to his feet again in a tremendous dither. He tried vainly to restore order. There was shouting all across the hall. Half a dozen people in the audience had risen to demand a vote.

Edward came to his senses and pulled at Dubarry's jacket.

'You must let me reply.'

The Chairman half-sat down.

'Edward. I don't know what to say. What can I do?'

Dubarry rose to his feet again and waved his arms to try to still the noise. Nothing happened, so he sat down.

'What on earth am I do?'

'If you won't then I shall.' Edward stood up and tried to speak.

'Ladies and gentlemen. I utterly reject . . .' The rest was lost in the noise. There was shouting for and against. The uproar was growing fiercer. It was most unlike Sussex.

'Let him speak.'

'Give him a chance.'

'Answer, answer.'

'Come on, Edward. Let's hear your side.'

But he was not given a chance. People were leaping up and down in their seats like football fans. One of the local newspaper reporters produced a camera from his pocket, and not for the first time that autumn Edward cursed its invention.

'Please. You must let me defend myself.'

But it was no good. The uproar and shouting continued. Derek Headley sat silent and triumphant in the second row, his arms re-folded. Major Peacock, at the front, was muttering to himself in silent fury.

It was ten minutes before Dubarry regained control of his meeting. He tried to let Edward speak again, but that merely promoted further shouting and no one heard his words.

'I'm sorry, Edward. I don't know what else I can do.'

In the show of hands which the Chairman counted as carefully as the contents of any cash register, Derek Headley's proposal was passed by 130 votes to 104.

Edward felt numb as the Chairman mournfully announced the result and accepted the new task thrust upon him. This was a most unfortunate and regrettable development, he said. He stood by his earlier comments. Nevertheless, the Executive would draw up a Committee of Selection the following day. Speed was essential. A candidate must be chosen quickly.

Edward got to his feet to leave the platform and find some way of quitting the hall. Dubarry was shaking his head. Edward looked for Rosemary but her chair was already empty. He scanned the audience anxiously and eventually saw her making her way quietly and efficiently towards the exit. A camera flashed as she passed. When she reached the door she turned for a moment to look back at him. Edward saw her face clearly. He knew what it meant. So far as Rosemary was concerned she had been given her answer.

32

On Thursday the telephone in Eaton Close rang every fifteen minutes, on Friday every hour, on Saturday hardly at all. Edward Dunsford, the man who brought down the Government, had been in demand everywhere. Edward Dunsford, the man whose seat was in danger, was also news, but not for long. Edward stayed in London, eating, broadcasting, drinking, sleeping, making up his mind. A curt telephone conversation with Rosemary established that he would stay in London, she in Long Meadow. For the time being, both said, though neither knew what might bring the time being to an end. On Saturday the first telephone call was from Major Peacock.

'Have you seen the *Telegraph*?'

'Not yet.' Edward wore a red towelled dressing-gown in the kitchen, where he was burning toast.

'Thank God for that. I wanted to reach you first. The Executive Meeting to choose a candidate is tomorrow afternoon. Four o'clock in the British Legion Hall. You know the one, just past the Feathers in Castle Street.'

There was a pause.

'Do you expect me?'

Another pause.

'I don't know. It's up to you.'

'Who else is on the list?'

'Well, of course, they – we rather – had to work pretty fast. Nominations have to be in by the middle of next week. Dubarry rang up the Party Chairman and got half a dozen likely names. They set up a small selection committee and went through the names on paper. A young man called Smythe came top.'

'Smythe?'

'Smythe. With an "e". London merchant banker. About twenty-eight, good-looking, wrote an excellent letter. I don't know much else about him. Headley praised him to the skies.'

'Headley not interested himself?'

'No, Smythe's his man. But there's Violet Stephenson as the local candidate.'

'In addition to me?'

'In addition to you.'

'Richard Peacock, do you really think I'm going to come down tomorrow and humble myself all over again before exactly the same crowd who humiliated me on Wednesday?'

'Some say they've changed their minds. Dubarry's still on your side. Many of them feel you didn't get a fair hearing. There's a swing back towards you.'

'Enough?'

'Not enough, but a start. It will depend on what you say, how you carry yourself.'

'Humble pie, you mean?'

'Certainly a promise to give priority to local issues in future.'

Edward suddenly imagined what it would be like, battling it out in the dimly lit, chilly British Legion Hall with old Violet Stephenson, who had always been a joke, and some smooth young oaf from the City. Battling it out for a nomination which in a just world would have been offered to him with gratitude and affection.

'I won't do it.'

A final pause.

'I don't blame you.' Richard Peacock cleared his throat. 'I have to soldier on, I'm afraid. You'll understand that. Can't do without the salary, piddling though it is. But you know how I feel. I'm damned sorry this . . .'

'Yes, I know how you feel. And when it's all over we'll have dinner and talk. Or go for a good walk above Firle Beacon. Meanwhile, we're both very busy.'

'Goodbye then, for the present.'

'Goodbye Richard, and thank you. For calling, and for the rest of it.'

Edward savagely buttered the burnt toast. The decision not to go for the nomination had come in a flash of intuition. It must be right. But after that decision, what was left?

The trouble about the Conservative Central Office in Smith Square was that there was no upstairs room of any size. To be precise, there was nowhere where the Prime Minister could hold a decent briefing meeting in advance of the first and all-important press conference of the campaign. So it was a squash. Everyone who wanted to be anything felt bound to attend, and there was no one with enough character to forbid them.

'The Foreign Secretary has rung for the fourth time to ask which days he's wanted at the press conference.'

'Please thank him and tell him I'm most grateful, but there is no need.'

'But you'll have a mass of questions about Meridia. Bound to.'

'There'll be fewer of them if Reid's not there. I do not wish to have to repeat it again. This is *not* going to be an election about Meridia.'

'You may get asked about Dunsford.'

'Yes, indeed, what's the position?'

'No one knows if he's going to try for the nomination. You remember they wouldn't let him have it automatically.'

'How wise. Who else is on the short list?'

'A local lady magistrate, and young Oliver Smythe from Lazards.'

'Not the youth who made a mess of the Sunderland by-election?'

'The same.'

'Good God. If I'm asked I'll put in a plug for the magistrate. Not that it ever does any good. But could someone please find out her name?'

But when it came to the point, there was no question about Edward Dunsford or the East Sussex seat, and the questions about Meridia were quickly dealt with. Life had moved on.

After they had decided against Edward's automatic adoption, many of the Executive thought that nevertheless they would choose him at the end of the day. He had taken them somewhat for granted, and undoubtedly had been remiss over the motorway. Once he had learned his lesson they could resume what had after all been a friendly relationship.

Most of the remainder were quite clear that this time they wanted a local candidate. Not someone who just bought a house in the constituency, as Edward had done, but someone Sussex born and bred. And someone with a good sound marriage.

Few people were interested in the names which came from Central Office. They went through the motions because the rules said that they should, and agreed to see Oliver Smythe. But only Derek Headley seemed keen.

Edward's refusal to stand came as a blow. Some felt he had let them down. He had certainly spoiled their fun. Worst of all, he had left them with a choice between Violet Stephenson and an unknown from London.

On Sunday afternoon in the British Legion Hall, Violet Stephenson, wearing her green tweeds, threw it away. Legs apart, crossing and uncrossing her arms, she talked for twenty minutes about her time as a magistrate, her time on the District Council, her work for the Red Cross and for saving the children. They all knew, she said, that she had not spared herself in serving Lewes, Sussex, and the Conservative Party. Yes, indeed, they all knew. They remembered that argument ten years ago over the council houses in Glynde. They remembered that her son had once been fined for speeding. They knew for certain that she was late paying her bills in the town. She had chaired too many meetings, overruled too many objections, had her way too often. No one had anything serious against her, but listening to her confident familiar voice that afternoon they knew that they did not want her as their MP.

Oliver Smythe was twenty-eight and looked five years younger. His smooth fair hair was just a little too long over his collar. He had a fresh boyish face and a voice with an attractive resonance which gave his views an apparent authority. He spoke briefly and well. Some of his most exciting holidays as a boy had been spent in Sussex. He had always longed to make his home there. He was in favour of restoring capital punishment. He was particularly keen on strengthening the laws against cruelty to animals. He had a great respect for Edward Dunsford, but was one hundred per cent behind the Prime Minister. He was a bachelor, and would need a lot of help from the ladies in learning about the constituency.

He won easily, getting three times as many votes as Violet Stephenson. Then they adopted him unanimously, though not before three or four members had left the meeting. Violet Stephenson wept briefly in the ladies' lavatory, pulled herself together and drove home to bake a cake for the Women's Institute.

Edward had never seen Richard Peacock in London, had never thought of him as a man who came to London. It was therefore a surprise to find him on the doorstep of Eaton Close on Monday morning.

'Thought I'd better come and have a word.'

'Come in.'

Major Peacock was wearing his town suit, a good, dark grey worsted, grown shiny and a little baggy. He took coffee. Edward was reverting fast to his bachelor days, mugs instead of cups, the furniture already slightly higgledy-piggledy in the room, bottles on the table instead of in the cabinet. He had just begun an article for next Sunday's *Observer*,

'I see Smythe won.'

'Easily.'

'What's he like?'

'Awful.'

'Young – good-looking – eloquent?'

'All three. He made me retch.'

'But it's too late to do anything about it.'

'Is it?'

Richard Peacock explained his plan. It was simple. Edward should stand as an independent Conservative. He, Richard Peacock, would act as his agent.

'Don't be silly, man. You'd be giving up your career. You need the money, you told me so the other day. I can't pay you anything.'

'I've got my pension. I'll rub along. One thing is clear – I can't work for that young reptile.'

'He'll learn – you'll teach him. He'll be nicer once he's got what he wants. Don't be too hard on him.'

Richard Peacock shook his head. Edward went on.

'And look at it from my point of view. I won't get in. But if I do, I'll have separated from my party. I'm not a loner by nature, you know.'

'They'll take you back when they need you.'

That was true enough. Edward began to think seriously about the proposition.

'Any financial backing?'

'Yes, I think I could get out and raise about half the expenses. You'd have to find the rest.'

Edward could manage that. His finances would soon be in a muddle, no doubt, without the ministerial salary, and with the uncertainty about Rosemary. But for the moment the bank manager was indulgent.

'Would we have a chance?'

'A chance, yes. I won't say more.'

Edward warmed to the notion. What else would he do during the next three weeks? Was it not the logical conclusion of everything he had recently said and done?

He rang Guy Carlton at Speyer's to ask his advice. As usual Guy was at his telephone. As usual he took the proposition calmly.

'I think you should do it. What else would you do during the next three weeks?'

'Thanks, Guy.'

'If it doesn't work, come and see me. Will you remember that?'

'If it doesn't work, you'll be the only person to give me the time of day.'

'By polling day you'll have been proved right about Meridia. Things are moving fast.'

'By polling day, no one will care.'

He turned back to Richard Peacock.

'Thank you, Richard. You've done me a better turn than you know. I agree.'

It seemed right to shake hands.

'It'll be fun, anyway,' said Edward.

'It'll be damned hard work. I've brought the nomination forms. We need a thousand pounds and a hundred signatures by Wednesday lunchtime.'

Neil Wainwright rang Bourton from his room in Brown's Hotel at 9 a.m. New York time. He had given up ringing every day. Bourton did not seem to mind this, or indeed that Neil had very little to say when they did talk. This time Bourton cut in before Neil produced his meagre scraps of news.

'Good news for you, boy. The bitch is dead.'

'What d'you mean, dead?'

'We heard last night that the Secretary of State in Washington, with full White House approval, has vetoed the MEECON project.'

'He has no legal power to do that.' They had often discussed the point.

Bourton laughed. 'Let me tell you something, Neil. These United States have a written constitution and a free-enterprise system. Our freedom is the envy of the world. We learn about it at school, particularly law school. But when it comes to swift executive action to reverse the decisions of US business, I guarantee there's no dictatorship in the world can match the ruthlessness of the US Administration. We make George III look like a weak-kneed civil-righter.' He paused. 'You still there? Of course the Secretary of State has no power of veto over Arkansas Oil and the rest of them. But they need him more than he needs them. They buckled under right away.'

'And you're pleased?'

'I'm not pleased, I'm not sore, I'm a corporation lawyer. Maybe you've still something to learn about the trade, Neil. These last few days MEECON has begun to stink. It's been dying before it was born. Now a putrefying project is no good to a corporation lawyer. It offends our sense of professional decency. But once the project is dead, we know where we stand. We bill the oil companies for our fees, making sure that we don't lose a dime. We bury the project, charging modestly for the coffin and the deaf mutes. Then we move on to the next one.'

Neil had nothing to say.

'D'you want to stay in England?'

Put like that, it was exactly what Neil did want.

'MEECON is dead, but Meridia is very much alive. The State Department doesn't want simply to frustrate the Soviets, it wants to replace them. That means a brand new aid package, international and certainly including the Brits. It means a strong private-enterprise element, and that certainly includes corporation lawyers. So keep hanging in there at the London end. I can't make head or tail of that political mess-up of theirs called an election. I hear contradictory things. I want to make sure we have the hang of it before our competitors. Are you game to stay?'

'I'm game.'

'And from now on, steer clear of the nightclubs. I want you back healthy, wealthy and wise.'

Bourton heard everything eventually. But Neil was too pleased to feel embarrassed.

Oliver Smythe was developing the knack of canvassing. He had borrowed a fiancée for the duration of the campaign, a nice, lively thirty-year-old with a job in publishing. This was a change in tactics since his success with the selection committee. But certain rumours which had been reported to him convinced him that he needed a girl in the entourage, and Ariadne managed it well. Together they trotted up and down garden paths, paraded with the loudspeaker van in shopping centres, and sidled up and down between the shelves of supermarkets. Occasionally they held hands, and once a day (not more, that was her bargain) they kissed in public, usually after a pub lunch. He also borrowed a retired agent to look after the expenses and legal requirements in place of Richard Peacock. Edward's decision to stand had come as a shock, but Smythe found that he was well received on the doorsteps.

Rain was a problem because neither Smythe nor Ariadne, being city folk, liked getting wet. That was why, on a wet Saturday morning, they abandoned a council estate across which the rain drove in horizontal sheets and took refuge in the village shop of Berwick St George. Smythe chose a tin of boot polish and a bottle of Alka-Seltzer from the shelves and stood, as if he were just an ordinary person, in the line of villagers waiting to pay. His huge blue rosette ensured that he was recogniscd. Canvassing was easier now that every household had received through the post his election address with photograph. Ariadne stood in the middle of the shop, rotating her wide smile between the cooked meats and the dairy counter.

In front of Smythe in the queue stood a woman perhaps even more beautiful than Ariadne. She wore black trousers and a thick fisherman's jersey in dark green, setting off a replica of a Sicilian coin which hung on a gold chain from her neck. Behind her stood a pale young man with reddish hair holding her wire basket.

The good lady at the counter fell into a social fluster when she saw her two next customers.

'Oh, Mrs Dunsford, I'm sure you know the new candidate, Mr Smythe. I expect you're old friends.'

'I don't know why you should suppose that, Mrs Braithwaite. We've never met before,' said Rosemary, hardly turning round. Long Meadow was just a mile away. 'I've never been really interested in politics.'

Smythe paid rapidly for his shoe polish and Alka-Seltzer, and hurried to catch her, glad that for the moment Ariadne was out of range.

'I'm so glad to meet you, Mrs Dunsford. I hoped that I might. I've felt very upset about the news of your splitting up with your husband. I've never met him. I know he's greatly respected hereabouts, but I wanted to say that my real sympathy lies with you. By all I hear, you've had a rotten time.'

Rosemary sized him up, accurately.

'I don't know what you've heard, Mr Smythe. Edward is impossible as a husband. If that's what you've heard, it's true. But as a Member of Parliament he's a giant. And you, Mr Smythe, are and will always be unworthy to lick his boots. Come along, Neil.'

It was less than elegant, but it sufficed. She drove away, wanting to cry, borrowing a handkerchief just in case, but actually happier than she had been for weeks.

33

The Foreign Secretary was rattled. It was a week into the election campaign. The grind of touring every town and village in his constituency in the Marches had begun. He could already feel the onset of the hoarseness which would soon catch up with him.

He could give a dozen reasons why he would rather not be in London that Tuesday morning. The Liberals were running him close. He needed every minute in the constituency. But he had been told his presence was necessary. Usually the Prime Minister liked to take his daily press conference at the party headquarters himself. But the Chief Whip had twisted the Foreign Secretary's arm. The problems at the Geneva arms talks were continuing. There might be detailed questions. The PM might need him. Patrick Reid had sighed, agreed, put down his telephone and asked someone to get hold of his Foreign Office driver. It was typical of every election he had ever known. There was no proper planning. First he was not wanted, then he was desperately needed. But there was no point in repining. He desperately wanted to keep his job as Foreign Secretary.

So it was doubly irritating to find that Michael Berinsfield had not needed him after all. There had indeed been questions on the Geneva talks, and the PM had taken them all himself. The Foreign Secretary had felt foolish and superfluous. He was not in a good mood when the Chief Whip, Francis Peretz, caught him in the entrance hall at Smith Square, took his arm and said he happened to be walking in the Foreign Secretary's direction.

'Thanks for coming up, Patrick. It's always a help.'

He wanted to say something by way of complaint. But it would not do, even for a Cabinet minister, to look childish before the Chief Whip, so Patrick Reid stayed silent.

They cut through side streets and into the courtyard behind Westminster Abbey and the school. The Foreign Secretary wore a black overcoat and hat, Peretz merely a muffler. The shrewd, bespectacled little man by Patrick Reid's side – a good three inches shorter and the Foreign Secretary was hardly tall – bided his time until they were in Dean's Yard.

'Does it not worry you just a little, Patrick,' he turned to glance at his companion, 'that all this really started in the Foreign Office?'

Patrick Reid needed no reminding of that.

'If I'd had my way at the outset, Francis, I would never have had Dunsford appointed. He's always been far too arrogant for his own good.'

'Actually, I've always liked him. An intelligent, honest mind I thought. It's a great shame. We need more like that in the House. But I'm afraid he won't survive in Sussex.'

They turned into the passageway which would bring them out in front of the Abbey, with the Foreign Secretary shaking his head in disagreement.

'I'm sorry. I find it difficult to feel any sympathy for him whatsoever.' He recalled the famous debate two weeks before. 'Now, if I'd had someone like Elliott in the Office it would have been a different matter entirely.'

'Charles Elliott? Sorry, Patrick, I don't agree. Charles is all envy and pride. Clever, yes. But he'll never make it into the Government. There's too much bitterness there which he can't control.'

A taxi slowed to allow them to cross Victoria Street.

'Anyway, it doesn't do for people like him to work out their personal grievances by sleeping with his opponent's secretary. It's cheap and sordid, even by our somewhat debatable standards.'

Patrick Reid was a man of strict family principles who was always taken by surprise when others failed to live up to his own code of personal conduct.

'I'm sorry, Francis, I have no idea what you mean.'

The Chief Whip halted them both in the middle of the pavement, a look of real surprise on his face.

'Come on, Patrick You're not telling me you haven't heard?'

The Foreign Secretary felt he had to be pompous.

'I don't listen to the gossip in the Members' Dining-Room, if that's what you mean, Francis. It's a habit I've never acquired, not having been a Whip myself.'

'This isn't idle gossip. It's fact. Charles Elliott has been sleeping for months with Edward Dunsford's Private Secretary in the Foreign Office. Surely you must know that?'

The Foreign Secretary was shaken.

'I can only repeat, Francis, that I never listen to gossip.'

They parted at the park door of the Foreign Office, Peretz to walk on up the steps and through the iron gate to his office in Downing Street, the Foreign Secretary to take the little Edwardian lift to his room on the first floor.

He walked through the corner of his Private Office and into his room without a word. He threw his hat and coat over an armchair. One of his Private Secretaries joined him immediately.

'Good morning, Secretary of State.'

'I want to see the Permanent Under-Secretary. I suppose he's here?'

'Yes, sir. He's coming up in ten minutes. He wants to talk to you about a number of things, including the Geneva negotiations and Meridia. There are papers on your desk dealing with the various points he wants to raise. And there are a number of recent telegrams which you haven't yet had in your box.'

Patrick Reid sat down wearily in his chair. Somehow it did not feel like his room. It had an unfamiliar, unused smell. He felt a stranger, that the place was not his in the way it usually was – like going back to school in the middle of the summer holidays.

His Private Secretary was hovering.

'Edward Dunsford's Private Secretary,' said the Foreign Secretary. 'Is she still in the office?'

'Yes. Without a minister, of course. But still around, certainly.'

'I've forgotten her name.' He had never known it.

'Sally Archer, Secretary of State.'

'Sally Archer, yes.'

'Why, is there . . . ?'

'No reason, none at all. That will be all, thank you. Show the Permanent Under-Secretary in as soon as he arrives.'

He added as an afterthought when the young man was leaving:

'I should prefer to see him alone.'

'Yes, sir.' The door closed.

Sir Reginald Anson entered the Secretary of State's room precisely ten minutes later. Patrick Reid's temper meanwhile had not improved. Although his meetings with the Permanent Under-Secretary were usually formal there was generally an opportunity to inject some warmth into them. Today there would not be.

'Good morning, Secretary of State. I trust you . . .'

'Good morning, Reginald. I am sorry, but we don't have a great deal of time so I fear we shall have to be brisk.'

'As you wish, Secretary of State.'

Twenty minutes later they had covered all the points on the Permanent Under-Secretary's list. They concluded on the subject of Meridia.

'So you see, Secretary of State, the situation has changed dramatically in the last fortnight. President Hamid has removed two-thirds of the Soviet Embassy. The chances are that relations will be broken shortly. So far as we can tell all the work on the MEECON project has come to a standstill. Washington is conducting a thorough review of its African policy and is keeping us closely informed. No decisions of policy are required by you at this stage but I should warn you that the Americans are likely to decide upon a substantial package of financial

418

aid, and will almost certainly ask us – at the highest level, and probably with little notice – to join with them. Obviously, we should have to look very carefully at anything they propose.'

'With what end, Reginald?'

The Permanent Under-Secretary cleared his throat.

'My own view is that our interests will almost certainly be best served by joining any Western move to help Hamid by contributing a significant additional sum of money ourselves.'

'I see.' Patrick Reid placed his hands on the desk and leant towards Sir Reginald. 'That's out of the question. A change of that sort now would put the Government in an impossible position. And my own position would be untenable.'

Sir Reginald gave the faintest possible sniff. 'I understand, Secretary of State. Though we must not forget,' he added, 'that Meridia has not become an election issue.'

'That is true, of course. Nevertheless, how on earth could we explain such a sudden change of mind on our part?'

'That aspect has been much on my mind, Secretary of State. We have come to no conclusions yet. But speaking personally, if I may, I can see reasons why it might be appropriate for a new government to take a bold step and pledge an increase in aid before the Americans. It would, in my opinion, be an imaginative decision from which the Government might derive much credit. There would be good arguments on our side to explain a change of policy. Events in Mangara speak for themselves.'

Patrick Reid looked into the future and smiled to

himself. What the PUS said had attractions, assuming he himself were reappointed after the election. He had still to make his mark on British foreign policy. This might be his chance. Indeed, there might be something to be said for making a move before the election.

'I take your point entirely. I shall reflect on it. Please make sure I see all the relevant papers.'

Sir Reginald was rising to take his leave. At the last moment the Foreign Secretary remembered what was on his mind.

'There is one other matter I should like to mention. A staff matter.'

Sir Reginald paused, wondering what it might be. They had been over the list of pending ambassadorial appointments. Everything else remained his own responsibility.

'It has come to my notice that Edward Dunsford's Private Secretary has been having an, er, a relationship with Charles Elliott, the Member of Parliament.'

The Permanent Under-Secretary cleared his throat. This was not the sort of housekeeping subject which he enjoyed discussing.

'Yes, that is unfortunately so, Secretary of State.'

'And do we know how long this has been going on for?'

'I think for some time. Perhaps as much as a year. Though it is, I understand, now at an end.'

'Reginald, it's no concern of mine what members of this Office care to do with their private lives unless their actions threaten the security of the state. Or,' he paused and looked sternly across the desk with his lawyer's eyes, 'unless they cause me personal embarrassment. In this case it strikes me as being, to say the least, less than desirable for a minister's Private Secretary to be behaving in such a fashion. Especially in the context of recent events. Wouldn't you agree?'

Sir Reginald found himself called upon to defend the honour of his profession.

'There is, of course, nothing against the rules, Foreign Secretary, in such behaviour. It is not, as such, a disciplinary matter. But there is, I agree, much in this particular case that was incautious and ill-advised, perhaps even irresponsible.'

The Foreign Secretary rose from his desk and walked to the window overlooking Horse Guards Parade. Red cloaks and plumed helmets in the middle distance showed that the guard in Whitehall was about to be changed. He turned his back on the scene.

'I should have much preferred to be told of this before learning of it from another parliamentary colleague. In fact, only this morning, when I presume the facts had been known in this building for some time.'

The Permanent Under-Secretary reddened just as much as his position and experience would allow.

'However, I shall say no more of that aspect. That is done now, though I would be grateful if you would ensure that if this sort of thing happens again I should be the first to know.'

'Of course, Secretary of State.'

'What is more important is the question in my mind as to whether it would be proper for this girl to continue in her present capacity as a Private Secretary. Would it not be more appropriate for her to be given work less intimately concerned with Parliament? I would not want any successor of Dunsford's to be placed in a similarly difficult position.'

He turned and smiled at his official. Sir Reginald nodded

'I shall look into it immediately, Foreign Secretary.'

Later that day Sally sat as usual almost totally unoccupied behind her desk four rooms away from Patrick Reid. She had done nothing all day. It had been the pattern of her life over the last three weeks, but for the hectic days which had followed Edward's departure.

Personnel Department rang three hours after Sir Reginald's interview with the Foreign Secretary. They had decided, they said, to post her sooner rather than later. She was overdue for a stint overseas. It would make better sense to move her now in the lull before a new government. If she waited to see in a new minister she could be trapped for up to a year more in London. Nothing specific to tell her over the telephone. They fixed a time for her to go over the following week.

She hardly cared what they might have in mind for her. She had made a mess of her own life over the last year, and she needed the chance to get it straight. Where she tried hardly mattered. This line of thought occupied her for much of the afternoon. She was silent and introverted. By four thirty she had begun to wonder whether she should remain in the Service at all. After all, what did the career have to offer her? There were other things to do. She still had time. Better to leave before it became too late. *She* did not want to grow old travelling round the world, collecting foreign bric-á-brac and ex-boyfriends as she left one capital for another. She had come across too many sad spinsters whom life had thus passed by.

She was putting on her coat when his call came. At first she had no recollection as to who it was.

'Sally Archer speaking . . . I'm sorry? Are you sure it's me you wanted and not . . . ? Oh yes, of course I do. I'm so sorry. How nice of you to ring, Mr Andrew . . . Yes. If you're really sure . . . Yes, I'd love to come. Of course I can. That would be lovely. Thank you very much . . . See you then.'

She put the phone down, smiling. James Harrison had been with Sally long enough not to worry about the pretence of private telephone calls.

'You've changed your tune a bit. Who was that?'

'A chap called Garth Andrew. A friend of Edward Dunsford. We met in the gallery at the famous debate.'

'Nice?'

'Interesting, I'd say. And different.'

'It sounded to me as though he was quite keen.'

Sally gathered together her things and prepared to leave for the evening.

'As usual, you're talking nonsense.'

She clattered along the tiles of the corridor outside, smiling.

34

In the pub they had actually given him three cheers – and that, of course, after paying for their own drinks. Richard Peacock would never have countenanced any breach of election rules.

'Mean anything?' asked Edward, as they drove away.

'They like you.'

'That's hardly enough.'

Major Peacock offered no further comment. What he thought to himself, as he negotiated the narrow lanes back to the main road, was that liking Edward was something new in the constituency. Respect he had always had, and a certain admiration; now the tone of the reception was warmer. A bit late.

Edward was enjoying the campaign. He was rediscovering the towns and villages which he thought he knew well. The truth was that in the last couple of years he had grown a bit bored with his constituency, with the surgeries, the civic dinners, the branch annual general meetings, the wet half-grapefruit with a cherry, cold chicken and Yugoslav hock. He had always despised those in the House of Commons who despised their constituents, thinking this ungrateful and silly. But he now admitted to himself that the zest had gone out of that part of his work in the past two or three years. Now, when the work might be taken from him for good, it became as attractive as it had been at the beginning. Stockbroker country was how the press described it, and of course that was half-true, as the crowded station platforms testified each morning. (Smythe, incidentally, had come down with strange ideas from some institute in London about scrapping rail subsidies, but a day or two at station entrances soon cured him of that.) Also to be mocked were the bogus timbered tea rooms, the gnomes in the gardens, the scruffiness of bus stations, the sameness of supermarkets, the second-rate design of almost everything modern. But all this was superficial. Peering for a sight of his window bills in the back streets of Lewes, navigating farm roads which suddenly ended, listening to old men at garden gates, watching the rain clear and a sharp evening light catch the edge of the Downs, listening to beaters and the guns in sodden woods, making little speeches to children and dogs on a village green, Edward was happy. Richard Peacock was the right companion for the venture, since he, too, enjoyed it. They never became close through all those miles driven side by side. Whenever the conversation veered towards the personal, Peacock became monosyllabic. But he never fussed, always provided sensible advice, never gave for one moment the impression that there were more sensible ways for two grown men to spend three weeks than following a lost cause.

Was it lost? Edward had no canvass returns, no organisation, no means of assessing progress. He aimed to be seen in every town and village at least twice a week. He had enough money for a few posters and window bills and a team of a dozen to distribute them. He had one evening meeting in Lewes, and there were two church meetings for all the candidates, but otherwise he went to bed early, either in Major Peacock's spare room with two rather good water-colours of Yorkshire moors, or back in London. Several times he found himself passing the gate of Long Meadow, but he never saw or heard from Rosemary. Often of course he met long-time supporters, but he felt no ill-will against those of them who had Smythe stickers on their cars, and they seemed to accept that he for his part had behaved reasonably.

Vote for Dunsford, the Conservative with an independent mind. It was a simple message and seemed to flourish. To begin with he talked about Meridia, and at the two church meetings that had gone well. But in the pubs and over the garden gate it evoked a look of puzzlement or distaste, and he soon gave it up. Smythe said a vote for Dunsford would split the Conservatives and let the Liberals in. The Liberal lady said the same, but hopefully. Edward said that the constituency wanted a member with a mind of his own. The Labour candidate said nothing. It was not an intellectually taxing campaign.

They found Miss Simpson about to close her shop. Elections, in her view, were *not* good for the antiques trade. Nevertheless she offered tea and private support. Mr Dunsford had always been so kind to people. Only that day Mrs Robins, a good customer, had told her how Mr Dunsford had sorted out her mother's tax affairs, passed away last winter poor soul, and left a tidy penny thanks, Mrs Robins had said, to Mr Dunsford keeping the taxman in his place. Mr Smythe was *not* popular, she had to say. Of course he was Conservative, and the Prime Minister and Mr Headley were supporting him. But he dashed up and down the High Street shaking hands and always in such a hurry he never listened to anyone except himself and that girl, and who knew where she had come from anyway, with that unlikely name. Not like Mrs Dunsford whom everyone knew; oh dear, she'd said the wrong thing. No, Miss Simpson could not put up a window bill, it might upset the customers, you couldn't be too careful with trade so uncertain, but she would vote for Mr Dunsford, and so would her sister over beyond Glynde, or was that in another constituency now . . .

They emerged eventually, full of sweet biscuits. Miss Simpson, though always polite, had never been so forthcoming in Edward's heyday.

'Have we a hope?' asked Edward.

'Early days yet,' said Major Peacock. He had been saying that for a fortnight. Now there was only a week to go.

During his election campaign the Prime Minister liked to retreat into 10 Downing Street for an hour or two every day. One columnist suggested that he wanted to savour to the full the last days of his tenure; but since he was six points ahead on the average of the opinion polls that was hardly a credible explanation. The truth was that Downing Street was quiet, the party faithful could not easily get at him, and anyway he preferred the company of the sardonic team of officials whom he had gathered round him to that of journalists, candidates and constituency chairmen.

'Awkward request from Washington,' said Monteith, offering a folder of Foreign Office telegrams.

Washington to FCO Telno 2930 of 1 December

1. The Secretary of State asked me to go to see him at the State Department at short notice this evening. He said that the realignment of US policy towards Meridia was moving fast. The oil companies had reacted without great indignation when he had told them that the Administration would no longer countenance the MEECON project. Now the President was anxious to put together a Western aid package as soon as possible to replace MEECON. Speed was essential because Hamid was a volatile man, who was perfectly capable of changing his mind again. He had been considering how to achieve the right momentum. The US would of course have to find most of the money, but there would be substantial political advantage if another country took the lead in putting the package together. If Britain could do this, then the chances of an excessive Soviet reaction would be reduced, and the opposition parties in Meridia might be less hostile than if the US was the protagonist.

2. I said I had no instructions, but I saw three considerable difficulties.

    a. HMG were in the middle of an election;

    b. that election had been called on the Meridian issue and the Government had resisted calls for increased aid;

    c. our budgetary constraints were very real.

3. The Secretary of State said that he had tried to explain

exactly these three points to the President. The President however had brushed them aside, and said he was confident his friend the Prime Minister could find a way through them. He had proposed to telephone the Prime Minister at once, but had been persuaded that a first approach should be made through me. The Secretary of State, with apologies for the inconveniences, suggested that you might fly out to Washington over the weekend for private discussion, with a view to HMG calling a conference of donor nations in London immediately after the election.

4. I promised to seek immediate instructions. Ends.

'Anything to avoid another transatlantic telephone call,' said the Prime Minister. He paused. 'What will they do if we say no?'

'Go to the Germans, perhaps. Or do it themselves and make a mess of it.'

'What would you all advise on this if Edward Dunsford had never existed?'

Monteith thought for a moment.

'The Treasury would be hostile, obviously. Everyone else would be in favour.'

The Prime Minister thought hard. His calculation had worked well. Meridia had not been an election issue. Dunsford had faded from the front pages, and would lose his seat. Although no election in Britain was a certainty, it seemed that only some sudden disaster could rob him of a good working majority and another five years in office. So far so good – a neat manoeuvre by a politician at the height of his abilities. But Berinsfield liked a touch of irony to salt his successes, and here it was, thanks to the Americans.

'Is the Foreign Secretary actually willing to fly to Washington straight away? His seat is not all that safe.'

'I gather that Sir Patrick feels he will get more favourable publicity on television by going to Washington than by canvassing in his own constituency.'

'That's the only shrewd political observation attributed to him these last five years. And he doesn't mind eating his own words? His speeches against giving more aid to Meridia were even more absolute than mine.'

'I gather the Foreign Secretary believes that the Foreign Office is worth a mass.' Only at Number 10 Downing Street were officials allowed to make sardonic political remarks. Monteith nevertheless hesitated before adding, 'I imagine that Sir Patrick judges that if you send him to Washington tonight you virtually preclude yourself from appointing a new foreign Secretary in six days' time.'

'Not at all, it doesn't follow,' said the Prime Minister who firmly intended to get rid of Patrick Reid when he appointed his new Government. 'But he must have something, certainly. He's worked hard.' He brightened. 'When it's all sorted out, this new programme for Meridia, we'll call it the Reid Plan. In that way he'll get at least one puzzled footnote in the history books. The Reid Plan, yes, it sounds admirably portentous. Much better, anyway, than the Dunsford Plan.'

So, after all, it was no good. The tellers had counted the total of votes cast to make sure that they tallied with the number recorded at the fifty-eight polling stations of the East Sussex constituency. Now they were well into the next process, sorting the votes into little piles for each candidate. They worked fast, because they were mostly recruited from the banks, and sorting bank notes was not all that different from sorting votes. Behind the tellers at their trestle tables in the town hall stood scrutineers from the main parties, most wearing blue, yellow or red rosettes. Edward had only himself, and Richard Peacock, and (recruited late in the day) Miss Simpson. Dubarry as Chairman of the Conservative Association wore an especially huge blue rosette on his plump chest. He had telephoned Edward two nights before to say that he had decided to vote for him, but not a word to anyone. As they passed he gave Edward a substantial wink.

Dubarry's telephone call, friendliness in the market, his own native self-confidence, had almost persuaded Edward that he had a chance. But the votes in his pile were not big enough. Not a disgrace, certainly higher than Labour or Liberal, but behind Smythe. As each candidate received a hundred votes the batch was tied with an elastic band and placed ceremoniously on the dais, at the feet of the returning officer. Smythe had several more batches than Edward.

Edward stood behind a ballot box which he knew came from the poorer streets round the railway station at Lewes. A good many Labour votes there, a few for Smythe, a few for him. He saw one on which the voter had scribbled, after putting an X against the name Dunsford, 'At least he thinks for himself.' Technically a spoiled vote, but the returning officer would allow it to him if the result was close.

But it would not be as close as that. An honourable result, the world would say, but Falstaff had said what had to be said about honour. For a moment, to his intense embarrassment, Edward's eyes filled with rage against

Oliver Smythe. There he stood, smiling smugly at Ariadne, wearing a rather loud sports jacket. At the election count in a county town, you should wear a suit, thought Edward savagely. What right had this smooth, fair-haired young nonentity to march in and take Edward's seat from him? And he had a pretty dark-haired girl into whose eyes he could smile.

Edward abstracted himself. He went into a tiny annex and listened to the first results from other constituencies on the radio. The Conservatives were holding their ground, gaining a seat here and there. Berinsfield had calculated well.

Then it was all over. They shuffled out into the moonlight. There was a small crowd of about fifty. The returning officer read the results in alphabetical order. Edward's figure came first – 25,116. There was a gasp from the more ignorant of the crowd, who thought that might be a winning hand. Then Liberal and Labour, both below 10,000. Then Smythe 31,376. A cheer from the blue rosettes, but not hearty.

'I hereby declare the aforesaid Oliver Smythe duly elected to serve as Member of Parliament for this constituency.'

A good short speech of thanks by Smythe to the returning officer and his staff. Probably after all he would make a perfectly good member. Edward stuttered something to second him, and there was a ragged farewell cheer from the crowd. Then he noticed Rosemary and Neil, two handsome faces out of the darkness, standing close together at the side of the steps. Neil half-raised a hand in greeting, then they disappeared. Edward could make nothing of this. It was a mystery which there was no point in investigating. They were both part of the past. He had to thank Richard Peacock, that was the next thing. After that all he wanted to do was drive fast, drive as fast as he could away from Lewes.

He drove fast and alone, listening to the election results. First along the foot of the Downs to Ditchling, crossing the path which, one day, the motorway might take. There was a token frost and sharp moonlight, but Edward had no eyes except for the road. He drove fast because of the pent-up energy inside him, not because he had an objective. He tried not to think of Rosemary, let alone Neil. He followed the familiar road to London because it was familiar, not because he had anywhere particular to go. After his resignation there had been the void in Cornwall, and then he had concentrated on the debate. After the debate there had been the void in Eaton Close, and then he had concentrated on the election campaign. He was now using up the last sparks of the energy which that had given him. There were no more short-term enterprises into which he could plunge to avoid the future. Ahead there was nothing but void, just cat's-eyes and anonymous road surrounded by darkness.

Cuckfield, then across to the main road and north, now up the hill out of Reigate. The radio reports gathered pace. The Prime Minister had calculated it shrewdly. It was not a landslide victory. Few seats were changing hands. The computer had hours ago predicted a Conservative majority of thirty-six, ten more than at present.

'One of the most interesting of the recent results came from East Sussex, where Edward Dunsford ran the official

Conservative candidate a close race to finish second. A gallant end to a notable career, for it was of course Edward Dunsford who precipitated the present election by his stand against government policy on Meridia. If he and the Opposition had managed to turn Meridia into a major election issue, then the result at Lewes might have been very different. But . . .'

'End to a career.' Edward heard the words but they did not really touch him. He lived in the interval between the blow and the pain from the blow. Tolworth, the Kingston by-pass, the edge of Richmond Park. He thought of stopping, slipping into the park by the pedestrian gate, and walking for a time in the cold moonlight among the deer and the ancient oaks. By the time the thought matured, the moment had passed. Roehampton, Putney High Street, Putney Bridge, Fulham and the Kings Road. Edward could not face the dark, empty house at Eaton Close, and the anticlimax which was all it now contained. Sloane Square, and straight on, then left past the stables of Buckingham Palace and out into the Mall. This was the beginning of Edward's London, the London of state visits and royalty, of resplendent parks, clubs and government departments, Parliament and Privy Council meetings within the palace he had just passed. Of course it was not the only London, perhaps not the real London, but there was good in its pretences and pageantries, and he did not regret his part in them. He parked the car, illegally he supposed, on the gravel by the garden wall of Lancaster House, locked it carefully, and walked briskly through the cold towards Trafalgar Square, vaguely remembering that on election nights this should be a scene of excitement. Whether because the night was cold, or the election result so predictable, there was only a small crowd in front of the loudspeakers. The fountains had been boarded up. The crowd groaned or cheered as each result was announced, but more from a sense of what was expected than from conviction. The Norwegian Christmas tree and its plain white lights, the façades of the National Gallery and St Martin's in the Fields, and Nelson in the centre of his lions gave the scene more interest and dignity than the human beings which it contained. Most of those present seemed to be Scots or Irish and/or drunk. No one recognised Edward.

Down Whitehall, then on foot past King Charles I and the darkened theatre and the Admiralty. There were few signs of approaching Christmas here, and none of the election just passed. But when Edward approached the turn into Downing Street he heard clapping and a shout of applause. By the time he reached the street the Prime Minister's car had swept in off Whitehall and vanished from sight round the bend. A friendly tall policeman at the barrier was explaining the scenario.

'Gone home to bed, now, he has. About time too. Been celebrating with his supporters at the Tory Central Office, down that way, past the Abbey, in Smith Square. Not usually one for a party, the Prime Minister, but I suppose tonight's an exception. It'll be getting light soon. Not long before he's up again and off to the palace.'

There in the darkness beyond the policeman loomed the Foreign Office. It seemed an immense time since Edward had taken for granted his office there, the long corridors and creaking lifts, the great staircase, the telegrams and friendly faces, the amazing assumption that Britain was actually part of a wider world.

Edward was between overcoats, having left his country tweed at Richard Peacock's and not yet refound his black at Eaton Close. The cold bit through his jacket.

There, at the foot of Whitehall, spread the towers and pinnacles of the Palace of Westminster. The moon had disappeared behind clouds, and a breeze had sprung up. Usually it was impossible because of the traffic to reach the garden in the middle of Parliament Square, but now it was easy. From there, by the huge statue of Churchill, you could see the full range of the palace, from Big Ben on the left to the House of Lords on the right.

No one had access now through the Members' Entrance because Parliament was dissolved. But soon, in a week or two, the members would be returning. The turnover would be small. Most faces would be familiar and present no problem to the policemen. But on the walls of a little booth would be pinned the election manifestos of Oliver Smythe and the other newcomers so that the police could learn their faces from the photographs.

Edward had lost it all. Lost the Foreign Office behind him, lost his place on the front bench of the Commons, lost his wife and daughters, lost the Private Secretary who might have been a friend, and today lost his seat in Parliament, and his very right to enter the Palace of Westminster. No doubt he would set foot in it again, but as a visitor and a guest, politely received but limited to certain unimportant rooms and corridors. The essence had gone, and he knew it had gone for good. Edward waited, and looked at what he had lost.

But with all these things had gone the burdens. He might find new ones, but at that moment for the first time in many years his shoulders were free. No letters to answer, no meetings to attend, no one to nag and criticise what he did and said, no one's feelings to watch and humour. In a way it was unjust. He had been foolish, rash, inept and in the eyes of the world had paid great penalties. But, at that moment, it seemed to Edward, with the keen perception which fatigue can bring, that foolishness had given him back his freedom.

The breeze freshened still further, and he was very cold. To the east beyond Westminster Bridge the darkness began to thin, and the dawn began modestly with a blue-green edge of light. Soon the Palace of Westminster would lose its magic and resume the garb of grey wintry day. The crowds would begin to shop and shoplift, the pavements would be littered with soft-drink cans, the cleaning ladies would cover the corridors of power with soapy water, and ordinary life would resume. But for the moment, for a small moment only, the magic held as a new day broke over London. Then it dissolved.

Edward proposed to cut across the park to retrieve the car from the Mall. There were, he thought, sausages in the refrigerator in Eaton Close. There would be plenty of time for a hot bath and a hot breakfast before he set out to see Guy Carlton in his office in the City.

THE SHAPE OF ICE
Douglas Hurd

Brilliantly conveying the unrelenting pressure of political existence at the highest level, *The Shape of Ice* shuttles the reader from routine parliamentary procedure to a media-fuelled international military crisis, from the G8 Summit to Prime Minister Simon Russell's most private moments, in a novel of stark authenticity and escalating tension.

'A consistent page turner . . . What makes *The Shape of Ice* so enjoyable is that you constantly feel you are getting the inside info on what it is like to hold high office in government. The writing is full of sharp observation and fascinating detail'
Sunday Telegraph

'The pace of the novel and the interweaving of plot lines are breathless . . . Hurd has done his old trade a service, by painting so vivid a picture of muddled, thrilling, frustrating, compulsive reality'
Max Hastings, *Evening Standard*

'Richly authentic . . . an intriguing, unusual and ambitious consideration of political life'
Mail on Sunday

VOTE TO KILL
Douglas Hurd

Sir James Percival is the world-weary veteran of Tory politics. When he becomes PM after seven years of Labour rule, he – and the rest of the country – feels justified in looking forward to a quiet time.

But life is not like that, and neither is politics. He must contend with a new wave of violence in Ireland and turmoil in his own party, in the form of maverick MP Jeremy Cornwall. And when the Government is betrayed from within, the new administration – and Percival himself – must fight for its life. Politics and personal relationships become irrevocably entwined and the sheer pace of events takes control. *Vote To Kill* is a dazzling portrait of politics as the most addictive of all drugs.

'Beautifully written, the atmosphere at No. 10 is well conveyed (and) amusingly topical. Once started it was impossible to put down and I finished it at a sitting'
Edward Heath

SCOTCH ON THE ROCKS
Douglas Hurd and Andrew Osmond

From the blackened, crumbling tenements of Glasgow come ugly rumours . . .

An army of separatist fanatics, recruited from the razor gangs of Europe's most violent city and funded and armed by an unknown power, are standing ready – waiting for the moment to strike. Is the nationalist tide about to turn? Will Prime Minister Harvey avert catastophe . . .?

A stunning political thriller set in the world of Scottish nationalism, Douglas Hurd and Andrew Osmond's classic novel remains as compelling and as timely as ever.

'Refreshingly original . . . an ingenious
and well-told tale'
Sunday Times

'Hurd and Osmond are a brilliantly
perceptive political team'
Economist

'The pace of the action never slackens
from beginning to end'
Daily Telegraph